IN COLD BLONDE

by

James L. Conway

ISBN: 978-0-9885499-2-0

Camel Press has granted permission to publish excerpts from *Dead and Not So Buried* (2012).

For more information check out: www.jameslconway.

For Sarah and Katie

PROLOGUE

She was hot.

A California girl, with long blonde hair pulled back in a ponytail, emerald green eyes and lips bathed in Revlon's Raspberry Mousse. The dress was by Calvin Klein, bright red, *notice* me red. It clung to her skin, served up the swell of her breasts, stopped at the top of her muscled thighs. Too short for most women, it looked perfect on her. Her long tanned legs curved down to a pair of Manolo Blahnik fuck-me pumps, her toes were painted to match her lips. And she had something else, attitude. She walked in long, confident strides, almost a swagger. She was on the prowl and tonight, this bar was her jungle.

If you'd glanced at your watch when she walked into Havoc, L.A.'s hottest body exchange, the little hand would have been on the one and the big hand just past the six; 1:32 a.m. to be exact.

Late, so the herd was cut by now, most everyone paired off and flirting. I say most everyone because one of the universe's absolute truths is that there are *always* more single guys in a bar than single girls. And tonight's loser was Colin Wood. He'd gotten to Havoc late, about 1:15, after all the available nubiles were taken. Frustrated, he'd ordered a Jack on the rocks, figuring he'd down it quickly and head home. He'd been working late, stuck on location in Redondo Beach, shooting in an abandoned power plant. Colin was an actor. Not a star, but a working actor; tall, handsome in a John Cusack sort of way, getting eight to ten jobs a year. Enough to pull down about 150 G's, including residuals. Enough to get recognized every so often, though no one could ever place his name. Enough to usually get him laid when he went clubbing. But not tonight; tonight he was too late. Frustrated, he finished his drink, dropped some money on the bar and turned to the door. And that's when she walked in.

Heads swiveled as she crossed the room, some drawn by her beauty, others just sensing her, well, sex. Colin could almost feel the regret as a lot of the now occupied guys reconsidered their hastily chosen partners. And to Colin's delight, she moved down the bar and took the stool next to him. "London or Paris?" he asked.

"Excuse me?" Daisy, Gatsby's wet dream, might have had a voice that was full of money; this babe's smoky timber sizzled sex.

"For our honeymoon. London or Paris?"

She actually smiled. "Does that line ever work?"

"No. But there's a first time for everything."

She appraised him slowly. Her green eyes drinking in his tousled brown hair, hazel eyes, freckled nose, dimpled chin. "Too hunky for a real job," she said. "Model or actor?"

"Brain surgeon."

An appreciative smile. "Too quick for a model. That means actor."

"Is that a bad thing?"

"For breeding, probably not, but most actors are shallow, self-absorbed egomaniacs who think an intelligent conversation starts and ends with me, me, me."

"Then, let's focus on the breeding part."

She laughed, and then she cocked her head to the side, tucked her chin into the palm of her right hand and said, "Okay."

"Okay, what?"

"Let's focus on the breeding part."

Yikes, Colin thought. Does she mean what I think she means? "Do you mean what I think you mean?" he asked.

She leaned forward and kissed him. Her tongue darted into his mouth, did a quick, tantalizing tango with his tongue, then slipped out again. "You got a car?"

"In the lot out back."

"Let me guess, Porsche?"

"Guilty."

She put her hand on his crotch and squeezed gently. She felt him stiffen through his jeans. "Stick shift?" she whispered.

"Yes," he answered thickly.

"Vroom. Vroom..."

They walked out of the club hand in hand. The Lady in Red leaned against him, her hip touching his hip, her thigh brushing against his thigh. He could smell flowers in her hair and Chanel on her skin. "I live nearby," Colin said. "A couple of miles up on Crescent."

"Perfect," she purred as he opened the door for her. She got in, sighed happily, her fingers relishing the hand-stitched leather. As Colin got in she wrapped her arms around him and kissed him again. Nothing playful this time; the kiss was pure lust. Her hand was back in his lap, rubbing his cock. His right hand went to her breasts, rubbing them through her dress. Real tits, he thought, thrilled. She even has real tits!

She moaned, took his left hand, put it under her dress, on her panties. He rubbed her mound, his finger searching, finding her clitoris. That brought a grateful groan and her right hand went to work on his belt, unfastening it. Colin lifted up and she slipped down his jeans.

Jesus Christ, Colin thought. This babe is unbelievable. She wants to do it right here, in this tiny fucking car. He pulled away from her voracious kiss. "Unless you work for Cirque du Soleil," he said, "we should wait 'til we get to my house."

"Don't want to wait," she said, her hand freeing his erect penis from his boxer shorts. "I want you now." She bent down, taking him in her mouth.

Okay, Colin thought. I can live with that. Now it was his turn to groan with pleasure as he laid his head back on the headrest and closed his eyes.

That's why he didn't see the last twenty seconds of his life.

He didn't see her hand slip into her purse and pull out the Colt Vest Pocket .25 automatic. He did feel the gun as she placed the muzzle under his balls, but he thought it was her finger and she was just kinky. He didn't see her pull the trigger.

POP. POP. POP.

The first bullet ripped through the sigmoid colon, shredded the small intestine, tore through the stomach and left lobe of the liver, finally severing the esophagus. Bullet two veered a little left, taking out the bladder, the ascending colon and the right lobe of the liver before imbedding itself in the spinal cord. Bullet three soared through the small intestine, took out the gallbladder, pulverized more liver, punched a hole in the diaphragm and did a victory dance in the right ventricle of the heart.

The lady in red leaned back in her seat, watching the little jerks and spasms his body made even though he was already dead. There was much more blood than she expected, and she was surprised to see he still had his hard-on, though it suddenly started to shrink, like a balloon losing air.

She put the Colt back in her purse, took out a pair of surgical gloves, put them on, and then pulled out a scalpel. She had work to do...

ONE

The phone woke Ryan, never a good sign. He opened one eye and looked out the window. Dark. Middle of the night dark. Shit.

He picked up the phone. "Hello."

"Duty calls, Ryan." He recognized the voice, his boss, Lieutenant Hanrahan. "Got a very dead body in a very bloody car on the always exciting Sunset Strip."

Ryan glanced at the clock, three-thirty. Fuck, he thought. Not because of the dead body, he was a homicide cop and it was hard to do his job without the occasional body or two. The fuck was for the hour. He liked his sleep.

Hanrahan coughed, a phlegm-filled hack from someone who gave up smoking twenty years too late. "Parking lot on the corner of Sunset and Martel. Oh, and call Syd, will you?"

Syd was Ryan's partner. "No problem," he said and hung up.

The sheets rustled then as a head popped out from under the pillow. Red hair cascaded past green eyes and a million adorable freckles. Syd. "That the bat signal?"

"Shining bright in the evening sky."

"Cool." Syd bounced naked from bed and bounded into the bathroom. She looked too young and innocent to be a cop, but Syd's combination of enthusiasm, street smarts and second- degree black belt more than made up for nature's disguise. "We're going to have to stop by my place for a minute so I can change. I can't very well show up at the crime scene in yesterday's Donna Karen... unless you're ready to go public with our relationship."

Syd and Ryan had been partners for eight weeks and sleeping together for four. They were in that wonderful pheromone-induced infatuation phase where they could barely keep their hands off each other.

It had been lust at first sight for Ryan. Whatever lizard brain criteria had been hardwired into Ryan for a sexual companion, this perky, freckled-face redhead was it. He literally got a hard-on the first time he shook her hand. Oh, shit, he thought. She's going to be trouble. He did everything he could to be business-like and professional around her. But they spent twelve to fifteen hours a day together; sitting across from each other in the Hollywood Division Homicide bullpen, sitting next to each other in their city issued Crown Vic, working the files together, conducting interviews, eating, brainstorming, and all the time, Ryan fantasized about her.

It must have been the same for Syd, Ryan realized, when late that fateful night four weeks later, they found themselves alone in the bullpen. Ryan went into the file room to return a murder book, and when he turned around he was nose to nose with Syd.

"I can't stand this," she whispered.

"What?"

"The game we're playing. Pretending to be totally professional when all we want to do is rip each other's clothes off and fuck like coked-up porn stars."

Don't do this, he thought. Be professional. You don't sleep with your partner.

"I should warn you," she said, her lips now brushing his. "I'm prone to multiple orgasms and I love anal sex."

Game. Set. Match. Ryan kissed her. They practically swallowed each other. They were naked in seconds and as Ryan entered Syd for the first time, he thought that doing something this wrong shouldn't feel so unbelievably good.

Back in Ryan's apartment, Ryan said, "Department policy states that partners aren't allowed to fondle each other's genitals."

Syd stuck her head out the bathroom doorway, toothpaste foaming at her mouth. "I remember doing a lot of things to you last night, but by no modern definition would any of them qualify as fondle." True, Ryan thought.

Sex with Syd was frantic, almost desperate. Always fantastic.

"I've got a good feeling about this one," she said ducking back into the bathroom. "This'll be the one that makes us famous."

That was Syd's one blind spot. Ambition. It had carried her in record time from street cop to Vice and now to Homicide. But she didn't want to just be a good cop; she wanted to be a *famous* cop. And that kind of ambition could be dangerous.

Ryan's right hand worked the stick as he steered all original 271 horses of his red '65 Mustang through the hairpin curves etched into the mountainside of Coldwater Canyon. They'd stopped at Syd's studio apartment and she'd changed clothes; now back on the road, Ryan relished the pre-dawn drive. The top was down, and though the temperature was only in the upper forties, typical for early May, the heater was blasting, modulating the chill enough so they could still savor the sweet, invigorating morning.

"Does it get any better than this?" Syd asked, her red hair whipping around her head. "A pre-dawn expedition into the belly of the beast, a fresh crime scene bursting with clues, a sprawling city hiding a cold-blooded murderer, intent on escape, but doomed because the world's best homicide detectives are on his ass."

Ryan smiled. "World's best homicide detectives?"

"Hey, we're undefeated. In eight weeks we've investigated four murders and solved them all."

True, Ryan thought, but they'd been lucky. Two of the killings had been a murder/suicide – a bitter ex-husband finalizing the divorce with a .9mm bullet to his wife's chest before blowing out the back of his skull. Another was a gas station robbery/murder, caught on a security camera – the tape was aired on the local news and the doer was ID'd by a heartbroken mother turning in her drug-addled son. Number four was a bit more challenging, a UCLA co-ed found dead, raped and strangled in the bathroom of her apartment. They spent four hours at the crime scene, working with SID collecting evidence, talking to her roommates, the neighbors. When they first arrived, Syd noticed a guy sitting in a battered blue pick-up, parked a half block north of the apartment. She pointed him out to Ryan. The guy in the pick-up stuck around for about twenty minutes, then left. Two hours later Ryan noticed him parked a block south of the apartment. Killers often return to the scene of the crime, so maybe. Ryan didn't dare risk approaching on foot – the suspect would see him coming and boogie. So he radioed for backup. The cops sealed off the street and then two black and whites swooped in trapping him. The suspect gave up without a fight. He was a convicted sex offender, released just two weeks earlier, working the neighborhood as a handyman. He'd arrived to do some work for the landlord, met the co-ed who excused herself to take a shower and well, the son of bitch couldn't help himself.

So, Ryan and Syd were four for four. Not bad for a Homicide department with just a thirty-four percent clearance rate. But with two out of every three murderers going free in the city of Los Angeles, Ryan knew it was just a matter of time before the odds caught up to them.

"You got any gum?" Syd asked.

"Check the glove box."

Syd popped it open, started rummaging around. "I hope you also have hand sanitizer in here because this is disgusting." She pulled out a grease-stained Taco Bell wrapper, a balled up Wienerschnitzel bag, a crushed Starbucks coffee cup, a half-eaten chocolate glazed Krispy Kreme, and a wadded up McDonalds napkin."

"In there," Ryan said. "The gum's in the napkin."

Syd peeled the napkin open. "It's already been chewed. You're offering me used gum?"

"Think of it as a symbol of our intimacy." Ryan laughed. Got you, he thought.

Syd looked at him, at the smug smile, and then she peeled the gum off the napkin, popped it in her mouth and began to chew.

"Yuck," Ryan said. "That's disgusting."

"I've had your tongue, ear, fingers, toes, balls and cock in my mouth. This is nothing."

That was the thing about Syd; Ryan never knew what she was going to do next.

She stuffed the detritus back in the glove box, and then noticed something. She pulled out a wrinkled lottery ticket. "I didn't know you played the lottery."

"I don't."

"Then what's this?"

"A lottery ticket," Ryan said, confused. Then a memory flooded back. One he wasn't very proud of. One he didn't want to tell Syd. "Oh, yeah, I remember," Ryan said, and then lied. "The jackpot was like forty million dollars or something so I took a flier."

She checked the date. "It's almost six months old. You ever check to see if it won?"

"No. I forgot all about it." That part was true.

Syd read the numbers, "14 19 20 23 36, and a mega of 18. Any significance to the numbers?"

Ryan didn't know, and then remembered, "No, it was a quick pick."

"Well, today may be your lucky day." She flipped the glove box closed. "A murder and a shot at unimaginable wealth; like I said, it doesn't get any better than this."

TWO

The Havoc parking lot had been taken over by the LAPD; yellow police tape and portable floodlights surrounded the Porsche, uniformed officers kept a few gawkers behind hastily erected LAPD plastic barricades. Two SID technicians worked the inside of the car. The Scientific Investigative Division was the LAPD's version of CSI. They dusted the car for prints, collected fibers, and bagged anything that might be considered evidence. Ryan and Syd joined Lieutenant Hanrahan and Liz Kettle, one of the L.A. County Coroners, outside the open driver's side door.

Syd looked at the victim. "Ok, that's gross." The victim lay slumped against the back of the driver's seat. His eyes were open and so was his mouth. Sticking out of his mouth, like a cheap cigar, was a penis.

"His junk, I presume," Ryan said, glancing down. The victim's pants were at his knees, blood soaked the exposed thighs and pubic hair and the ragged end of a once proud penis.

"Is that what killed him?" Syd asked.

"No," Ryan said. "Not enough blood. Isn't that right, Liz?"

Liz was Ryan's favorite coroner. She had the body of a linebacker and the mouth of a marine. In her early fifties, thrice divorced, Liz was on the handsome side of attractive. She wore her salt and pepper hair pulled back and the only make-up she wore was a touch of eyeliner to frame her piercing blue eyes. Liz had no patience for laziness or stupidity and her sharp tongue scared the shit out of almost everyone. Everyone but Ryan. But Ryan knew Liz better than most other cops – she was his stepmother. Well, one of them, anyway. Ryan's mother died when he was just two years old and his dad married four more times. Liz had been wife number three. She lasted six years, six of the most important years for Ryan, age eight through fourteen. So Ryan was used to the bluster; in fact, he cherished it. She'd been his favorite stepmom.

"Oh, there's plenty of blood, but not enough to indicate he bled out. Something stopped his heart, which stopped the blood flow. Move your fat ass, Hanrahan," she snapped. "You're blocking the light."

Hanrahan shifted to his right as Liz plucked the penis out of the victim's mouth then held it up to the light.

"How humiliating," Hanrahan mumbled.

"Sort of puts everything into perspective if you ask me," Liz said. "All the murder and mayhem created because you Neanderthals are always trying to prove who has the bigger dick. Well, here it is, fellas, in all its flaccid glory. Four and a half inches of shriveled meat..." Liz's voice trailed off as she noticed something. "Huh, look at that, there are no hesitation cuts before the actual amputation."

"So the killer had medical training?" Ryan ventured.

"Or was used to handling knives," Liz said.

"Or has done it before," Syd said.

"Grizzly thought but possible," Hanrahan said, unwrapping a grape Tootsie Roll Pop. He'd taken to sucking the Pops when he quit smoking his beloved Marlboros. He turned to Ryan, "Be sure and run the specifics through VICAP." The FBI's Violent Crime Apprehension Program was an online database used by the county's law enforcement agency to collect and compare violent crimes.

"The bartender said the victim met a woman inside the club, they flirted for a few minutes then left. About twenty minutes later a couple noticed the body when they got to their car."

Ryan asked, "Could the bartender tell if they knew each other?"

Hanrahan shook his head. "She sat down next to him and he started talking. Could have been a prearranged date, could have been an old friend, could have been two strangers in the night."

"The woman's the doer?" Syd asked.

"Or she was working with someone who was waiting out here," Hanrahan said.

"Robbery?" Syd asked.

Tony Ramirez, the lead SID tech, held up an evidence bag. Ramirez was one of the department's best. A chess champion as a kid, Ramirez was brilliant if a bit anal compulsive, which actually came in handy in his line of work. Forensics was all about the details.

Inside the evidence bag was a wallet. "Found it in his front left pocket," Tony said. "It's got three hundred eleven dollars in cash but here's where it gets interesting; there are credit cards in all the slots except one."

"She left his money but took a credit card?" Syd asked.

"Which cards did he carry?" Ryan asked.

Tony checked his inventory. "Master Card, Visa, Nordstrom and Barney's."

"No American Express?" Ryan asked.

"Nope."

"Then that's what she took," Ryan said. "Everybody who drives a Porsche carries American Express; they are all about status."

Syd made a note. "I'll contact American Express. If she uses it, we can trace her."

"I don't think she took the card to use it," Tony said. "This wasn't about money. Besides the cash in his wallet, there is a nine-hundred-dollar Patik Phillip watch on his wrist and a gold signet on the pinkie of his left hand."

Syd was confused. "Then why take the credit card?"

"Souvenir?" Liz asked.

"Maybe he just left it somewhere the last time he used it," Hanrahan said.

"We'll check," Ryan said.

"His name was Colin Wood," Ramirez said. "Registration in the glove box confirms it's his car." He ripped a page out of his notebook, held it out. "I wrote down his address for you."

"Thanks," Syd said then turned to Ryan. "It should be easier to find a premeditated murderer than a random robbery."

"Right," Ryan said. "Though it is a little troubling the killer didn't even try to pretend it was a robbery. It would have been so easy to take the wallet and watch. It's like the killer *wants* us to know it was murder..."

"I think the dick in the mouth is message enough," Liz said. "Sounds *very* personal to me."

"Old girlfriend?" Syd asked.

"Sounds like a great place to start," Hanrahan said.

"What about a cell phone," Ryan asked. "Did you find a cell phone?"

Tony held up another evidence bag. "iPhone. I've already dusted it, so if you want to check it, it's yours."

"If it was an old girlfriend, her number or picture could be in that phone," Syd said. Cell phones were a treasure trove of evidence, from the phone directory to the picture and video files. And the cell phone cameras came in handy, too. There were a number of cases when victims have taken pictures of their attackers as they fled.

Ryan took the iPhone, turned to Liz. "Do you know what killed him?"

Liz dropped the penis in an evidence bag. "Not until I get him on the table." Liz glanced at Ramirez, "How long before you're finished, Tony?"

"We're done," Ramirez said.

"First impressions?" Ryan asked.

"We've got a little bit to work with. The killer wiped off any fingerprints, but we did find a long strand of blonde hair caught under aforementioned Patik Phillip."

"The woman in the bar was a blonde," Hanrahan said.

"And there was a smudge of lipstick at the corner of his mouth, bright red. We swabbed a sample."

"Can you get DNA?" Hanrahan asked.

"Only if there is any saliva which, sorry to say, is rare. But we'll check. Otherwise, we didn't find much else."

"Check out where they were sitting at the bar," Ryan said. "Maybe she left a print there."

"We're on it," Tony said. The SID techs left as Liz waved over the two morgue attendants waiting by a gurney at the morgue van.

"I stopped by and saw your dad yesterday," Liz said to Ryan.

"Really," Ryan said, surprised. His dad had been dead for three years.

"My Uncle Elwood died; remember Elwood, he was the dentist."

"Right," Ryan said. "He had twin boys, and they both became dentists, too." Ryan remembered because Ryan's father had been a lawyer, as had his grandfather. And the expectation had been that Ryan would follow in the family's footsteps. But life got in the way.

Ryan fell in love his junior year at UCLA. Her name was Anne Reich, a pretty brunette who grew up dirt poor in a Riverside trailer park. Ryan flipped for Anne; they had similar tastes in books, movies, food. She was smart, funny, attentive, and ambitious. They were the perfect couple, everyone said so, and they were soon daydreaming about getting married. Ryan wanted to wait until after law school, once their careers were safely on their way. But Anne got pregnant, and taking it as a sign, the happy couple got married the summer before their senior year.

Then life threw a one-two punch. First, Anne lost the baby. A miscarriage. Ryan consoled Anne, told her not to worry they would have plenty of babies.

Then the knockout punch; Ryan's father was charged with tax fraud. Under financial strain from paying four alimonies and caught short by the bursting tech bubble, Ryan's father had played a little fast and loose with the IRS. He was caught, convicted, disbarred and sentenced to six years in jail.

Ryan scraped together enough money for his last year of UCLA and Anne had her scholarship, but now there was no money for law school. So Ryan made a decision. He'd work while Anne went to law school. When she graduated, she'd go to work and pay for his education.

Not only had Ryan loved his six years with stepmom

Liz, her stories about the Coroner's office and police work intrigued him. So he joined the LAPD. Anne thrived at UCLA law school and Ryan loved the police force. But it was a financial struggle. A patrolman's salary barely covered the studio apartment, groceries and incidentals.

The summer after her second year of law school Anne got a job as an intern at a big L.A. firm, Rogers, Middleton and Roberts. There she met Rick Rogers, son of founding partner, Edward Rogers. He was five years Anne's senior and an associate on the fast track to making partner. He was handsome, Harvard-educated, and rich. He also had a huge crush on Anne and pursued her relentlessly.

And then one night, Anne never came home. Frantic, Ryan worked the phone calling hospitals, friends, family, desperately trying to find her. She called in the morning to say she'd fallen in love with Rick Rogers and she wanted a divorce. Rick sent movers to clean her things out of the apartment while a shell-shocked Ryan looked on. Two weeks after the divorce was final, Rick married Anne.

Ryan was devastated. He tortured himself, wondering what he'd done wrong. Wondering what he could have done to keep Anne. His well-planned life had come completely unraveled. He was supposed to quit the police force and go to law school next year. But without Anne's salary to support them, how would he afford it?

And suddenly, the idea of becoming a lawyer didn't appeal to him very much. It hadn't done much to insure his father's happiness. And indirectly, law school had ruined his life with Anne. Besides, he loved being a cop. He was good at it. And it was his brothers in blue who gathered round him when Anne dumped him. So Ryan stayed a cop and never thought about becoming a lawyer again.

"Elwood was buried at Calvary," Liz said. "Not far from your dad. So after the service I stopped by his grave." Ryan's father died of a heart attack while in prison.

"How's he doing?"

"Still dead, but there were fresh flowers on the grave."

Ryan nodded. "Maggie never stopped loving him." Maggie was Ryan's father's second wife. She only lasted two years. "Not even after he dumped her for you, Liz. Maggie visits the grave every week."

"Epic love," Syd said. "Even in the teeth of a gale. That's so romantic."

"Pathetic if you ask me," Liz said. "Ryan's father was a self-centered son of a bitch who couldn't keep his dick in his pants. I'm just sorry it took me six years to realize it." Liz started for her car. "I'll call you guys when I know something."

Hanrahan shook his head. "I can't imagine waking up to that every morning. How'd your dad do it?"

"She makes a mean blueberry pancake," Ryan said. "She's also smart, informed and passionate about life."

"Yet she spends her days sticking her hands in dead people, go figure." Hanrahan sucked the last bit of chocolate off his Tootsie Roll Pop. "Anyway, the bartender's inside along with a few of the customers who got a look at the blonde."

"Don't suppose the bar or parking lot had a surveillance camera?" Ryan asked.

"No," Hanrahan said.

Syd pointed across the street. "There's a 7-Eleven. I'll check to see if they have a camera pointed in this direction."

"Great idea," Ryan said. Syd hurried off.

Hanrahan watched Syd cross the street. "If she was my partner, I'd have trouble keeping my dick in my pants."

Ryan studied Hanrahan for any sign of suspicion, found none. "I've never had a thing for redheads," Ryan said, not crazy about lying to his boss. Then he sprinkled on a little extra seasoning. "Besides, she's got a boyfriend."

"Good," Hanrahan said, turning back to Ryan. "Because fucking your partner always ends the same way. You end up fucking yourself."

THREE

Syd was excited. She just had a feeling. Not about the security camera. 7-Eleven's have their cameras inside, trained on the aisles and cash register, not on the parking lot. There was probably no way there was a security camera to help in their murder investigation. No, she was excited about Ryan's lottery ticket. She just had this feeling.

"Can I help you?" the clerk asked as Syd approached the counter. He was smiling, but he didn't mean it. Syd could just tell. He was Middle Eastern, of course, late thirties to early forties, and he just oozed resentment. He was probably a doctor or an engineer in his native country but in America he's stuck behind a sticky, slurpee-stained counter.

"Yes," Syd said, handing him Ryan's Lotto ticket, beaming him her brightest smile. "Could you check this for me, tell me if I've won anything?"

"Certainly," he said, perking up. No man, no matter where he is from, can resist a pretty girl. He tried to put it in the Lotto reader, but it was so wrinkled the machine rejected it.

"Sorry," Syd said. "It was sort of forgotten about, stuffed in a glove compartment."

"No problem," he said, smoothing it out. "You'd be surprised how many millions of dollars go unclaimed because people forgot about their tickets." He carefully placed the ticket in the machine and, with a mechanical whir, the machine sucked it in.

Syd couldn't see the screen from her angle so she watched the clerk's face. He stared at the screen, expressionless, and then shook his head. "Sorry, miss, no luck today." He hit a button, the machine spit the ticket out and the clerk threw it into the trashcan behind the counter.

"Can I have my ticket?" Syd asked.

"No need, miss, it's a loser. I've thrown it away for you."

Syd pulled her .9mm Glock and stuck it in his face.

"Shit," he gasped, raising his hands. "Take whatever you want. But, please, don't shoot."

"I'm a cop, you jackass, and all I want is my Lotto ticket."

Looking even more worried than when Syd pulled the gun, the clerk leaned down, plucked the ticket out of the trash and handed it to her.

"You lied to me," Syd said. "I could see it in your eyes. What came up on the screen?"

"Nothing, I swear. It was like I said, the screen said, no winner."

Syd walked behind the counter, stopped in front of the Lotto machine. "Let's just double check, shall we?" Syd smoothed the edges and slipped it into the machine. The screen flashed: CALL 800 465-9586.

"What's that mean?" Syd asked.

The clerk hesitated, then, "It means you've won a very large jackpot. The 800 number comes up whenever the ticket is worth more than fifty thousand dollars."

"And if I'd left after you threw my 'losing' ticket away, you were going to take it out of the trash and claim it yourself?"

He just stared at her, sullenly silent.

"One final question," Syd said, writing down the 800 number. "Do any of your security cameras point toward the parking lot across the street?"

The question was so out of left field, confusion filled his face. "What?"

"Look there," Syd said pointing out the window, losing patience. "See all the police cars? That's a crime scene. Do any of your security cameras point toward that parking lot?"

"No, they only point inside."

"At you, ripping off your customers?"

"It was an honest mistake, I swear."

"Yeah, right," Syd said. She was tempted to arrest him for attempted robbery or fraud, or whatever the hell you call trying to fuck someone out of their Lotto winnings. But deep down she understood the clerk's survival instinct. He was a cliché stuck in a xenophobic wasteland, a Middle Eastern man running a 7-Eleven. He's mocked in pop culture in everything from *The Simpsons* to *South Park.* And in return for his humiliation he makes minimum wage. So he plays a few angles and, if the locals are dumb enough to fall for his act, more power to him. So Syd simply withered him with a look, holstered her weapon and left.

Syd was used to guys trying to take advantage of her. She had such a sweet, girl-next- door look that most guys thought she was naïve, or worse, nice. At her core, Syd was neither. She outgrew naïve when her stepfather raped her on her fourteenth birthday. She outgrew nice when she killed him two years later after countless molestations. Well, that's not exactly true, it was one hundred and thirty-eight molestations. Syd kept count.

Ryan didn't know about the rapes or the murder. No one did. In fact, no one even knew Syd's real background. She lied to everyone.

Syd walked out of the 7-Eleven, pulled out her cell phone and called the Lotto 800 number. A woman answered on the third ring. "California Lottery."

"Yes, hi, I hope you can help me. I've got a Lotto ticket and when I checked to see if it was a winner, a screen came up telling me to call this number."

"There is a serial number on the ticket, just below the date. Do you see it?" Syd could hear a change in the woman's voice, a thrum of excitement.

"Yes."

"Read the number to me please."

"193-036806682-086035." Syd heard her type the numbers into a keyboard.

"Oh my God, congratulations, you have a winner with a capital W!" The thrum had turned into a marching band. "Where are you calling from?"

"Hollywood."

"There's a Lotto office in Van Nuys. Bring the ticket, answer a couple of questions and we can begin to process your check. But you better hurry. The jackpot must be picked up within one hundred and eighty days of the drawing date; you've only got two days left. The ticket expires on the twenty-sixth, that's Thursday, the day after tomorrow."

Thank God I found it when I did, thought Syd. "Actually, I'm calling for a friend, it's his ticket," she said.

"Well, you got a very lucky friend."

"How lucky, how much has he won?"

The woman laughed. "Oh, of course, sorry; the jackpot is forty seven million dollars."

FOUR

Syd walked in Havoc with a big smile on her face. Ryan was at a corner table conducting an interview with the bartender.

Syd loved Ryan's looks. He was tall, six-two to be exact, with jet-black hair, straight nose and strong chin. But what sent her heart a thumping were his dimples, one in each cheek, and his boyish, self-deprecating style. Like he had no idea how cute he was.

And Ryan loved his work. He practically oozed enthusiasm. His hazel eyes looked almost incandescent as he asked questions, made notes. He was one of the few truly happy people she'd ever met.

"Okay," Ryan said joining Syd in the doorway of Havoc. "The victim met a beautiful blonde somewhere around one-thirty. The bartender knew Colin Wood, knew his face at least, not so much his name. He'd come in every so often looking for a hook-up. He'd never seen the woman before. He'd remember, he said."

"Did the blonde and the victim know each other?" Syd asked.

"The bartender wasn't sure. When she came in, everyone noticed her. Even the ladies; she was that hot. The bartender saw her look around for a beat then head in Mr. Wood's direction. But she was alone and he was the only guy without a girl at that point."

"So she might have been looking for any single guy or him specifically."

"Exactly," Ryan said.

"Did she have a drink, any chance for a fingerprint?"

Ryan shook his head. "She didn't order anything. How about you, any luck at the 7-Eleven?"

A mischievous smile tugged her lips. "No security

camera aimed in this direction. But as for luck..." Syd handed him the piece of paper. "Call this number."

"Forty-seven million dollars!" Ryan said into the cell phone after reciting the serial number on the Lotto ticket.

"That's right, sir," the Lotto operator told him. "But you chose cash value, so after taxes you'll only net about thirty-four million."

"Only..." Ryan laughed. A few cops still working the crime scene began to gather as word spread. "So how do I get the money?"

"Just come down to the office, answer a few questions to verify it's your ticket, and we'll issue a check."

Warning bells went off in Ryan's head. "What do you mean verify it's mine?"

"Just answer a couple of questions. Where you bought the ticket, was it a quick pick or did you choose the numbers? We often check the store's video tape to see you buying it, but with a ticket this old, I doubt there would be a tape."

"Probably not," Ryan said, praying there wouldn't be.

"And like I told your friend, you need to hurry. This ticket expires on Thursday. It's only good for one hundred and eighty days after the drawing so you've only got two days left. After close of business Thursday, that's 6:00 p.m., it'll be worthless."

"Thursday, got it," Ryan said.

In point of fact, Ryan hadn't bought the ticket at all. Someone else did, a guy wearing grease-stained coveralls. He was in front of Ryan at the 7-Eleven; bought a six-pack of Bud light, a beef jerky and a pack of Marlboros. When he got his change, he had a buck left so he bought a Lotto ticket. He asked for a quick pick, cash value ticket, got it and left.

Ryan remembered because he was late for a court hearing but desperately needed some Rolaids for an excruciating attack of heartburn. The counterman and the guy in the coveralls took forever, talking about the Lakers, the Dodgers and even the fucking Angels while a volcano burbled in Ryan's stomach.

Finally, after the guy left, Ryan bought the antacids and headed out the door. He saw the guy in overalls climb into a tow truck. Ryan also noticed a Lotto ticket fluttering on the ground. He picked it up as the guy started his tow truck. Ryan thought about calling out to him, telling him he dropped his Lotto ticket, but Ryan was so annoyed that the jerk had taken so long at the counter that he just let him drive off.

Ryan had no idea who he was, didn't bother looking at the license plate, so had no way of tracking him down. And why would he bother? What were the odds a lottery ticket was actually worth anything? A hundred million to one odds, more? Fuck it, Ryan thought as he climbed into his Mustang. He shoved the ticket in his glove box and forgot about it.

Now the goddamn thing was worth millions and Ryan wasn't sure what he should do. File it under finders/keepers and claim the prize, or be honest and try and track down the guy in overalls. He needed time to think. "Look," he said to the Lotto lady, "I'm a police officer in the middle of a murder investigation. I'm not sure when I'll be able to stop by."

"Just get here by close of business Thursday or you can kiss your millions goodbye. Oh, and have you signed the ticket?"

"No."

"Nobody does. But do it, right now. That way no one can steal it from you."

"Okay," Ryan said, pulling out his pen, signing the back of the ticket. "Done."

"Great. Be sure to call and let us know when you're coming in. I'm sure some of the press will want to cover it. And be sure to keep the ticket someplace safe. Be a shame if you lost it."

"Don't worry," Ryan said. "I won't lose it. Thank you." Ryan hung up as Lieutenant Hanrahan and a couple of uniforms entered the bar.

"Is it true?" Hanrahan asked. "You just won the

Lotto?"

"He sure did, Chief," Syd said. "Forty-seven million cash dollars!"

"Actually, just thirty-four million after taxes," Ryan said.

"Hot damn!" Hanrahan said, high fiving a less than enthusiastic Ryan. "You going to clear this case for me before you quit?"

"I'm not going to quit."

"You're rich, Ryan. Why would you want to be a cop?"

"I love being a cop, Lieutenant. I don't give a shit about the money."

"Yeah, right."

"It's true."

Hanrahan reached out and grabbed the ticket. "Then give me it me."

Ryan grabbed it back. "No fucking way!"

"You see," Hanrahan said, laughing. "Money changes everything, take my word for it. Everything." A buzz rippled through the assembled cops agreeing with Hanrahan.

"Well, I don't have the money yet," Ryan said, carefully folding the Lotto ticket in half and slipping it into his wallet. "But I do have a murder to solve. Syd, you have the victim's address?"

She held up the paper Ramirez gave her. "He lives a couple of miles away, on Crescent."

"Let's go," Ryan said, heading for the door.

"There's a Bentley dealership on your way, Ryan," Hanrahan called after him. "You should stop by."

Ryan held up his hand, flipped Hanrahan the bird and walked out the door.

FIVE

"I thought you'd be happier."

"It's kind of hard to wrap your head around," Ryan said. "I mean, all that money…"

They were driving south on Sunset in Ryan's Mustang. The sun was up, and so was the temperature. They drove with the top down but the heater was off.

Syd turned to Ryan. "You've just been handed the keys to the kingdom. Money means freedom. You can do *anything* you want. Be *anything* you want. Go *anywhere* you want. Live anywhere, drive anything, eat anything, fuck anything… "

"I like fucking you."

"Good answer. You definitely deserve the money."

Ryan laughed. He wanted to tell Syd about the Lotto ticket. How he got it, his guilt, his confusion. But something held him back. What? He tried to put his finger on it. Was he ashamed that he lied to her when he told her he'd bought it? Was he afraid she'd be disappointed in him? Judge him? Would she stop trusting him? Or was he afraid she would tell him he shouldn't keep the ticket, that he had to be honest with the Lotto people and help them find the righteous winner?

Well, all of them actually. And he was very confused about his relationship with her in the first place. He'd only known her for eight weeks. Knew he was crazy about her. But was it lust or love?

Syd told him she loved him a week after they slept together. And she had said it practically every day since then. And the subtle plea was there; tell me you love me, too.

Then, just a week ago, walking out of a movie, hand in hand, in a great mood after a Reese Witherspoon romantic comedy, Ryan said it. "I love you, Syd." Just like that. It popped out spontaneously.

But was it really heartfelt or the result of Syd's subtle pressure? Or was it just the afterglow of the stupid movie?

Ryan hadn't loved anyone since Anne, hadn't really committed himself since Anne, and Lord knows how badly that turned out. Did he really want to risk it again?

Fuck, he thought. Life was so simple when he woke up this morning. How'd it get so confusing so fast?

"There," Syd said, pointing. "That's his house on the left."

Colin Wood lived in a small, one story Spanish style stucco. Two small palm trees sprouted out of a well-tended lawn. Ryan picked the morning paper up off the sidewalk, carried it to the front door. They could hear noise inside, a TV. Ryan rang the bell.

"Hold on, I'm coming," a male voice called. The door was pulled open and revealed a barefoot man wearing a USC tee shirt and gym shorts. He was a little goofy looking, Ryan thought, and he looked familiar. Tall, somewhere between six foot two or three, he was rail thin, blonde but balding, with a horse face. He looked like someone out of a Norman Rockwell painting. Then Ryan realized, he was a character actor. Ryan had seen him on TV.

"Can I help you?" the man asked.

Ryan handed him the newspaper, then badged him. "I'm Detective Magee, this is Detective Curtis. May we come in?"

"Sure," the man said warily, stepping aside. "What's this about?"

"Colin Wood," Ryan said. "Is he a friend of yours?"

The man nodded. "We're roommates." Then it dawned on him. "Oh, my God, something's happened, hasn't it?"

"He's been the victim of a crime. A murder." Ryan watched the man carefully looking for a sign of genuine surprise. At this point, everyone was a suspect.

The reaction had two parts. The first was concern

about Colin being involved in a crime, then the word, *murder,* settled in and shock filled the long face. "He's dead?"

"I'm afraid so."

"Who? Why?"

"That's what we're trying to find out," Syd said. "Could we ask you some questions, Mr..."

"Dodd. Sorry, I'm Reggie Dodd." He shook their hands, led them into the kitchen. The house was cluttered and looked like two men lived it in, two men with an aversion to cleaning up.

"You're an actor, aren't you?" Ryan asked. "You look familiar."

Dodd nodded. "That's how Colin and I met, on a movie."

"He was an actor, too?" Syd asked.

"Yeah." Dodd dug something out of a pile on the kitchen counter and handed it Syd. It was what was called a Head Shot, a picture of Colin Wood on the front and a list of his credits on the back. "We did that George Clooney picture last year. I was just splitting from my wife, Colin's girlfriend had just moved out, so he asked if I needed a place to crash. I've been here about six months."

Ryan studied the picture, recognized the face. He might have recognized him in the car, but all he was focused on then was the penis in his mouth.

"Can you tell me what happened?" Dodd asked.

Hanrahan had instructed everyone to keep the amputated appendage a secret, not so much as a courtesy to the victim, but holding back key evidence often helps separate real suspects from the nut jobs.

"He was found dead in his car."

"Where?"

"Outside a nightclub, the Havoc parking lot."

"Colin loved that place," Dodd said. "We both did. Great place to meet chicks." Dodd suddenly remembered Syd. "Sorry, I mean women. Meet women."

Syd smiled. "Chicks works, don't sweat it. You mentioned Colin broke up with a girlfriend. Tell us about

27

her."

"Abby, Abigail something or other; I don't remember her last name. I only met her once, when she stopped by to pick up some stuff she'd left behind."

"Pretty girl?" Ryan asked.

"Beautiful. Blonde, great body. She's a wannabe actress. Colin said it was the perfect job for her; she's a total drama queen."

Syd leaned forward. "So she had a temper."

"Did she ever. Colin said she caught him cheating on her and went ballistic."

"She got violent?"

"Colin said she practically trashed the place. Hit him in the head with a frying pan." Then it dawned on him. "Wait, you don't think Abby did this?"

"Just trying to narrow down the suspect list," Ryan said. "What about other people who might have wanted to hurt him; were there other women, maybe someone with a grudge?"

"There were plenty of other women, Colin was a total slut and proud of it. But lately they've all been happy hookups, if you know what I mean. He never mentioned any trouble."

Syd asked, "No threatening phone calls, letters, anything like that?"

"Not that I know of; Colin was a great guy. Everybody loved him."

"Not quite everybody," Ryan said. "Let me ask you something, did Colin have an American Express card?"

"Sure, a Platinum card. He loved to flash it, thought it impressed his dates."

"Is it here?" Syd asked. "Or had he mentioned losing it recently?"

"No, we went out to Flemings for dinner the other night and Colin used it to pay the check. I mean, I think I remember him putting it back in his wallet. Why, is it missing?"

"Yes," Ryan said. "Look, we need to go through Colin's things: computer, phone book, bills. We could get a warrant, but…"

"No, no problem. It's all right here."

"And next of kin," Syd said. "Who should we notify?"

"His mom's dead, but his dad is still alive, lives in Orange County."

Syd asked, "Do you have his number?"

Dodd shook his head. "But it'll be on his cell. Did you find that?"

"It was in the car," Syd said.

"He kept everything on his iPhone," Dodd said. "But he's got a phone book, too; I'll get it." Dodd got up to fetch it. Ryan's phone rang.

"Ryan."

"The plot thickens," Liz said from her examining room. "I'm looking down at the remains of Colin Wood, and you'll never guess what I found when I took his shirt off."

"Another penis?"

Liz snorted a laugh. "Funny. No, I found something carved into his chest. The number 2. My guess, it was probably the same blade that Benihana'd his penis."

Syd saw the shock on Ryan's face. "What? What is it?"

"The number 2 was carved into Colin Wood's chest," Ryan said checking to make sure Dodd was out of earshot.

"No shit," Syd said, the implication clear. "Which means the killer's done it before."

"And will probably do it again," Ryan said.

Syd's eyes lit up. "We've got ourselves a serial killer, Ryan. How cool is that!"

SIX

She stood naked in the shower. The make-up washed off. The nail and toe polish removed. The green contacts taken out. The Lady in Red was stripped bare, restored to her natural state.

Her name was Alice Waterman. She was pretty in a fresh-scrubbed, studious sort of way. But Alice never thought of herself as pretty. She thought of herself as smart. It had been beaten into her head ever since she was a little girl growing up in Santa Ana, California. Her brains were going to get her into a great college, good career and, one day, a solid marriage.

Her dad worked at the nearby Knotts Berry Farm theme park; he did maintenance on the thrill rides. Her mom worked at Sears in ladies apparel. A typical hard working blue collar family barely getting by, but they had a dream, a dream that one day their smart, gifted daughter would join the corporate culture as an executive and be able to live a life of privilege and luxury. And to succeed in a world run by men, her father told her she had to be able to compete with men out of the office, too. So while her friends took dance lessons, Dad taught her golf. He took her hunting; she even learned to box.

Alice wasn't popular in high school. She was heavy; judged a little plump if you were kind, fat if you were the typical high school kid. And the extra weight hid the simple beauty of the face that would one day emerge.

She hung with the nerds, and the boys liked her because she was promiscuous. She started giving hand jobs in eighth grade, blow jobs freshman year and was sleeping with a variety of boys by her sophomore year. But she dreamt of running with the cool kids, and even though word had spread that she was easy, there were plenty of prettier girls willing to put out. Alice was sentenced to high school Siberia and was miserable.

Alice turned off the water, pulled back the shower curtain and stepped out of the tub. The bathroom was tiny and smelled of mildew. The wallpaper was peeling away and the bowl of the once-white toilet bowl was stained a disgusting yellow. The sink was cracked and the counter was barely big enough to hold her prescription bottles. She even had to open the bathroom door so she'd have room to dry herself with the coarse towel.

But it was her bathroom and hers alone. She didn't have to share it with anyone, a definite improvement over her circumstances for the last few years. The dingy studio apartment, one of eight units above an army surplus store on Vine Street in Hollywood, smelled too, courtesy of the Thai fast food joint next door. But the apartment was hers alone. She didn't have a roommate. She could eat whenever she wanted. She could come and go as she pleased because the door locked from the inside, not the outside.

So much better than the fucking Institute.

Her parents had visited the apartment when she first moved in a month ago, and were disgusted. Her dad offered her money to get a nicer place. But she didn't want any more of his money. His money was *their* money and she wanted nothing to do with it.

Her mom had noticed the bottles of pills and Alice told her they were antidepressants prescribed at the Institute. No reason to freak her out with the truth; Stage IV breast cancer metastasized to the liver, lungs, bone and brain. The doctors told her she had six months to live, maybe a little longer with luck.

So, little girl, what did you do with the last six months of your life? Why I got even with the dirty bastards who ruined my life.

Two more men had to die. Two more souls rendered to balance the scales of justice.

Alice walked into the cramped living room/dining

room/kitchen/bedroom. Her war room. Four pictures were pinned to the dingy white walls. The late Colin Wood was picture number two. She picked up a red magic marker, drew a circle around his face, then a slash through the middle.

The picture to the immediate left of Colin also had a circle and slash scrawled across his face. Victim number one, Zachary Stone. He had been as easy to seduce as Colin. Not surprising, he was another horn dog asshole.

Stone was a lawyer.

The lawyer.

The cocksucker who orchestrated the Great Escape.

That's why he had to die first.

Stone lived in Newport Beach. He had a fancy suite of offices, drove a Silver Cloud convertible, wore three-thousand-dollar suits, got two-hundred-dollar haircuts, lived on the beach in an eight-million-dollar home and dated Southern California's most beautiful woman. He was slick, handsome and rich with the three most important ingredients for success: intelligence, charisma and ambition.

Stone had a powerful voice and an infectious personality that won over clients, jurors and judges; it was a wonderful asset for a criminal defense attorney who represented the rich, the very rich and ultra rich of Orange County from charges of bribery, fraud, embezzlement, assault, rape or murder. He'd even stoop to a DUI defense if the client was wealthy enough.

Alice had called his office, told the assistant she was referred by her close family friend, the Governor, and she'd like an appointment. She explained that she and her husband had been accused of stealing eighty million dollars from his investors and she needed a good lawyer. She wanted to be the last appointment of the day, so she asked if he could see her at 6:00 p.m. The assistant checked and told her that would be fine.

Alice dressed to kill, in red, of course. She watched his eyes as she walked into the office. They flicked from her blonde hair, to her face, to her tits, to her legs, to her

Manolo Blahnik's then back to her tits. She had him.

He indicated for her to sit on the couch, asked if her husband would be joining them. She said, no, the son of a bitch had fled the country. She was scared, confused and now alone. Would he help her?

Stone sat across from her, took her hands in his and said, "Absolutely, you can count on me."

She spun a sad story, a modified version of the ponzi scam Bernie Madoff used to rip off billions. In Alice's version she was the innocent victim of an evil husband who bilked millions and left her holding the bag.

She touched his arm, as she told her story, then a leg, for emphasis. Finally she started crying which prompted an embrace from Stone. She hugged him tightly, making sure he got a chest load of her tits and a nose full of her Chanel.

"For the first time in a long time," she said as they separated, "I feel that someone finally cares about me." She looked deeply, gratefully into his eyes then suddenly leaned forward and kissed him. It was practically platonic. Closed mouth, tender, sweet, but promising oh so much more. "I'm sorry," she said pulling back. "I shouldn't have done that."

Stone's face was flushed, and she was sure blood rushed to another part of his body as well. "It's all right," he said. "I understand. These are stressful times for you. Look, there's a wonderful restaurant just down the street, Gerard's. You know it?"

She did. When she researched Zachary Stone, the *L.A. Times* interview was actually conducted from what the interviewer described as Stone's favorite restaurant, Gerard's. The food was great, Stone said, but what he liked most was it was walking distance from his office. She was hoping he'd ask her to dinner there.   "Yes," she said. "They make a wicked martini."

"I'd love to buy you that martini, and dinner. We can talk some more about the case. Get to know each other a little better," he said, serving up a sexual innuendo.

Her eyes met his, message received. "That would be wonderful."

"I need some time to finish up here. Can you meet me there in say, an hour?"

She gave him her most promising smile. "See you then."

Walking distance. Gerard's was just a quarter of a mile from Stone's office. You simply walk down West Balboa Boulevard, turn right on 41st then cut through the alley which brings you to River Avenue and the restaurant.

And that's where Alice was waiting, hidden in the alley. When she saw Stone cross 41st, she crouched behind a dumpster, the Colt .25 in her right hand. Her ears did the work now. Just like her dad taught her when they went deer hunting. *You'll hear them first, in the brush. A few steps, nibble, a few more steps.*

At first she just heard the muted sounds of the city: the hum of traffic, the beeping of a truck backing up somewhere, a far off siren. Then she heard his footsteps. The crisp click of an expensive leather heel, then the click of another. The footfalls grew louder, the gait even, confident.

Then Stone passed the dumpster. Alice stepped out, said, "Zachary."

He stopped, turned, surprised to see her. "Hi."

She raised the Colt and shot him in the face.

POP.

The bullet went through his forehead, plowed through his frontal lobe, tumbled a bit taking out the septum pellucidum, thalmus and hypothalamus before coming to rest in the middle of his spinal cord. Catastrophic injuries and death was instantaneous. He hit the ground as a corpse.

Alice stood there, waiting to see if she'd feel any regret, any remorse. She'd killed before: birds, deer, an elk on a Colorado vacation when she was twelve. But this was her first human being.

Nope, she felt fine. Better than fine, actually, she felt great. Endorphins were released and did a waltz with the adrenaline coursing through her veins. It felt better than sex.

She slipped on a pair of surgical gloves, searched the alley for the spent cartridge, found it and slipped it in her pocket. Next she bent over the body, and slipped the wallet out of his Armani jacket. It was filled with hundreds, eleven of them, plus three twenties, a five and two ones. Good, she thought. She took eight of the hundreds; she needed some working capital, but left enough cash in the wallet so cops wouldn't think it was a robbery. He had all the major credit cards and her eyes settled on his Platinum American Express card. She slipped it out, not to use it, but as a souvenir, something to remember him by. Then she plucked a one dollar bill out of the wallet, and stuffed it into his right hand.

These murders were going to be Alice's legacy. And she wanted the story to be a colorful one. So she planned to leave a few subtle clues along the way to be deciphered later, clever nuggets that in hindsight would let everyone know how carefully she planned her revenge.

But she had to be careful. Because Alice wasn't afraid of getting caught, she was afraid of getting caught too soon. She needed time to kill all four.

Back in her apartment, Alice stared at the picture of Zachary Stone, at the circle and slash across his face. Then at Colin Wood's photo also marred with the red circle and slash.

Two down and two to go.

Her eyes drifted to the next picture, an old high school yearbook picture of a handsome blonde man in a Speedo. He had a lean, muscled body and an easy smile. Adam Devlin.

She had a wild crush on him in high school. Everyone knew because she'd stare at him like a lovesick puppy whenever she saw him. Adam was just nice enough to her to give her hope. Just nice enough to trick her into going over to Colin's house that night eleven years ago. That horrible night that changed everything.

Alice had no trouble locating Adam. He was all over the Internet; pictures of him at the Super Bowl, the World Series, the NBA Finals and Wimbledon. There was even a picture of Adam in front of his office building in Santa Monica.

That's where she planned to meet him. That's where she planned to kill him.

SEVEN

"Oh, I absolutely recognize him now," Syd said, staring down at Colin Wood's body. Ryan and Liz stood next to her in the morgue examination room. "He did this great guest shot on *Grey's Anatomy*. Gave head to Ellen Pompeo in a Starbuck's bathroom."

"Did he take his shirt off in the episode?" Liz asked.

"Actually, yes."

"Did he have this 2 carved into it?"

"Not so much."

"Then let's stay focused, shall we?"

"I've got Higgins searching VICAP for any recent victims with numbers carved on their corpses," Ryan said. "I know we've got no open LAPD files that match. You determine the cause of death?"

"There are two gunshot entrance wounds beneath the scrotum, the bullets ripped through just about every internal organ; one was imbedded in his spinal cord, the other in his heart. Death was probably instantaneous. The slugs were small, looked like .25's. I sent them to Forensics."

Ryan and Syd exchanged a confused look, tried to picture the murder. Ryan asked, "Did you find any evidence of fabric in the wounds?"

Liz smiled, the game was on. "No. The gun was pressed against bare skin."

"Bare skin," Syd said, the possibilities swirling in her brain. Something stuck. She asked, "Did you autopsy the penis?"

"Yes," Liz said, thinking, she's got it.

Realization dawned on Ryan. "Did you find any seminal fluid?"

"The vans deferens was swimming in it." Liz said, thinking, they made a pretty good team.

"She was blowing him," Ryan said, the picture now crystal clear.

"Wow," Syd said. "This chick has got some serious *cohones* of her own."

"Any chance of DNA on the penis?" Ryan asked.

Liz shook her head. "Just his. I found traces of an antiseptic on the skin. Looks like she wiped it down before cutting it off."

"She must've really hated this dude," Syd said. "I mean, talk about premeditated. She picks him up in a bar, seduces him in his car, gives him head before killing him, takes out a scalpel, gloves and antiseptic and goes to work. And then taunts *us* with a 2 carved into his chest."

Ryan shook his head. "Something's not making sense. If she hated him enough to rearrange his body parts, wouldn't he have recognized her? Known her?"

"You thinking Colin's girlfriend, Abigail?" Syd asked.

"An obvious place to start, but maybe too obvious."

Liz said, "She could just be a freak who hates men. Then the 2 would make more sense. She's decided to rid the world of men, one cock at a time and she's keeping count."

Ryan considered. "Makes more sense than someone killing all her old boyfriends, but at this point, anything's possible. I just hope we find victim number one before there is a victim number three." Ryan started for the door, Syd on his tail.

"Hey, Ryan," Liz called after him. "One more thing."

Ryan turned. "Anything, Liz."

"Can I borrow a million bucks?"

"Oh, shit, you heard."

"Everyone's heard, Ryan. Congratulations, baby. But be careful, you're about to have a whole bunch of new best friends."

The L.A. County Morgue is on Mission Road near downtown L.A., about a fifteen- minute drive from Ryan and Syd's Hollywood office. They were still in Ryan's

Mustang; they hadn't had a chance to go the station and switch to their LAPD issued Crown Vic. But they were headed there now.

"You ever hate a guy enough to want to cut his dick off?" Ryan asked.

"Yes," Syd said before she could stop herself. Syd's stepfather wasn't the only one to have abused her. There were scores of men.

But Syd wasn't ready to tell Ryan about that part of her life, yet.

If ever.

"Whose dick would you have cut off? Have you mentioned him?"

"No," Syd said, then she fashioned a lie. "He was just some creep from high school; he pretended to like me just to win a bet with some friends. Broke my heart."

"Asshole."

"Do me a favor, Ryan. Don't ever break my heart."

Ryan answered without thinking about it. "I won't, I promise."

Four words. I won't, I promise. Ryan said them because it's the kind of thing you say when you're really just telling someone what they want to hear.

Syd heard an oath.

They would both remember those four words for a long time.

EIGHT

"Something's up," Ryan said as they pulled up to the Hollywood Station. News vans clogged the street and a pack of cameras and reporters blocked the sidewalk.

"Maybe the mayor's inside," Syd said, then noticed the hungry look in the reporter's eyes. "Or the governor." They parked in the lot, climbed out of the car. Ryan carried Colin Wood's laptop, Syd had Wood's check and appointment books. They headed for the back door.

"That's him," one of the reporters called, pointing. "Hey, Ryan!" she started jogging toward Ryan and the others followed, also calling out to him.

"This can't be good," Ryan muttered as they were surrounded. Ryan knew most of the reporters; he'd given many interviews over the years.

The pretty blonde from CBS asked, "How's it feel to be the richest cop in L.A.?"

The redhead from ABC, "The richest cop in the world!"

NBC's brunette, a former beauty pageant winner who Ryan dated briefly asked, "We heard you won fifty million dollars."

FOX's ponytail, "I heard a hundred million."

Syd watched the chaos, amused as Ryan held up his hands. "Hold on, everyone. Quiet, please!"

Reluctantly, they all shut up. Ryan's eyes flicked from one reporter to another, from one camera to another, all staring at him, expectantly. He milked the moment then said, "No comment," and plowed through the cameras.

"What about the murder, this morning?" NBC's brunette asked. "What can you tell us?"

Ryan turned back to the pack. "Nothing yet, we're still awaiting notification of next of kin."

"The bartender said he was an actor."

"In this town, isn't everyone?"

"One last question," ABC's redhead called out. "Are you married?"

"Only to my work," Ryan said. Then he swiped his ID card in the reader, threw open the back door and disappeared inside, Syd in his wake. He slammed the door behind them. "Fuck, how'd they find out about the lottery?"

"Good news travels fast."

Ryan wasn't so sure it was good news.

"Think about it," Syd said as they headed for the Homicide bullpen. "A few hours ago a handful of cops at the crime scene heard you won the lottery. So one cop tips someone in the media, whose assistant texts her friend at another station and in a cyber second *everyone* knows."

"Cop wins money. BFD. Aren't there more important stories to cover?"

"You don't get it, do you? Everybody dreams of hitting the jackpot. Everybody. And whenever someone hits the Lotto for twenty or thirty or forty-six million dollars, the winners are paraded on the *TODAY* show, profiled in *US Weekly*, and trotted out in front of an eager public. It's wish fulfillment, Ryan. People want to share your joy."

Ryan wasn't feeling too joyful. He was conflicted. Not only about whether he should take the money, but also whether he should he tell Syd the truth.

Syd, meanwhile, had worries of her own. "I'm not sure I liked the way they were looking at you."

"Who?"

"Those female reporters. Usually we're just information sources; they look at us for a story. But those prom queens with microphones were eyeing you for dinner. You just got a lot better looking, Ryan."

"I do feel taller."

Syd cupped her hand over his crotch. "And this definitely feels bigger."

Ryan laughed as Syd dropped her hand and they turned

into the bullpen. It was 10:00 a.m., rush hour in a homicide bureau, because even though most of the detectives spent the day on the streets conducting investigations, they started and ended each day in the bullpen. And almost every one of the sixteen desks was occupied. A hum of busy conversation filled the air, punctuated by an occasional burst of laughter. But as Ryan and Syd crossed to their desks, the conversation slowly died and then the room was quiet, all eyes on Detective Ryan Magee.

"What?" he asked.

Suddenly everyone started clapping and cheering. Ryan was popular, but now he was forty-seven million times more popular. These men and women were Ryan's friends, and they were genuinely happy for him. And that just made Ryan feel even worse. He realized that if he said, *the ticket isn't mine, give the money to someone else,* he'd be letting them down.

"Okay, okay, thank you," he said, holding his hands up. "But tell me you don't just love me for my money."

That got a laugh, and after a spattering of "congratulations," everyone got back to work.

Syd checked her email. "We got a preliminary report from VICAP on the amputated penis." Her voice trailed off as she read. "Jeez, Louise, there are a lot of freaks out there who like to slice and dice. Ryan, there are like, fifty cases going back over twenty-five years."

"What's the most recent?"

Syd checked. "Nine months ago in Miami." Syd quickly scanned the summary. "Victim was a Columbian drug runner; they caught the killer, a shooter from a rival gang trying to send a message."

"Can't imagine that's related; print them all out and we'll take a look." Ryan picked up his phone, called Ramirez at SID. "Hey, Tony, it's Ryan."

"Great, I'm glad you called."

Ryan had heard that excited tone in Ramirez's voice before, usually before Ramirez dropped a bomb that broke a case wide open. Ryan could feel his pulse quicken. "Talk to me, Tony."

"You know how much you love my mother's albondigas?"

"The world's best meatballs, absolutely," Ryan said, confused.

"Well, I've put together a business plan for a national franchise, Maribel's Meatballs. We'll just have restaurants, to start; but I've got plans for canned and frozen food, cookbooks, and a line of Mexican spices. And all we need is a little seed money, say two hundred thousand dollars."

Oh shit, Ryan thought. Suddenly everyone thinks I'm an ATM. But he liked Tony and wanted to be polite. "Sounds like a great idea, Tony. But I haven't even thought about what I'm going to do with the Lotto money, so this is way too soon for me to be looking at investment opportunities."

"But you won forty-seven million bucks, what's two hundred thousand?"

"Thirty-four after taxes, but that's not the point. It's too soon, Tony, okay?"

Tony paused then said, "Okay."

Ryan heard the disappointment in his voice. Ryan could imagine how much Tony and his mom had invested in this dream, a dream they had no way to realize. Then, out of nowhere, someone Tony knew morphed into a potential sugar daddy and suddenly *anything* was possible. Of course he had to ask Ryan for the money. "Look, Tony," Ryan said, regretting the words even as he said them. "I'm not saying no. I'm just saying you need to give me a little time."

"Oh, Ryan, that's great," Ramirez said, his excitement palpable. "You won't be sorry, man."

"Hold it, I haven't said yes, yet; I just said we'll talk about it later."

"I know, I know, but when you read the business plan, you'll realize this is a no brainer. I'll send it right over."

"Wait, whoa, what about the Colin Wood crime scene? You got anything for me?"

"Oh yeah, I almost forgot. Not sure it'll help much,

but the blonde hair we found, it's human all right, dyed, but no root. No root, no follicle, no DNA. It could also have come from a wig, so we're can't even say for certain the woman was blond. So, sorry Ryan, we've got nothing."

Ryan didn't expect much from Ramirez, but he was still disappointed. "Okay Tony, thanks." Ryan hung up, he looked up to find Syd staring at him, Colin Wood's iPhone in her hand. She'd checked for pictures and video; the phone had none. But it was loaded with music and the phone directory was extensive.

"I've got two numbers for you: Andrew Wood, the victim's father, and Abigail Granger, former girlfriend."

"Let's try the father first," Ryan said. Syd brought it up on the iPhone, tapped the number, handed the phone to Ryan. He got an answering machine.

"Sorry I missed your call," a male voice said. "Please leave your name and number and I'll call you back."

"He's not home," Ryan said to Syd, and then left his name and cell phone number on the machine. Ryan looked up Abigail's number on the iPhone and called. It rang.

The first contact with a prime suspect was critical, so Ryan always weighed his words and listened to their words very carefully.

It rang again and was answered. "Hello, asshole. What the fuck do you want?"

Ryan had to smile. Abigail obviously checked her caller ID and thought Colin was calling her. "Ms. Granger, this is Detective Ryan Magee of the Los Angeles Police Department."

There was silence for a moment, then, "Police Department...?"

"I'm afraid Colin Wood has been the victim of a crime, Ms. Granger, and we'd like to talk to you."

Ryan could almost hear her stiffen over the phone. "What kind of crime?"

"He's been murdered."

There was a sharp intake of breath, and then fear coated her next words. "Why do you want to talk to me?"

"Just routine, Ms. Granger. We understand you used

to be close to Mr. Wood; hopefully you can give us information that will aid our investigation."

Another pause, she was thinking. "Okay, I guess; I'm a hostess at the Ivy. I'll be here all day."

"My partner and I can be there in an hour."

"You don't wear uniforms or anything, do you? I mean, it won't look good if I'm seen talking to a couple of cops."

"We're plainclothes detectives, Mr. Granger. We blend in just fine."

A hesitant pause, then, "Okay. Oh, can you tell me how he died?"

A logical question, Ryan thought. The killer, of course, would have known he was shot, but this could also be another way to deflect suspicion. "He was shot," Ryan said.

"Do you think he suffered?"

"No, death was probably instantaneous."

"Too bad," she snapped and hung up.

Ryan handed Syd back her cell phone. "That's one angry woman."

"Do you think she did it?"

"No. But hopefully she'll be able to help us figure out who did." Ryan noticed Lieutenant Hanrahan at the door of his office. Hanrahan crocked his finger in a come-here motion. "The boss wants us," Ryan said and led Syd to the Lieutenant's office.

"I heard about the 2 carved in Colin Wood's chest," Hanrahan said. "You think we've got a serial killer?"

"Not sure yet," Ryan answered. "The perp could have put it there to throw us off."

"No way, Chief," Syd said, excited. "She put it there to mark her second victim. Two down and more to come. We've got a serial killer."

"Try not to sound so happy about it," Hanrahan said. "You positive it's a she?"

"I am," Syd said.

Hanrahan turned to Ryan. "How about you?"

"Probably. She may be working with someone else, a

guy, maybe; too soon to tell."

"Any precedent to numbers carved on a body?"

Ryan shook his head. "Nothing in our database, we're checking VICAP."

"The press have any idea yet?"

Syd laughed. "They're too obsessed with Ryan's windfall. A pack of L.A.'s most beautiful reporters ambushed us on our way in, bombarding Ryan with questions and wedding proposals."

Hanrahan coughed up a throat full of phlegm, pulled a handful of Tootsie Roll Pops out of his desk drawer. He offered them to Ryan and Syd who both shook their head. Hanrahan unwrapped a cherry one for himself. "Well, I got a feeling serial killer will trump millionaire cop, right Ryan?" But when Hanrahan and Syd glanced at Ryan, Ryan was looking past them into the bullpen.

Syd followed his gaze to a beautiful brunette standing in the middle of the room. She had a Visitor's badge pinned to her silk collar and was obviously searching for someone. Her eyes came to rest on Ryan. They looked at each other in silence for a moment, and then she gave him a tentative smile. Syd's radar spiked. "Let me guess," she said, keeping her tone neutral, "Your ex-wife?"

Ryan nodded. "Anne. I wonder what she's doing here."

Ryan had never told Syd much about his marriage. Just said they got married too young and it didn't work out. But Ryan looked wounded right now. Vulnerable. Jealousy surged through Syd. But she couldn't let Hanrahan sense it, or Ryan for that matter. So, as nonchalant as she could muster, Syd said, "Only one way to find out."

Without ever taking his eyes from Anne, Ryan nodded again and walked into the bullpen.

"That is one beautiful woman," Hanrahan said.

"She sure is," Syd said, hating her.

Ryan reached Anne and gave her a polite hug. Same cologne, he thought. When she left him, Ryan used to smell her pillow at night to get a whiff of that cologne. It made him ache. "This is a surprise," he said.

"I was in the station on business, so I thought I'd stop by and say hello," she said, her eyes taking an inventory of his face. "God, you look great. You've really been taking care of yourself, Ryan."

His eyes went from her brown eyes to her patrician nose and lingered on the small cleft in her chin. "You, too," he said. "How's Rick?" Ryan asked, hoping Anne's husband had choked to death on a chicken bone or gotten stomach cancer and died a horrible death.

"He's great. And you, are you with someone now?"

"No," Ryan said, feeling guilty about Syd, but he could hardly admit to sleeping with his partner.

"I'd love to catch up, Ryan, you got a few minutes for a cup of coffee?"

"Not now, no. I'm in the middle of something. But I'd like that too; maybe in a day or so. Can I call you?"

"Absolutely," Anne said, handing him her card. "And if you don't call me, I'll call you." Anne leaned forward, kissed Ryan on the cheek. "Till then..."

Ryan watched her walk out the door. "Nice ass," Syd said, joining Ryan.

"Not really," Ryan said. "It's riddled with cellulite."

"Liar."

"Okay, she's got a great ass, and the rest of her ain't too bad either, but she's got one problem."

"What's that?"

"She's not you."

Syd smiled. "You're sweet. I'd kiss you if it wouldn't get us fired."

Ryan looked into Syd's adorable freckled face. "It would almost be worth it. Now come on, we've got a murder to solve."

NINE

Adam Devlin was going to die today.

He didn't know it of course; he was firmly entrenched in his typical Tuesday routine. The day had started with the alarm waking him at five forty-five. He rolled over on his 1020 thread count, 100% spun Egyptian Cotton Sateen Jacurard sheets and looked into the sleeping face of his wife, Emily. Emily was cheerleader pretty, blonde, athletic, perky. They'd been college sweethearts at USC and gotten married the same June they graduated. And after seven years of marriage, they were still happy. Well, L.A. happy. She was having an affair with the eighteen-year-old boy living next door and Adam cheated regularly with an array of willing participants.

They lived in a five-million-dollar house in Brentwood, bought with the money Adam made as a wildly successful sports agent. Adam's best friend in college was the USC quarterback, who went on to win the Heisman trophy, and then signed an eighty-million-dollar contract with the Washington Redskins. The quarterback signed on as Adam's first client and after a blizzard of commercials and endorsements, other clients soon followed.

Adam rolled out of bed, slipped on a pair of Nike workout shorts, Under Armor tee shirt, Reebok socks and Adidas running shoes, all gifts from his many sponsors, and walked down the hall to his home gym. He jumped on his Precor treadmill, did twenty minutes at 4.5 miles an hour at 5% elevation, and then did twenty more minutes on his Parabody weight machine, also gifts from sponsors. He checked his email on his Samsung Galaxy then watched a 32 inch Sony LCD flat screen as he worked out, switching between ESPN and CNBC to catch up on two of his favorite things, sports and money.

Next he shaved with a Gillette Fusion razor, brushed his teeth with Crest toothpaste, showered with Irish Spring soap, shampooed with Pantene and dressed in his usual blue Levi 501's, a pale yellow Tommy Hilfiger dress shirt, then slipped, barefoot, into a pair of Kenneth Cole loafers. Emily was up by then and had poured Adam a bowl of Grape Nuts, sliced him a Chiquita banana and made him a Starbucks decaf latte with nonfat Alta Dena milk and half a pack of Splenda. And yes, they were all sponsor gifts.

Adam and Emily chatted about their upcoming day. Emily had her tennis league at Riviera and a lunch at Geoffrey's with Ellen and JoAnne.

Adam had a meeting with an NBA official in the morning, lunch with a golf pro client at Mr. Chow's, then a meeting at the Bel Air Regent Hotel with some execs from BMW who wanted his clients in their cars.

So, with exactly eleven hours left to inhale oxygen, Adam steered his Salsa Red XKR 4.2 Supercharged Jag convertible into the parking lot of his Santa Monica office building. As he spun the wheel to pull into his assigned parking spot, a white Prius suddenly backed out of a spot in front of him and they collided.

"God damn it," Adam said leaping out of his car to inspect the damage. It was minor, a small dent on his bumper, a bigger ding on the Prius, but he was still pissed. As the door to the Prius opened, he prepared a verbal assault that died in his throat when he saw the driver.

She was blonde, tall and beautiful. She wore a white halter-top, red shorts and sandals. She was more skin than cloth and Adam wasn't complaining. This girl was hot.

"I'm so sorry," the blonde said. "I'm such an idiot. Oh, and look at your beautiful car, it's ruined."

"Not at all, it's just a scratch," Adam said. "Your car took most to the damage."

"I hope we don't have to call the police or involve the insurance companies," she said, her green eyes locked on his face. "My rates are already sky high and I couldn't afford another hike."

Adam could feel this woman's sexuality. It practically radiated off of her. He had to have her, so he pulled out one of his favorite lines. "Are you an actress, or something," Adam blurted out. "I mean, you are just *so* beautiful."

The blonde blushed, embarrassed. "Me? No, no; I'm, well, to be honest, I'm out of work at the moment. I was hoping to find a job, something in fashion or advertising, but I just moved to town, so I don't know anybody, and I'm having a hard time getting started."

"I have a lot of contacts in advertising," Adam said. "Maybe I could help you. My name is Adam, by the way..." Adam extended his hand.

The blonde took it, gave him a firm handshake. "Susie," Alice said. "My name is Susie."

Adam loved the feel of her skin, he let the handshake linger, and then reluctantly let go. "Tell you what, Susie, I've got a meeting at the Bel Air Regent Hotel this afternoon but I'll be done about five-thirty. If you'll meet me in the bar, we can talk and I bet I can help you get that job."

"That's fantastic! Adam, thank you so much," then her eyes dropped to the damaged fenders. "But what about your car?"

"Don't worry about it. In fact," Adam said, pulling out a thick roll of hundreds and peeling off five. "Use this to get your bumper fixed. If I hadn't been going so fast, you never would have hit me."

"I can't take your money."

"You can and will," Adam said, closing her hand around the handful of bills. "And that's just the beginning. You've got a friend in L.A. now, me. So will I see you at the Bel Air Regent?"

Alice scrunched up her face pretending to think about it, and then nodded. "Yes. Thank you, Adam." She stuffed the money in purse. "Thank you so much."

Adam had a smile on his face as he got back into his car. A smile and a hard-on.

TEN

The Crown Vic smelled like pepperoni pizza. Ryan and Syd were sharing the car with a team from the vice squad that had been staking out a strip club waiting for a certain pimp to show up, and each morning Ryan and Syd knew what the team ate for dinner. They had eclectic taste, Chinese, Mexican, and last night, Italian.

Ryan was behind the wheel, talking on his cell phone. "Yes, that'll be fine sir, and again, my sympathies." Ryan disconnected. "Colin Wood's father will meet us at the morgue at four o'clock to ID the body."

Syd had the VICAP printout on her lap. "Good," she said as Ryan drove down Robertson Boulevard en route to the Ivy restaurant. "Did you know there is actually a medical term for having your cock cut off, penectomy."

"No way."

"Way. That's when doctors do it, if the patient has cancer or something. But when it's involved in a crime, it's just called mutilation. By the way, the killer of that drug dealer I mentioned in the office was caught and is currently in prison. And so is this guy in Germany who cut off some guy's penis, watched him bleed to death, and then ate him."

"Ate the guy's penis?"

"Yeah, and other stuff. What a freak."

"How about cases where the doer was a woman?"

"Been a while," Syd said flipping through the pages. "You might've heard of Lorena Bobbitt; in 1993 she cut off her husband's penis while he was asleep then threw it out the car window."

"Why?"

"She was pissed he wouldn't give her an orgasm."

"In that case, I've got nothing to worry about," Ryan

said.

Syd smiled. With Ryan, she had multiple orgasms. "Nothing at all. Anyway, doctors were able to reattach Bobbitt's penis and he went on to become a porn star. And Mrs. Penis Remover was found not guilty by reason of temporary insanity. So a happy ending for everyone involved. Well, everyone but us." She flipped through the report. "There are no cases of a woman killing a man and cutting off his you know what. Just a few angry women hacking away at lovers and boyfriends."

"And nothing in the last few weeks or months?"

"No."

"Shit." Ryan's cell phone rang. He answered. "Hello."

"Hey Ryan, its Johnny."

Ryan tried to place the name, couldn't. "Johnny?"

"Johnny Grayson, you dope. Your one and only brother."

My one and only *step*brother, Ryan thought, and for only eighteen months. Johnny was the son of Maggie, wife number two. A couple of years older than Ryan he had picked on Ryan relentlessly. Now he was a manager at Home Depot but spent every spare moment at the racetrack. Ryan thought the guy was a total loser and hadn't spoken to him in a couple of years.

"Hey, Johnny, what's up?"

"You are, bro. You are forty-seven million smackers worth of up."

Fuck, Ryan thought. "Actually it's only thirty-four after taxes."

"Still enough to start that stable of horses we always talked about."

"We never talked about a stable of horses, Johnny."

"Okay, you may not have, but it's something I've always dreamt of. And I figured it would be the perfect way for you to share your wealth with the family."

Ryan wasn't sure about a lot of things, including whether he was even going to take the money; but one thing he was sure of, there was no way Johnny Grayson was going to see a penny of it. "Look, Johnny, I can't talk about this right now. I'm on a case. But I'll call you back, I promise," Ryan hung up, and then muttered, "When hell freezes over."

"And so it begins," Syd said.

"Oh, it's begun all right," Ryan said. "Tony Ramirez called me earlier about a meatball franchise, in the men's room Chen begged me for *just* eighty-three thousand dollars so he could save his mother's house from foreclosure, in the locker room Katz showed me a picture of the fishing boat he's always dreamed of and it only cost one hundred and eighteen thousand dollars." Ryan pulled to a stop in front of the Ivy. "God damn lottery ticket."

"Speaking of which," Syd said, climbing out of the car. "When do you want to stop by the Lotto office and pick up your check? You don't have much time."

"I'm not sure," Ryan said, his eyes searching the restaurant's patio. He picked out a pretty blonde ushering a couple to their table. "That looks like her."

Syd spotted her. Actress pretty, Syd thought, with a bit of attitude. She fit the roommate's description. "Let's go find out," she said.

They caught up to Abigail Granger at the hostess stand, introduced themselves and Abigail led them to a small office behind the bar. Her eyes were bloodshot; it looked like she'd been crying. She may have hated Colin Wood, Ryan thought. But there was a lot of love there, too.

"I'm sorry for your loss," Ryan said.

"Yeah, yeah; fuck him," she said, fighting back tears. "He was a selfish SOB, you know, and was always cheating on me. And I'd catch him and we'd fight, and I'd leave... then a few days later he would call, or stop by with flowers, or send some guy with a mandolin who'd sing kitschy Barry Manilow love songs and I'd melt and go back to Colin and he'd promise to never cheat on me again."

"But he would," Syd said sympathetically.

Abby nodded. "I'm such a sap. And now," she said, the tears flowing, "and now he'll never call again."

Ryan had seen a lot of people grieve. Some of the

most anguished and heartfelt had actually turned out to be the killer, so Ryan never let himself be swayed by public displays of emotion.

Ryan had taught Syd this, but needn't have bothered. Syd's own life lessons had taught her to never trust anyone. And as she and Ryan watched Abigail Granger weep, Syd looked at her blonde hair, remembered Colin Wood's roommate's story about Abigail hitting Colin with a frying pan and Abigail's notorious temper. When Abigail regained her composure, Syd asked, "Do you have any idea who may have wanted to kill Colin?"

Abigail looked confused. "I thought you said it was a robbery?"

"There were certain elements at the crime scene to suggest it might have actually been a premeditated murder," Ryan said.

"Just for the record," Syd said as casually as possible while she flipped open her notepad, "where were you between the hours of midnight and two a.m.?"

"In bed, asleep."

"Can anyone confirm that?" Syd asked.

Anger flashed in Abigail's blue eyes. "Are you saying I'm a suspect?"

"You can't be a suspect if you have an alibi," Ryan said.

Abigail stuck out her hands. "Then lock me up officer because I was alone in my apartment and unless you can get my cat to talk, I've got no way to prove it."

"We're not here to arrest anyone," Syd said. "We're just trying to get some information."

"Oh, I get it," Abigail said. "You heard about some of the fights Colin and I had. Well just because I hit him with a frying pan, backed over his foot in my car and stabbed him in the hand with a fork doesn't mean I killed him." Abigail let the words hang in the air, then seemed to hear what she said and started laughing. "Okay, maybe it does sound like I killed him."

Syd laughed too. "Actually, we'd heard only about the frying pan."

"Okay, look," Abigail said. "I've got a temper, and I can be a bitch, I admit it. But I didn't kill Colin, I swear."

Syd believed her. And it would be easy enough to show Abigail's picture to the bartender to confirm it. She glanced at Ryan who seemed to agree.

"You have any idea who might have wanted him dead?" Ryan asked.

"If it helps," Syd said, "he was spotted at the crime scene with a beautiful blonde."

Abigail's hand involuntarily touched her hair. "Ah, now I get it. 'Beautiful blonde,' guess I should be complimented."

"Do you know of any women who hated Colin," Ryan pressed. "And forget hair color; people wear wigs."

Abigail concentrated then revelation lit up her face. "Something happened a year or so before I met Colin, which would make it like three years ago – he was accused of date rape. He wasn't arrested or anything, but I know there was an investigation, and she threatened to sue him, but Colin's dad ending up paying her off and the whole thing went away."

"Do you think Colin was capable of date rape?" Syd asked.

"Date rape all depends on your definition of no, doesn't it? There are a few times in my life when I'd say no, but the guy didn't listen, kept kissing, rubbing, begging and I'd eventually give in; well, in my head that's still date rape." She looked at Syd. "That ever happen to you?"

Syd thought of her stepfather. "More than a few times."

"So," Abigail said. "Sure, I can see Colin crossing someone *else's* line. It's all perception, after all, isn't it?"

"Do you know this woman's name?" Ryan asked.

"No, sorry, I only know the story because Colin got drunk one night and told me. Not one of his proudest moments. But I'm sure his dad knows the name, he wrote her a check, right?"

"We'll ask him," Ryan said.

"Look," Abigail said, glancing into the restaurant. "Is

there anything else, I've really got to get back to work."

"You're an actress, right?" Ryan asked.

"Yes."

"And I bet you keep some headshots here, just in case you meet a producer or director."

"And you'd like one to show that bartender or whoever to see if I was the one that killed Colin. Sure, no problem, I'll be right back."

Abigail hurried off.

"The date rape sounds promising," Syd said.

"Speaking of which, did you mean what you told her. About being date raped?"

"Of course not," Syd said. "I was just trying to earn her confidence."

"Good," he said, taking her hand. "I hate thinking anything terrible ever happened to you."

Anything terrible, indeed, Syd thought.

Syd grew up in Kansas City, Missouri, daughter of Todd Curtis, an eighth grade science teacher and Amanda Curtis, a registered nurse. The first nine years of young Syd's life were blissfully normal until her father fell in love with the school principal, another man, and they ran off together.

Feelings of abandonment rocked young Syd. Not to mention confusion; her daddy left home for another man?

Her mother didn't fare any better. Humiliated, she started self medicating from the hospital's pharmacy. And drinking. And ignoring her daughter.

Then a white knight showed up, Doctor Jay Stevens, an ER doctor Syd's mother met at work. He had a drug problem, too. Speed. And he drank more than a bit. So they had a lot in common. When Syd was twelve, they got married.

Syd never liked Doctor Jay. He had this way of looking at her that made her skin crawl. She learned the perfect word for him when she was older. Smarmy.

Doctor Jay was, of course, lusting after the sweet, redheaded darling. And on her fourteenth birthday, when

Syd was asleep in her bed, and her mother was passed out on the couch, a drunk Doctor Jay stumbled into the birthday girl's room, took off his clothes and climbed into bed next to her. She awoke with a start; Doctor Jay clasped his hand over her mouth, told her to do what he said or he'd kill her mother.

And so it went for three years. A thoroughly confused and conflicted Syd, afraid for her mother's life, afraid to lose another father figure, submitted her body to repeated abuse. Once she tried to tell her mother, but as soon as Mom realized where the conversation was going, she shut her daughter up. She didn't want to hear what she suspected. She didn't want to lose another husband, no matter how high a price her daughter had to pay.

Always a loner with few friends, the shame and guilt of her stepfather's abuse isolated Syd even more. She felt trapped and truly alone.

Then, late one cold February night, Syd heard Doctor Jay pull into the garage. On nights when Doctor Jay worked this late, he usually came upstairs to Syd's bedroom and stinking of bourbon, would slip into her bed. But tonight, she didn't hear the dreaded sound of the car being shut off, the garage door closing, the kitchen door opening and his feet on the staircase. Tonight she just heard the sound of the car, idling in the garage.

She realized he'd probably fallen asleep after pulling into the garage. It had happened before. Too bad he didn't close the garage door, she thought. Then the car's exhaust would've filled the garage and he'd die of carbon monoxide poisoning.

Epiphany. Just because he didn't close the door didn't mean someone else couldn't. She tiptoed into the hallway and peaked in her mother's room – she was out, snoring. Syd snuck down the stairs and silently opened the door to the garage. Yep, there he was, asleep behind the wheel of his BMW.

Syd put her finger on the garage door button and hesitated. She knew pushing it meant going through a one-way door. She'd be a murderer. If caught, she could go to jail. If God was more than a psychological crutch, she could go to hell. But if Doctor Jay was dead, she'd be free.

She pushed the button.

His asphyxiation was ruled an accidental death. Syd had gotten away with murder.

But if Syd thought getting rid of Doctor Jay would fix her life, she was wrong. Her mother plummeted into alcohol-drenched mourning. She took her grief out on Syd, snapping at her, hitting her. Then her Mom had the audacity to throw Doctor Jay's molestations at Syd, accusing her daughter of trying to seduce her husband, trying to steal him away. That did it. After committing cold-blooded murder, the decision to run away seemed easy.

Where to go? Why Hollywood, of course. Syd had always daydreamed about being a famous actress. That's where her mind would flee when Doctor Jay would paw her.

Syd had some money saved, almost two thousand dollars, enough to get to L.A. The rest; finding a place to live, getting a car, finding an agent, Syd figured, would take care of themselves. The next morning, instead of going to school, Syd boarded a Greyhound bus.

Three days later, a stiff and bleary-eyed Syd finally pulled into Hollywood. It was midnight when she stepped into a practically deserted bus station. She looked at a wall full of hotel advertisements, found a cheap motel about three blocks away and started walking down Cahuenga Boulevard.

The adrenaline that had fueled Syd's escape had drained by now, leaving her bedraggled, inside and out. She had a purse, a backpack and a suitcase which she rolled behind her.

A van suddenly screeched to a stop next to her, the side door slid open and three men leapt out. They grabbed Syd, shoved her into an alley. One guy snatched the suitcase, another used a knife to cut the straps of the backpack and the third ripped the purse out of her hands.

They were Hispanic, wired on something, twitchy.

Two of the men tossed the goods in the van as the third man pressed Syd against the alley wall, shoved his hand under her blouse and said, "Don't scream, don't fight and you might live." His pupils were the size of golf balls. He pressed himself against her as the other two returned, lust in their eyes. Syd realized she was going to be gang-raped.

Then a shot rang out. All heads spun to see a man standing in the mouth of the alley, backlit by a street light, a huge automatic in his hand, pointed at Syd's attackers. He pistol whipped the man closest to him, shoved the barrel of the gun against the forehead of another and hissed at them in Spanish. Clearly terrified, the men scrambled back into their van and with a screech of rubber, fled.

"You all right?" the man asked his voice now gentle, concerned.

Syd nodded, grateful. The man was tall, lanky and shaved bald. And though he seemed scary as hell with that gun in his hand, there was something incredibly soulful about him. His eyes were dark brown with a few flecks of green and he had thick, sensuous lips. Then she realized, "Oh, my God. They got all my stuff. My clothes, my money…"

"Do you have any friends in L.A.? Is someone waiting for you?"

She shook her head as tears formed. "No."

"Then let me be your friend," he said, sticking out his hand. "My name is Ernesto."

Ernesto.

Her savior.

Oh, that first night, the night he *rescued* her, Ernesto was so charming. So caring and gentle. He gave her a glass of wine, scrambled her eggs, told her he was a musician, singer-songwriter, and he was just a couple of weeks from recording his first CD. Then he kissed her. It seemed so natural, so right. Then they were naked. Ernesto was the first man she'd ever made love to she'd *wanted* to make love to.

Afterward, he pulled a joint out of the bedside table and lit it up. He took a deep drag and offered it to Syd.

She'd never had grass, though most of her friends had been smoking for years. She didn't like what the booze and pills did to her mother, didn't want to be like her. But now, she had a new life, maybe even her first boyfriend, and she didn't want to offend him, so… she took a hit. It was an A-bomb. A joint laced with heroin. The smoke filled her lungs, and as the heroin invaded her brain, it metabolized into morphine, the sweetest of all drugs, and she was transported to a blissful euphoria she didn't know could exist.

She was hooked. Just like Ernesto knew she would be. And he had another runaway for his stable of young hookers, willing to do *anything* to keep the sweet nowhere flowing through her synapses.

Ernesto ran anywhere from three to six girls. The number fluctuated depending on who found God that week, OD'd or crawled home. They lived in a cramped two-bedroom apartment in the same building.

He recruited his girls from the Greyhound bus stop. It was the loaves and fishes of desperate females, delivering a seemingly endless bounty. And he usually recruited them the same way he'd *rescued* Syd.

The three guys who robbed Syd worked for Ernesto. His miraculous appearance in the nick of time was all part of the plan. The grateful teens almost always went home with Ernesto. So not only was he able to steal all their valuables, within a few days he'd usually absconded with their souls.

Syd went to Ernesto's best customers first – the guys willing to pay extra for a seventeen-year-old girl. These were guys he knew, guys he could trust. Because even though he was willing to whore her out, Ernesto actually kind of had a crush on the cute redhead, and didn't want anything too horrible to happen to her. They lived together as boyfriend and girlfriend, and Syd couldn't be happier.

Looking back, Syd realized she was living in a drug-induced haze. It numbed her to the strange men who violated her body two or three times a day. It numbed her to the life Ernesto's other girls were leading – sent out to the streets to give blowjobs in front seats or spread their legs in rent-by-the-hour motels. Or the girls sent out on *special assignments* and came back battered and bruised by Ernesto's more violent customers.

It took almost eight months before Ernesto got tired of Syd. And he moved Syd out the same way he always did – he gave her something she'd love more than him. The needle.

Ernesto was always very careful to make sure Syd only smoked or occasionally snorted her heroin. You get hooked, but it's a manageable situation. Two to three times a day at the most, and you can live an almost normal life, for a hooker. But once you mainline, once that pretty poison is shot directly into your veins, the jolt is all you live for. *All* that matters.

So when Ernesto was ready to move Syd out and another pretty young thing in, he convinced a stoned Syd to try the needle, just once, just to see what it feels like. Of course it felt *wonderful*.

And suddenly, when Ernesto said, if you move into the apartment with the other girls, I'll give you another fix. *Sure.* I'll give you another fix if you troll Hollywood Boulevard for blowjobs. *Love to.* There's a frat party that wants someone to strip and gang bang. *I'm your girl.* I've got a friend who's into a little S&M. *Bring him on.*

Syd did anything and everything. She ate little, living on Chablis and potato chips. Soon Syd was bone thin and had the same glazed pod-person stare as her roommates. She was eighteen years old. A drugged-out sexual automaton going through the motions and her expiration date was coming due.

Then she OD'd. It was an accident, and if one of Syd's roommates hadn't been there when it happened, she would have died.

Enter Eric, EMT.

Eric Templeton, to be exact. An army vet, Eric was just twenty-five when he wheeled Syd out of the apartment. He had served two tours in Iraq as a medic, and then joined the fire department when he got home.

Eric fell in love with Syd on the ride to the hospital. Sitting in the back with her, wiping the sweat off her face he stared, beguiled, at all the freckles. She looked so beautiful but so broken.

Eric had been to the Vine Street apartment before; another OD. They saved a young black girl; as soon as she was revived at the hospital, a slick bald dude paid her bill and walked her out the door. A cop filled him in; the girl was a hooker, the guy her pimp. Eric and his partner were called back to the apartment two months later; the black girl had OD'd again. This time they were too late; she was dead.

Well, not again, Eric vowed to himself. This time he was going to save her. Once Syd was stabilized at St. John's, he grabbed her chart, wheeled her to the fifth floor and hid her out on the maternity ward.

Eric watched, amused, as the blustering Ernesto freaked out when the hospital couldn't find her, but what was he going to do, call a cop? The pimp finally stormed out yelling that he'd be back and they better have his niece. Niece, right.

When Syd regained consciousness, Eric was at her side.

"Where's Ernesto?" she asked through chapped lips.

"Gone. But I'm going to help you."

Panic filled her eyes, sweat beaded on her body, muscle spasms rippled her body. She was in withdrawal. "I need a fix…"

"You keep shooting heroin you're going to die. You know that, right?"

"I'll do whatever you want. Suck you, fuck you. Anything."

"I can get you in a program, get you drugs, methadone. Get you cleaned up. Give you a fresh start. Would you like that?"

Syd started crying. "But it hurts so bad."

"Let me help you, please."

Syd looked into the face of the paramedic. She'd stared into a lot of men's faces during the last eighteen months; embarrassed, lonely, desperate, faces. Arrogant, angry, cruel faces. But the paramedic's face was different. His face was honest, caring, genuine. Syd realized she could trust him.

"What's your name?" she asked.

"Eric."

"Okay, Eric. Do what you've got to do."

It took three weeks for Eric to flush the poison out of Syd. He moved her to his apartment. She suffered mightily, tried to escape twice, but Eric was resolute, firm when he had to be, always nurturing, and most of all, loving.

And as Syd got stronger, as the chemical haze cleared her consciousness, she felt the first stirring of hope. She could envision a life beyond the next fix. She could envision a new life, a *real* life, all because of Eric.

And Eric had all sorts of plans for her. He wanted her to take the high school equivalency exam and enroll at Santa Monica College. He wanted her to find a career, become a nurse or a doctor or lawyer.

And in the three weeks they had been together, he had never come on to her, never touched her inappropriately; he'd been the perfect gentleman. Because if Syd was going to fall in love with him, Eric wanted the clean and sober Syd, not the drug-addicted girl who would glom on to the closest hero figure.

But Eric had made a mortal enemy. Ernesto. He didn't like having his girls taken from him, especially not one of his favorites. So while Eric was nursing Syd back to health, Ernesto and his minions were combing the streets, asking questions, doing whatever they could to find Syd.

They came on a Monday night. Syd had made dinner, macaroni and cheese. Syd and Eric were just sitting down when the front door burst open.

Rodolfo and Santiago came through first. They were Ernesto's muscle, tatted out and brutal. They were two of the men who robbed her that first night in Hollywood. Syd had been forced to fuck them numerous times when she was on the needle. They each had a .9mm pointed at Eric's head.

Then Ernesto walked in. It was more like an entrance, the conquering hero capturing a city. He glanced at Syd then walked right up to Eric, leaned forward so they were just inches apart. Ernesto said, "I think you have something that belongs to me."

Syd knew there was only one chance to save Eric's life and she took it. "Thank God," Syd said, rushing to Ernesto, throwing her arms around him. "Take me home, baby. I've had enough of this goody two shoes."

Ernesto grabbed Syd by the hair, pulled back her head and kissed her. He jammed his tongue into her mouth and she responded, groaning with pleasure, pressing her body against his. "I've missed you, sweetie," Syd whispered.

Ernesto turned back to Eric. "You like fucking her? You like fucking my girl?"

"I've never touched her," Eric said, surprised by his own calm. He'd been shot at in Iraq, but always from a distance, faceless snipers; now he was staring directly into the face of evil. Sure he was scared, but he was also proud. He knew he was probably going to die and he didn't want Syd's last image of him to be that of a sniveling coward.

"It's true, Ernesto," Syd said. "Never once. I think he's gay."

Ernesto leaned in to Eric, "You a faggot?"

"No, sir."

"Who cares what he is," Syd said. "I'm just happy you're here. Come on, baby," Syd said, pulling Ernesto toward the door. "Take me home."

Ernesto let Syd drag him across the room. The further Ernesto got from Eric, the better Syd felt. She'd spend the rest of her life with Ernesto if it would save Eric's life.

Eric would have loved to stop them. The thought of Syd going back to the pimp sickened him. But Eric was smart enough to know if he took even one step forward, the thugs would shoot him. He'd figure out a way to rescue her later. So right now, discretion was the better part of valor.

When they reached the doorway Ernesto snapped a

few Spanish words to his men. They holstered their guns and left the apartment. Syd could feel the tension leaving the room.

"Oh, just one more thing," Ernesto said. He slipped a throwing knife out of his pocket and with a practiced flip of the wrist he sent it flying across the room and into Eric's chest.

Syd screamed, "No!"

Eric dropped to his knees. His hands clutched the knife. He tried to pull it out, but it had pierced his heart. His strength ebbed as blood flooded his chest cavity. He was dying, and he knew it.

Syd rushed to Eric's side, pulled the knife from his chest. "Call 911!"

"Yeah, like that's going to happen," Ernesto scoffed.

Syd put her arms around Eric. "I'm so sorry," she said, crying.

Eric took one last look into Syd's eyes. "Thanks for the best three weeks of my life."

Syd leaned down and kissed Eric, their first kiss. And last. He died in her arms.

"Let's go, Syd," Ernesto said. "Time to boogie."

Syd stood, the bloody knife in her right hand. She looked at the malevolent smirk on Ernesto's face and charged him, the knife sweeping up towards his chest. He easily caught her hand, twisted the knife free.

But Syd wasn't really trying to stab him; she was using the knife as a diversion. As Ernesto concentrated on getting the knife, Syd slipped her other hand into his jacket and pulled out the Beretta he always carried there. She stuck the .9mm under his chin and pulled the trigger.

The top of Ernesto's head exploded and his blood and brains sprayed the ceiling.

Syd heard footsteps, then Rodolfo and Santiago appeared in the doorway. They looked at Ernesto's corpse, the gun in Syd's hand now pointed at them, and the crazed look in her eyes. Wordlessly they spun on their heels and ran.

Syd was surprisingly calm. She knew the gunfire

would bring the cops, but she had a few things to do first. She picked up the knife and dropped the gun and knife in her purse. Then she dug out Ernesto's wallet, it was filled, as always, with hundreds. She took most of them, leaving a couple for the cops to find. Then she put the wallet back, took a last look at Eric, and walked out the door.

Syd was two blocks away when she heard the sirens. She was clean, had a little money and the hope that Eric had instilled in her. Heartbroken, yes, but instinctively she knew that this was truly the first day in the rest of her life.

Back in the Ivy restaurant, Syd took Ryan's other hand. "Worry not, Ryan. I've had a blessed life." Then she sealed the lie with a kiss.

ELEVEN

Anne Rogers sat behind her massive mahogany desk in her plush corner office nestled fifty stories high in the L.A. skyline. On a clear day, she could see from the Hollywood sign to the Pacific Ocean. She cherished the view, loved her office and well, hated everything else about her life.

"Dad's refusing to help," Anne's husband, Rick Rogers said. "He can be such a self- righteous bastard. He even threatened to go to the D.A."

"The payment's due in two weeks, Rick. What do you suggest we do?"

"Fuck 'em. Send the keys back to the bank and we'll move into a hotel until I can sort all this out."

A balloon payment was due on their Santa Monica condo, one point one million dollars, just the latest catastrophe in a three-year financial disaster. It started when Rick got a stock tip from one of his clients, a biotech firm that was about to announce a new wonder drug. Rick talked Anne into investing everything they had in the stock, ride it up, then cash out with a big profit. But the FDA discovered the research data was rigged, banned the drug and fined the company. The stock tanked.

Anne and Rick lost everything. They had no money for the beach house mortgage, owed tens of thousands more to credit card companies and were on the brink of declaring bankruptcy when Rick's father stepped in to bail them out.

They sold the beach house, downsized to the condo and were put on a strict budget. But Anne and Rick were so humiliated by being saved by Rick's father, and suddenly having to report to him about every nickel and dime they spent, that Rick convinced Anne they should take a final shot at financial independence. They secretly mortgaged the condo, forging Rick's father's signature, took the money and gambled it on a tip Rick got on a new stock – and lost it all. They were broke, penniless; Anne's worst nightmares come true.

"Sort this out?" Anne said, furious. "Rick, there is nothing to sort out. We'll be forced to declare bankruptcy. And if the D.A. finds out we forged your father's signature, we'll be disbarred."

"Dad's agreed not to report the forgery but his silence did come with a price – he wants us to resign, quit the firm."

"What?"

"We don't need Rogers, Middleton and Roberts," Rick said. "We'll start our own firm.

I'm sure we can take a ton of clients with us."

Anne looked at her husband. The stress of the last few years had taken a toll. He'd been drinking too much, eating too much and his once lean body had twenty extra pounds. Worse, his once almost arrogant self-confidence was so badly shaken he practically reeked of anxiety and desperation.

She wasn't in love with him anymore. She wasn't sure she was ever in love with him. She hated to admit it, but she had really been in love with his money, his power. And as he had squandered both in the last few years, the lie of their marriage became crystal clear.

She'd had a few affairs over the years, one-night stands when she'd been away on business. The sex had been fine, but the illicit adventure appealed to her even more. Sitting in a bar, alone, knowing all the men were checking you out. Scoping each of them out, imagining what they might be like in bed. Then the magical moment, she would choose one, meet his eyes and smile. It was such a turn on to watch them stand up and walk over to her. The power a beautiful woman has in a bar is truly amazing. And, if they were smart enough or charming enough or funny enough, she'd sleep with them.

But for Anne, it wasn't about the sex; it was the power. It was nice to know she still had it. And she also realized that sex appeal had an expiration date. She'd been in bars and seen older women sitting alone, attractive women in their fifties and sixties *available* written all over them; but the men's hungry eyes invariably landed on the younger, sexier Anne.

One day, Anne knew, she would be in her fifties and sixties, and she'd be the ignored one. When you've lost the power, there is only one thing left; money.

Money had been the driving force of her life; she'd been determined to flee her trailer trash roots. Growing up, Anne hated her life. She watched the glamorous life of other teens on TV shows like *Dawson's Creek* and *Felicity* on a crappy 20-inch Phillips from the dreary living room of her double-wide. She promised herself then she would do whatever it takes to make money. She studied hard and earned a scholarship to UCLA and had her heart set on law school.

When Anne met Ryan, she found a man who embodied all her teenage daydreams. He was tall with craggy good looks and those adorable dimples.

Then she found out Ryan's dad was a rich Beverly Hills attorney, and she knew Ryan was definitely the man for her. Once they started dating junior year of college, Anne wanted to close the deal, get married right away. But Ryan wanted to wait. Anne suspected Ryan was skittish because of his dad's profligate ways; he was just divorcing wife number four at that point. So Anne decided to speed up the process. She told him she was pregnant. A lie, but it worked; she read Ryan's integrity perfectly and they got married.

When she *lost* the baby a few weeks later, Anne was worried that Ryan would be suspicious, but of course, he wasn't. He loved her too much to suspect treachery.

They might have stayed married if his stupid father hadn't lost all his money. But suddenly Anne found herself living like a pauper, having to count every frickin' penny.

That's why she was so vulnerable when she first met Rick the summer she interned at Rogers, Middleton and Roberts. He pursued her relentlessly, giving her flowers, jewelry, and clothes. Then one night he invited her to dinner and she accepted.

Rick picked her up in his two-hundred-thousand-dollar Lamborghini, took her to Granita, Wolfgang Puck's swanky Malibu restaurant. After two twelve-dollar martinis, two thirty-dollar appetizers, two fifty-six-dollar steaks, one three-hundred-dollar bottle of Cabernet, one eighteen-dollar dessert and two ten-dollar lattes, he drove them to his Malibu beach house for after-dinner drinks. The house was almost three thousand square feet of luxury with a huge redwood deck facing the moonlit Pacific.

For someone as admittedly materialistic as Anne, all this wealth was like a junkie's first jolt of heroin. This was so far from her mother's crappy trailer, so far from Anne and Ryan's cramped studio apartment. This was the life she wanted. The life she deserved. When Rick leaned in to kiss her, she eagerly met his lips.

Anne never went back to the apartment.

Money. It always came back to money. Money is why she married Ryan. Money is why she left Ryan for Rick. And now Rick had lost all his money.

There was no way she was going to stay with a penniless Rick if he left the firm. But she wasn't ready to drop that bomb quite yet. So she said, "Starting our own practice sounds great, honey. And you're right, plenty of clients will follow us." Not a chance, she thought. Dear old dad would make sure every client knew the embarrassing truth behind their exit.

"Okay, good. Great," Rick said, relieved at her loyalty, and then he headed back to his office.

Anne should have been panicked by Rick's catastrophic news. But Fate seemed to be coming to her rescue. Why else would she have been driving not four blocks from the LAPD Hollywood Division when she heard a Hollywood Homicide detective named Ryan Magee had hit the lottery? Why else would he have been in the bullpen when she dropped by? Why else would she have seen the desire in Ryan's eyes when they talked?

Ryan wasn't married. He told her he didn't even have a girlfriend. So all she had to do was win Ryan's heart back. And how hard could that be; she always could wrap him around her little finger.

TWELVE

The Windows Lounge at the Bel Air Regent Hotel lists eighteen vodka martinis on its menu. Vodka mixed with Triple Sec, vodka mixed with cranberry juice, orange liqueur, watermelon pucker, blue Curacao, absinthe, crème de fucking menthe, for Christ's sake, thought Adam Devlin as he perused the menu, all these inventive ways to ruin a martini. A martini should be served very dry, in a chilled martini glass with a twist. Simple elegance. And that's what Adam ordered when the pretty waitress stopped by, a Chopin martini, very dry with a twist. Then he sat back in his booth and smiled.

Adam was in a great mood. His meeting with the BMW reps had been successful; he put two golfers and a tennis player under contract for three years, total value six million dollars and he took home ten percent. Not bad for an hour of his time. What a business.

And now for a little fun. He glanced at his Rolex Cosmograph Daytona; five twenty-five. The very sexy Susie should be here any minute. He'd been fantasizing about the blonde most of the day. If things went as planned, he could get a room here at the hotel, or take her to the company's apartment in Century City. Either way, this was going to be fun.

"I love martinis," a voice said over his shoulder. "Mind if I join you?"

Adam turned to find Susie standing there. She'd changed out of the shorts and halter-top and replaced them with a more appropriate, but equally sexy, red skirt and blouse. Her hair was down, a devil danced in her green eyes and a smile played on her lips. He stood, ever the gentlemen. "Please," he said, "sit." She did. "What would you like to drink?"

"Whatever you're having," she said, sliding close to him. "In fact," she said picking up his drink. "I can't wait." Alice sipped from Adam's drink leaving a lipstick imprint on the rim of the glass. She shivered as the vodka hit bottom. "God, that's good."

"You're unbelievable," Adam said, laughing. Then he carefully fit his lips around her lipstick imprint and sipped. "It's almost like a kiss," he said.

"Now, now," she said. "I thought we were here to talk business."

"We are," Adam said, getting the waitress's attention and signaling for two more drinks. "You want a job in advertising, our biggest problem will be deciding which of the fifteen or twenty companies I routinely work with will be the best fit for you."

"It can't be that easy."

"It is, trust me. But first, tell me about yourself. Where are you from?"

Alice had a biography all ready. One she cooked up just for Adam, one that should resonate with him. "Well, I grew up in Dayton, Ohio. My dad was a pharmacist and Mom was a teacher."

"Brothers? Sisters?"

"Nope, only child."

"Hey, me too," Adam said.

"I always wished I had a sister. Someone I could trust with all my secrets."

Adam reacted, surprised. "That's unbelievable. I always wanted a brother for the same reason. I felt so alone growing up."

Alice knew this. Eleven years earlier, when she was a senior in high school, she spent a two-hour school bus trip sitting next to a seventeen-year-old Adam Devlin. They were on a field trip to the Getty Center in Los Angeles, and Adam got stuck sitting next to the dumpy Alice Waterman. He'd sort of seen her around, had heard some rumors about her being easy, but never paid her much attention. Not pretty enough, not popular enough, not anything enough for his clique. But it was a long trip and they got to talking.

She fell in love with him on that trip. Played over their conversation a thousand times in her head, spent weeks hoping he'd call or acknowledge her at school. Of course, he never did. He completely ignored her.

Until that terrible day.

But she'd gleaned enough information to serve her purposes today. The waitress arrived with their drinks; when she left, Alice said, "Anyway, I loved high school. I was an athlete, a tennis player, and I actually thought about turning pro, but I blew my knee out senior year and that ended that."

"Okay, now this is freaky," he said. "I was an athlete too, a football player. Until a linebacker cut my knees out from under me and shredded my ACL."

"It's awful, isn't it? Not just the pain, but also the shattering of all your dreams, all your expectations. It was like starting over at seventeen."

Those were Adam Devlin's exact words eleven years ago and he stared at her in wonder. "That's *exactly* what it was like," he said, looking at her as if for the first time. There was something special about this woman, something wonderful. And this was going to be more than a one night stand, he decided. Much more.

THIRTEEN

Looking at a dead body is never easy. Looking at your dead son is agony. "That's him," Nick Wood said grimly. "That's Colin."

Nick Wood was an impressive-looking guy. Ryan guessed he was sixty, and in great shape. Trim, handsome, with a long face and bushy eyebrows, he dressed casually in khakis and a blue Polo golf shirt. He wore a thick gold bracelet on one hand and a ruby encrusted school ring on another. Expensive jewelry, but he could afford it. He was a very successful contractor, Ryan knew, building many of Orange County's most prestigious high rises.

Ryan waited to see what Nick Wood would do next. Some people kiss their loved ones; others take a hand or stroke the face. Nick Wood just stared, shook his head as if disappointed, then asked, "Do you know who did this?"

"No, not yet," Ryan said leading Nick Wood into the hallway where Syd waited. "We've got some leads we're following, and we were hoping you might be able to shed some light."

"You said it was a murder."

"A woman met him in a bar, they went back to his car and we believe she shot him."

Ryan could almost hear the gears working as Wood digested the information. Something complicated was going on in there, more than just grief. "Is something bothering you, sir," Ryan asked.

"Could it have been self defense?" Nick Wood asked.

"Self defense," Syd asked. "Why would you think that?"

Ryan connected the dots. "You're thinking about the date rape three years ago."

Nick Wood was surprised. "You know about that?"

Ryan nodded. "We heard Colin avoided prosecution because you settled out of court."

Wood shook his head. "Colin had this... problem with women. My fault, I guess, I don't know."

"Why would it be your fault?" Syd asked.

"Colin's mother died when he was six years old. I never remarried, but I dated, a lot. And I was never shy about bringing the women back to the house."

"So Colin grew up watching a parade of women march in and out of your bedroom," Ryan said.

"And we used to joke about it. Grade them on a scale, 1-10, that sort of thing. Colin would grade them on looks and I'd grade them on performance. Then, when he got into high school and started dating, I'd grade *his* dates on their looks and he'd grade them on performance."

"How charming," Syd said.

Wood glanced at her, shrugged. "I'm a pig, I know. Or was. Karma has a way of catching up with all of us. I got prostate cancer, the operation left me, well, let's just say I'm incapable of judging performance anymore."

"And now that you can't fuck anymore, you've stopped thinking of women as sex objects?" Syd snapped.

"Syd..." Ryan said, his tone telling her to shut up. She knew better. Never let your personal feeling affect an interview.

"No, it's all right, Detective," Wood said. "She has a right to be angry. I treated women like shit for years. And so did Colin. That's why I asked if it could have been self-defense."

"It's possible," Ryan said. "But under the circumstances, it's doubtful. It doesn't feel like a spur of the moment attack. We think it was planned. Perhaps by a woman he offended in the past."

"We'd like the name of the woman you paid off three years ago," Syd said. "And any other women you know who may have had a grudge."

"Kathy Tuttle was the woman three years ago. She lived in Santa Monica, I think, but I sent the check to her lawyer. I can call my office and get you the information."

"Thank you," Ryan said. "Can you think of any other women?"

Wood considered for a long time, and then shook his head. "I don't know. The Tuttle girl was the only one he told me about, because he had to. He needed the money. If there were others in the last few years, I'd have no way of knowing."

Ryan and Syd stood in the doorway watching Nick Wood get in his Lexus. They had gotten the name and number of Kathy Tuttle's attorney and Ryan had called LAPD Media Relations to let them know they could issue a press release with Colin Wood's identity.

As Wood drove off, Syd asked, "You believe in karma, Ryan? Like Casanova there and his prostate cancer."

"Actually, I do," Ryan said, then realized that was one of the reasons he was hesitating about picking up the Lotto money. Enough, he thought. Time to tell Syd, at least get her advice about what he should do. He looked at Syd. "I need to tell you something."

Syd looked at him expectantly. "What?"

Before Ryan could answer, his cell phone rang. "Damn it," he said pulling it out of his pocket, ready to turn it off – then he noticed the name of the caller, Anne. "I better take this," Ryan said. "Why don't you call that lawyer and see if you can get an address for Kathy Tuttle."

Ryan looked a little flummoxed, Syd thought, and she immediately suspected that the call was from Ryan's ex-wife. But she wasn't going to say anything. Not yet, anyway. "You got it," Syd said, stepping into the parking lot. "I'll meet you at the car."

Ryan answered his phone. "Hello," he said, "This is a surprise."

"I know you said you were busy and we should wait a couple of days before getting together," Anne said. "But, I don't know, seeing you today made me realize how much I've missed talking to you. Any chance you can squeeze in a quick drink a little later? I'll be in Hollywood; we could meet at Musso and Frank, in like an hour or something.

But if you're too busy, I understand, no pressure."

Ryan was torn. Part of him wanted to drop everything and meet her. Another part of him wanted to tell her to go fuck herself. She had broken his heart.

But she was a lawyer and he did have some legal questions he'd like answered about his Lotto ticket. And he was curious about what she wanted. So... "You know what, Anne. I could probably use a break. Sure let's get together. I'll meet you at Musso's, how's seven o'clock?"

"Perfect," Anne said, "Just perfect."

FOURTEEN

There are three TVs behind the bar of the Windows Lounge, all tuned to the same station. The time was six-fifteen, and the local NBC affiliate was in the middle of their news broadcast. The sound was muted, of course, can't have TV chatter interrupting drunken conversation, and the three 42-inch flat screens all cut to a picture of Colin Wood. If those in the bar could have heard the anchor, they would have heard that the victim of the murder last night in the Havoc parking lot has just been identified as Hollywood actor, Colin Wood.

Adam and Alice were on their second round. Adam's back was to the TV's, so he couldn't see Colin's picture. Alice, however, had a front row seat. She expected the police to ID Colin, so she wasn't surprised. She was interested to see what else they were reporting, how good a description of her they had and what the police were saying about the investigation. But there would be plenty of time for that later.

She turned her attention back to Adam. He was rambling on about his business now, how he had a personal hotline to the CEO's of America's top companies, and he could set her up with the job of her dreams. Yeah, yeah, yeah, she thought. Let's just cut to the chase. Rent us a room already.

"So, are you hungry?" Adam asked. "We could go somewhere, Spago's or Matsuhisa if you like sushi."

Alice slid closer to Adam, dropped her voice to a sexy whisper. "You know what I really like?" she asked.

Adam could feel her breath on his face. "What?" he asked.

"Room service." Then she touched his hand. Voltage seemed to flow through her fingers and shoot through

Adam's body. He was caught a little off guard but Adam was quick on the uptake. "Rumor has it they have room service in this hotel."

"Really? Such a shame we don't have a room."

He smiled. "That's a problem easily solved." Adam got up. "I'll be right back."

Adam got a key from the front desk, bought a bottle of Cristal champagne from the bar, grabbed two glasses and led Alice into the elevator. They were alone and when the door closed, he stepped into her arms and kissed her.

As a teenager Alice fantasized about the first time she'd kiss Adam Devlin. Sometimes she'd be at her locker, alone in an empty corridor and, when she turned around, he'd be standing in front of her. They'd look lovingly into each other's eyes, and then kiss. Other times she'd be on the staircase going up and he'd be coming down and they'd bump into each other. They stare wordlessly at each other and then kiss. Or she'd be in her bedroom doing homework and he'd crawl in through the window, take her in his arms and kiss.

Silly schoolgirl fantasies that never came true.

But now she was kissing him and it was, surprisingly, wonderful. They melted into each other. Their tongues found a perfect rhythm, their bodies fit seamlessly, and even their breathing was in sync. It felt like they *belonged* together.

With a Ding, the elevator glided to a stop. The door opened and their lips parted, but their eyes were still locked together. "You are unbelievable," Adam whispered.

"You ain't seen nothing yet," Alice said, grabbed his hand and led him off the elevator. "What's our room number?"

"1224," Adam said, stopping in front of the door.

"My new lucky number," she said.

He opened the door. As they stepped inside, he put down the champagne and glasses. Alice dropped her purse on a chair and then turned back to the door. It was a big, heavy door on a pneumatic hinge and took a few seconds to close. Once it snapped shut Alice threw the dead bolt.

"Now where were we?" he asked. Adam took her hands, pulled her to him and kissed her.

It felt so good, she thought. She knew it shouldn't. And she knew she shouldn't be so aroused, but she was, in fact, soaking wet.

It wasn't supposed to be like this. She hated this man. Hated what he had done to her. She was there to kill him, not fuck him.

But, still this was the fulfillment of that schoolgirl fantasy; why not let it play itself out.

His hands slipped under her blouse. She wore no bra and he cupped her breasts, his fingers massaging her nipples. She groaned with pleasure.

Suddenly Adam picked her up, carried her across the room and gently dropped her on the king size bed. He pulled off her blouse, her skirt and finally her shoes. He kissed the soles of both her feet then slowly kissed his way along her ankle, past her knee, up the thigh. He spread her legs and kissed the outside of her panties. She arched her back shoving her pussy into his face. He inhaled her scent, nibbling her clitoris through the thin, red fabric.

"Jesus, God," she murmured.

Adam pulled off her panties. She was bare, smooth, soft. Perfect. He sunk his face into her, taking her clitoris between his lips, his tongue gentle but insistent. He wanted to make this beautiful woman come. He wanted her to think he was the greatest lover she'd ever had. This was not the norm for Adam, who usually just took what he wanted and moved on. But he wanted to make love to this woman, not just fuck her. He wanted tonight to be special.

"Oh, yes," Alice groaned as the first wonderful thrumming of an orgasm stirred deep inside her. She wrapped her legs around his back, dug her fingers into the sheets. "Fuck, yes," she breathed, her hips now moving in rhythm with his tongue.

Suddenly Alice realized how much she loved him then, and still loved him now. Maybe she misjudged him that night. Maybe he only did what he did because he was drunk.

"Oh, God," she moaned, the wonderful moment was here. "Yes, yes, yes..." Her toes curled as the orgasm rocked her. "Oh, God!"

Adam felt her convulse as she climaxed. It was an incredible turn-on to watch her ecstasy, to feel her body vibrate as pleasure surged through her. He rolled over, stripping off his shirt, pants, and Calvin Klein Briefs. He was hard, Viagra hard, without the chemicals. She was the drug tonight and he was hoping to overdose.

Adam planted one arm on either side and suspended himself over her. "You are so beautiful," he said, staring into her sparkling green eyes.

"Shut up and fuck me." She said it with a desperate urgency that thrilled him.

He lowered his hips and ever so slowly entered her. Making love to this incredible woman was monumental and Adam wanted to cherish every millimeter of this first time inside her. She was tight, warm. Delicious.

Then they were moving together, slowly at first but within moments their lovemaking intensified as mouths met, hands groped, legs flayed and a frenzied, almost desperate need gripped them both.

Soon, oh, way too soon, Adam felt his orgasm coming. He tried to think it away but failed and gave himself into its power. He thrust, deeper and deeper until he practically exploded inside her.

He clung to her as he came, finishing with a deep, passionate kiss. He was still deep inside her. "Jesus fucking Christ," he muttered. "That was unbelievable."

"It sure was," she said. "And the best part is we're just getting started."

Adam smiled. "I was hoping you'd say that."

Alice rolled them over so she was on top. "Only this time," she said. "I'll do all the work."

And she began to make love to him.

FIFTEEN

Ryan and Syd drove to the Hollywood station. Syd knew something was up. Ryan had been unusually quiet. She'd expected him to finish the conversation he'd started before his ex-wife called. What could be a more provocative opening then, *I need to tell you something*? But they'd driven in silence while her imagination rifled through a horrifying catalog of possibilities: *We have to stop dating. I want a new partner. I'm going back to my ex-wife. I have herpes.*

Finally, unhappily, Syd prompted him. "What was it you had to tell me?"

Ryan looked at her, confused; he'd been so preoccupied with the upcoming meeting with Anne that he'd blanked. "I'm sorry, sweetie, what?"

"You said you had something to tell me."

Oh yeah, Ryan thought. The Lotto ticket. He briefly reconsidered, almost ashamed by the truth. Then glanced at Syd, at the fear in her eyes. Of course, he realized, she assumes I'm going to say something about us. The last thing in the world he wanted to do was hurt Syd, so he took a breath then told her about the garrulous guy in greasy coveralls who took forever in the 7-Eleven buying beef jerky, a six pack and a lottery ticket with his one dollar change. And how, after the tow truck driver left, Ryan bought a pack of Rolaids and walked into the parking lot to see the Lotto ticket on the ground and the tow truck driver getting in his vehicle. It would have been easy for Ryan to pick up the ticket and get the guy's attention, but his stomach hurt and Ryan was so annoyed with the big-mouthed driver that he just let the guy drive off. Then he picked up the Lotto ticket and stuck it in his glove box.

"The Lotto ticket may be worth millions of dollars," he

concluded. "But it's not mine."

"Holy shit."

"And then some."

Syd sat back in her seat and let the implications settle in. "Let me ask you a few questions."

"Shoot."

"Was there a name on the tow truck driver's coveralls?"

"Probably, but I didn't notice."

"On his truck?"

"I'm sure, but I didn't pay any attention. Same for the license plate, I didn't even look."

"So you have no way of tracking him down?"

"No."

"And did he ask the clerk for certain numbers or was it a quick pick."

"A quick pick."

"So the tow truck driver would have no idea what the numbers were or that he actually bought a winning ticket?"

"That's right. And it was six months ago, I doubt he even remembers buying or losing it."

Ryan had been through the identical thought process countless times himself since he found out the ticket was a winner, but it was nice to get someone else's take on his dilemma.

"So no one would ever know that you didn't buy the Lotto ticket."

"That's right."

Syd liked to think she had a reliable moral compass. Well, except for murdering the motherfuckers who have done her wrong. And, like Ryan, she was a cop. She knew the law. "If I remember my Academy law classes properly," Syd said, "lost property, in this case, the Lotto ticket, belongs to whoever owns it, in this case, the tow truck driver. Just because you find something doesn't mean you now own it. The law requires that all lost property be turned in to the police. If you keep lost property and don't disclose it, it's theft. That applies to a bag of diamonds, an envelope full of money or a quarter lying on the ground. Finders are not legally entitled to be keepers."

"Exactly. Even when, like in this case, no one knows its lost property. Even when, like in this case, the lost item is worth millions of dollars."

"If you don't claim the money, what happens to it?"

"I don't know."

"So, multimillion dollar question time; what're you going to do?"

Ryan sighed. "I don't know." He pulled into the parking lot of the Hollywood Division, turned off the car. "I'm going to meet with Anne at seven, get a legal opinion."

Anger flared inside Syd. She didn't know Anne, didn't know any of the details of their marriage, but instinctively Syd didn't trust her. "You sure that's a good idea? I mean, she's your ex-wife, she could have an agenda."

Ryan realized Syd was jealous, though in his mind she had no reason to be. "Don't worry, I'll be careful."

"Want me to wait for you here?" Loaded question, he better, Syd thought.

"If you don't mind, I shouldn't be more than an hour or so."

"No problem," Syd said, relieved. "I've got plenty of work to do." Syd wanted to lean over and kiss him, but other cops were in the parking lot so she just squeezed his hand and opened her car door.

"By the way," Ryan said, stopping her. "What would you do?"

Syd thought about it for a moment. "What would I do or what do I think you should do?"

"What would you do?"

Syd smiled. "It doesn't matter, I don't have the ticket. You do."

Ryan laughed. "Bitch. Okay, what do you think I should do?"

Syd may have only known Ryan for eight weeks but she felt she had a firm fix on his moral compass. This was a man who knew right from wrong. "There's only one thing you can do," she said.

That surprised him. "What?"

"Think about it," Syd said and shut the door.

"What kind of answer is that?" Ryan called after her.

But Syd just smiled, turned her back and walked into the station.

SIXTEEN

It was all so confusing. She felt so good, so *satisfied*. Alice could never remember feeling such bliss. And it had nothing to do with the three incredible orgasms – her first orgasms with a man. In the past they had all come from masturbation.

No, her joy, yes, that's what she was feeling, joy, came from lying next to a man she'd dreamt about for years. And now she lay naked, entwined in his arms as he slept peacefully. A dream comes true. Amazing.

This was the first truly good thing that had happened to her in years. Maybe ever, for that matter and she wanted to play it out. He was married, she knew, but she also knew that something happened to Adam, as well. She saw it in his eyes, the way he touched her, the way he kissed her. She wasn't just another affair for him, she could tell. He was going to want to see her again, make her a part of his life.

And to her surprise, that's what she wanted, too. Time was limited, of course. But all the more reason to make every minute count.

Alice slipped out of bed, grabbed her purse and walked into the bathroom then quietly closed and locked the door.

She looked at herself in the mirror. It always surprised her a bit seeing herself as a hot blonde with green eyes. In her mind's eye she was always the dumpy, brunette Alice. But Alice had simply been the chrysalis before her metamorphosis into the Lady in Red.

She reached into her purse. Her hand passed the Colt Vest Pocket .25, passed the scalpel and grabbed her pill holder. She took it out, flipped open the afternoon dose, dumped the four pills in her hand: Arimidex, Tamoxifen and Cytoxan for the cancer and Aprepitant to control the nausea. She washed them down with sink water.

Seemed like a waste of time to her, but the Doctor said miracles happen. And now, suddenly, she wanted to milk this life of hers for every additional day.

She peed, winced a bit as she wiped. It was a little tender down there. Overuse, she thought, smiling. But the discomfort brought back the memories of that night eleven years ago when the pain was so agonizing.

It started so innocently. Alice had earned a scholarship to Camden Hall, a top of the line private school for the prodigy of Orange County's wealthiest residents. She was sitting under a tree in the high school quad reading the latest Harry Potter. She heard laughter and looked up to find three boys looking at her: Adam Devlin, Colin Wood and Blake Hunter. They were seniors, like her. Adam, of course, she knew. The fateful bus trip to the Getty Center was only a month before and she was seriously, albeit secretly, in love with him. She'd seen Colin and Blake around. They were BMOC, handsome but spoiled sons of rich fathers who hung with the cool kids. Alice was on scholarship since her parents made so little money.

The three boys were looking at her, whispering among themselves, laughing, and then Colin and Blake shoved Adam in her direction. With an annoyed glance back at his friends, Adam reluctantly walked up to her.

Her heart did flip-flops as Adam got closer.

"Hi," he said as he knelt down next to her. "It's Alice, right?"

"Right," she said, so nervous she was barely able to speak.

"My friends and I – you know Colin and Blake, don't you?"

"I've seen them around."

"We're having a party later at Colin's house. We wondered if you'd like to stop by."

She couldn't believe her ears. She wanted to scream, yes, but fought to stay cool. "Tonight?"

"Yeah, say seven o'clock."

She was free, but wanted to stay cool. She pretended

to consider it for a few moments, then said, "There are a few things I'll need to move around, but I'd love to come."

Adam gave her the address, and then returned to his friends who greeted him with high fives. That struck Alice as a little odd, but she ignored it and started thinking about what she was going to wear.

Alice spent the rest of the day deciding between skirt or jeans? Heels or sandals? Thong or boyshorts? She finally decided on black jeans, her favorite blue tank top, black boyshorts and her rainbow strap wedge sandals.

She was hoping to sleep with Adam. At least be able to jerk him off or blow him. All the boys she did it with told her how good she was, so if she could impress Adam, well, before she knew it she could be finally be hanging with the cool kids.

So with sex a distinct possibility, Alice sprinkled a little J'adore by Christian Dior on her nipples and pubes for a little unexpected treat for Adam.

She arrived at seven-fifteen; can't seem too anxious after all. The house was a typical ten-thousand-square-foot Orange County McMansion. She was surprised that there wasn't a line of cars parked on the street. School parties tended to attract big crowds. She rang the doorbell and Colin answered. He had a beer in one hand a joint in the other.

"Alice," he said, all smiles. "So glad you could make it. Come in, come in. We're in the game room. My dad's in Cabo so we've got the house to ourselves."

He led her through the sprawling house to an oak-paneled room dominated by a nine-foot pool table. Adam and Blake were in the middle of a game.

"Hi," Blake said. "Can I get you a drink?"

She looked at Adam, the only boy she really cared about, but he was preoccupied with lining up a shot.

"Yeah, sure," she said. "I'd like a coke, diet if you've got it."

"Want a little rum with that?"

Alice had had a few glasses of wine before, beer and drinks with some of the boys she'd dated, but never really liked it. But she didn't want to seem a prude, so she said, "Sure. Rum and coke it is." Then she looked around, confused. "Where is everyone? I thought there was going to be a party."

Colin and Blake exchanged a look. "More kids are coming later," Colin said. "But we wanted a chance to get to know you first."

Blake handed her a rum and coke. "Cheers."

She clinked her glass with his beer and drank. The rum and coke didn't taste too good. Too much rum, not enough coke, she guessed. Oh, well, she thought, maybe it'll help me relax. She took another big sip.

"You play pool?" Blake asked.

"No," she said. "It looks like fun, though."

"Adam," Blake said. "Why don't you show Alice here how to hold your shaft – I mean cue."

Colin and Blake snickered as Adam shot them a disapproving look.

Alice caught the double entendre; a couple of warning bells went off in the back of her mind, but the thought of spending time with Adam was too tempting. "Please, Adam," she said. "I'd love to learn to play pool."

"All right," Adam said finally looking at her. She saw something in his eyes, what was it, regret? "Here," he said handing her a cue.

She had her drink in her right hand. She moved to set it down.

"Just go ahead and finish your drink, Alice," Colin said. "I'll make you another."

Alice downed the rest of her drink and handed Colin her glass. "Not so much rum this time," she said.

"Sure, no problem," Colin said, grinning. "Rum and coke, light, coming up." That got another laugh out of Blake who joined Colin at the bar.

"Okay," Adam said. "The key to a good pool shot is the bridge." He spread his fingers on the table forming a circle with his thumb and index finger. "You try."

Alice spread her fingers, but as she tried to form the circle, she was hit by a wave of dizziness. She looked at

Adam, but his face blurred, and then she felt herself falling.

All she remembers next are fragments.

Hands pulling off her clothes...

Blake's face looming over her...

Cold hands on her bare skin as she was dropped onto the pool table...

Her legs being spread...

Whoops of laughter...

Sharp, stinging, pain...

She woke up hours later. She was alone in the game room. A clock over the bar said it was three-thirty. She was on the pool table, naked. Her clothes were scattered on the floor. She climbed off the table then crumpled to the ground as pain swept through her. Her head spun and she vomited. She hurt everywhere, her head, stomach, her vagina, her butt.

Dear God what did they do to her?

Terrified, humiliated, she scrambled into her clothes and staggered out of the house. Tears ran down her face as she drove home. Alice snuck in the back door and crept silently into her room. She wasn't going to tell her parents what happened. She wasn't going to tell anyone.

Then she found out about the video.

Back in the hotel bathroom, Alice touched up her lipstick. She heard the TV come on in the hotel room. Adam must be awake. She slipped into the plush white terrycloth hotel robe and stepped into the hotel room.

Adam was on the bed, the remote control in his hand, channel surfing. "I must've dozed off," he said. He grinned. "No surprise, you wore me out."

Alice laughed, slid onto the bed next to him. "That makes two of us."

He kissed her sweetly. "Thank you."

"No, thank you." She kissed him, playfully sucking his lower lip. "Now, you promised me some food. I'm starving."

Adam looked around, spotted the room service menu on the end table, handed it to her. "Order the five most expensive items on the menu."

"Really?"

"Really."

She scanned the menu as Adam went back to the TV. "Hey," he said, turning up the volume. "I know him."

Alice glanced up to see a clip of Colin Wood on the TV. "Hollywood actor, Colin Wood, was murdered last night in the parking lot of Havoc, a Hollywood nightclub," the announcer said. "Witnesses say he was seen leaving the nightclub with a blonde woman, she is being sought by authorities for questioning." The picture cut to video of a building on fire. "A fire engulfed a warehouse in Culver City…"

Adam muted the TV. "Unbelievable," he said.

Alice enjoyed watching Adam's reaction. He was shocked for sure; if he only knew. "Was he a client?" she asked.

"No, no, we went to high school together. He was a really great guy."

"Were you friends?"

"Oh, yeah. We had some good times. Crazy times."

"Tell me."

Adam shook his head. "Just stupid high school stuff."

Alice wanted to probe further, but sensed that now wasn't the time. "Did you stay in touch?"

"No, we drifted apart when we went to college. I've seen him in a few movies, since then, always meant to call him, say hello, congratulate him, but never did." He shook his head. "Murdered, wow."

"Guess you've got to be careful who you pick up in bars these days."

"Tell me about it." Then he turned back to Alice. "Good thing I met you in a parking lot."

She smiled. "Much safer." And then she kissed him.

SEVENTEEN

Musso and Frank Grill was the oldest restaurant in Hollywood, and felt like it. It's got wood-paneled walls, red leather booths and the same menu as when it opened in 1919. Want Turkey a la King, liver with onions, broiled squab with bacon, lamb kidney sauté; this is your place. But old-fashioned is the charm of the place. And they've got a great bar.

Anne sat at far end of the bar nursing a vodka tonic. She was surprised how nervous she was. Anne was never nervous. Not in a boardroom or courtroom. But she could feel an anxiety buzz, and she didn't like it.

Of course, her life was in turmoil, her marriage over, her job gone. Rick's father may bail them out but Anne was sure rumors would leak about her and Rick forging his father's signature and her reputation was sure to take a big time hit. What a fucking mess.

"Hey, Beautiful."

Anne turned to find Ryan behind her. "Hey, Handsome."

That's how they used to greet each other when they first started dating, those intoxicating wonderful days of young love.

"Sit, please," she said. "What're you drinking?"

"I'll have a beer."

Anne caught the eye of the bartender. "Michelob draft for him," she said, and then looked at Ryan. "That all right?"

"I'm surprised you remember."

It was easy for Anne to remember, Rick drank the same thing. But she smiled shyly and ordered another vodka tonic for herself.

"Amazing," Ryan said. "I haven't seen you in seven

years and now twice in one day."

"You complaining?" she teased.

"No, not at all."

The bartender delivered the drinks. No reason to beat around the bush, Anne thought. "A toast," she said, holding up her glass, "in honor of your Lotto winnings. To wealth, wisdom and happiness."

"One down, two to go," Ryan said. They both laughed and drank.

Anne had to be careful here. She wanted to seem helpful without being predatory; friendly and just a hint flirtatious. But she couldn't seem opportunistic. She had to play this just right.

"You know our firm has represented a number of Lotto winners over the years."

"Really?"

She nodded. "Believe it or not, winning the lottery is a dangerous proposition. Sometimes winning the lottery is the *un*luckiest thing in the world. One third of all Lotto winners are bankrupt in five years. One client won eleven million dollars, ignored our advice and plowed it all into slot machines and crap tables. He now lives in a trailer park. The brother of another client hired hit men to kill him so he would get the inheritance."

"Jesus."

"There's story after story. Another guy won fifteen million, so bought a house for his mom, cars for all his relatives, gave hundreds of thousands to his church, tens of thousands to his friends, sent money to people who wrote him sob stores; he ended up spending it all. Died of a heart attack and there wasn't enough left to pay for the burial. And I read about this woman who won twenty million, went out to celebrate and was killed driving home."

"Okay, that's it, I'm ripping the damn thing up."

"No! There are also plenty of stories about people whose lives have been blessed by the money. All I'm saying is, you have to be careful. Get a team around you: lawyer, CPA, people you can trust." As soon as she said the word trust, Anne regretted it. How would he ever trust the woman who betrayed and dumped him? "People who know and care about you," she added.

Even in college Ryan knew Anne was going to be a great lawyer. She was articulate and convincing. And smart. Hearing all the potential downsides of winning the lottery made him very glad he'd agreed to meet her.

And she was so damn beautiful. When they were together, he used to spend hours staring at her face; when she talked, while she read, as she slept. He used to tell her that her face massaged his eyes. And looking at her now he realized that nothing had changed.

"I do need some advice," he said. "You see, my winning the Lotto is a little more complicated than normal."

"Complicated how?"

Ryan took a sip of his beer and told her about the tow truck driver and finding the ticket on the ground. "And I know enough law," he said finishing, "to know that the ticket is not legally mine."

Anne listened to the story with an increasing sense of doom. She knew Ryan well enough to know that he would probably want to do the *right* thing. Turn the ticket in and let the Lotto officials try and find the tow truck driver.

But it's hard for anyone, even Ryan, to turn down tens of millions of dollars that no one could prove *wasn't* his. And she needed him to claim that money. A rich Ryan would solve so many of her problems.

Then she had an idea, a brainstorm really, something that Ryan would probably find irresistible. So she went to work. "Okay, we've got a real conundrum here, don't we?"

"Yes and no. I mean, it's simple, really, isn't it? The ticket is not mine. I have to turn it in."

"Do you know what will happen if you turn it in?"

"Not really. I'm mean, I guess they'll try and find the tow truck driver."

"You're a detective. Any chance they'll find him?"

"I didn't pay that much attention to his face. I'm sure there was a company name on the tow truck but I don't remember it and I didn't even glance at the license plate. So no, I could never identify him."

"And since it was a quick pick, no one could prove these were numbers he played every week. And since it was six months ago, the 7-Eleven won't have a video tape."

"Right. So if they can't find the real owner, what happens to the money?"

"It goes back into the State general budget fund. Meaning no one gets it."

Ryan slumped; that's what he was afraid of. "What a waste," he said.

Okay, Anne thought. Got to go careful here. "Ryan, who else knows the truth about the lottery ticket?"

Ryan looked at her. He knew where she was going. She was going to try and find a way to justify keeping it. And so was he. That's the real reason he was here, wasn't it?

"Just my partner."

"Can you trust him?"

"Her. And yes, totally."

She didn't like that answer; too quick, too definitive. There was only one reason he could be so sure, he was probably involved with her. Anne wanted to probe further, but there would be time for that later.

"What does she think you should so do with the ticket?"

"She hasn't told me. She says it's my decision."

Good, Anne thought. Smart girl. "Then let's look at a couple of options. I know you used to look at life in absolutes, Ryan, your John Wayne syndrome; right is right, wrong is wrong, life is black and white, period. Has nine years in law enforcement dulled your integrity?"

Nine years on the streets usually turned the biggest idealist into a jaded cynic. And Ryan had seen enough injustices, corruption and abuse of power to rattle his belief system, but it still worked, somehow. "Dulled, perhaps, destroyed, no."

"But I'm sure you now realize that there is a lot of gray mixed in with the black and white."

"Oh yeah."

"Well, that's what we've got here, Ryan. A gray area. In a perfect world you'd turn the ticket in, the rightful owner would get it and the angels in heaven sing a chorus of Halleluiah. But, since turning in the ticket would mean *no one* gets the money, those angels have got nothing to sing about. If you did claim the lottery and used the millions for the greater good, those angels could unleash their voices."

"The greater good?"

"Charities, friends in need; Ryan, we're talking forty-seven million dollars!"

"Thirty-four after taxes."

Anne laughed. "Okay, thirty-four. That's still a boatload of cash. Think of all the great things you could do with that money. All the people you could help. You could be a one-man United Way, giving help and money to whomever *you* want."

Ryan hadn't thought of that. And taking the money for charitable purposes didn't seem as dishonest somehow.

"Look, I'm just spit-balling here, I need to get back to my office and check a few things. How much time do we have? When does the ticket expire?"

"Thursday."

Anne's jaw dropped. "The day after tomorrow? Aren't you cutting this a little bit close?"

"We just found the ticket. Syd, that's my partner, wanted some gum so I told her to look in my glove compartment. And there it was, buried in a few years worth of crap."

"Sounds like she's the real hero in this story," Anne said. Then something occurred to her. "Wait a minute, you don't still drive the Mustang, do you?"

"It was my dream car in college and it's my dream car now."

And then Anne remembered a night long ago. They were driving back from Malibu the night Ryan proposed, the top was down, their hair was blowing and he said, "I'm in my dream car with my dream girl. Does it get any better than this?" The memory filled her with such a sense of melancholy that she looked away, oddly embarrassed.

Ryan noticed. "You okay?"

"Fine," she said, and then regrouped. "You know," she said, getting back to the heart of her idea, the heart of her salvation. "I could help you set up this foundation. I've been living the life of a greedy corporate attorney for long enough. Taking and never giving back. This could be a great opportunity for both of us. You'd resign from the police department and we could run it together."

"Wait, hold it. Who said anything about leaving the police department?"

"You'd have millions of dollars, why would you want to still be a cop?"

"I love being a cop."

He said it with such conviction Anne was envious. She wished she loved something that much. "Then you remain a cop and oversee the foundation on the side. The important thing is we put that money to good use."

"You make it sound so simple."

"It is simple, Ryan. You've been given an incredible opportunity to help thousands of people. Frankly, it's a no brainer. In fact, as I fully unwind my powers of rationalization, I could make a case that you winning the Lotto and using the money for charity is much more humane than some beer guzzling tow truck driver who would no doubt piss away all the money. It's better for everyone."

"Well, almost everyone," Ryan said.

"Sure. But what the tow truck driver doesn't know can't possibly hurt him."

Anne made so much sense. And for the first time since he'd found out about the winning lottery ticket, Ryan began to see a way he could actually justify keeping the money. And the idea of working with Anne every day, seeing Anne every day, was surprisingly appealing.

"You have time for one more drink?" he asked.

Anne shook her head. "No, if we've got a Thursday deadline, I've got a ton of work to do." She slid a twenty-dollar bill onto the bar. "You have time tomorrow if I need you?"

"I'll make time."

Anne stood. "I've missed you, Handsome." And then she kissed him gently on the lips.

The kiss surprised Ryan. It felt good. It felt familiar. It felt right. Ryan suddenly realized how much he had missed her. "Talk to you soon, Beautiful."

Anne walked out of the bar, a smile on her lips. She had him.

EIGHTEEN

Syd sat at her desk in the deserted bullpen, eyes focused on her computer screen. The more Syd read about Anne Rogers, formerly Anne Magee, formerly Anne Reich, the less she liked her. Syd had Googled her, checked her Facebook page and the Rogers, Middleton and Roberts homepage. What emerged was an up-from-the-bootstraps story of a poor young girl raised in a trailer park by an alcoholic mother who made it to the top with pluck, brains and determination. There is no mention of her brief college marriage to Ryan Magee, but blog after blog accompanied by the appropriate pictures, chronicled her worldwide travels to the far-flung capitals of the world, Zurich, Dubai, Paris, etc., with her wonderful husband Rick. They were always photographed either hand in hand or with arms around each other; clearly two people in love.

That was a bit consoling; at least she was happily married.

Anne's legal career seemed successful but uneventful. She represented Fortune 500 firms in a variety of corporate litigations; lawsuits that make money, not headlines. Syd double-clicked on Anne's picture on the Rogers, Middleton Roberts homepage and the smiling brunette face filled the screen. She was pretty, if anything, too perfect; almost like she was trying too hard.

Syd had met a few women like her in the Police Academy. Overachievers, who studied harder and worked out longer than all the other cadets. Syd knew the type well; she was one of them.

In a way, becoming a cop was a going away present from EMT Eric Templeton. At Eric's funeral, Syd met his sister, Andrea. She was a vet, too, an MP in the Army who joined the LAPD after her discharge. Eric had told Andrea all about Syd, and the two women hit it off immediately.

Andrea saw the same potential in Syd that Eric had, and helped her get her high school GED, enroll in Santa Monica City College and even got Syd a part-time job working at a friend's cafe.

Andrea wasn't pretty. She had a nose that was a bit small on a face that was a bit too long and eyes that were just a tad too close together. She kept her brown hair cut short and wore almost no make-up. She was tall and skinny, but strong. She spent five hours a week in the gym and was a first-degree black belt.

She was also gay. In the Army, nobody asked and she didn't tell. In the LAPD, it was nobody's fucking business.

Andrea lived in a three-bedroom house in Burbank she inherited from her folks. She offered Syd one of the spare bedrooms until she got on her feet. They became lovers a month later.

Syd was smart enough to realize a pattern was developing; she was using sex as the glue to cement important relationships. It happened with Ernesto and now Andrea. But she didn't care; she was so desperate for security, for stability that sex seemed a small price to pay.

Syd didn't think of herself as gay; bi-sexual at best. When she was a hooker she'd had to do a number of threesomes; guys always loved to see two girls get it on. Syd liked it okay; women certainly were better lovers than men. However given a choice, Syd preferred men.

But Andrea was so much more than a lover. She was teacher, friend, and inspiration. She took Syd to the gym, to the dojo so she could learn karate, to museums and art galleries. And Andrea instilled in Syd her love for law enforcement. Andrea relished running into a dangerous situation when everyone else was running away. She felt she made a difference every day. There were millions of people living in L.A. just trying to mind their own business, raise their children and get safely through the day. Millions of people who are preyed on by thugs, thieves, rapists and murderers. Andrea was proud to man the wall that separated good from evil. And what better way for Syd to get over her former life as a victim than by becoming an advocate for justice.

She never told Andrea that she'd killed two men. In Syd's mind those weren't crimes, they were clear-cut cases of self-defense. Besides, she feared Andrea's sense of justice would land her in jail.

Syd joined the LAPD as soon as she graduated from Santa Monica City College. She was determined to be number one in her Academy class and make Andrea proud. So she was an overachiever.

But Andrea didn't live to see Syd's graduation. Andrea was killed by a gangbanger trying to hold up a Wendy's.

Syd's reaction was surprising. She was heartbroken, of course, but a part of her was relieved. Syd was hoping to start her LAPD career on her own. She was ready to move on with her life and that meant breaking up with Andrea. Andrea would have been devastated, so a valiant death in the line of duty was at the very least, a consolation.

Syd's success as a cop was due, in great deal, to the lessons learned from Andrea and the ambition seared into her soul by her late lover. And though Syd had dated a few times in the ensuing years, men only now, nothing stuck until Syd met Ryan.

But at times like this she really missed Andrea. Andrea was a great judge of character and Syd would love Andrea's take on ex-wife Anne and the whole lottery mess.

The bullpen door swung open and Ryan walked in. He had a bounce to his step and a smile on his face.

"You look happy," Syd said clicking a window on her computer banishing the picture of Anne Rogers.

"I do? Well, I guess I kind of am. Anne was very helpful."

"What, tell me?"

He plopped into his chair, facing her. "You first; any luck finding the Tuttle girl?"

"Of course, nobody can hide from me. She's a wannabe actress working nights as a waitress at Tony

Roma's."

"I love Tony Roma's."

"I know you do. I thought we could stop for a little third degree and a side of baby back ribs."

"Genius."

"I also got the VICAP report on numbers scrawled into corpses. 666 seem to be the numerals of choice, often left on corpses, walls, floors or cars."

"Devil worship."

"Right, which is what we don't have here. Aside from the 666 freaks, I couldn't find any reports of a body found with the number 1 carved or painted on it, or the numbers 2, 3 or 4 for that matter."

"Okay. Guess we'll have to crack this case the old fashioned way." Ryan stood. "So, we good to go?"

"Wait, what about your ex-wife and the lottery ticket?"

"I'll tell you on the way," Ryan said heading for the door. "But here's the headline: Ryan Magee saves the world." And he walked out the door.

Intrigued, and more than a little worried, Syd followed.

NINTEEN

The five most expensive items on the Bel Air Regent Hotel room service menu were: Iranian Ostera Caviar, three hundred and sixty-five dollars an ounce; Lobster Thermador with Wilted Baby Spinach, sixty-five dollars; Crispy Duck Confit with Sautéed Fingerling Potatoes, Smoked Mushrooms and Wild Mushrooms, fifty-five dollars; a twenty-four ounce Rib Eye at fifty-two dollars and finally, Duo of Foie Gras with Scented Wild mushrooms a paltry forty-five dollars.

Of course, the *most* expensive things on any restaurant menu are the wines and the Bel Air Regent room service menu was no exception. So Adam also ordered the priciest wine, a six hundred dollars bottle of Chateau Margaux '89 to wash it all down.

Adam watched Susie gobble up the caviar. And that's exactly what it looked like. He'd never seen anyone enjoy something so much. It was a far cry from her reaction when she first saw the jet-black pile of fish eggs.

"I've never had caviar," she said staring at the caviar warily. "Why would anyone want to eat fish eggs?"

"Because they're good. Here, let me make you one." Adam picked up a cracker, doled out a small scoop of caviar, added a little chopped onion, chopped egg and a dollop of sour cream. He handed it to her; she took it cautiously but made no motion toward her mouth.

Adam smiled. "They don't charge hundreds of dollars an ounce because it's bad, Susie. Go ahead, you'll love it, I promise."

She closed her eyes, slipped the cracker into her mouth and took a tentative bite. First her eyes popped open, then a smile spread as the miraculous mixture of salty eggs, crunchy onions, sour cream and egg engulfed her taste buds. "Oh, my God," she said, her mouth still full. "This definitely does not suck."

"Told you."

She closed her eyes relishing the flavor. Only one word could describe her reaction, ecstasy. And watching her bliss was thrilling for Adam. His wife Emily was a spoiled bitch who grew up in Beverly Hills and had probably been spoon-fed caviar as a baby. Nothing seemed to delight her any more. She'd seen it all, done it all. She was totally jaded.

But not Susie. She was like a kid with a new toy and Adam was surprised how much pleasure *he* was getting from Susie's happiness. Then he had an epiphany.

"Come work for me."

"What?"

"Now that I've found you I don't want to let you go. If I get you a job with one of my clients who knows when I'll see you again. I want you all to myself."

Alice looked at him and smiled provocatively. "What kind of job do you have in mind?"

"No, I'm serious. I'll train you to become an agent. You're smart, beautiful, and ambitious; you would make a fantastic sports agent."

Alice realized he was serious. "You're offering me a job?"

"Not just a job, a career. You could make enough money to order caviar whenever you liked."

She threw her arms around him. "Yes, I'd love to; Adam, thank you so much." She kissed him.

"Of course," he said slipping his hand under the robe, rubbing his finger on her nipple, "we're going to need to spend a lot of time together while I train you."

"I suppose I could stomach it," she said, nibbling his ear.

"And I travel a lot, all over the world. You'd need to come with me." His hand moved to her other breast.

She purred. "Sounds exhausting, but I'm game." She kissed his neck.

Then Adam realized something. "I can't believe it, I'm hard again."

"Then I guess we're just going to have to do something about that," she said, slipping off her robe.

"Four times in one night!" Adam reached past her to put down his glass of wine. "Okay, I've haven't had sex four times in one day since college. Whoops..." his hand hit her purse, knocking it to the floor. It landed upside down, spilling most of its contents. "Shit, I'm sorry, I'll get it."

"No!" Alice blurted, leaping off the bed. "Let me."

But she was too late, Adam picked up the purse revealing a pile of purse detritus – including the Colt Vest Pocket .25.

"Is that a gun?"

"Yes," she said, picking it up. "A girl can't be too careful these days."

Something else caught Adam's eye; he picked it up. "And a scalpel, what's this for?"

Alice said the first thing that came to mind. "They're great for getting stains out of clothes. Just scrape them off and good as new."

"What a great idea." Adam looked at the blade. "Guess you spilled some red wine recently, this blade is filthy."

Colin Wood's dried blood, Alice thought. She'd meant to wipe it off when she got back to the apartment after killing him, but forgot. Shit. "I spilled wine on a sweater the other day, worked like a charm." She took the scalpel from him, dropped it in the purse along with the gun.

Adam reached into the pile to help her refill her purse, coming up with a Platinum American Express card. He stared at the name, confused. It said Colin Wood. "What the hell?"

Alice looked up. Fuck, she thought, Colin's credit card. She'd stolen it as a souvenir to go along with the card she stole from Zachary Stone and forgotten to take it out of her purse.

Adam stood up, the Platinum card clutched in his hand. He glanced at the TV remembering the news report of Colin's murder. His face clouded as pieces of an impossible puzzle tried to fall into place. When he looked back at Alice, she had the gun pointed at him.

TWENTY

"Where were you last night between midnight and 2:00 a.m.?"

"I was in the Havoc parking lot killing that pig, Colin Wood."

Ryan and Syd exchanged astonished look.

Then Kathy Tuttle laughed. "Just kidding," she said. "I was home, asleep like almost everyone else in L.A." They were standing in the Tony Roma's manager's office. Kathy Tuttle was beautiful; jet black hair, blue eyes, sex appeal that sizzled through her low cut, tuxedo-style waitress uniform and an effusive personality.

Ryan asked, "Can anyone confirm that?"

"Sure, the guy who sits in this office, Cameron, the manager. We've been dating about six months."

Syd made a note to confirm the alibi. "We understand you got a check from Colin's father for half a million dollars three years ago," Syd said. "With all that money, why are you working as a waitress?"

Kathy laughed. "Because the money's gone. I spent every last penny and then some."

Kathy took a pack of cigarettes out of her pocket, tapped one out. "You mind if I smoke?" She lit up without waiting for an answer, opened a desk drawer and pulled out an ashtray. "I was poor all my life and had this list of things I would buy myself if I ever hit the Lotto, which was stupid because I never even played the Lotto. Then Colin rapes me, and deep down I wanted to send that prick to jail, but then his father offered me all that money, and well, I sold out. Half a million dollars, I mean," she looked at Syd. "What would you have done?" Then, without waiting for an answer, she went on. "Exactly, it was a no brainer, right. I mean all that money!"

"Irresistible, absolutely," Syd said and shot Ryan a look. Ryan had explained his ex-wife's idea for keeping the money to Syd on the drive over. Syd hated the idea but had kept her feeling to herself, for the time being.

"So I bought shoes, clothes, a new car – a red Mini if you must know, went to Hawaii, Vegas – Vegas was a huge mistake; I lost thousands playing blackjack." Kathy breathed in a lung full of smoke, shook her head. "I was, in a word, incredibly idiotic. Wait, that's two words, isn't it?"

"Money is the ultimate temptation," Ryan said, the resonance not lost on him. "Could you tell us more about what Colin Wood did to you, about the rape itself?"

Kathy eyed him suspiciously. "Why? I told you I didn't kill him."

"His father suggested the murder might have been self defense," Syd said. "Maybe he picked up a girl in the bar, tried to force himself on her and she killed him protecting herself."

Kathy sucked in another lung full of smoke. "I wouldn't know about that," she said. "He raped me in my apartment and it was a slow motion sort of rape, not groping me in a car."

"I don't understand," Syd said.

"We met at a wrap party for this movie a friend of mine worked on and Colin was there. We talked, he was charming and all, but I drank too much, and he offered to drive me home. When we got there, I invited him in for a drink, to be polite you know; I never sleep with a guy on the first night. We had some wine, made out for a little while, and then I asked him to leave because I had to get up early. He said he'd come to bed with me, and I said no; I'd just met him. Please leave. He didn't budge, just kissed me again. So I kiss him back then said, now I'm going to bed, goodnight. But he doesn't move, just pulls me to him and kisses me again. He's trying to wear me down, you know," she said to Syd. "Just keep making out until I fuck him to get rid of him. But I'm not that drunk and now I'm starting to get mad. I tell him to leave. Instead, he tried to kiss me again, but I'm not playing anymore and I turn away from him. That pisses him off; he calls me a prick teaser and tears at my clothes, forcing my legs open and that's when the son of a bitch raped me. When he's done, he pulls his clothes back on and actually asked for my phone number. Can you believe it?"

"Did you go to the police?" Syd asked.

"Almost. I mean, I was going to but Jenny, that's the friend I called after he left, suggested going to a lawyer first. She'd been through a similar situation and the cops made it all sound like her fault. She said date rape was almost impossible to prove, especially since I invited him into my apartment, and I needed a lawyer to protect myself. So we call her uncle, he's a lawyer down in Orange County, tell him the story, give him Colin's name and he says he wants to check a few things out and he'll get back to me. He calls back the next day, says we could go to the police if I want, but he thought if we threatened a lawsuit, we'd collect a lot money."

"Just because Colin was an actor?" Syd asked.

"Well, a date rape charge can certainly be a career killer, and Colin's father was rich, so he'd probably be willing to step up to save his son. But my lawyer also said Colin had been in trouble before for the same thing."

"Date rape?" Ryan asked.

"I guess; I never heard the specifics. It happened a long time ago, in high school, I think. My lawyer had heard some rumors, thought we could pressure Colin and his dad. And he was right." She stubbed out her cigarette. "The case was settled after just a couple of phone calls."

"Sounds like he had something to hide," Ryan said, cutting his eyes to Syd. "Did you talk to the lawyer when you got Kathy's phone number?"

"No, he was out of town. His assistant gave me Kathy's number."

Ryan checked his notes. "I'm going to call Nick Wood and ask him." Ryan found the number, pulled out his cell phone and dialed. After a moment he frowned, "Voice mail," he said to Syd. Then he spoke into his phone, "Mr. Wood this is Detective Ryan Magee; something has come up and I need to talk to you immediately." Ryan left his number and hung up.

"You know it's kind of funny," Kathy Tuttle said. "If I had pressed charges and Colin Wood was sent to jail three years ago, he'd still be alive. Ironic, huh?"

TWENTY-ONE

"Damn it, Adam, you've ruined everything."

"What? I don't understand." He held out the Platinum card. "How did you get this? Did you kill Colin?"

She nodded.

"And you're going to kill me?"

Any thoughts of sparing Adam were dashed now. How could she build a life with him once he knew she was a murderer? There will be no happy ending tonight.

His eyes went from the gun to her face. "Are you?"

Another nod.

"Why?"

And then she realized her previous mistakes. Colin Wood and Zachary Stone died without knowing why. Stone was happily walking to a restaurant to meet a hot blonde. Wood was getting a blowjob from the same hot blonde. What good was revenge if the victim doesn't know retribution is at hand? Well, Adam would know.

"Look at me Adam, really look at me."

He did. This was Adam's first brush with death and, while some people report an almost supernatural clarity giving them time to react, Adam's usually nimble brain ramped to slow motion. Panic swept through him: his vision narrowed, his heart pounded, he could barely catch his breath. "Don't kill me, please. Take my wallet, my watch, anything you want. Just, please, don't kill me."

How pathetic, Alice thought. How could I have been in love with such a pussy? "Don't beg, Adam. Concentrate. Look at me. I need you to remember."

"Remember what?"

"Me. Alice. Alice Waterman."

Adam's mind was glue. Alice Waterman? Who the fuck was Alice Waterman? And then he remembered. It was Blake's eighteenth birthday and they wanted to have a little fun. They'd gotten a bottle of Rohypnol, the date rape drug, from Blake's older brother. Colin had noticed how that loser Alice Waterman was always following Adam around like a puppy dog. She wasn't very pretty but she did have decent tits and word was, she put out. So they came up with this stupid plan to get her drugged up, and play around with her a little bit. But it had gotten out of hand. Way out of hand.

The woman in front of him was a beautiful blonde. Alice was a mousey brunette. He looked at her trying to remember Alice's face. Nothing.

"Do you remember the bus trip we took together senior year? The field trip to the Getty center?"

It's amazing how an incident can mean so much to one person and nothing to the other. Alice fell in love with Adam on that two-hour trip. He had absolutely no memory of it. But he was staring at a woman with a gun leveled at his head so he said, "Yes, of course."

She smiled, sadly. "No, you don't."

He deflated. "No, I don't."

"We sat next to each other. We talked. You were very nice to me. You told me you were an only child, that you always wanted a brother."

He remembered their conversation in the bar earlier. "And that's why you said you always wanted a sister."

She nodded.

Adam was starting to get his bearings now, his brain finally kicking into gear. He had to talk his way out of this or she was going to shoot him. And a successful agent is nothing if not a great salesman. "Look, Alice, I am so sorry for what happened in high school. I never meant to hurt you. But you can't deny that something happened between us tonight, something wonderful."

"It did," she said. "I felt it, too."

A ray of hope lit a corner of Colin's brain. "So that's all that matters. Us. You and me. Fuck Colin Wood. I'm glad he's dead. I won't tell anyone you killed him, I swear. Put down the gun, let's talk and try to figure this out."

"Ever wish you had a time machine, Adam?"

"What?"

"A time machine, like in the movies. I do. And I always go back to the same moment in time. I'm sitting on the quad that day in high school when you came up to me and asked if I wanted to go to a party. I saw Colin and Blake behind you, these evil grins on their faces. Deep down I knew it was too good to be true. But I was such a sap, and so in love with you I ignored all the warning bells and said yes. That's my destination, Adam, that moment my lips formed the word *yes.* If I'd only said *no,* you wouldn't have drugged me. You wouldn't have raped me. I wouldn't have spent all those years locked up in that hell hole."

"I want to take that time travel trip with you," Adam said. "Because if I could, I never would have let Blake talk me into asking you in the first place."

"It was all Blake's idea?"

"Yes, absolutely." Then something occurred to Adam. "Is he, I mean, have you killed him, too?"

"No, not yet. He's on my To Do list for tomorrow."

My To Do list for tomorrow. She said it as matter of fact as saying she needed to pick up a gallon of milk. This woman is absolutely nuts, Adam realized. And if he didn't get that gun away from her, he was dead. "Tell you what, this is all Blake's fault anyway, right? I mean he talked me into asking you over that night. So, let me help you kill Blake. Let me prove to you how much I care about you."

Interesting idea, Alice thought. She cocked her head, weighing Adam's commitment. "You would do that for me? Help me kill Blake?"

"Yes, absolutely."

"Commit murder?"

He was willing to say whatever he had to. "Yes."

Alice was starting to enjoy this. He was like a puppet on a string. Ask a question that he thinks only has one answer and watch him perform. "Do you love me, Adam?"

Just the slightest hesitation before he said, "Yes."

"Are you willing to spend eternity with me?"

"Yes. Eternity."

"Good. But you go first." She pulled the trigger.

The Colt Vest Pocket .25 made a delicate POP and sent a 6.4mm bullet at 815 feet per second into Adam's left eye. The POP of the gun was not much louder than a champagne cork being popped, a sound that would certainly go unnoticed in the plush hallways of the Bel Air Regent Hotel. But because the 45 grain bullet had a soft tissue route into Adam's brain, it inflicted maximum damage as it shredded the septum pellucidum, corpus callosum and a good part of the cerebrum.

Alice watched Adam's lifeless body crumble to the ground. Poor Adam, she couldn't blame him for lying to save his life, but she did wish he'd gone out with a little more dignity.

Tears fell as she looked at the lips that had kissed her, the arms that had held her and the hands that had caressed her. Tonight was a night she would cherish for the rest of her life. Right up until the moment she'd had to kill the only man she ever loved.

TWENTY-TWO

"Tell me about your marriage."

"I've told you. We were just kids, still in college; it was a bad idea and when we both realized it, we split up. End of story."

Ryan and Syd were eating dinner at Tony Roma's. They'd both ordered the baby back ribs and were sharing sides of coleslaw and the corn fritter casserole. Ryan nursed a Michelob, iced tea for Syd. She didn't drink. She'd told Ryan it was because she just never had a taste for it; he knew nothing about her drug-addicted days and she wasn't ready to tell him yet, if ever.

And even though Syd had a suitcase full of secrets she kept from Ryan, she felt entitled to know everything about him. "Were you in love with her?"

"I guess. Or thought I was." He'd been crazy in love with Anne, corny-greeting-card kind of love. And the memory of her dumping him still hurt. But Ryan wasn't about to tell Syd that. Not because he was necessarily hiding something from her, he'd just never verbalized it to anyone. The closest he came was a drunken night with his ex-stepmom, Liz. Liz never liked Anne, told Ryan she was a mercenary, gold-digging bitch, and he was better off without her. Ryan tried to embrace that anger and it kept him going for a little while, but deep down there was still an open sore on his heart.

"And how did you feel when you broke up?"

Ryan put down his rib, looked at Syd. "What's with all the questions about Anne, sweetie? Don't tell me you're jealous."

"Isn't every girlfriend jealous of the ex-wife?"

"I guess so. But trust me, you have nothing to worry

about." Ryan went back to work on his ribs, a not so subtle signal that she should change the subject. Because the truth was, Syd had a lot to worry about. The time Ryan spent with Anne at Musso and Frank had left him wanting more. The idea of starting a foundation with her, or spending time with her every day excited him. Deep down he felt their earlier relationship was unfinished. He'd invested a lot of hopes and dreams in that marriage and when she ended it so abruptly, he was left at sea. He not only lost his wife, but his life's plan. He wasn't supposed to be a cop forever; he was going to be a lawyer. And as much as he loved being a cop, he often wondered what would have happened if he'd found a way to go to law school. And now with the lottery money, he might be able to find out.

"I guess you're right, I'm being silly, sorry," Syd said, knowing she should just shut the fuck up but unable to stop herself. "Besides, she's happily married."

"Exactly," Ryan said, not thrilled to be reminded of that. "So now let's talk about something important, murder and our Lady in Red. The way I see it we've got two possibilities. One, Colin Wood was the only victim and the 2 carved into his chest was misdirection."

"Since we've found no evidence of a victim number one, a definite possibility."

"Or, two, there was a victim one, still unaccounted for, and there is going to be a victim three or there has already been a victim three and our phones will ring any second with the location of a new crime scene."

"Be still my heart," Syd said. "A new crime scene is *exactly* what we need. A new body means new clues. But if this crime was revenge for a rape of some sort, what's with multiple victims?"

"A gang rape?"

"Maybe, but does Colin Wood seem the type to be involved in a gang rape? I don't know; I'm still leaning toward a nutjob going after all her old boyfriends. But that raises the question, why now?"

Ryan finished his last rib, dropped the bone on the table. "God, that was good." Syd was done too, even though she only ate half her rack. Ryan asked for a check and a takeout carton. "Well," Ryan said. "Until Colin Wood's father or Kathy Tuttle's attorney call us back, there's nothing more we can do tonight."

Actually there was, Syd thought. They could talk about the lottery and Anne's idea to set up a foundation. Syd hated the idea. The Lotto ticket wasn't Ryan's and he had no right to take the money. But she could see Ryan was a bit fragile tonight, so Syd decided to wait and stay in safer waters.

"Then you won't mind if I ask you a favor?" Syd said, her green eyes flashing.

"No, sweetie, what?"

"Take me home and fuck my brains out."

Ryan laughed. There was something so sexy about this innocent girl next door talking dirty. And in bed there wasn't an innocent bone in her body. "I have a better idea," he said. "Let's leave your brain intact and I'll fuck everything else."

Ryan thought making love to Syd was like starring in porno. She was so enthusiastic it was almost like she was being paid for it. And she would do anything, wanted to do everything. Take tonight, for example. As soon as they walked in the door of Ryan's apartment, Syd kicked off her shoes, pulled off her blouse, stepped out of her dress and yanked off her panties. Then she stood before him, stark naked, threw her arms out by her side, turned a slow circle and said, "Where would you like to start?"

He chose her belly button. It was an innie; he kissed it, flicked his tongue into it a couple of times, then blew a raspberry. She laughed, pulled Ryan to his feet and kissed him. It was a hungry kiss that seemed to inhale him, not just into her mouth but into her body.

Her hands expertly undid his belt buckle and his pants fell to the floor. She pulled his shirt off as he stepped out of his pants, then she dropped to her knees, yanked off his boxer shorts and took him into her mouth.

When Syd gave him head, she seemed to enjoy it more

than Ryan. She groaned with pleasure as her hands caressed his balls.

Suddenly the thought of another woman giving him head invaded Ryan's brain. Anne. The first time they made love was in her crappy studio apartment shared by three broke co-eds. All four of them were in the apartment that night, Ryan and Anne, plus Anne's two roommates. Ryan and Anne had finished off a bottle of Merlot and been making out while her roommates watched *American Idol* and pretended to ignore the horny lovers. Ryan and Anne had their hands all over each other and Ryan ached for them to be alone. Anne got the message and led them into the bathroom. As soon as the door closed she dropped to her knees, freed Ryan's hard- on from his pants and wrapped her mouth around it. Ryan was so turned on that he immediately felt himself ready to blow. *Oh, God* he'd said then, gripping the back of Anne's head.

"Oh, God," he said now, gripping the back of Syd's head.

Back in college, as Kelly Clarkson sang a song on *Idol*, and Anne's lips and tongue worked him to a climax, he said, *Oh, Anne, yes, baby, yes.*

And now, as Syd expertly brought him to an orgasm he blurted, "Oh, Anne, yes baby, yes."

Syd's eyes popped open.

Ryan's eyes popped open.

And they both thought the same thing.

"Oh, shit."

TWENTY-THREE

Alice's fingerprints were everywhere. Wearing her surgical gloves, Alice wiped down the entire hotel room: the bathroom, the champagne bottle, glasses, plates, silverware, end table, doorknob, light switches. She knew she'd probably left DNA in the bed but she didn't care. Her DNA wasn't on file anywhere, so it couldn't be used to catch her, just convict her. And right now, she was only concerned with avoiding capture and, since her fingerprints were on file, she had to be sure to get rid of every single one.

She glanced down at Adam's body, but that's all it was now. A slab of meat. Adam was gone, he was obliterated a few milliseconds after the bullet pulped his brain. So it didn't bother her to cut off his penis and stick it in his mouth. She did it more for her legacy than out of rage at this point. If the brutality of her revenge made another potential rapist stop and think, mission accomplished. If it made another woman fight back, mission accomplished.

Alice didn't believe in God anymore, but she did believe in Satan. She couldn't understand the people who thought you couldn't have one without the other. One look at all the evil in the world should be all it takes for everyone to realize we were living in Satan's playground. You always read about schools or churches collapsing during earthquakes killing scores of innocents. When was the last time you read about a whorehouse going down in a natural catastrophe? Wake up people!

Three down and one to go. But Alice needed time. Once Adam's body was found, it wouldn't be long until the police connected him to Colin Wood and Zachary Stone. From there, with a little research, they'd be able to predict her next victim. So the Lady in Red needed to buy as much time as possible before Adam's body was found.

She rolled the room service cart into the hall and then called down and told room service the food was fantastic and they'd find the cart in the corridor.

Then she called the hotel operator and told her she and her husband had just flown in from Shanghai and needed to sleep. Please hold all their calls until further notice.

She wiped off the telephone, took a final look around the room to make sure she hadn't forgotten anything, and then saw Colin's Platinum card lying a few inches from Adam's outstretched hand. Damn, so much to remember.

She picked it up, shoved the credit card in her purse and then fished Adam's wallet out of his discarded pants pocket. She knew he had a Black American Express card, she'd seen him use it to pay for the drinks. She would have preferred a Platinum one so they would all match, but the black one would do.

She also took the wad of hundreds out of his other pants pocket; the extra money might come in handy.

And now just one final touch remained. She bent down to his right hand. She took the thumb and folded it into his palm and then folded his pinkie on top of his thumb. Then she laid his hand, palm down on the floor. She looked at the result and smiled. Perfect.

She triple checked the room; satisfied, she grabbed the Do Not Disturb sign. The sign hanging on the doorknob should keep the housekeepers at bay in the morning and perhaps throughout the afternoon. With luck, the body wouldn't be found for at least twenty-four hours.

Alice pulled opened the heavy door with the pneumatic hinge and stepped into the hall. An elderly woman was walking with her dog, a yappy little Maltese, who was clearly unhappy and tugging at its leash.

Alice smiled at the guest, dropped the Do Not Disturb sign on the doorknob and pulled on the door to hasten its closing.

And then the shit hit the fan.

The dog barked and jerked the leash out of its owner's

hand and bolted down the hall. "Maggie, no!" screamed the woman, running after the dog. She looked at Alice, called, "Stop her!"

Alice instinctively used her arms and legs to block the corridor, so the dog skittered left toward the only avenue of escape left open, the slowly closing door of Alice's room.

The dog shot inside just as the door hissed closed. There was silence for a moment, and then they heard the muffled barks of the dog.

"I'm so sorry," the elderly woman said. "If you'll just open up, I'll get Maggie and we'll be on our way."

"I don't have the key," Alice said, realizing how the captain of the Titanic must have felt seconds after striking the iceberg. "I left it inside the room." Which was true, it was on the end table right next to Adam's dead body.

"Tell you what," Alice said. "I'll go down to the desk, get another key and then come right back up."

"Thank you so much," the old woman said. "And again, I'm so sorry."

Tell me about it, Alice thought as she hurried to the elevator. She used her knuckle to hit the call button so as not to leave a fingerprint, and then realized she still had her surgical gloves on. She stripped them off.

She had no intention of stopping by the desk. She was going to walk straight out the door. It would probably be fifteen or twenty minutes until the old lady made her way downstairs wondering what happened to her; plenty of time for Alice to get far from the Bel Air Regent. The elevator arrived. She got in and hit the Lobby button with her knuckle. So much for a twenty-four hour grace period, Alice thought, as the elevator door slid shut.

TWENTY-FOUR

A crossroad. Syd knew that Ryan's slip of the tongue had put their relationship at a critical crossroad, and what Syd said and did in the next few seconds would affect the rest of her life. Throw a fit? Storm out of the apartment? Pretend she didn't hear it? Accept his inevitable apology?

Well, first things first; she swallowed.

Ryan dropped to his knees, took Syd's face in his hands and said, "Jesus, sweetheart, I am so sorry."

Syd could see the pain in his face, the embarrassment, the humiliation. And he couldn't have sounded more sincere. Syd loved Ryan, and, Erich Segal be damned, but sometimes love means *letting* someone say they're sorry.

"Well," she said, "So much for me not being jealous of Anne."

Ryan laughed. Now it was his turn to say just the right thing. But it couldn't be the truth, could it? He was thinking about his ex-wife while having sex with his girlfriend. Syd would freak out. But what other explanation could he give her? Syd was not stupid and expected the truth, deserved the truth. And Ryan knew if he said the wrong thing, he might lose her forever.

"I don't know what to say. I guess seeing Anne today stirred up some old memories. While you were giving me head, I flashed back to the first time Anne gave me head. And before I could refocus on you, I came. I don't fantasize about Anne; I'm crazy about you, I love you, and I am so sorry."

Syd could hear the truth in every word. And she wasn't into playing games. So she let Ryan off the hook.

"To tell you the truth," she said. "I was fantasizing about Lieutenant Hanrahan."

Ryan laughed, relieved, and hugged her.

"Now," Syd said, playfully shoving Ryan back onto the floor, "where were we?"

Anne sat on the balcony of her soon-to-be-foreclosed Santa Monica condo staring out at the black glob of the Pacific Ocean. There wasn't much to see at night unless the moon was cycling through its more incandescent phases. Tonight a feeble crescent hung tentatively in the sky turning the sea into a murky mess. But the view was glorious during the day, and the sunsets were breathtaking.

Unfortunately, the only nice thing about the condo was the view. It was a boxy three- bedroom two-bath unit on the fourth floor of a twelve story building. And it wasn't even a full- on view; you had to sit on the far edge of the balcony and look around the edge of the building.

It had been tough for Anne to move out of the Malibu house. Trading three thousand square feet of beachfront for eleven hundred feet of poured concrete was humiliating. And now, having to trade this rat hole for what, a studio in the Valley? Dear God, what a mess.

Rick came onto the patio, beer in hand. "I've found some office space we can look at tomorrow, decent building, just off Washington in Culver City."

Oh yeah, she wasn't only losing her home, she was getting kicked out of her office, too. Trading a corner office on the fiftieth floor of L.A.'s most prestigious high-rise to what, Culver fucking City? Well, Anne always had a plan and now was no exception. She turned to her husband. "I'm not going to start a law firm with you, Rick," she said. "And I'm not going to move into a hotel with you. We're done."

"You mean, now that you've sucked me dry, you need to go find another sugar daddy?"

"How dare you."

"Don't get self-righteous with me, Anne. You're the one with a Gucci closet, you're the one who has to fly in private jets, rent villas on the Riviera, drive a Bentley, and flash a fistful of diamonds."

"Don't you dare make this about me. *You* lost all our money in the market."

"And *you're* the one who came up with the idea of forging dad's signature."

Anne shook her head. It was the same argument they'd been having for months. She was sick of it. "Look, Rick, let's make this simple. I want a divorce. Let's just split what few things we've got left down the middle and call it a day."

"Where will you live?"

"I don't know."

"What will you do?"

"I have no idea." But she did have an idea. First thing in the morning she was going to call the California Lottery and make an appointment for Thursday morning. There should be plenty of press there so what better place to announce that honest, hardworking homicide detective, Ryan Magee, was going to set up a foundation and give millions of dollars to charity. And she'd be sure to mention that she'd be heading up the foundation. It would be a great way to launch her new law firm and get plenty of priceless publicity.

Of course, with thirty-four million dollars to play with, you could give away ten million and still have twenty-four million. Hell you could give away twenty-four million and still have ten million. Point being, Ryan was now rich. Gold-plated rich. If she could win Ryan back, they could afford to buy a house on the beach. Her new offices would be in Beverly Hills, not Culver City, and she could continue to live the life of luxury she always dreamed about.

With a man she actually loves.

That's right, because something happened to Anne while she was having that drink with Ryan. She realized she still loved him.

They didn't get divorced because they fought or he was cruel, or inattentive or boring. They got divorced because Ryan was poor and she met someone who was rich. But that didn't mean Ryan and his adorable dimples weren't handsome, smart and charming.

But he had something else, something she rarely encountered in her law practice, integrity. Oh sure, there were honest lawyers out there, but a lawyer, by definition, was somebody who was always looking for a way to parse the truth. Ryan didn't parse. He stood on a razor blade with two sides, right and wrong. He was going to give up a Lotto ticket worth tens of millions because technically it wasn't his. Who would do that?!

Ryan.

And sitting with him tonight she realized how much she admired him. Here was a guy who loved his job, believed in right and wrong, and was honorable. There was absolutely no bullshit in Ryan Magee.

Now admittedly, she tricked Ryan into taking the Lotto money with the foundation idea, but Anne had no pretense about who or what she was.

So, part one of her plan was to get her hands on Ryan's Lotto money. But part two of her plan was even more important; getting her hands on Ryan.

TWENTY-FIVE

Edna Kaye paced anxiously in front of room 1224. She could hear her dear sweet Maggie whining inside. It had been almost fifteen minutes since that pretty blonde woman had gone down to the desk and still no one had come to let Maggie out of the room. She was about to get on the elevator herself when it dinged and a room service waiter stepped into the corridor.

Edna recognized him; he'd been the same waiter who delivered her Oolong tea and sherry a couple of hours ago. "Oh, thank God you've come," she said. "Maggie is trapped in that room there, 1224. The woman who's staying there went to get security but it's taking forever and Maggie is simply miserable."

The room service waiter, Jorge, was actually there to pick up the room service cart for 1224, which he saw in the hallway across from the room. He also saw the Do Not Disturb sign on 1224's door. A good way to get fired from the Bel Air Regent was to knock on the door, or walk into a room that had a Do Not Disturb sign.

"Please, won't you please open the door so I can get my Maggie?"

Jorge remembered Edna and remembered her dog. Edna had tipped him ten dollars cash, which he liked. The dog had nipped his ankle, which he didn't. But he could hear the dog clawing at the door.

"How long ago did she leave?" Jorge asked. Though born in Mexico, he was raised in Fresno and spoke with no accent. He was a senior at UCLA, on scholarship, and desperately needed this job to make ends meet.

"At least fifteen minutes. Does it usually take that long for security to respond? What if someone was in real trouble? Please, can't you help me?"

Actually, security usually responded very quickly but they must have their hands full tonight, he thought. He had an electronic pass card, of course; he was always going into guest rooms to retrieve trays and carts. And who could he possibly disturb by opening the door now? That dog was making so much noise, that if there was a guest inside, he'd have to be awake.

Still, you never knew. He looked at Edna, saw the desperation on her face and made a decision. He took out his pass card, slid it in the door and slowly pushed.

The door was only open six or seven inches when Maggie shot out of there like a cannon ball and leapt into Edna's outstretched arms. "Oh, my poor baby, it's okay, momma's here."

The door to 1224 was barely open and Jorge couldn't see inside. He thought about walking in and checking it out, but the Do Not Disturb sign haunted him and since the dog was freed, he saw no reason. Jorge let go of the door and it hissed shut.

Alice's bloody secret was safe, for now.

Alice didn't know that, of course. She was back in her apartment about five miles from the Bel Air Regent. She liked to think in the shower. And that's what she was doing now; Alice was thinking about the rape. Or more precisely, what happened after the rape.

As she lay in bed that night eleven years ago, hurting inside and out, she tried to figure out exactly what had happened. She must have been drugged, she hadn't drunk that much. And it hit her so fast. It had to be a Roofie. She'd heard about the date rape drug on TV and in Human Sexuality class. Mrs. Brillstein warned about never taking a drink at a party unless you made it yourself. But who expects your own classmates to drug you?

She knew she should go to the police. Make those bastards pay for what they'd done to her. She just wished she'd known what exactly they had done to her. She had no semen in her vagina, but she had been raped, she knew that. So they must've worn condoms. And though she'd never had anal sex before, she could tell that she had now.

Mrs. Brillstein had been very clear what a woman should do if she was ever raped. Get to a hospital emergency room. Don't bathe or change your clothes. Once there, call the police. Then they'd check you for injuries, put together a rape kit and collect evidence they could use in court.

But Alice had already showered. It's the first thing she did when she got home. Stood under the shower and wept. She felt so guilty about what had happened. She actually thought it was her fault.

The truth is, if Adam had said he wanted to have sex with her, she would have said yes. And if Adam said he also wanted her to have sex with his friends, the answer, pathetically, would probably have been yes. She'd have done whatever Adam asked her.

And she'd actually had sex with more than one boy at a time once before, with Tommy Chapman and his friend David. She'd slept with Tommy a few times and did the twosome on a dare. It was kind of fun at the time in a porn-star-wannabe, slightly perverted, sort of way. But she'd felt cheap and used the next day and hadn't done it again.

Lying in bed that night eleven years ago, Alice was ashamed of herself. She knew deep down that she'd been using sex to be more popular. And she hated that about herself. She wished she could just be satisfied at being a brainiac and not care what others thought about her. But she couldn't.

And deep down, in that moral, guilt-ridden consciousness that we're either born with or our parents poison us with, she felt that being drugged and raped was God's way of punishing her for being a slut.

So as she lay in bed, she decided not to go to the hospital. Not to go to the cops. Just to go to school and act as if nothing had happened. And in that twisted, adolescent way of thinking, she actually decided that if she said nothing, showed up at school as if nothing had happened, Adam might be so impressed he would begin to respect her. Maybe even like her.

She had a class with Adam first period, English. Alice got to school earlier, took her seat and waited. A few seconds after the bell Adam hurried in, he looked ragged, hung over. Good, Alice thought, I'm not the only one in pain.

His eyes immediately went to Alice; he seemed surprised she was in class, and then he quickly looked away, embarrassed, Alice thought, guilty.

She wanted to catch up to him after class, tell him it was okay, she wasn't going to say anything, but he hurried out the door as soon as the bell rang. She got a couple of glimpses of Blake and Colin during the day as they were changing classes but they ignored her.

The final bell rang and everyone went about business as usual. Alice felt a great sense of relief. She was terrified the boys would tell their friends a sanitized version of what they'd done last night and she'd be besieged by snide looks, whispers and ridicule. But as she walked home, alone as usual, everyone ignored her, as usual.

Everything changed the next morning. When she got to school she could almost feel it in the air.

A buzz.

About her.

Boys were looking at her, whispering, smirking. Girls were staring with a mix of disgust and pity.

They know, she thought. Adam, Blake and Colin had told everyone. But no, it was even worse. Lizzy Grinaldi, a fuzzy-haired member of the nerd herd, and the closest thing to a friend Alice had, grabbed her in the hallway and pulled her into an empty classroom.

"How could you?" she said.

"How could I what? What have you heard?"

"You mean, what have you *seen*, don't you?" she said, showing Alice her cell phone. There was a picture on the screen of Alice, naked, spread-eagle on the pool table. She hit a button, a new shot, this time of Alice with a penis in her mouth. Then a shot of Alice making love with a man. The image only showed the man's butt, so there was no telling who it was. And a final shot of Alice being penetrated by a pool cue.

"Oh, my God," Alice mumbled. "Where did you get these?"

"They were emailed to a few guys last night who turned around and emailed them to all their friends who emailed them to their friends. It's gone totally viral, Alice. Everyone has seen them, and there are even rumors of a video. What were you thinking?"

"I was drugged, Lizzy. Raped. I don't remember any of this."

"Did you go to the police?"

"No."

Lizzy was shocked. "Why not?"

"You wouldn't understand," she said, fighting back tears. Then Alice ran out of the classroom.

Lizzy chased her, calling out, "Who did this to you?"

Alice ignored her, racing past startled students out of the school, all the way home.

But a tsunami built in her wake. Lizzy told her friends that Alice was drugged and raped and they told their friends and by lunch Blake, Colin and Adam heard. Colin was afraid Alice might go the police so he called his dad who called his lawyer, Zachary Stone.

Meanwhile, Alice told her mother what happened when she got home from school. Her mother had called her father at work at Knotts Berry Farm, who listened, furious, to the story and promised they'd talk about it and decide what to do when he got home.

And that's what they were preparing to do that night when the doorbell rang. Zachary Stone was at the door and needed to speak to them urgently. Once he determined that they hadn't yet contacted the police, he launched into his pitch. The parents of the boys involved are so sorry for what happened to Alice. They would like the ability to punish the boys themselves without calling in the authorities and were offering a five-hundred-thousand-dollar settlement fee in return for the Waterman family's cooperation.

"A half a million dollars could make a lot of dreams come true," Stone said. "You'd be able to pay for Alice's college education and still have plenty of money left to buy a new car, put an addition onto the house or take a family vacation to anywhere in the world."

Alice's Mom exploded. "My daughter is not a whore who can be bought for half a million dollars!"

"All right then," Stone said calmly. "Go to the police and let's take the case to court. But I should warn you, there is a very good chance that because of your daughter's sexual history, the boys will be acquitted while your daughter's reputation will suffer irreparable harm."

"What the hell are you talking about?" Cliff, Alice's father, demanded.

Alice had told her parents about the rape at Colin Wood's house, but her parents had no idea that she was sexually active. In fact, she'd given them every reason to believe she was still a virgin. Her heart sank as Stone turned to her and asked, "Do you want to tell them or should I?"

"Tell us what?" her mother asked.

So Alice told them. Told them she'd been having sex since sophomore year with a number of boys. And that even before then, she'd been with boys in others ways.

Her father turned beet red listening to her. He finally held out a hand, saying, "Stop." He turned to his wife. "Did you know all this?"

Alice's horrified mother said, "No."

"But a lot of kids at school know it, Mr. Waterman," Stone said. "And if we go to court, the whole world will know. Your daughter may claim she was raped and drugged but the boys say she came willingly, drank too much on her own volition and wanted to have sex with them."

"That's a lie," a mortified Alice said, her voice barely above a whisper.

"And with her sexual history," Stone went on, "What jury is going to disagree?"

Alice's Mom and Dad exchanged a defeated look.

"But we can avoid the legal circus. The families are very sorry for what happened, and like I said, are willing to pay five hundred thousand dollars to make the matter disappear."

Alice was about to say *no, I'm going to the police* when her father said, "Make it a million. Make it a million dollars and we won't file charges."

A shocked Alice looked on as Stone took out his cell phone, made a brief phone call. She tried to catch her father's eye, but he was pointedly looking away from her.

"Deal," Stone said.

But no one was happy in the Waterman household. Alice's father took her promiscuity as a betrayal and shunned her. Alice's mother was ashamed of her and worse, knew that all the other mothers would badger her about her slutty daughter. She started sniping at Alice, relentlessly criticizing her.

At school, it was worse. Everyone knew her parents got a huge cash settlement. Some kids thought Alice's parents sold her out. Others thought the boys should never have paid a cent. She was mocked, the butt of jokes, ostracized.

Her first suicide attempt was three days later.

Alice turned off the water, grabbed a towel and dried herself off. She had her TV tuned to NBC. It was 11:00 p.m. and the newscaster led with the day's top local stories: a fire in Culver City, a metro bus collision in Van Nuys, and a robbery in a Denny's restaurant on Wilshire Boulevard. Nothing about a body found at the Bel Air Regent. So far, so good.

She slipped into a worn Angels tee shirt and walked into the living room/dining room/kitchen/bedroom. She picked up the red magic marker and stared at the picture of Adam Devlin. "Sorry, baby." She drew a circle and a slash through his face.

She turned to the final picture, Blake Hunter. The rape had been his idea. He'd been the one to shoot the video. He was the one who sent the disgusting pictures of her to all his friends.

    She had saved the best, or worst, for last.

TWENTY-SIX

Ryan was in a great mood. He walked down the hallway of the Hollywood Division anxious to get the day started. The place was bustling and everyone seemed to be happy.

He strolled into the bullpen, then stopped dead in his tracks. A man was sitting in the guest chair at the edge of his desk. The man's back was to him but Ryan recognized what he was wearing, a mechanic's coveralls. Then the man turned to face him – it was the tow truck driver.

The driver leapt to his feet, rushed up to Ryan. "I saw you on TV, thought I recognized you."

Ryan was literally speechless.

The driver continued. "Saw how you won this huge lottery. About six months ago I bought this Lotto ticket at a 7-Eleven, and there was this real impatient dude behind me. I glanced back and got a good look at him and, I swear to Christ, it was you. See, the thing is, I dropped that ticket as I came out of the store, didn't realize it until I got home, then sort of forgot about it until I saw the news last night. So I'm thinking maybe this giant jackpot isn't yours at all. That it actually belongs to me. You didn't happen to find that ticket, did you? Maybe pick it up as you came out of the store?"

Ryan looked at him for a long time before finally answering. "No," he said. "I bought that ticket myself. And I'm sorry but I don't recognize you."

The tow truck driver flushed with anger. "Liar." Then he pulled out a knife and plunged it into Ryan's chest.

"No!" Ryan screamed, sitting up in bed.

Syd sat up next to him. "Ryan? You okay?"

He looked around, disoriented. He was at home. The lights were out. The clock on the bedside table said 3:17.

It had been a dream.

"What happened, sweetie, you have a nightmare?"

"Yeah, weird. I haven't had a nightmare since I was a kid."

"Want to talk about it?"

He looked at her. "The tow truck driver showed up, wanted to know if I found his Lotto ticket. I lied to him, told him I bought the ticket and he pulled a knife."

"Wow, gotta love the subconscious."

"Not really." Ryan got out of bed, walked into the bathroom, ran cold water into his hand, splashed it onto his face. Ryan didn't usually remember his dreams and rarely had anxiety dreams, so the stark reality of this one upset him.

"You must really want that money."

Ryan glanced in the mirror, saw Syd standing behind him.

"I guess I do," he said turning to her. "You know, I never thought that much about money. Sure my dad had it when I was growing up; we lived in a huge house in Beverly Hills and I went to an expensive private school, but I was just a kid growing up. I honestly didn't pay that much attention. When I went to UCLA I had my mustang and lived in a tiny dorm, didn't bother me a bit. And when dad lost his money and Anne and I had to make do with a small studio apartment, I didn't mind. I was happy. When Anne left, I stayed in that studio for three years, never dreamed of a bigger place, never wanted another car; I was busy at work, happy, satisfied. I only moved to this apartment because the other building went condo. And I like the extra room, but I didn't lie in bed dreaming of a big house, swimming pool and three-car garage."

"And now you do?"

"No, not exactly. But suddenly I'm *noticing* things. As we walked into Tony Roma's there was a guy getting into a Bentley; royal blue, luscious leather interior. I bet it was fast as hell. And driving home we passed this house on Valleyheart, an old Tudor with outdoor lights illuminating the walkway and trees. It looked so…comfortable."

"Uh oh," Syd said. "The infection is spreading Ryan, a new car and house today, a private jet tomorrow."

Ryan laughed and then said, "You never told me what you thought of Anne's idea, about me keeping the money and setting up a foundation."

"It doesn't matter what I think."

"Of course it does. I value your opinion."

Syd considered, not what she thought about his taking the Lotto ticket, but whether she would tell Ryan. She didn't want to become the bad guy to Anne's good guy. She didn't want to become a spoilsport. Nobody likes a party pooper. Still, if he did value her opinion, maybe she could stop him from making a mistake. "Even if I tell you taking the money is a terrible idea?"

Ryan looked at Syd like she was crazy. "It's not a terrible idea. In fact, it's the only *sane* thing to do. If I don't take it, no one does. The money disappears into the California general fund."

"So taking something that isn't rightfully yours is okay because you're going to use it to help people?"

"Yes, exactly."

"Then why not rob a bank and distribute the money to the poor? Or steal a car and give it to someone stuck taking the bus?"

"It's not the same thing."

"Yes, it is, Ryan. The ticket isn't yours! Hey, according to your rules, it's actually mine. I'm the one who found it in the glove box."

That caught him by surprise. "Do you want the ticket?"

"Fuck no. Anyway, I found it in your car so technically it's still yours – if you don't count the tow truck driver, I mean."

"So, you think I should just tear the Lotto ticket up, burn it; what? Syd, I've been on TV; all my friends think I've won millions of dollars, friends I want to help, and you want me to say, hey everybody, actually I just found the ticket on the sidewalk so I can't accept the forty-seven million dollars."

"Thirty-four after taxes."

Ryan smiled. "Thirty-four after taxes," he repeated. Somehow that brought the argument back down to earth but one fact remained. "Syd, if I don't take the money, everyone will think I'm a chump."

"And if you take it, you're a thief."

Ryan let out a long sigh. Technically he knew she was right, but god damn it, Anne was right, too. The world isn't black and white; we have to live in the gray. It wasn't until then, that moment, that Ryan realized how much he *wanted* to take the money. But he also wanted Syd's approval, her blessing. "Don't you think I could do a better job of redistributing this wealth than a bunch of crooked politicians?"

"Yes."

"So what's the problem?"

Syd sighed, knowing she'd lost. "There is no problem, Ryan. Take the money. I know you'll do great things with it. And, frankly, I'd love to ride in a Bentley and live in that house on Valleyheart."

"But I want you to be as excited as I am."

Not going to happen, she thought. But that's not what Ryan needs to hear right now so she said, "I will be, I promise." Then something occurred to her. "Did we just have our first fight?"

"I guess we did."

"Good," she said slipping into his arms. "I just love make-up sex."

"Is there any kind of sex you don't like?"

A montage of images fluttered through Syd's mind, things she'd had to do as a hooker and hated: being beaten by bondage freaks, getting pissed on, getting shat on, fucking a dwarf in front of a bunch of drunk fraternity brothers, having everything from carrots to dildos to cigars stuck up her vagina, having everything from carrots to dildos to cigars stuck up her ass.

Syd focused on the hazel eyes of the man she loved, her finger traced his dimple. "If it's with you, sweetie, there is no kind of sex I don't like." She kissed him. "Now shut up and fuck me."

TWENTY-SEVEN

Blake Hunter woke up staring at a huge pair of tits. He rolled over to find another huge pair of tits. Ah, what a way to start the day.

The breasts belonged to two hookers, Emmy and Amy, or was it Annie and Erin? No matter, he was sure those weren't their real names anyway.

He'd ordered them up at the last minute, sort of a spur of the moment celebratory reward after one of his photographers scored a topless photo of pop sensation, Tiffany Brooks. Mario had been hiding in a tree across the street from Tiffany's estate for two days, hoping for a shot of her sunbathing topless or fucking the pool boy or just watering the flowers. Something, anything of Tiffany in her new house would be tabloid gold. But she'd never left the house. Then yesterday, she finally came out for a swim. Topless. And a delighted Mario started shooting the first ever topless photos of Tiffany Brooks.

The pictures were worth a fortune. Blake would sell them worldwide through BHPIX, his photo news company that fed the voracious hunger of the worldwide tabloids.

Blake sat atop the paparazzi pyramid with a staff of six highly paid photographers willing to harass, intimidate, lie, cheat and steal to get a marketable shot. Blake also had a network of waiters and waitresses, bartenders, hostesses, valets and salesclerks who, for a cash commission, would call in when a celebrity showed up. Not to mention an army of publicists and agents who *wanted* their clients photographed.

It was a great business but not the one Blake had hoped for. He'd wanted to be a director. As far back as high school he always had his video camera with him, shooting events at school and small movies with friends.

He went to USC Film School, distinguished himself with a couple of student films and got a job directing a low budget independent movie right after graduation. There was this adorable teenage girl in the cast, only fifteen, and Blake flipped for her. He pursued her relentlessly during shooting, finally getting into her pants the last day of shooting.

And that's exactly how her mother found her daughter when she unexpectedly walked into her trailer; her daughter's pants off, Blake's pants off and Blake's reproductive organ inserted snuggly in her fifteen-year-old daughter's reproductive organ.

Statutory Rape.

No matter that Blake was her tenth or eleventh lover, the girl couldn't be sure. No matter that the girl tried to convince her mother not to press charges to protect her reputation and career. Her mother called the cops, Blake was arrested and on advice of his consul, Zachary Stone, he pled out to two years in state prison for statutory rape. The girl spoke in Blake's defense at the sentencing, and Stone managed to convince the judge to send Blake to Avenal State Prison, a minimum security facility, where he wouldn't be gang-raped, tortured or killed.

But talk about a career ender. When Blake got out of prison, he couldn't get arrested. As a director, that is. He'd become friends with the guy who shot publicity pictures on his movie and the photographer moonlighted as a paparazzi. He asked Blake if he wanted to work with him and Blake was a natural. He was also an entrepreneur and within a couple of years put together his network of photographers and snitches.

He was also a master at digitally manipulating the pictures his staff shot, highlighting and sometimes enhancing things such as cellulite for magazines looking for Stars-at-their-Worst shots, or thinning a thigh here or increasing a breast size there for a Stars-at-their-Best story.

Blake lived in small beach house on Carbon Beach, one of the twenty-four beaches that make up the twenty-seven mile Malibu coastline. He got the down payment selling pictures of Angelina Jolie going down on Brad Pitt. No matter that the photo was later proved fake, a product of his digital mastery; he'd already raked in three quarters of a million dollars.

Blake was short, with jet-black hair and thick eyebrows. He spoke in rapid, profanity-laden bursts of words and was unabashedly rude.

He put one hand on the breast of each girl then twisted the nipple. With a start, both girls yelped and sat up in bed. They were both blonde and billed themselves as a sister act, but they weren't related.

They'd treated Blake to an incredibly hot lesbian love fest, fueled by Stoli shots and cocaine, before he finally dove in and screwed them both. And he woke up horny.

"The snake needs servicing girls," he said. It's amazing how crude you're allowed to be when you pay two thousand dollars a girl. "But first, do me a favor and warm up on each other."

The girls were actually in love with one another so they happily fell into each other's arms and began to make out.

Blake grabbed the remote control and turned on the 60-inch LCD hanging on the wall. As they girls ravished each other in front of him, the muted news played behind them. There was a weather map on the screen, another beautiful Southern California day in the offing and then the screen cut to a picture of Colin Wood.

It took Blake a couple of seconds to register it was the picture of his friend, Colin Wood. Blake hit the Mute button. "...found dead in his car outside the Havoc nightclub. Police aren't speculating on a motive for the murder right now, but are asking for the public's help in identifying a blonde woman who was last seen with the actor. Ironically, one of the detectives investigating the murder has just hit the Lotto. His name is..."

Blake hit the mute button. Colin was dead. Jesus. They'd been friends since high school and would still hang out every once in a while. Blake remembered Colin's old girlfriend, Abigail. She was hot. Blake always wanted to take a shot at her, but resisted because he knew it would bug Colin. But now that Colin was dead…

Blake smiled; Abigail was a struggling actress so it would easy to get her number. His eyes shifted to the girls who now had their faces planted in each other's vaginas. He watched them gobble each other up, but he was thinking about Abigail.

TWENTY-EIGHT

"I've got a good feeling about today," Syd said. She was working her cell phone as Ryan threaded his way through morning rush hour traffic. She checked her notebook, and dialed. "Today we take one more step on the road to immortality. Today we're going to get a lead on the Lady in Red case, we're going to tenaciously follow that lead using intuition, skill and a little luck, and after a stunning revelation or two, we'll break the case wide open, bringing the murdering bitch to justice."

Ryan smiled, got to love her enthusiasm. "Before or after lunch?"

"That depends on when," she glanced at the bottlenecked traffic, "or *if* you finally get us to the office. Yes, hello," she said shifting to her official voice as the cell phone was answered. "This is Detective Syd Curtis, Los Angeles Police Department; I'd like to speak to Mr. Reade please." Chris Reade was Kathy Tuttle's lawyer, the attorney who handled the half-million-dollar settlement she received from Colin Wood's father. "Yes, I know I've called before," Syd said patiently. "In fact, I think I left two voice mails on your phone last night which speaks to the urgency of our situation. We're in the middle of an ongoing murder investigation and Mr. Reade may have information critical to the case." Syd listened for a few moments, scribbled down a note then said, "That would be great, thank you." She hung up, turned to Ryan. "He's out of town. He's been in Miami for the last few days and is now on a flight to New York, scheduled to land in less than an hour. She'll make sure he calls as soon as he checks in."

"Great."

Syd called Colin Wood's father but just got his voice

mail, again. "Still not answering," she said. "Hello, this is Detective Syd Curtis, LAPD, we need to speak to you as soon as possible, Mr. Wood, so please call us back." She left her number and disconnected. "Why is this guy so hard to get a hold of?"

"Think he's hiding something?"

"Hard to say. I can't imagine he's involved in his own son's murder, but I did get the feeling he knew more than he told us at the morgue yesterday."

Ryan sensed the same thing. "Me, too." Ryan's cell phone rang; he glanced at the caller ID, Anne. An excited thrill shot through him, surprising him. Was he excited because of the money or because he'd be talking to her?

Syd read the same reaction. "Let me guess," she said. "The former Mrs. Magee."

"You'd make a pretty good detective, you know that," Ryan said and then he answered the phone. "Good morning."

"Morning, Handsome. I've got some papers I need you to sign this morning. I'm just leaving my CPA's office now and I can be at the Hollywood Division in about fifteen minutes. You going to be there?"

"I'm about five minutes away."

"Good. And, Ryan, things are going to move kind of fast the next couple of days. We've got a lot of work to do setting up this foundation before tomorrow afternoon."

"No problem."

"And keep tomorrow morning clear, I'm calling the lottery office as soon as we hang up and asking for an eleven o'clock presentation."

"Eleven o'clock, got it."

"Good. I'll see you in a few minutes." Anne hung up.

Syd unhappily watched Ryan's side of the phone call. Ryan was hanging on Anne's every word and his excitement was palpable. "She's coming to the station?"

Ryan nodded. "I've got some papers to sign."

Syd simply nodded.

Ryan picked up her mood. "You said last night you were okay with this."

"I am," she said, smiling at Ryan. But she wasn't. She'd accepted his taking the money, sort of. At least there was some logic to that. But she had a major problem with Ryan spending so much time with his ex-wife. She just didn't know what to do about it. Yet.

Every cop on the force had heard about Ryan's Lotto ticket by now so he was besieged by well-wishers at the station, high-fiving him as he made his way down the hallway. When Ryan and Syd stepped into the bullpen, Ryan's eyes went to the guest chair next to his desk. It was empty. No coverall-clad tow truck driver to ruin his day.

But a pile of yellow phone messages were piled on his desk.

"Jesus Christ," he said picking up the stack. "There must be a hundred of them." He thumbed through a few. "Calls from the *Today Show*, *Good Morning America*, CBS, CNN, Fox News."

"Ah, the official start of your fifteen minutes of fame."

"*Time, Newsweek, New York Times, L.A. Times, Chicago Tribune*; don't these guys have real news to write about?"

Syd picked up the one message on her desk. "I got a call from my hairdresser."

Ryan rifled through the messages. "There are calls from stock brokers, financial planners, girls I dated in high school, and guys I haven't seen in years."

"And they all want your money. Tell me, Ryan, just how are you going to decide who is entitled to share your bounty?"

"Hell if I know." Then Ryan cocked his head. "Do you smell something?"

"What's that?" Syd asked pointing to a paper bag sitting on the corner of Ryan's desk.

Ryan opened the bag, took out a plastic covered dish. "Meatball soup." Something else was in the bag. Ryan pulled it out. "And a business plan for Maribel's Meatballs."

Hanrahan stepped up. "I love albondigas."

"Here," Ryan said shoving the dish into the

Lieutenant's hands.

"Thanks," Hanrahan said. "Anything new on the Lady in Red?"

"Apparently Colin Wood didn't believe that no means no."

"There are two cases of date rape we know of so far," Syd said. "And we're guessing that we'll find more."

"And you think the Lady in Red was one of his victims?"

Syd nodded. "Don't suppose any bodies turned up last night with a relocated penis?"

"No." Hanrahan eyed Ryan's pile of messages. "I'm hoping those are from concerned citizens with tips on the Colin Wood murder, but I'm guessing they're from people hoping to pick your newly enriched pockets."

"Yep."

"Just remember to save a little for your brothers in blue."

"And the inspirational man you work for," Syd said.

"I couldn't have said it better myself." Hanrahan took his meatballs and headed back to his office passing Anne who walked in, spotted Ryan, smiled and joined him.

"Good morning," she said giving him a peck on the cheek, but her eyes were on Syd. She didn't like what she saw. Way too cute, and from the way Syd was looking back at her, way too possessive.

Syd wanted to strangle Anne right there and then. She hated the all too familiar way she kissed Ryan on the cheek. And she was so fucking beautiful.

"Anne," Ryan said, "I want you to meet my partner, Syd Curtis."

"How do you do," Anne said extending her hand. Syd took it and they shook, both squeezing a bit too hard.

"A pleasure," Syd said, smiling so insincerely it could only mean one thing.

She's fucking him, Anne realized. The little bitch is fucking Ryan. This may complicate things. "Look, I know you guys are busy, so if I can just borrow Ryan for a few minutes..."

Ryan indicted the empty conference room. "This way."

Syd watched them cross the room. Anne was everything Syd admired in a woman: smart, confidant, successful. And one thing she hated; predatory. Anne had her sights set on Ryan, Syd could tell.

Shit, Syd thought, this woman was going to be trouble.

"Syd seems nice," Anne said as Ryan closed the conference room door. Anne opened her attaché case, pulled out some papers. "How long have you been partners?"

"Just a couple of months," Ryan said, nonchalantly. He didn't want to give any indication they were having an affair. But Anne had always been able to read him like a book, so he suspected she had already figured it out. "Syd transferred in after making a name for herself in Vice."

Anne wanted to probe further, but resisted the temptation. First things first, she decided; getting the lottery money was priority one. "You're going to get a check for thirty-four million dollars tomorrow," she said laying the papers out on the table, "and the immediate problem becomes what you do with it. Individual bank accounts are only insured for two hundred and fifty thousand dollars per account per bank, so we're going to spread some of the money to a network of banks and buy thirty-day T-bills with the rest. These documents give me your power-of-attorney to open the accounts and buy the T-bills, but nothing can be sold or withdrawn without *your* signature."

"So you can't steal my money."

Anne looked at him to see if he was kidding, realized he wasn't. "That's right. Only you can get at the money. Ryan, you do trust me, don't you?"

If they were going to be working together, Ryan needed to clear the air. He knew how he felt, but he wasn't the kind of man who liked to vocalize his insecurities or fears. Like many men, he bottled everything up. But this was an extraordinary circumstance and called for extraordinary candor. "I trusted you with my life and you broke my heart."

If there was ever a doubt Anne still loved Ryan, it vanished with those words. Now it was time to start winning that heart back. "And I've regretted it ever since," Anne said. "To be honest, I've never been happier than I was those three years we were married. I was a fool to leave you. And if it makes you feel any better, Rick and I are getting a divorce."

Ryan's heart leapt, catching him by surprise. Suddenly Anne was available again. And part of Ryan wanted to win her back. Prove to her that leaving him was a terrible idea. And part of him was still loyal to Syd. He had no idea what to say, so he settled on, "I'm sorry."

"Don't be, it was a long time coming. A fresh start is just what I need, personally and professionally. Ryan, your winning the Lotto couldn't have come at a better time." She took out a pen, handed it to him and then with her best courtroom closing argument sincerity she said, "You can trust me, Ryan. I promise."

Ryan looked into the face he loved for so long, missed for so long. He believed her. "Okay." He took the pen.

"Just sign here and here and I'll get to work on opening these accounts."

He signed.

In the bullpen, a worried Syd tried to work at her desk but her attention kept drifting to the closed conference room door. Her cell phone rang, she answered. "Hello."

"Detective Curtis, this is Chris Reade; my office told me you called."

"Yes, Mr. Reade, Kathy Tuttle told us you represented her in a transaction with Colin Wood and his father."

"I did."

"She told us about the date rape, Mr. Reade, and she said you told her Colin Wood had trouble before, in high school."

"My assistant told me this was a murder investigation; could you tell me who was murdered?"

"Colin Wood."

There was long pause, then Reade said, "Now that's

interesting."

"Why?"

And when Reade told Syd, she thanked him and rushed to the conference room, knocked on the door and entered. Anne was slipping some papers back into her attaché case. "Sorry to bother you," Syd said. "But we just got a break."

"Great. Anne and I were finishing up."

"I'll call you later with an update," Anne said to Ryan. "And I'll probably have more papers to sign. I'm moving into the Beverly Hilton this afternoon, we can meet there tonight to sign the papers and go over everything for tomorrow morning." She turned to Syd. "Nice to meet you, Detective." Anne swept out the door.

A worried Syd asked, "Why is she moving into a hotel?"

Ryan knew the answer would upset her. "She's getting a divorce."

A silent moment registered between them as the implications settled in. "Should I be worried?" Syd asked.

I honestly don't know, Ryan thought. "No," he said and then got back to business. "Tell me the news."

"I just spoke to the lawyer, Chris Reade. There was a rumored date rape incident involving Colin Wood in high school. In fact a few boys might have been involved. Reade knew the lawyer that handled the case, a man named Zachary Stone."

"Did you get a number, can we talk to him?"

"No, and that's the good part. For us, not him. He's dead. Shot to death in Newport Beach on Sunday."

"The day before Colin Wood's murder," Ryan said, excited.

"We've got a conference call scheduled with Newport Beach Homicide in fifteen minutes."

TWENTY-NINE

Technically there were no private beaches in Malibu, much to the chagrin of the rich beach house owners. The courts ruled that the public had a right to build sandcastles wherever they wanted. But for all intents and purposes, many of the beaches were rendered private by the lack of public parking. And the closest public parking to Carbon Beach was miles away.

So Alice had to figure out a way to get close to Blake Hunter. There was plenty of information about Blake online. His company, BHPIX, was one of the largest suppliers of paparazzi photos in the world. There was a profile published in *L.A. Magazine* that talked about his statutory rape conviction, which didn't surprise Alice at all. The fact that when Blake got out of jail and actually dated the victim, who had finally turned eighteen, did. The relationship didn't last but it certainly made Blake infamous.

According to all her online research, Blake worked from home and though he often went out, there was no schedule, no rhyme or reason to his comings and goings.

And Alice knew there was a clock on her now. She checked the news when she got up this morning. There was a story about the lucky homicide detective who won the lottery and is investigating the Colin Wood murder, but there was still no report of a dead body at the Bel Air Regent. The old lady should have come down to the desk fifteen minutes after the Lady in Red had left the hotel looking for a way to retrieve her dog. What happened? Did the old lady die? Not likely. Did they find the body and decide to keep it quiet? No, the cops didn't work that way. Alice knew there were security cameras all over the hotel and the cops would use them to get video of her. And they would want that video on television as soon as possible hoping someone would see her and turn her in.

So what? Never one to look a gift horse in the mouth, Alice accepted the extra time gratefully.

Now her research did mention that Blake liked to go for a run every morning, a three mile jog up and down the beach. Since she couldn't park nearby, Alice rented a kayak at Paradise Beach and paddled two miles to a spot about one hundred yards off shore of Blake's house. Then she waited.

Blake, meanwhile, had sent the hookers home and was now hard at work. He'd converted one of his bedrooms into an office. It had a full on ocean view. A huge desk sat in the middle of the room dominated by a 27-inch iMac. This is where Blake worked and did his photo editing. A 42-inch flat screen TV hung on the wall across from the desk. Two bookcases flanked the TV filled with a mixture of books and DVD's. Another wall was filled with photos, shots of celebrities that had helped make BHPIX so successful: Lara snorting coke in a nightclub bathroom; Britney climbing out of a car sans panties and flashing the world; Tara, drunk, throwing up on the sidewalk.

Blake had no guilt about what he did for a living. Stars needed publicity to pimp their movies and TV shows. And most of the celebs who adorned the *Enquirer, Star, People,* and *US* were people who asked for it. Everyone knows the paparazzi hang out at certain restaurants; if you don't want to be mobbed, don't go to the fucking restaurant. Eat somewhere else! Yet the twits continue to go to the Ivy, to Skybar, to Morton's and act annoyed when the paparazzi descend.

And yes, some photographers went too far. Blake didn't really condone extreme behavior publicly, but he paid his people huge bonuses for those priceless snaps and never asked how they got them.

Blake checked his email and then turned to look out the picture window. It was a beautiful spring day, temperature in the low sixties, a calm sea. He checked his watch. He had a meeting in about an hour, but he still had time for a run.

Blake noticed a girl in a red bikini kayaking nearby as he jogged down the beach but didn't pay too much attention. He was jogging away from her so couldn't see her for long. But after he turned around and was jogging back up the beach, he saw plenty of her. Kind of hot, he thought, but she was too far away to be sure.

She seemed to be having trouble paddling and then as he got closer, the kayak suddenly flipped and she disappeared under water. Kayaks are supposed to flip back over but this one didn't. And moments later the girl popped to the surface, arms flailing, obviously in distress.

Blake kicked off his sneakers and dove in. He was a good swimmer and a few powerful strokes quickly brought him to her. Her eyes were panicked, wild. She must've swallowed a mouthful of water when she flipped over, because she was coughing, having trouble breathing.

"It's okay, I've got you," Blake said, wrapping an arm around her. "Stay calm and I'll get you to shore." The woman obeyed, relaxed, and Blake paddled.

When they got to shore, the women bent over coughing as Blake's retrieved his shoes. When he came back, the woman stood up and he got his first real good look at her.

She was blonde, with green eyes, great tits and incredible legs. The ocean was cold, goose bumps covered her body and she was shivering. "You saved my life," she said.

"But it looks like you're about to freeze to death. I live right there," he said pointing at his house. "Come inside and let me get you warmed up."

She dazzled him with a smile. "I'd like that. Thank you."

THIRTY

Newport Beach was only fifty miles from Hollywood, but in heavy traffic it could take over two hours to get there, so when time was an issue and the LAPD had to interface with an Orange County law enforcement agency on a murder investigation, they used the phone, fax and internet. Newport Beach PD faxed the initial crime scene report to Hollywood, and the Medical Examiner's Office would email their report later in the day.

Ryan, Syd and Lieutenant Hanrahan were on a speakerphone in the conference room. Ramirez was patched in from his office at SID and the lead detective from Newport Beach, Alex Cortez, was on the phone in his Captain's office. "His body was found at a little after 7:00 p.m. by a storekeeper taking out the trash," Cortez said. "Shot once in the face. The Medical Examiner put the time of death between 6:00 p.m. and when he was found."

"Was there any mutilation of the body?" Ryan asked.

"What kind of mutilation?"

"A missing or rearranged body part?"

"No. But you've sure got my attention."

Ryan and Syd exchanged disappointed looks. "Was there anything carved onto his body?"

Cortez laughed. "No. Man, you must have some freak up there."

"Maybe it's not her," Hanrahan said to Ryan and Syd.

Ramirez asked, "What caliber bullet was he shot with?"

".25"

"Same here," Ramirez said. "I think your SID and I need to compare our lands and grooves."

"I'm hoping they match." Ryan said. "Detective

Cortez, were there any reports of a beautiful blonde in the area."

"Hey, this is the OC, man, we got beautiful blondes all over the place," Cortez said, and then remembered something. "But Stone's last client of the day was blonde. His assistant told us she was very attractive."

"Wearing red?" Syd asked.

"As a matter of fact, yes she was."

"You get a name?"

Cortez flipped some notebook pages. "Susan Rafferty. That's all the assistant got. No address, no phone number."

"Have you run her?" Hanrahan asked.

"Not yet. Without an address or phone number I didn't see how much good it would do, but hell, you never know. Hey, Billy," Cortez yelled out. "Run the name Susan Rafferty, will you, tell me what you find."

"I'm guessing it's a phony," Syd said.

"Did the assistant know what the blonde and Stone talked about?"

Cortez checked his notes. "No. They talked for about fifteen minutes and she left. He worked for an hour longer then left for the day. She had no idea what his plans were for the rest of the evening. To be honest guys, Stone was a criminal defense attorney so we've been focusing on any old clients who might've had a grudge. The blonde wasn't even on our radar."

"Not surprising," Ryan said. "I would have done the same thing."

"If you don't mind my asking," Cortez said. "What's with the mutilation and carving questions?"

Ryan glanced at Hanrahan for permission to tell them, Hanrahan nodded his assent. "Our victim's penis was cut off and stuffed in his mouth," Ryan said.

"No way!"

"And the number 2 was carved in his chest."

"The number 2..." Cortez digested this, made a connection. "Son of a bitch, that may explain the dollar bill."

"Dollar bill?" Syd asked.

"Yeah, Stone had three hundred and sixty-six dollars in his wallet, but he also had a one dollar bill in his hand."

"*One* dollar bill," Syd said. "It's her, I'm sure of it. Zachary Stone was first, Colin Wood was second."

"But why mutilate Wood and not Stone?" Cortez asked.

"If this is revenge for a rape, Stone was just the lawyer," Syd said. "He probably never touched her. But Wood was another story."

"And since she's numbering her victims," Ryan said, "we're thinking there will be more. We spoke to an Orange County attorney, Chris Reade, who'd heard that Stone represented Colin Wood in a case when Wood was in high school. There were rumors that money was paid to a date rape victim. Any way to get information on a case Stone handled ten or eleven years ago?"

"It's tricky, you know that. I'll give it a shot but its privileged information."

A uniformed cop appeared in the conference room doorway, signaled for Hanrahan. The Lieutenant joined him as Syd said, "There's one guy who knows who knows for sure, Colin Wood's father."

"We've been trying to call him without luck," Ryan said. "Detective Cortez, maybe you can put a Be On the Lookout for him."

"Consider it done. And we'll pay a visit to his home and office. I'll find him, don't worry. Wait, hold on," Cortez took a printout from Billy. "Okay, we've got six Susan Raffertys in Southern California." He scanned the list, frowned. "Two in their forties, three in their sixties and one is eighty-eight."

"Told you," Syd said. "It's a phony. Smart lady."

"And dangerous," Hanrahan said. Ryan and Syd looked at him. "They just found a body at the Bel Air Regent Hotel with a missing body part."

"On my way," Ramirez said and hung up.

"Good luck," Cortez said and hung up.

But they were talking to no one. Ryan and Syd were already out the door.

THIRTY-ONE

"I bet Mr. Magee is very happy."

"He's thrilled, believe me," Anne said. She was on the phone with Lucinda McCarthy, a vice president of the California Lottery. They loved giving out big jackpots almost as much the winner loved getting the money. Big, highly publicized payouts always led to a spike in sales.

Anne was in her office at Rogers, Middleton and Roberts, staring out at a crystal clear Los Angeles morning.

Lucinda, a cheerful bundle of energy, sat in front of her computer in the Van Nuys district office. "I saw Detective Magee on television; he's quite good looking isn't he?"

"Adorable."

"Is he nice?"

"Very."

"Is he married?"

"Divorced, I think," Anne said.

"Some dumb woman's going to regret that," Lucinda said, laughing.

"Tell me about it," Anne said.

Lucinda hit a couple of keys, finished inputting the Lotto ticket serial number Anne had provided. "Oh, my, Mr. Magee likes to cut things close, doesn't he? This ticket expires tomorrow."

"Actually," Anne said. "He just found it, forgot he even bought it."

"It happens all the time," Lucinda said. "We've had almost a hundred million dollars in unclaimed jackpots in the last twenty years. Now would Mr. Magee like to receive his check privately or would he prefer a press conference?"

"Oh, I didn't know there was a choice." Contrary to what Anne told Ryan, neither she nor her firm had ever represented a Lotto winner. But she figured her credibility would be enhanced if she'd actually represented lottery winners so she'd gone online to get the statistics and case studies she'd described to Ryan.

"We only hold a press conference if the winner wants one. We like to respect everyone's privacy. Many winners wish to remain anonymous. But if someone wants a press conference then we rent a small ballroom in a local hotel, invite the media, the owner of the outlet that sold the ticket, and of course, the lucky winner."

"Well," Anne said. "Anonymity is out of the question at this point, the press has already learned that Mr. Magee won. His name is actually Detective Ryan Magee, he's an LAPD Homicide detective."

"Yes, I know, I saw it on the news. Isn't it wonderful! To be honest we have a hard time getting the local press interested in Lotto winners these days. We've been giving out jackpots for over twenty years so you need something extraordinary to pique their interest. But they do love the hard-working-public-servant-strikes-it-rich angle."

"Well, you'll be happy to know that besides Detective Magee being a cop, he's also planning to donate much of his winnings to charity. We plan to announce the formation of a charitable foundation at the press conference."

"That'll get the media's attention. How generous of him. There is a Holiday Inn in Studio City we often use for press conferences. I'll check with them and make sure the ballroom's available. Did you have a time in mind?"

"I was thinking late morning, say eleven."

"Excellent. Late morning usually gets our best press turnout."

"Good."

"Now if Mr. Magee needs a CPA, I've got a cousin who has handled the finances of a number of lottery winners."

"No, he's got a CPA."

"How about a real estate agent? I'm sure Mr. Magee's thinking about a new home right about now and my cousin, Ed, has put a number of lottery winners into the home of their dreams."

"We got that handled, too."

"Bet he needs a new car. My cousin, Teddy, owns the Cadillac dealership in Burbank and he's helped a lot of lottery winners into their first Escalade."

How big is your frickin' family lady, thought Anne. "No, Mr. Magee's got everything he needs."

"All right then," Lucinda said, disappointed but undeterred. "But I know how difficult it is to navigate the sudden wealth landscape so if you or Mr. Magee need anything, don't hesitate to call. Now just give me a couple of hours to coordinate things on my end and confirm the hotel, then I'll call you back with all the particulars."

"That'll be great, Lucinda. Thank you," Anne said and hung up.

"What the fuck are you doing?"

Startled, Anne looked up to find Rick standing in her doorway. "Excuse me?"

"I know you went to see Ryan Magee this morning." Rick was flushed, panicked. "Were you telling him about the mortgage papers? Trying to cut a deal with the cops to save your own ass?"

Anne stood up, a cold fury seething through every cell of her body. "How do you know I saw Ryan this morning?"

"Doesn't matter. Were you selling me out?"

"First of all," she said, ice coating every word. "It's none of your fucking business what I was doing with Ryan. Second, no, I was not selling out your sorry ass. Your father has agreed not to go to the cops if we resign and I'll be writing my letter of resignation as soon as you get out of my office. And third, tell me how you knew I saw Ryan this morning or I *will* tell the California Bar about the forgery."

The air seemed to go out of Rick. He was ashamed, embarrassed. "I had you followed."

"What?"

"I hired Cal Fisher to follow you." Cal Fisher was one of the private detectives Rogers,

Middleton and Roberts employed when necessary. "You freaked me out last night, Anne. I mean, my world's coming apart, losing the house, my job... I thought I'd at least have you. That we were a team, that somehow we'd weather all this together. So when you said you were leaving, I just, I don't know, got paranoid. I figured you must be up to something so I called Cal and asked him to keep an eye on you. I'm sorry." Then a light bulb went off in Rick's head. "Wait a minute. Didn't I see something on TV about a homicide cop winning the lottery? It was Ryan, wasn't it?"

Anne stiffened, feeling caught somehow. "Yes."

Rick gave her a cruel smile. "You always knew how to follow the money, baby." He laughed bitterly. "You're unbelievable."

"Get out of my office."

He did the opposite. He stepped closer. "Was it all a lie? The years we had together. Did you ever love me or was it just my money?"

She'd asked herself that question a lot lately and answered honestly. "I loved you. But the rich successful you was a different guy than the one standing in front of me now. You used to be funny, now you're morose. You were cocky, now you're scared. I used to cuddle in your arms and feel so safe, now I dread being alone in a room with you. It's like you've morphed into a bad impression of yourself." Anne could see her words hit home. "You can't *not* know this, Rick."

"You know, I was hoping you were going to say you never loved me and then I could get on with my life, hating you." He looked at her, as vulnerable as she'd even seen him. "Now, I guess, I have to hate myself. I'm sorry, Anne. I loved you so much. I loved *us*. It just all got away from me somehow. And yes, I miss me, too."

"You'll bounce back, Rick. I know it."

Neither one of them believed it. "Thanks. And good

luck; I mean it."

"Thank you."

With the saddest smile she'd ever seen, he left.

Anne watched him go, a little ashamed at the emotional flailing she'd given him. But he'd pissed her off. The nerve, having her followed.

And then she had a brainstorm. She needed her own PI. Anne sat down, opened her phone book, found the number she wanted and dialed.

"Travis Taylor."

"Travis, its Anne Rogers, how are you?"

"Fine, Anne, nice to hear from you." Travis was a retired FBI agent, expensive but thorough.

"Travis I need you to run a background check on someone. And I want to know *everything*."

"Absolutely, what's the name?" "Curtis. Detective Syd Curtis. She's an LAPD homicide detective."

"No problem. I should be able to get back to you later today."

"Excellent." Anne hung up. If she was going to have to fight the pretty redhead for

Ryan's affections, Anne wanted to be prepared.

THIRTY-TWO

"I've paddled by these houses every day for three weeks and never been inside one," Alice said. She was sitting at Blake's kitchen counter, sipping a cup of coffee Blake had made her. She had a thick terry cloth towel draped over her shoulders but the ocean chill had passed.

After getting her a towel and making coffee, Blake had gone back outside and retrieved the kayak and paddle. Now, back in the house, Blake stared at Alice. He'd had countless women in his home but never one washed in from the sea. And though he didn't know her, there was something vaguely familiar about her. She intrigued him.

He said, "I grew up in Orange County, south of here, and surfed every day as a kid. And as I sat out in the water, waiting for a wave, I'd stare at the houses nestled into Shaw's Cove and dream about one day owning my own beach house."

"And now you do."

"And now I do."

"I saw the surfboards on the patio, do you still surf every day?"

"That's the funny part. I hardly surf anymore. No time. But from time to time I force myself to take an afternoon off and paddle out."

"I'd love to learn. I grew up in Denver. Not too many gnarly waves back there." She laughed. "But it sure looks like fun."

Blake hated teaching people how to surf. It was a lot harder than it looked so it took forever, and most people totally spazzed out, never getting to their feet. But the prospect of teaching this blonde in the red bikini to surf excited him. "Maybe I could teach you sometime," he said.

"That would be great," Alice said, getting off the stool and roaming through the large living room. It was comfortable with wood floors, a plush leather couch, and two overstuffed leather side chairs. They faced the huge picture window featuring a delicious view of the ocean. "And is it everything you dreamed about? Living here, I mean?"

"Yes and no. The good is obvious: great view, I love the smell of the ocean, it's cooler in summer and warmer in winter, and staring at that big beautiful sea soothes my soul. But there's the bad, too. You end up with sand everywhere, the salt corrodes everything, traffic on the PCH totally sucks; during a storm, the crashing waves sound like artillery shells so sleeping is impossible. Oh and there are fires, floods and in June, the fog is so heavy you can go weeks without seeing the sun."

"You poor baby."

Blake laughed. "Yeah, pity me." He thought the blonde looked so cute with his big towel wrapped around her. Blake's eyes went from her bare feet, up her legs to her bikini clad ass. Nice. "So you're from Colorado, how long have you been in L.A.?"

"Just under a month. I'm an actress; big shock, huh? I starred in all the plays in college, I went to the University of Colorado at Boulder, and then spent a couple years doing regional theatre in Denver." The fake biography was easy for Alice. It was based on the life of her friend, Dawn, from the Institute. Dawn came to Hollywood full of hope and confidence but after six months and countless failed auditions – and running a gauntlet of men promising her anything to get into her pants but delivering nothing – Dawn swallowed a full bottle of Xanax. Her parents sent her to the Institute to get better. And it worked. Dawn realized that being a big fish in a small pond was better than being bait in L.A. and she returned to Denver.

"I did a three week revival of *Sweet Charity* and got these great reviews. The director said I should go to Hollywood; he knew an agent there, so I figured, hey, you only go around once in life so why not take a chance? But it's a lot harder than I imagined. His agent friend turned out to be a sixty-year-old letch that only represented cameramen and crew people. And getting an audition with a real agent is tough. To be honest, I'm thinking about going home."

Blake knew a lot of agents. It was vital to a young career to be photographed at all the right movie premieres and A-list parties, so Hollywood's ten-percenters needed coverage from Blake's photographers. And this was definitely a you-scratch-my-back-and-I'll-scratch-yours kind of town. "I know some people, some agents I could set you up with."

If she hadn't known Blake in high school, she would have been convinced by his sincerity. But Blake Hunter was a player. He'd say and do anything in high school to get laid. It had been *his* idea to invite her over to Colin's house and drug and rape her. *He'd* been the one to email those horrible pictures of her. He might have been trying to charm her now, but in his mind, she was the antelope and he was the lion.

But if he was acting, she could act, too. So she cocked her head and looked at him suspiciously. "How do I you know you're not a letch who just wants to get into my pants?"

She said it playfully and Blake laughed. "Well, let's start with this simple statement of fact: I do want to get into your pants." His eyes dropped to her bathing suit, "Or, bottoms as the case may be. But I *do* know a lot of agents and quite a few owe me favors. And I don't expect anything from you. I'll get you a meeting at CAA, WME and UTA, no strings attached."

"Really?"

"Really." He stepped forward, took the coffee cup out of her hands. "Can I get you some more coffee?"

"Yes, please."

Her eyes tracked him into the kitchen. She wasn't able to bring her gun with her but Alice figured there would be knives in the house she could use to kill him. And sure enough there was a wood block filled with knives on the counter.

Her dad made her clean the deer and elk she shot as a kid, and cutting through the skin, muscle and bone hadn't bothered her as much as she thought it would. She wasn't crazy about the blood, but it washed off easily enough, so the prospect of sliding a butcher knife into Blake's back or slitting his throat open with a paring knife didn't bother her. In fact, the vision of his blood squirting onto his shiny kitchen floor thrilled her.

"You have a beautiful kitchen," she said, following him into the kitchen. "Do you cook?"

"No," he said, adding Splenda and milk to her mug. "But my decorator was a great chef and she insisted I have a top notch kitchen."

Alice leaned on the counter, the set of knives behind her. She reached back, wrapped her right hand around the butcher knife. She was about to slide it out when Blake turned around with her coffee.

"Here you go," he said. "With milk and Splenda, just like before."

Her hand dropped off the knife, took the cup. "Thank you."

"Are you hungry? I've got bananas here somewhere, and apples in the refrigerator, I think."

"An apple would be great."

Blake opened the Sub Zero, bent over and slid open a bottom drawer. His back was to her now, and a perfect target.

Alice silently slid the butcher knife out of the block, turned toward Blake raising the knife over her head.

Crash! The front door burst open. "Hey, Blake, we're here!"

Alice dropped her hand, slid the knife back into the block and three guys came around the corner.

"Sorry we're late, but..." the guy who was talking stopped when he saw Alice standing in the kitchen. A moment later Blake stood up with an apple. The guy, Joel, one of Blake's photographers who looked like a Hell's Angel motorcycle outlaw said, "I thought Eve was the one with the apple, but hey, I was kicked out of bible studies for wacking off to an illustration of Delilah."

The other two men laughed. One was tall in a luau shirt and cargo shorts, the other in jeans and a torn tee shirt. All three had multiple cameras draped around their necks.

"Funny, Joel," Blake said. "Guys, this is Dawn. Dawn, the guys."

"Hi," she said.

"I'm sorry," Blake said to Alice. "But we've got to be in Hollywood by noon. Can we drop you somewhere?"

Shit, Alice thought. Shit, shit, shit. "No, I've got my kayak, I'll be fine."

Blake took her by the arm, led her onto the deck. "Look," he said. "I feel like we're just getting started here and I'd love to see you again. Are you free tonight?"

Alice wasn't sure how much time she had left before the cops found Adam and started putting all the pieces together, but she didn't have much choice, now, did she? "I could be," she said. "In fact, I happen to be a wonderful cook. What say I put that fancy dancy kitchen of yours to work and make us dinner?"

"That would be great," he said. And then I'm going to fuck you silly, he thought. "Say, seven o'clock."

"I'll be here. In a car this time."

Blake laughed. "Good idea." He kissed her on the cheek. "Be safe."

"I will. Oh, and thanks for saving my life."

"All in a day's work."

Alice held his look for a long, provocative moment. "I'm happy I met you, Blake Hunter." Then she ran down the beach toward her kayak thinking: But I'm going to be even happier to kill you.

THIRTY-THREE

"Look at the fingers," Syd said. "What do you see?"

Ryan saw the index, middle and ring finger spread out, the thumb and pinkie folded into Adam Devlin's palm. "Three fingers," then it hit him. "3. The three fingers mean 3."

"Her third victim. I love a worthy opponent," Syd said. "Be a shame when we finally catch her."

They stood in the middle of suite 1224 looking at Adam's dead body. He was naked. There was a single bullet wound which obliterated his left eye, blew out the back of his skull and left a Rorschach-like blood spray on the wall behind him. His penis had been removed but wasn't in his mouth.

Ramirez and his team were hard at work dusting the room for prints, vacuuming samples from the floor, taking hair and fibers from the bed.

Liz knelt at Adam's head examining the gunshot wound. Then she moved to his mouth. "There's blood on his lips. But no penis." She looked at the cops spread throughout the room. "Anyone see a severed cock?"

"Okay," Hanrahan said, a cherry Tootsie Roll Pop jammed in his mouth. "That's something you don't hear at every crime scene."

"We have an ID on the victim?" Ryan asked.

"The room's registered to Adam Devlin." Hanrahan held up a plastic evidence bag holding Adam's wallet. "The driver's license confirms the ID. He's a sports agent according to the business cards in his wallet. And, FYI, there is an empty credit card slot and no American Express."

"And he's somehow connected to Zachary Stone and

Colin Wood," Syd said. "Three down, how many more to go?"

"We ran Devlin's name, and a missing person report was filed this morning by his wife. He never came home last night." Hanrahan ripped a page out of his notebook, handed it to Ryan. "Here's the address."

"Brentwood," Ryan said looking around the room. "And he rented a suite. This guy had money."

Ramirez sidled up to Ryan. "Speaking of money, you get a chance to look over the business plan yet?"

"Hey, great meatballs, Tony," Hanrahan said. "Give him the money, Ryan, I'd eat there."

"I did glance at it," Ryan said. "And frankly, I don't know shit about business. But I'll be setting up a foundation and hiring some experts, so I'll give them your proposal; promise. But in return, I want a solid piece of evidence from this crime scene."

"Tell me you're not serious, because this babe is good. You know our problem in a hotel room is *eliminating* fingerprints; there are usually hundreds of them, guests, maids, bellboys. But not here. Every surface has been wiped down; doorknobs, light switches, end tables, in the bathroom she wiped the sink handles and even remembered the toilet handles. A lot of people forget that. They had sex before he killed her. There are semen stains on the bed. We've found pubic hair in the sheets, black and they all look identical, and they all match him." Ramirez cut his eyes to Adam's corpse. "And since I didn't find any of her pubic hair, I'm guessing she shaves. So we've got no prints, no hair, no nothing."

"Then I guess Mirabelle's Meatballs is out of luck."

Ramirez's face fell. "But ..."

Ryan laughed. "Just kidding. It'll be the first thing I give to the CPA."

"Thanks, Ryan."

"We may not have DNA on her," Hanrahan said. "But we may be just a few minutes from getting a look at her. The desk clerk who checked Mr. Devlin in is going through the hotel security videos to see if they've got the Lady in

Red on camera. So with any luck…"

Liz stood up. "Ryan, tell me again about this foundation of yours."

"I've decided to give away most of the Lotto money. Friends and family have first shot at it. But nothing frivolous, just people in need of a life changing monetary infusion."

A surprised Liz looked at Syd. "When did it happen?"

"When did what happen?"

"When did Ryan lose his mind?"

Ryan was confused. "Liz, I thought you'd like the idea. When I was a kid, I remember you nagging Dad at the holidays to give money to the United Way, Salvation Army, Red Cross."

"That's right. I wanted him to give money to *professional* charitable organizations who knew how to equitably distribute the money. But let's back up a bit. Why the hell do you feel the need to give the money away in the first place?"

Ryan and Syd exchanged a quick look and then Ryan said, "It just seems a bit… obscene. Thirty-four million dollars. That's way too much for one person."

"I'll take ten million off your hands," Hanrahan said.

"Count me in for five," an SID tech said.

"And I'll take the rest if you insist," Liz said. "Look, Ryan, the truth is you're in shock. *Anyone* would be. Winning that much money is beyond your comprehension, you're justifiably confused. So do me a favor; before you piss away your windfall, just stick it in the bank and wait. Put your brain on simmer and let the implications of all that money marinate for a little while. Your life has just changed forever and you're going to need time to adjust. Find a new equilibrium. Then in six months, a year, if you still want to give it away, there will be plenty of takers, believe me."

"Talk about a buzz kill," Hanrahan muttered.

Ryan respected Liz and under normal circumstances would have listened to her. But the only way in Ryan's mind to assuage the guilty he felt taking the money in the first place was the rationalization that he'd be giving it away. "Liz, I respect your opinion, I do, but Anne and I have given this a lot of thought and -- "

"Anne?" asked Liz. "As in ex-wife Anne?"

"That's right."

"When did she get back in the picture?" Liz asked distastefully.

Before Ryan could answer, a uniform guarding the door waved, trying to get their attention. In the hallway behind him Ryan saw an older woman standing with a small dog in her arms.

"I think we're being paged," Hanrahan said. He headed for the door, Ryan followed.

Syd remained with Liz. The way Liz had said *Anne,* was filled with attitude, and Syd realized that if anyone could give her the real story of what happened between Ryan and Anne, it was Liz. "Liz, could I talk with you privately?"

Liz looked at her, curiously. "Sure." She led them to a corner of the room.

Syd spoke quietly, "I'd like to ask you something in confidence."

"Okay," Liz answered, warily.

"What happened between Anne and Ryan? What happened to their marriage?"

"I was afraid you were going to ask me that."

"Afraid, why?"

"Because you and Ryan are a great team. But if you're dating, it's just a matter of time until Hanrahan finds out and is forced to spilt you up."

"Getting a new partner is the least of my problems right now. Ryan *reteaming* with Anne is at the top of my list."

"Reteaming how?"

"Anne's going to run the foundation for Ryan. So they'll be spending all sorts of time together. And, she's getting a divorce. Should I be worried?"

Liz answered instantly. "Oh, yeah."

"Why?"

"What did Ryan tell you about their marriage?"

"That they were kids; after a couple of years they realized it was a mistake and split up. He didn't make it sound like a very big deal."

Liz shook her head. "Men. If men would learn to vocalize their feelings, they'd live longer and we'd all be happier."

"So what happened?"

"If you tell him I told you this, I'll take a skull saw to your sweet little neck."

"Pinkie promise." Syd took out her notebook, flipped it open, started writing notes.

"What're you doing?"

"If Ryan looks over, it'll look like I'm working. So what happened?"

"She broke his heart. Called him up one day, said she'd met someone else and never went back to their apartment. Her new boyfriend sent movers to clean out her stuff. Ryan never got over it. It's been like seven years, and he hasn't had a serious girlfriend since. A few dates here and there, but I think he's been afraid to commit. I think he's afraid he's going to be hurt again. How long have you guys been involved?"

"A month."

"That's a modern day record for Ryan."

"And I'm crazy about him."

"He cares about you, too. I can tell."

That pleased Syd. "Really?"

"I see the way he looks at you. There is that lovely mix of admiration and adoration. God, I miss that."

"What's Anne like?"

"Let me put it this way. The first time Ryan brought Anne to my house, she spent the entire dinner asking me how much things cost. How much had I paid for the house? How much for the couch? My Lexus. My necklace. She was obsessed with money. And if you ask me, that's why she left Ryan. When they got married, his dad was rich. Ryan was on track to become a lawyer, too. The future was gold-plated. Then his dad lost all his money. It didn't seem to matter to Ryan, but Anne was beside herself; you'd have thought it was *her* money that disappeared. Then she meets Rick Rogers, *rich* Rick Rogers, and Ryan's out and Rick is in."

"But now Ryan's suddenly rich," Syd said.

"Richer than rich," Liz said. "Anne suddenly reappears in Ryan's life *and* is getting divorced. Coincidence?"

Every fear Syd had was suddenly confirmed. "So what do I do?"

Liz looked past Syd to Ryan. "I love that boy, but he's got a soft spot in his heart and head for Anne." Liz looked back at Syd. "You want the truth?"

No, Syd thought, because it doesn't sound like I'll like it. But she nodded.

"He's always loved Anne. He'll always love Anne. If she wants him back, he's hers."

The words hit Syd like a body blow. She didn't just want Ryan. She wanted Ryan to love her. Pick her over Anne. And if Liz was right, that would never happen.

"He's waving at you," Liz said.

"What?" Syd asked, jolted out of her reverie.

"Ryan, he's signaling to you."

Syd turned. Ryan waved for her to join him. Syd looked back to Liz. "Thanks for your honesty. I think."

"Maybe I'm wrong. I hope I'm wrong, I really do."

"Me, too." Syd closed the notebook, joined Ryan, Hanrahan and the older woman in the hallway.

"Syd," Ryan said. "This is Edna Kaye, she saw the Lady in Red. Talked to her."

That fact jolted Syd's love life to the backburner; she was first and foremost a cop. Syd extended her hand, "Nice to meet you, I'm Detective Syd Curtis."

Maggie, the dog, barked as Syd extended her hand. "Quiet, Maggie," Edna said, taking Syd's hand. "Sorry, she's gets a little excited sometimes."

"Tell me about her," Syd said. "The Lady in Red."

"Blonde, very pretty. Sultry, I think that's the word. Did she really kill someone? Is there a body in there?"

"All we can tell you is we're conducting a murder investigation," Hanrahan said.

"Edna was walking down the hall with her dog when the Lady in Red came out of the suite," Ryan said. "Maggie ran into the suite just as the door was closing."

"No wonder she wouldn't open the door for me," Edna said. "I thought she was a little suspicious, but I never dreamt she was a cold-blooded killer."

"Why did you think she was suspicious?" Syd asked.

"The way she acted when Maggie got locked inside. She got, what's the word, discombobulated. Very nervous. Oh, and did I mention the gloves?"

"No," Ryan said. "She was wearing gloves?"

Edna nodded. The kind you see on TV all the time, on *CSI* and such. The kind doctors wear. And some of the police I see here."

Syd pulled her pair of surgical gloves out of her pocket. "Like these?"

"Exactly. Criminals wear them so they won't leave fingerprints, right?"

"That's right, ma'am," Hanrahan said.

Edna's eyes drifted to the body on the floor. "Seeing that poor man must be what made Maggie sick."

"What's that? Sick, how?" Syd asked.

Edna grimaced at the memory. "She threw up when I got her back into my room. Coughed up some food."

Hanrahan, Ryan and Syd exchanged a knowing look. The dog must've eaten the missing penis. "Well," Hanrahan said. "That's one mystery solved."

"What did you do with the... with whatever Maggie threw up?" Ryan asked.

"Wrapped it in a bunch of toilet paper and flushed it down the toilet." Edna saw the cops disappointed reaction. "Did I do something wrong?"

"No, ma'am," Syd said.

Ryan looked at Syd. "This happened last night by the way, about nine-thirty. A room service attendant opened the door to get the dog for Mrs. Kaye, but he never entered the room because there was a Do Not Disturb sign on the door."

"Damn, that's fifteen hours ago," Syd said. "We could have figured out her next victim by now."

Hanrahan's cell phone rang. He answered, listened, said, "Thanks," and snapped it shut. He looked at Ryan and Syd, "Ready to meet the Lady in Red?"

They had caught her three times on two cameras. The Lady in Red and Adam Devlin passed through the lobby crossing from the Windows Lounge toward the bank of elevators. He held a bottle of champagne in one hand, two flutes in the other. The Lady in Red had her left arm entwined in his and leaned against him as they walked. But there was no good view of her face from this angle. Adam was taller than the Lady in Red, and since they were walking side-by-side, he blocked her face.

"You think she did it on purpose?" Hanrahan asked. "Scoped out the cameras ahead of time and tucked behind him to hide her face?"

"It wouldn't surprise me, Chief," Syd said. "She's been one step ahead of us from the beginning."

"There is one more shot from this angle," the head of security said. They were in his office. Hanrahan, Ryan and Syd stood behind him looking at the monitor. The head of security fast-forwarded. "This is three hours and six minutes later." The Lady in Red entered the left side of frame and walked out the front door. Her back was to camera the entire time.

"That's no help," Hanrahan said.

"Let's see the other angle," Ryan said. The head of security hit a few buttons and the scene shifted to a bank of elevators. Adam Devlin and the Lady in Red turned a corner and walked straight for the camera.

"Gotcha," Hanrahan said.

The video was silent but you could see the Lady in Red's mouth moving and Adam Devlin smiling. "Okay, freeze it there," Ryan said.

The tape froze with a big clear shot of the Lady in Red and Adam Devlin.

"She's pretty," Ryan said.

"And diabolical," Syd said. "Imagine, she's walking arm-in-arm, flirting up a storm with a guy who she knows she's going to kill and mutilate in just a few minutes." Syd crossed to the screen, looked closely at Adam. "What did you do to her, you bastard?"

"You're calling him a bastard?" Hanrahan asked. "She's the nutbag rearranging their anatomy."

"That's right. She's methodically killing certain handpicked men. She has planned this for a long, long time. And when we find the connection between these victims, I guarantee you we're going find out that she," Syd pointed at the frozen image of the Lady in Red, "was the first victim."

Ryan looked at his partner. "She's a murderer, Syd. No matter what they did to her, you can't take the law into your own hands."

"Of course not," Syd said. "I'm just saying as bad as I want to catch her, I'm dying to find out why."

"Well let's start with catching her," Hanrahan said. He turned to the head of security. "I'll need a copy of that tape. Media Relations will make copies for all the news outlets. We should have her face on every TV in Southern California by dinner."

"And we'll talk to the widow," Ryan said. "Maybe she'll know what Zachary Stone, Colin Wood and Adam Devlin have in common."

THIRTY-FOUR

Anne sat across from Travis Taylor. The private detective was a good looking man, reminding Anne of a young Clint Eastwood. He had steel-gray hair and a trace of Texas in his gravelly speech. He dressed in a dark blue suit, probably a throwback to his FBI days, and smelled of Old Spice.

They sat in a quiet corner of the Beverly Hilton lobby bar. Anne had checked into the hotel, treating herself to a suite, but the room wasn't ready yet. She still had to move out of the Santa Monica apartment and her office at Rogers, Middleton and Roberts, but two things took priority; getting ready for the California Lottery in the morning, and finding out about Syd Curtis.

"She's a good cop," Travis said. "She was only on the street for five years before getting bumped to detective. She had a solid rep as a uniform. She earned three commendations before actually winning a Medal of Valor last year."

The Medal of Valor was the highest honor an LAPD officer could earn, not given out lightly and always involving bravery and heroism above and beyond the call of duty. "What did she do?" Anne asked.

Travis read from his notes, paraphrasing the police report. "A man started beating his pregnant wife in a grocery store in Sherman Oaks. One of the customers tried to stop him; the husband pulled a gun and shot the customer, killing him. Chaos erupted inside the store, panicked people running out the doors, employees fleeing out the back and one of them called 911.

"Officer Syd Curtis and her partner, Bruce Carroll, were the first to arrive at the scene. Witnesses told them that the man with the gun and his pregnant wife were still inside the store and he'd also taken a teenage girl hostage. The hysterical mother begged the officers to save her daughter.

"Officers Curtis and Carroll entered the store with weapons drawn and spread out trying to find the suspect. As Officer Curtis turned down an aisle, she found the husband holding his wife and the teenage girl at gunpoint. He immediately put the gun to the back of the teenage girl's head and said if the police didn't leave immediately, he was going to shoot the girl. The man was clearly unstable and Officer Curtis feared for the lives of the hostages.

"Then she spotted her partner moving up behind the suspect. But her partner was unable to risk apprehending the suspect because of the imminent threat of the suspect's gun to the teenager's head.

"So Officer Curtis lowered her gun to the floor and placed her hands above her head. Then she began to slowly approach the suspect. The official language reads, 'With disregard for her own safety and a high degree of courage and bravery,' she asked the suspect to please release the hostages and take her instead. Closer and closer she stepped, gently urging him to let the hostages go.

"Finally the suspect took the gun away from the teenage girl's head and pointed it at Officer Curtis. That gave her partner the opening he'd been waiting for. He fired, killing the suspect."

"Wow," Anne said, impressed. The diminutive, freckled-faced little red head was full of surprises.

"She got her detective shield and was transferred to Vice. She distinguished herself both as an undercover officer soliciting johns on the street and in a deep cover operation to break up a Russian white slavery ring. The brass was impressed and she got her pick of assignments. She chose Homicide."

What Travis didn't tell Anne was that he also checked on Syd Curtis's new partner in Homicide, Ryan Magee, and discovered that Ryan and Anne used to be married. And

Travis heard that Magee had just hit the Lotto. Judging by her LAPD photo, Syd Curtis was a looker; so, like any trained detective, Travis put two and two together and figured Magee was fucking his partner and now that he was rich, Anne wanted Magee back. And since Anne was paying Travis six hundred dollars a day, he was perfectly willing to help her for as long as possible.

"Now that's all official file stuff," Travis said, sipping his club soda. "But I did find out some intriguing inconsistencies. On her police application she lists her name as Syd Curtis from Riverside, California. She claims to have attended Arlington High School before getting an AA at Santa Monica College. Santa Monica College does list her as a graduate but there is no record of her ever attending Arlington High School. In fact, there is no record for her in the State of California before she got a driver's license ten years ago when she was eighteen."

"Kind of old to get your first driver's license," Anne said.

"That's what I thought," Travis said. "And there's more. A friend of mine works at the Police Academy and I had him pull her application. A letter of recommendation accompanied the application, written by an LAPD officer, Andrea Templeton. Syd Curtis's address while she attended the Police Academy was the same as Andrea Templeton's."

"They were living together?"

"Apparently. Officer Templeton was killed in the line of duty a few days before Syd Curtis graduated from the Academy. I checked her obituary; one line stuck out to me." He referred to his notes again. "In lieu of flowers please send a donation to the Gay and Lesbian Alliance against Defamation."

Anne tried to make sense of this. "GLAAD? What're you saying, Andrea Templeton was gay?"

"I don't know. But that kind of obit is generally a pretty good indicator."

"Do you think she and Syd Curtis were lovers?"

Travis shrugged. "I don't know. I've only been on the

case for a few hours. But I could try and find out. I'm also curious about Syd Curtis's life before she suddenly appeared at Santa Monica College. We know she lied about going to Arlington High School, I'd like to know what else she's lied about."

"Me, too," Anne said. "How much time do you need?"

"One day, maybe two."

"Excellent. And, Travis, don't bill Rogers, Middleton and Roberts for this; I'll be taking care of it personally."

"Of course," he said, her request confirming his suspicions. "I'll call you when I've got something." Travis collected his files and left.

Secrets and lies. Everybody's got them, thought Anne. It was one of her favorite things about being a lawyer, finding those lies, exposing the secrets, exploiting a weakness. And sometimes what you found even surprised someone as cynical as Anne.

Surprise me Syd, thought Anne.

Surprise the hell out of me.

THIRTY-FIVE

Alice was staring at herself on television. Surveillance footage taken at the Bel Air Regent Hotel showed her walking to the elevator with Adam.

Adam looked so, what was the word, expectant, yes, expectant. Look at that smile on his face, she thought. Joyful but still a little bit naughty. You could almost feel his enthusiasm as they walked. Here was a man who ruled his world. Here was a man about to get laid.

The blonde didn't look so bad either, if she did say so herself. The short skirt showed off her long legs, the low cut blouse showcased her tits, and the sexy way she walked promised carnal delights.

She owed it all to Charlotte, her look, that is. Charlotte came to the Institute three years ago; she was bi-polar and a sex addict. They had all sorts of fancy theories for sexual addiction these days – compulsion, disease, impulse control disorder, sexual desire disorder – but Charlotte happily called herself a nymphomaniac. In fact, during her three-month stay, Charlotte seduced three of the doctors (two men and a woman), four nurses (all women), three orderlies (men), six patients (four women and two men) and a husband she found in the atrium who was waiting to visit his wife.

And here was the thing; Charlotte wasn't that pretty. Average at best. And for a long time she had trouble seducing the people she wanted to have sex with. So she taught herself how to use clothes, make-up and attitude to become irresistible.

"But it takes discipline," she told Alice as they lay naked together. Alice had watched Charlotte sleep her way through the Institute, and though not gay, Alice was so fascinated by Charlotte and her spellbinding sexuality that Alice slept with her just to experience it. And the pillow talk afterward changed Alice's life.

"You have tons of potential, Alice. But right now you're dumpy, frumpy and grumpy. You need to lose weight, look and dress better and learn to *exude*. Exude fun. Exude mystery. Exude sex."

Charlotte made Alice her personal project. She worked out with her at the gym and taught her what to eat; Alice lost twenty pounds in a month. Alice's brown hair was blah, so Charlotte convinced Alice to dye it blonde. Her brown eyes were dull so Charlotte got her green contact lenses. Losing the weight brought out Alice's cheekbones; Charlotte taught her how to use make-up to accent them. And, of course, clothes make the woman. So Charlotte worked with Alice using pictures from magazines to design an ideal wardrobe. But color was the key. With Alice's blonde hair and green eyes, her new dominant color had to be red.

Last but most important was attitude. It's tough to get depressed, suicidal people to simply change their personality, so Charlotte made it a game. Alice needed to pretend she was someone else. A movie star blend, if you will. Charlotte taught Alice to walk like Charlize Theron, flirt like Angela Jolie, listen like Anne Hathaway and laugh like Scarlett Johanssen.

As Alice perfected her skills, she didn't realize that one day she would be using them for revenge. But she could have never ensnared the fearsome foursome without Charlotte's life lessons.

The image on the television switched to a blow up of the surveillance photo, now just a close up of Alice, with a phone number beneath it. The announcer said, "These images were just released by the Los Angeles Police Department and this woman is being sought for questioning in a number of homicides. The Police request that if you've seen this Lady in Red or know her identity, please contact the LAPD at the number on the bottom of your screen."

The picture switched back to the two shot of Alice and Adam. Then the camera zoomed in on Adam. "Once again, sports agent Adam Devlin has been found dead at the Bel Air Regent Hotel."

Alice muted the TV as the announcer handed off to the weatherman. Okay, she thought, my picture is finally out there. But the shot isn't great and I had my hair down when I was with Adam. Anticipating this, Alice wore her hair tied back for this morning's encounter with Blake, and would keep it back for tonight's rendezvous.

But since the police had found Adam's body it was just a matter of time until they tumble to her. And if they were smart enough to put two and two together, they could soon predict Blake would be her next victim. It might take them some time, a day or so at least she hoped, but just in case they were waiting for her when she went back to Blake's beach house, it was time to leave the message.

Her manifesto.

Alice took out the cell phone she bought last week at Best Buy, switched on the video recorder, turned it toward herself and said, "Test, test, test, this is a test." She shut it off, spun the phone around and hit play. Her face filled the screen and was slightly distorted because she held the phone so close. "Test, test, test, this is a test." Her recorded image said.

Alice was satisfied. She erased the test, turned on the video recorder, held the phone a little further away, a final surrender to vanity, and started talking.

THIRTY-SIX

"Who is she?"

"We don't know, yet," Ryan said to Emily Devlin. "But, with your help, we're hoping to find out."

Emily Devlin, Adam's widow, sat in the living room of their Brentwood home in her tennis outfit, a tight, pink Adidas Response Court tank and white Response Court skirt. Her Adidas Barricade V tennis shoes completed the ensemble given to the Devlin's by a grateful Adidas Corporation after Adam signed his superstar client, Olga, to an exclusive contract.

Though she'd been worried enough about Adam to report him missing early that morning, Emily wasn't so worried she'd miss her Wednesday tennis league. She was just returning home, having kicked Alisha's butt 6-3, 6-1, when Ryan and Syd drove up.

Emily correctly assumed they were cops as they climbed out of the Crown Vic, and the grim expressions on their faces told her Adam must be dead. Tears were already flowing as the cops introduced themselves and the pretty female officer told her that they were sorry but her husband was dead, murdered.

They followed her inside, allowing her silent time to digest the news. She led them into the living room, dropped onto her white Thomasville Affinity sofa and stopped crying long enough to ask, "How did it… what happened?"

Ryan and Syd exchanged a glance. This is where is got delicate. Hearing your husband was dead was one thing, finding out he was killed by a woman, in a hotel room, after they had sex, and then had his penis cut off was something completely different.

"Mrs. Devlin," Syd said. "Your husband was at the

Bel Air Regent Hotel with another woman."

The tears seemed to stop falling midstream and freeze on Emily's pretty face.

"We believe she may have killed him." Syd took out a color printout of the close-up of the Lady in Red from the security camera. She showed it to Emily. "Do you recognize this woman?"

Emily wiped away the tears, looked at the picture. She shook her head. "Who is she?"

"We don't know, yet," Ryan said. "But, with your help, we're hoping to find out."

Emily looked at the picture again. "Was she a client?"

"We don't think so," Syd said. Then gently, "They had sex, Mrs. Devlin. In a hotel suite. That's where your husband's body was found." No reason to dump the mutilation on her right now, Syd decided. She'll find out soon enough. "Are you sure you've never seen her before."

Emily stared at the photo. "No, I've never seen her before." Then a few gears meshed as Syd's words sunk in. "My husband was having an affair?"

"Yes, ma'am," Syd said.

Emily looked first at Syd, then at Ryan. Her brain was processing the information, the implications of Adam's affair and death. "Where did you get this picture?"

Ryan answered. "It's from a hotel security camera, taped last night at six twenty-two."

"There is a video of them together?" Emily asked.

"Yes," Syd answered.

"Do you have a copy of it with you?" Ryan had asked security to burn them a DVD before they left the hotel. "We do," Ryan said.

The Devlins had a screening room; video projector, Blue-Ray DVD player, and surround sound system provided by Sony. The six theatre chairs were supplied by La-Z-Boy; Orville Redenbacher's company donated the popcorn maker, but the Devlins actually paid for the 15-foot Draper projection screen.

And it was on that giant screen that Emily Devlin watched her eager husband and the Lady in Red stroll toward the elevator.

"He looks happy," Emily said icily. "And I see he's got his favorite champagne, Cristal. Nothing but the best for Adam. Is she a hooker?"

"We don't know," Syd said.

"She looks like a hooker, don't you think? Cheap, tawdry."

Actually, Syd thought, the Lady in Red looks anything but cheap and tawdry. She looked classy, confident, and sexy as hell.

Then a horrifying realization dawned on Emily. "What are you going to do with this video?"

"Use it to find your husband's killer," Ryan said. "We've distributed it to all the news outlets. We're hoping someone recognizes the Lady in Red and tells us who and where she is."

Panic seized Emily. "But you can't! You've got to get those videos back!"

Ryan threw a confused look to Syd. "It's too late, Mrs. Devlin, I'm sorry. They're already running."

"Then stop them, immediately."

"We can't," Syd said.

"But don't you see, it's so embarrassing! Everyone's going to know Adam was cheating on me. I'll be a laughing stock!"

Ryan caught Syd's eye, clocked her surprise. People, Ryan thought. You just never knew how they'd react. "With all due respect, Mrs. Devlin, this is a murder investigation. We think this woman has killed three men and may kill more. Our first priority is to find her and stop her."

Any trace of grief was gone. Humiliation and anger fueled her words. "Look, let's be honest. I knew Adam had the occasional affair," then with a defiant look to Ryan she added, "We *both* had affairs."

Syd found it interesting Emily aimed that comment at Ryan. A *fuck you* to men or a provocative statement to flirt?

"But I have the decency to keep mine private," Emily

said. Then another realization rocked Emily. "Could this woman have been a girlfriend? Someone he's been seeing for a long time?"

"We have no way of knowing that yet," Ryan said.

"Motherfucker," Emily said racing for the phone. "Shit, what's his number?" she said to herself and then apparently remembered because she quickly dialed. "Thomas, its Emily Devlin... Adam's dead... Yeah, yeah, me, too. Listen, has he made any changes to his will since we did the Trust papers... Oh, thank God... What... Murdered, it's on TV apparently... yes, yes, let's talk later." She hung up. "I'm sorry," she said to Ryan and Syd, "Where were we?"

Watching you make sure you'll get to keep all of your husband's money, Ryan thought. "We were trying to find your husband's killer," Ryan said. "Do you know Zachary Stone?"

"Who's Zachary Stone?"

"He is, or was, a lawyer in Orange County."

Emily thought about it and then shook her head. "No. The only people I know in Orange County are Adam's parents. He makes air conditioning ducts, I think, and she's a big muckity-muck at one of the banks."

"Orange County," Syd said, jumping on the connection. "Was your husband raised in Orange County?"

"Yes." Emily saw the excited reaction from Ryan and Syd. "Why, is that important?"

"How about Colin Wood?" asked Syd. "Did your husband know Colin Wood."

"Colin Wood, wasn't he the actor that was killed yesterday?"

"Yes," Ryan said. "Did your husband know him?"

Emily considered. "You know, I actually think I remember Adam mentioning Colin Wood a few months ago. He was in a movie we saw; Adam said he knew him."

"How old was your husband?" Syd asked.

The rapid-fire questions were unsettling Emily. "Twenty-nine."

Syd looked at Ryan. "Same age as Colin. And Kathy

Tuttle's lawyer said he heard rumors about trouble when Colin was in high school."

Ryan looked at Emily. "Did your husband go to school with Colin Wood?"

"I don't know."

Then Ryan had a brainstorm. "I don't suppose Adam kept any of his high school yearbooks?"

Adam Devlin's office was a mahogany and leather delight. The room smelled of cigar smoke and floor-to-ceiling bookcases encircled a custom made Parnian desk.

It took a while to find the yearbooks. Ryan enjoyed the search because many of Adam Devlin's books were first editions. There was a shelf of American classics by F. Scott Fitzgerald, Hemingway, Faulkner; Adam Devlin even had a signed first edition of *Moby Dick* by Melville.

Then there was a shelf of classic detective novels: *The Big Sleep*, by Raymond Chandler, *The Thin Man* by Dashiell Hammett, *The Postman Always Rings Twice*, by James M. Cain. Devlin owned scores of books from the world's most renowned detective writers: Agatha Christie, John D. MacDonald, Rex Stout, Erle Stanley Gardner, Graham Greene, Cornell Woolrich, Ross Thomas, Ruth Rendell; even signed first editions from contemporary masters like Elmore Leonard, John Grisham, John Sanford, James Lee Burke and Michael Connelly.

Ryan loved books and always dreamed of collecting first editions. Of course, he never had the money to buy them or the library necessary to house them.

Until now.

As Ryan scoured through the books, a strange feeling took hold. Now he could buy any book he wanted. He could even buy Devlin's entire library and it wouldn't make a dent in his money.

For the first time Ryan really understood the magnitude of his Lotto winnings.

He could have a room like this.

He could have a house like this.

He could have all the toys.

He could have anything he wanted.

He had originally planned to give away all the money, but for the first time he reconsidered. Why did he have to give it *all* away? If he kept just ten percent, or twenty percent, even thirty percent would still leave tens of millions for the foundation.

"Got it," Syd said, excited. "I found the yearbooks."

Ryan and Emily joined Syd. She knelt in a far corner of the library, pulled out a yearbook from the bottom shelf. "Here's the last one, his senior year." She handed it to Ryan. He flipped through the senior pictures, found the one for Adam Devlin. He wore a yellow sweater and a warm, open smile.

"Hasn't changed much," Syd said.

Emily touched the picture with her finger. "He was wearing that sweater when I met him freshman year at USC," Emily said, tearing up, suddenly nostalgic.

She's going to go through a lot of emotions for the next few weeks, Ryan knew. Losing someone to murder, no matter how ambivalent you might feel toward them, was always a jolting experience.

He flipped through the alphabetical pages of photos until he got to the W's. "Bingo," Ryan said. Colin Wood's picture was in the middle of the page. "Mrs. Devlin," Ryan said. "Did Adam ever mention any trouble he might have had in high school?"

She thought about it. "No, not really. He told me his dad caught him with dope one time, and his mom walked in on him masturbating. I have too, by the way, but that's another story."

"I'll bet the next victim's in that book. Hell," Syd said. "I'll bet the Lady in Red's in that book."

"Can we borrow this," Ryan asked Emily

"Of course."

"We'll also need access to your husband's address book and computer."

"They're both there on his desk," Emily said, looking at Ryan as if she was seeing him for the first time. "Detective, have we met before?"

Oh, shit, Ryan thought. Here it comes. "I don't think

so."

"Are you an actor on the side or something?"

Syd knew where she was going, too. "No," she said. "But you may have seen him on TV recently."

Then it hit her. "You're the Lotto winner, right. The cop who struck it rich."

"That's right," Ryan said.

"How much did you win?"

"Thirty-four million."

Emily's eye's dropped to Ryan's ring finger. "I don't see a wedding ring."

"Oh, he's single," Syd said, enjoying Ryan's discomfort.

"Well," Emily said, a little of her old perkiness reemerging. "I'd be foolish not to mention I'm suddenly single."

"This guy knows everybody in sports," Syd said, thumbing through Adam Devlin's address book. They were driving east on Olympic from Brentwood to Hollywood, suffering the fits and starts of rush hours. "Tiger Woods, Maria Sharapova, Tony Romo, Michael Phelps. And even most A list actors: George Clooney, Tom Cruise, Will Smith and, saving the best for last... Colin Wood."

"He may not have been on Hollywood's A-list, but he's certainly on mine."

"So, how's this for a plan?" Syd asked. "I'll check Colin Wood's cell phone and phone book for Adam Devlin's number; if it's there, then I'll cross reference all the names in both men's phone books looking for matching names. Then I'll cross reference any matches to the names in Adam Devlin's high school yearbook. And if we get lucky, maybe, just maybe, we can get the names of a few more potential victims."

Ryan looked at Syd, impressed. "Brilliant."

"Look, I know you need to meet Anne to go over stuff for the Lotto tomorrow, so drop me at the station and I'll call you if I find a match."

"No," Ryan said, instinctively. "Fuck the Lotto. This is too important. I'll help."

"Don't be silly, Ryan, I can do this alone. And you don't really mean that, do you? Fuck the Lotto?" Please say yes, Syd thought.

Ryan did feel guilty leaving Syd alone to work. All his adult life, work was priority one. But, at the same time, he was only a few hours from getting the Lotto money and surprisingly found himself focused on all the things that could go wrong. What if he loses the ticket? What if the tow truck driver shows up at the presentation? What if the 7-Eleven clerk is there and says Ryan didn't buy the ticket? What if they find the video of the tow truck driver buying the ticket? What if he oversleeps? What if he has a car accident in the morning and misses the presentation? What if Anne steals the money from him?

What if? What if? What if?

The growing obsession should have been enough warning to Ryan that his life would probably be much better off if he *didn't* take the money. If he *never* took the money.

But he was far too gone for that.

In spite of himself, Ryan was dreaming about first edition books and hand crafted desks. He'd noticed all the *things* in the Devlin house: the plush carpets, state of the art appliances, beautiful furniture. And the familiar smells of freshly polished furniture and fresh flowers. Sights, sounds and smells that all reminded Ryan of his father's house.

Ryan may not have cared much about money growing up, but living in luxury sure leaves a mark. His childhood memories of that house were like comfort food for the brain. His bedroom was filled with toys as a boy, gadgets and the latest computers as a teenager. His meals were prepared by Vivian, their black housekeeper. And with the musical chair nature of his father's wives, Vivian was the only constant female influence on young Ryan's life. The house was always clean, the bathrooms spotless, windows and mirrors sparkled, and furniture glistened. Each new wife would want to redecorate, so the carpets, drapes, pictures and furniture changed as fast as his father's wedding rings. But it was always home.

After his father lost all his money and went to jail, Ryan rejected that part of his life. It wouldn't take much time on a shrink's couch to find out how betrayed Ryan felt by his father's fraud. His father putting money before everything, including Ryan. So Ryan enjoyed his monastic life of a small apartment and forty-year-old car. Money wasn't an issue because he didn't have any, didn't make any, and didn't want any.

But that was all a lie, Ryan realized. It had to be because Ryan found himself more and more obsessed with the Lotto ticket. How it could change his life, how it was going to change the life of so many of his friends and family.

So the answer to Syd's simple question, *You don't really mean that, do you? Fuck the Lotto?* was simple. "No, Syd, I don't mean it. It's become too important to too many people."

Like your money grubbing ex-wife, Anne, thought Syd. And Tony Ramirez and his mother's meatballs, Chen and his mother's mortgage, Katz's fishing boat, your fucking stepbrother's horses and sadly, you too, my dear Ryan.

But Syd said none of this. What she did say was, "Exactly. So go to your meeting with Anne; I'll call you if I come up with something. And I think I better sleep at home, tonight," Syd said. "I promised Eleanor I'd meet her for dinner and it might go late." Eleanor had been Syd's partner at Vice, and they got together every couple of weeks.

"Okay," Ryan said. "But I'll miss you."

"Me too, you." But Syd wasn't planning on meeting Eleanor for dinner. She had other plans for this evening.

Plans she hoped Ryan never found out about.

THIRTY-SEVEN

Blake Hunter rarely dated. There were much easier ways to get laid and he couldn't stand the hassle of wining, dining and being charming just to get into some girls panties. Hookers were expensive, but as actor Charlie Sheen said, "I don't pay them for sex, I pay them to leave."

Blake *hated* being stuck with some girl in his bed all night, then having to be civil in the morning, giving them coffee or a muffin and, worst of all, driving them home.

He hadn't had a real girlfriend since college and that was just fine. A long-term relationship wasn't on his radar right now. And though plenty of young girls wanted to date him – he was, after all, the Prince of the paparazzi and therefore able to get ambitious actresses plenty of face time in the world's most-read magazines – Blake decided it just wasn't worth the effort. For a thousand bucks, he could do whatever he wanted to whatever flavor of luscious young lady he desired; professional women who were only there to satisfy their client with every sensual trick they knew, and having relieved him of all his precious bodily fluids, would happily leave.

So Blake's deigning to have the blonde in the red bathing suit come back tonight was unusual. No doubt he could order up a girl just like her from Millie, his madam. But there was something intriguing about the girl, and it was always fun to actually seduce a woman. It was thrilling when a woman surrendered herself to you with genuine passion. Besides, the blonde was not only going to cook him dinner but she was driving herself over, so getting rid of her should be easy.

Blake worked at his computer, checking shots of Jennifer Lopez nipple slip while getting out of a swimming pool, when he noticed the time, six fifty-five. Shit, she was due at seven. He saved his work on Photoshop and hurried into the bedroom. He grabbed the remote, clicked on the TV and started changing clothes as the news wrapped up. He was in his closet slipping out of shorts and into a pair of khakis, sandals and a Grateful Dead tee shirt when his synapses plowed through the meaningless blah blah blah of the newscast and focused in on the words "...Adam Devlin's murder..."

Blake stepped into the bedroom in time to see the surveillance video from the Bel Air Regent Hotel and hear: "Police say this woman is a suspect in not only Adam Devlin's murder, but also the murder of Colin Wood two nights ago and Orange County attorney Zachary Stone earlier this week. If you know the identity or whereabouts of this Lady in Red, please call the number at the bottom of your screen."

Blake hit the pause button, freezing the image on his DVR.

Adam Devlin was dead, too? Murdered just like Colin? Blake had spoken to Adam just six months ago. One of Adam's clients, a beautiful ice skater with four Olympic Gold Medals and a squeaky-clean-girl-next-door rep that had netted her millions in endorsements had been photographed giving the finger to an obnoxious paparazzi, Joel, as a matter of fact, Blake's number one shooter.

Adam called Blake, asked him to kill the picture as a favor. Blake always liked Adam; they had great times in high school. So Blake did his old friend a favor and killed the picture. Now Adam was dead, too. What the fuck was going on?

Blake studied the frozen image of the blonde on his TV and a cold chill ran through him. It looked like that girl he met this morning in the red bikini. Her hair was down in the video and pulled back in a ponytail today, but it sure looked like the same girl who washed up on his beach.

Then with a jolt the implications rocked him. She'd killed Adam and Colin and now she wanted to kill him.

Kill him!

But who the hell was she? He studied her face. He didn't recognize her, though he remembered thinking there was something familiar about her when they first talked.

Then he thought about her victims; Colin, Adam and an Orange County attorney... and then it hit him. Zachary Stone was the lawyer who handled the payoff to that girl from high school, Annie, Angie, no wait, Alice. Alice Waterman.

He studied the picture again. That woman looked *nothing* like Alice Waterman. Well, not that he really remembered what that slut looked like. But wasn't she brunette and chunky? He could quickly check the video he made that night. He kept it, of course; he kept everything he shot.

But if she dyed her hair and lost weight... He studied the surveillance shot one more time, it could be her.

Could be, hell, it *must* be her, otherwise why would she be killing everyone who was there that night?

And what was with the damsel in distress act this morning? She must have been researching him. Knew where he lived, knew he liked to run in the mornings. She had to have been waiting for him in that kayak, waiting for him to take his run on the beach so he'd be able to *rescue* her.

But then why didn't she kill him this morning? And then he remembered standing with her in the kitchen making her some more coffee and getting her an apple. She was standing behind him; he pictured the kitchen, the counter...the spice rack...the jar of utensils...and the knives. She was standing in front of the fucking knives!

He vaguely remembered sensing movement behind him when he bent over to get her that apple, but then Joel and the guys suddenly walked in.

Was she going to kill him then? Had the guys interrupted her, saving his life?

Now Blake was starting to get mad.

That bitch. She tried to kill him this morning, failed, so she was coming back tonight to finish the job. He picked up his phone, started punching in the number on the bottom of the TV screen, then stopped as an idea struck him. A brainstorm, actually.

There may be an incredible opportunity here.

It would be risky; she was a killer, after all. But she didn't know that he knew who she was. And that should buy him both time and opportunity.

The doorbell rang. She was here. Decision time. The more he thought about his plan, the more he liked it. He hung up the phone.

Alice drove her Prius to Malibu. It was a gift from her parents when she got out of the Institute a month ago. She hated taking gifts from them since they were all bought with the blood money.

She'd driven by Blake's house twice, looking for any sign of police. She saw none. Relieved she was still a couple of steps ahead of the cops, she pulled into Blake's driveway.

She'd chosen a red skirt that was just a little too short and a white tank top that was a little too tight. She'd had sex with Adam and given head to Colin but she wanted nothing to do with this sleazebag. She didn't mind tempting him, but she sure as hell wasn't going to sleep with him.

She'd come prepared. The scalpel was washed. Her .25 Colt was cleaned and loaded. And she had a grocery bag filled with the makings for dinner. Pasta, sauce, bread, premixed salad from Whole Foods and a low calorie Italian dressing.

She almost made a mistake this morning. She was just going to kill him and be done with it. But it occurred to her that Blake was the one shooting the video on that terrible night. She'd really like to finally see that video. Find out once and for all what really happened to her. So she was going to flirt, and cook and pry and hopefully find out where he kept his old videos. And then finally, with her gun pressed to his forehead, as he was begging for his life, she might even get an apology.

She walked to his door filled with hope. Hope that she'd finally learn what those boys did to her and hope that her bloody revenge would finally come to an end. Fixing a smile firmly in place, Alice rang the bell.

Blake opened the door. "Right on time," Blake said, motioning her inside.

"My mother taught me to never keep a man waiting," she said walking in.

Blake eyed the grocery bag. "What's for dinner?"

"My specialty," Alice said heading for the kitchen. "Pasta." She dropped her purse on a chair in the living room and giggled. "To be honest, it's about the only thing I know how to cook. But it'll be good, I promise."

"I love pasta." Blake said as he watched her unpack the food. He studied her face, tried to see Alice in there. Couldn't. This woman has the most dazzling green eyes, did Alice have green eyes? He didn't think so. Contacts?

"So," he said, joining her in the kitchen. "Before you start cooking," he said looking deeply into her eyes, "I insist we have a drink on the deck. The sun sets in a few minutes and, with that mountain of cumulous clouds on the horizon, it should be spectacular."

God, he's intense, Alice thought as Blake stared into her eyes. And a little bit creepy. But she had a job to do so she raised a perfectly plucked eyebrow, tilted her head and said, "Sounds wonderful."

Yep, contacts, Blake thought as he finally discerned a bit of the edge. "You go out on the deck and I'll make us a drink. What'll you have?"

"Wine, white if you have it."

"I've got a Chardonnay with your name on it."

"Thank you," Alice said, sliding open the French doors and stepping outside. It was like stepping into a postcard. The sea was calm and the sun hung like a huge crimson sphere just above the surface. Alice breathed in the air, allowed herself to enjoy the smell of the sea, the sound of the surf, the visual splendor of nature's charismatic swan song.

There was this one doctor at the Institute who was experimenting with aural psychology and would make her lie on a waterbed listening to sounds of the surf, waves breaking and seagulls singing and watch her brainwaves. He showed her the results and they were amazing. Her alpha wave went from a network of huge hills and valleys to an almost smooth line. She was revved up now and could do with a little modulating, so Alice breathed deeply, closed her eyes and let her ears take over.

Blake watched the blonde from kitchen. As soon as her back was to him, he inched toward her purse. He opened it and looked inside. He moved a wallet aside and saw a handgun. It was small, easy to conceal. Good.

With a quick glance to make sure she still wasn't looking, he snatched the gun, slipped it into his pocket. Then he put the wallet back in place, closed the purse and walked to the Sub Zero. The blonde's eyes were closed. She looked peaceful, he thought.

Enjoy it while you can, baby.

He took out a bottle of Cakebread chardonnay and set it on the counter. Then he took the gun and surreptitiously slipped it into the dishtowel drawer, shoving it well back and out of sight. He closed the drawer.

His eyes went back to the blonde on the deck, still in her trance. He had to admit she was beautiful. Hard to believe she's killed three people. He didn't want to become number four and thought briefly about calling 911. But, hell, he had her gun, what could she do to him?

He picked up his Nikon D90 and started taking pictures of her. She was in profile, and looked spectacular silhouetted against the setting sun. Her eyes were closed and she had just a hint of a smile on her lips.

Candid shots of the notorious Lady in Red. They would be worth a fortune in worldwide sales. But the stills were just the appetizer in Blake's plan. He had something much more spectacular in mind. He had the actual video of the Lady in Red having sex with the men she would kill eleven years later!

The commercial implications were staggering. Besides

the millions of dollars it could gross in DVD, internet and licensing sales, it would be a great way for him to re-introduce himself to mainstream Hollywood. Hollywood was a sucker for comeback stories and what better comeback was there than capturing the notorious Lady in Red?

He zoomed in for an extreme close-up just as she opened her eyes, turned her head and looked right at him.

CLICK. CLICK. CLICK.

He took shot after shot. A dazzling smile lit up her face as the sunset scorched the sky behind her. Photographers wait hours for this kind of light. It was called the magic hour even though it usually only lasted about twenty minutes each day as the sun set.

"What are you doing?" she asked.

"Taking pictures of a beautiful woman. Do you mind?"

She thought about it, decided she had nothing to lose at this point; he'd be dead soon and she could take the camera. On second thought, she might leave the camera for the police to find, these pictures should look a lot better than those lousy surveillance shots they're showing on TV. So she posed, playfully. "Not at all."

CLICK. CLICK. CLICK.

"Did you ever model while you were in Denver?" Since Blake knew her *wannabe actress from Denver* story was bullshit, he thought it'd be fun to poke at the lie.

Actually, Alice's actress friend, Dawn, did some modeling in Denver and had told her all about it. "I did," Alice said, turning her head from one side to the other like she'd seen so many models do on TV. "Mostly print ads for Khol's Department Store."

"You should think about modeling in L.A.; you're fabulous."

"Thank you," she said, sweetly.

All right, Blake thought. Enough of this; she is a cold-blooded killer after all, don't get too cocky. He lowered the camera. "Time for that drink I promised." He traded the Nikon for the bottle of Cakebread. "Would you get the glasses while I open the wine?" He pointed to a row of wine glasses hanging above the bar in the den.

"Sure," she said, turning for the bar.

As soon as her back was turned, Blake swung the bottle.

Alice sensed the movement, started to turn but too late, the bottle whacked into the back of her skull. Her head snapped back and she went down.

Blake looked down at the unconscious woman at his feet. He'd done it!

Now the fun would begin.

THIRTY-EIGHT

Syd wrote down a name: Blake Hunter.

Could he be the next victim, Syd wondered? It was written on her yellow legal pad beneath six other names: Kris Adams, Jonathan Battle, Edward Bartowski, John Crystal, Ted Dearborn, and James Eagleton.

Syd was alone in the bullpen, comparing the names in the address books of Colin Wood and Adam Devlin, and had found seven matches through the first five letters of the alphabet. And all seven names were also listed in the yearbook. A notation in Colin Wood's appointment book explained it; they'd had a ten-year high school reunion last year. So they gotten together with all their old friends and exchanged numbers.

Syd was sure the names of other potential victims were on that list, but the way it was going, there were going to be twenty or thirty names on the list before she finished. Far more names than she'd expected, which disappointed her. She was hoping the combination of the two address books and yearbook would point her at just one or two people. But even twenty or thirty names did help narrow their focus and at this point, every little bit helped.

Syd leaned back in her chair and stretched. She was stiff. She hadn't been to the gym or dojo in almost a week. She depended on her workouts, not only to stay fit, but also to help throttle back her stress. And she could feel her anxiety level building. Not the case so much; Syd was confident they were close to finding the Lady in Red. It was Ryan. Well, Ryan and Anne to be more precise. Syd could live with Ryan taking the Lotto money; she didn't agree with it but she understood the money's irresistible appeal. Hell, there was a fresh stack of messages piled on

Ryan's desk from friends, relatives and complete strangers hitting him up for some of that precious money.

Anne was another story. She was truly dangerous.

Syd's cell phone rang. She answered. "Syd Curtis."

"It's Alex Cortez from Newport Beach."

"Hey, how you doing, Detective?"

"A little frustrated to be honest. I've come up empty on Colin Wood's dad. His office says he is in seclusion due to the death of his son. I stopped by his house and he's either not there or refusing to come to the door. Short of getting a warrant and breaking down the door, I'm not sure what else we can do."

Something didn't feel right. "What kind of man won't help the police find his son's killer?" asked Syd.

"One who can't deal with his feelings," Cortez said, not convinced. "Or has something to hide."

"Yeah, my spidey sense is tingling, too."

"I do have some good news, though," Cortez said. "I showed the surveillance photo of the Lady in Red to Zachary Stone's assistant, and she positively ID'd her as the woman who met him."

"Great. And we've had some other interesting developments." She brought him up to date on the interview with Emily Devlin and the yearbook discovery. "I should have twenty names or so by morning. So far, half the numbers I've found have OC area codes, so we could use your help contacting them."

"You mean warning them, don't you?"

"And then some. Something happened in high school, I'm sure of it, some kind of brutal humiliation or gang rape, something horrible enough for a woman to kill and mutilate her attackers years later. So if any of the guys we go see were involved, they may lie about it. I think we should do a lot more than just warn these guys, we should interrogate them."

"Good point."

"I'll finish some time tonight and email you a list of the OC names. But here are two to get you started tonight." Syd grabbed her list. "Blake Hunter, oh, wait, no, he lives in Malibu. Here, Jonathan Battle and John Crystal." She told him the phone numbers.

"Thanks, Detective. I'll let you know what I find. And hey, I hope we can all actually meet face to face one of these days."

"Oh, we'll meet," Syd said. "At the Lady in Red's trial."

Cortez laughed. "I like the way you think. Have a good night."

"Yeah, you, too," Syd said and hung up.

At the Lady in Red's trial, Syd thought. They were going to catch her, Syd was more certain of that than ever before. But she wondered if they should be in such a hurry. As she just told Cortez, something dreadful went down eleven years ago. These guys must have done terrible things to the Lady in Red. Syd didn't know why she waited so long to seek her revenge, but she understood, firsthand, the Lady in Red's *desire* for revenge. Syd, herself, had killed twice.

Syd felt her murders were justified. In court she would probably be acquitted of Ernesto's murder; a self-defense plea would certainly fly. But her stepfather was another story. She planned that one. She intentionally closed that garage door knowing the fumes would kill him, clearly pre-meditated murder.

And the thing was, Syd had no regrets. Given the chance, she would kill them both again.

Syd was sure that the Lady in Red felt the same way. Her murders are totally justified in her mind. The Lady in Red must know she's going to get caught and has decided that revenge is worth any incarceration or execution.

And here was the irony; these boys broke the law when they attacked her in high school, but didn't get punished. And now, because of *their* crime, the innocent victim has become a serial killer. Yeah, yeah, Syd knew that two wrongs don't make a right; but she also knew that sometimes revenge sure makes you feel better.

She glanced at the clock, seven-fifteen; almost time for Ryan's dinner meeting with Anne at the Beverly Hilton.

And that meant it was time for Syd to take a break. Syd would get back to the appointment books later, but first, a little surveillance.

On Ryan and Anne.

Ryan would freak if he found out, Syd knew. But hey, a girl's got to protect herself, doesn't she?

THIRTY-NINE

Alice woke up with a start. And then she panicked. She was blind. Something was stuffed in her mouth, her hands were tied behind her and her feet were bound. She tried to scream, kicked her feet, fought to free her hands.

"Take it easy, Alice, you're going to hurt yourself," a voice said. Blake's voice. And he called her Alice. Shit, she thought, he knows who I am.

He did indeed. Blake had dragged Alice into his office after knocking her out, and then grabbed a pair of handcuffs from his bedroom. Fur-lined, of course, and usually used for Blake's kinkier call girls, but the handcuffs were real so he pulled Alice's arms behind her back, snapped the cuffs snuggly around her wrists and slipped the key into his pocket. He used rope from his bedroom to bind her ankles. The rope had been used to bind feet before, but usually to his bedpost.

And to Blake's surprise, the whole thing was turning him on. "Freak," he mumbled to himself, laughing at his own perversions.

He finished off by gagging her with a washcloth held in place with a bandana then slipped her head inside a cloth, eco-friendly grocery bag from Whole Foods.

She was out for a long time. At first Blake was grateful as he used the time to find the infamous video in one of the storage boxes stacked in his office closet and set up his video camera. After fifteen minutes, she was still unconscious and he began to worry that he'd hit her too hard. He actually put his hand on her chest to check her breathing, and once he determined it was slow but steady, he copped a quick feel of her tits. Very nice.

She finally woke up a few minutes later kicking and screaming into her gag. After he calmed her down, he pulled the sack off her head. He expected her eyes to be wild with fear, but instead they burned with a fierce hatred as she continued to curse at him through the gag.

"Whoa, throttle back the venom, dude," Blake said. "I'll take the gag off if you promise not to scream. No one can hear you anyway, so chill, Alice. And if you're nice, I've got a surprise for you."

But Alice wasn't done venting yet. In an incomprehensible rant into her gag, she bitched him out then called herself a fucking idiot for letting him get the drop on her. Finally, she leaned back against the wall, her vitriol spent.

"Feel better?"

He could clearly make out the half-hearted, but still muffled, "Fuck you."

Then Alice took in her surroundings. She was on the floor of an office placed in front of a big screen TV. There was also a video camera pointed at her. What the hell?

"You're wondering what I've got up my sleeve, aren't you? Well, promise not to scream, I'll take your gag off and we can talk about it."

Alice realized yelling wasn't going to get her anywhere so she nodded. Blake untied the bandana and removed the washcloth. "My head hurts," she said.

"I'm not surprised, you've got a lump the size of a softball on your scalp."

"Asshole." She didn't yell, just a quiet statement of fact. Then she asked, "What'd you hit me with?"

"The bottle of wine."

"Prick."

"Wait a minute, you came here to kill me, right? A man's got a right to self-defense."

"Cocksucker."

"Funny you should say that," Blake said. "Because I've got a tape here of someone sucking cock, but it's not me, Alice, it's you." Blake hit a remote control and the video began to play.

A hand held camera sweeps across Colin Wood's

game room and comes to rest on an unconscious Alice Waterman. Adam and Colin kneel next to her. "Fuck, that shit works fast," Colin says. "Help me get her on the pool table, Adam."

They pick her off the floor and lay her on the pool table. Colin holds her neck but he lets go too soon and her head thuds on the table.

"Careful," Adam says, looking very uncomfortable. He looks directly into the lens. "You sure taping this is a good idea, Blake?"

"It's a brilliant idea, bro. When we're old and gray and snorting Viagra, we're going to cherish the chance to relive our glory days."

Blake froze the image and looked at Alice. "How much of that night do you remember?"

Alice stared at the screen. At last. The tape. Answers.

"How much?" Blake repeated.

Alice knew she'd have to pretend to cooperate to see the tape, so she said, "After I passed out, nothing. Did you record everything that happened to me that night?"

"Yes."

The Lady in Red turned back to the frozen image. "Let me see it. I want to know."

Blake went over to the video camera aimed at Alice and turned it on.

Alice eyed the camera suspiciously. "What're you doing?"

"How would you like a chance to tell the whole world why you murdered Colin Wood, Adam Devlin and Zachary Stone? How would you like the whole world to watch your reaction as you watch your own rape?"

"But you're on that tape. You'd be implicating yourself."

"Actually, there is a ten year statute of limitations on rape in California. Our… party was shot *eleven* years ago. So while this tape confirms I was a sleazebag in high school, I won't be putting myself into any legal jeopardy."

"You want to tape me watching myself get raped?

You are one sick fuck."

"No argument there, Alice. But I'm also a filmmaker, and we've got a chance here for a mind-blowing documentary. Wouldn't you like a chance to set the record straight, tell the world in your own words why you decided to kill those men. *Show* the world what happened to you eleven years ago."

Yes, she thought. "What happens after I watch the tape?"

"I interview you. You walk us through each murder, the more detail the better."

"And then?"

Blake shrugged. "I call the cops."

"Kind of sucks for me."

"I can't let you go, Alice. You're a murderer. Hell, you came here to kill me, right?"

She nodded.

"And if I let you go, you'll try again."

"I see your point," she said.

"So, do we have a deal?"

Alice pretended to think about it. She didn't mind him turning her over to the police. Getting arrested had always been her plan, but only after killing all *four* of the bastards. So she needed time to figure a way out of the handcuffs. And, more than anything, she wanted to see that video.

She looked at Blake watching her expectantly. God he looked desperate. She milked the suspense for a few more seconds and then said, "Okay, you scumbag. Deal."

What a fucking coup! This film was going to resurrect his movie career. Blake could hardly contain his glee. He hit Play on the remote.

FORTY

Detective Syd Curtis was one interesting woman, Travis Taylor decided. The private detective sat in his Century City office surrounded by an array of computers screens linking him to mainframes and databases across the planet. But even in the wired age, good old fashion police work and instincts were needed to crack a case. And that meant personal relationships with people who had personal relationships with people who had personal relationships with people. And it was *that* network, the human network that had helped Travis crack open Syd Curtis.

And his investigation only confirmed an old axiom he believed in, you *never* know what you're going to find.

He'd started with the Department of Motor Vehicles. The only real paper trail he had. When you apply for a driver's license you are required to provide proof of a birth date and social security number and, if you have a valid driver's license from another state, the driving portion of the test can be waived.

Travis spent the last two years of his FBI career on loan to Homeland Security and he spent a lot of time interfacing with DMVs all across the country. Valid driver's licenses were prized possessions for illegal aliens and potential terrorists so tough new measures were instituted to make the licenses themselves much harder to forge.

And he became quite friendly with Deputy Director Warren Welch of the California Department of Transportation. He called Warren who called his friend, Joyce, who called her sister-in-law, Bella, and got Syd's application file pulled. Elapsed time from Travis's first call to Warren's call back with the goods, eighteen minutes.

Syd Curtis's Social Security Number was 492-43-

7490. The number alone told Travis something. The first three numbers of a Social Security Number are determined by the ZIP code of the mailing address of the application. And these three numbers, 492, indicated a Missouri address. That was confirmed by the birth certificate, issued by Truman Medical Center in Kansas City, Missouri. The birth certificate listed the birth mother as Amanda Curtis and the father as Todd Curtis.

The date of birth matched her LAPD application. But on the application she's claimed to be from Riverside, California. Now it was certainly possible that she was born in Kansas City and her parents moved to Riverside, but since she lied about attending Arlington High School, there was a good chance she'd never moved at all.

Judging by her age, Travis figured Syd had to be in high school ten to fifteen years ago. Syd was a very uncommon name so he was hoping to get lucky. He accessed the Kansas City School District database and searched for Syd Curtis. There were three students named Syd Curtis in the district but two were male. The only female, Syd Curtis, attended Lincoln High School but dropped out her junior year.

Her home address was 1876 Tracy Avenue. He checked the tax records. The property was owned in joint tenancy by Amanda and Jay Stevens, M.D.

A wrinkle. The last name was Stevens, not Curtis. If the mother divorced and remarried, that would explain the different last name, or there was a chance the Curtis family moved. Maybe they moved Syd's junior year, which would mean she actually transferred, not dropped out.

Travis logged into the Missouri Vital Records marriage certificate database for the name Jay Stevens in Kansas City. Travis had to set broad parameters; Syd's mother could have remarried as early as the year Syd was born until last year. That's twenty-seven years and he was afraid he'd get too many hits. But only thirty matches came up and it took Travis less than a minute to find the only Jay Stevens that married an Amanda Curtis. They were married on June 3, 1986.

So the Stevens still lived in the same house. Good.

Next Travis Googled Jay Stevens + Kansas City, Missouri. There were a few hits about a boy named Jay Stevens who was the star of his little league team, but then a slew of hits from the *Kansas City Star* about Dr. Jay Stevens. More specifically about his tragic death when he fell asleep in his car after closing the garage door, but left the engine running.

The police ruled the death an accident. Dr. Stevens was an emergency room physician and kept very long hours. His tearful wife told officers it wasn't the first time he'd fallen asleep in the garage, but it was the first time he'd forgotten to turn off the car.

Travis found the date of the accident,

The same year Syd dropped out of school.

Interesting.

On a hunch Travis ran Syd Curtis's name through the National Center for Missing and Exploited Children website and got a hit. Syd Curtis was reported missing by her mother, Amanda, on February 18, 2001. There was also a picture of a cute sixteen-year-old red head, undoubtedly Syd Curtis.

So Travis had a few questions. Syd left home just one week after her stepfather died. Why?

Syd Curtis is alive and well in Los Angeles but is *still* listed as missing on the database. Why?

Does Syd's mother even know she's alive? And if not, why?

One way to find out, Travis thought. He used the FBI's Reverse Directory to input 1876 Tracy Avenue and get the home's phone number. He dialed, heard the ring, then a tentative, "Hello?"

"Yes, hello, my name is Don Wofford, I'm a writer for the *Kansas City Star* and I'm doing a Sunday feature on runaway kids." Travis decided it wasn't his place to tell Amanda Stevens that her daughter was alive. At least, not yet. And he replaced his natural Texas twang with a flat Midwestern accent.

There was a long pause, then, "And why, exactly,

would you be calling me?" She pronounced her words very carefully but Travis could tell she'd been drinking.

"I'll be honest with you, Mrs. Stevens. I was in school with Syd, and we were friends. I remember that terrible accident, when Dr. Stevens was killed, and I remember how upset Syd was. A bunch of us tried to be there for her, but I guess we let her down, because just a few days later..." He trailed off, letting her fill in the obvious blanks. "Did you ever hear from her, Mrs. Stevens? Do you know where she is now?"

A long pause, Travis was afraid she'd hang up, but then, finally he heard, "No." Amanda Stevens' voice was brittle, she was fighting back tears. "I never heard from Syd. To be honest, I wasn't that worried at first; I was sure she'd get scared or run out of money and come running home. Every time the phone rang, I was sure it would be Syd. But the days stretched to weeks, then months, then... Did anyone at school ever hear from her? A phone call, an email?"

"No ma'am. It was like she dropped off the face of the earth."

"I think about her all the time, you know. Wondering how she is. What she looks like. Praying that she's even alive." The tears were flowing now. "If God would just give me a second chance with Syd, I would do things so differently."

She blames herself, Travis thought. Interesting. "That's actually the point of my piece," Travis said. "How parents handle the child's disappearance. How much blame the parents place on themselves; what, if anything, they think they could have done to keep their child home."

"I could have listened more," Amanda Stevens said. "I could have chosen better."

"Chosen better, I don't understand."

"My husband was a... demanding man. He was an emergency room doctor, under enormous stress, kept terrible hours. Syd's real father deserted us and it was real hard on Syd and me until Dr. Jay came along. Real hard." Travis could hear ice rattle as she took a drink of something. "I couldn't risk losing Jay. No matter what..." she trailed off, leaving the phrase unfinished. Then she hurriedly added, "It was best for both of us."

But the unfinished phrase stuck with Travis. No matter what...

No matter what he did to her, Travis wondered. Travis knew better than to come right out and ask, so he tread carefully. "So you chose Jay over Syd?"

A long silent pause then, "Yes." And then the dam broke. Amanda Stevens was sobbing now, years of guilt and shame pouring out of her. "She tried to tell me, but I wouldn't listen. Couldn't *afford* to listen. You understand that, don't you? If Jay had gone to jail, what would we have done?"

And then Travis knew. The stepfather was abusing Syd. He'd heard different versions of the same story so many heartbreaking times before. Abused by one parent, betrayed by the other, the only choice the child sees is escape. Some place different, any place different, no matter what the risk.

There was nothing more Travis needed from Amanda Stevens at the moment so he thanked her for her time and promised to let her know when the article would run.

Part one of the Syd Curtis mystery was solved. Syd ran away from home when she was seventeen years old and ended up in Los Angeles. Now most kids with the same resume end up on the streets or doing porn, drug addicted and all too often, dead.

But Syd Curtis ended up a cop. How did that happen?

The only lead Travis had was the woman Syd was living with when she applied to the Police Academy, Andrea Templeton. How did Syd and Andrea meet?

Travis went online and Googled Andrea Templeton. He wanted to review the articles written about Andrea after her death. And he found a clue in a *Daily News* piece about Iraq war vets killed on the streets of Los Angeles after surviving war in the Middle East. It mentioned that a brother and sister, both Iraq vets, were killed three years apart. Amanda Templeton, a cop, shot in the line of duty.

And her brother, Eric, a paramedic, killed in a drug deal gone bad.

Interesting. So Travis Googled Eric Templeton, and found three pages of articles on Eric's murder. Templeton was stationed at Fire Station 82 in Hollywood, and lived in an apartment nearby. He was found stabbed to death in that apartment along with another man, Ernesto Sian, who had been shot once through the head. No weapons were found in the apartment. The articles described Sian as a known pimp who had two prior arrests but no convictions. Eric Templeton had no police record. And as far as Travis could tell from the articles, no one was ever arrested for the crime.

Something didn't sound right. What was Eric Templeton doing in the same room with a scumbag like Ernesto Sian?

So Travis called a friend of his, LAPD Deputy Chief Randy Tuttle. Tuttle worked Vice for a decade before moving up to head Robbery Homicide. Travis asked him if he remembered a pimp named Ernesto Sian.

"Sure, he ran a string of young girls out of Hollywood about ten years ago. Used to pick them up at the bus station, get them hooked and put them on the street."

"You remember anything about his murder?"

"He was murdered?"

Travis laughed. "Guess that's a no."

"I could pull the file, take a look if you like."

Travis told him he wasn't sure it was necessary at this point, but would get back to Randy if he needed more help.

Travis didn't believe in coincidences. And Andrea Templeton's brother being found dead in the same room with a pimp who preyed on runaways seemed like a big coincidence. Travis went back to the Internet and checked the date of the murders; November 16, 2003. Just over eighteen months after Syd ran away from Kansas City.

Was Ernesto Sian waiting at the bus station the night Syd Curtis arrived? Could this decorated cop have actually been a hooker?

Had Eric Templeton somehow come between Ernesto

Sian and Syd?   Was he a client?   Had he met her professionally?

If Ernesto Sian kept his girls drugged up, Syd could have overdosed.   If an ambulance was called, Eric Templeton could have responded.

Travis looked up the number for Fire Station 82, called them and asked where they take drug overdose victims. They told him St. John's Hospital.

All Travis had to do now was find someone who knew someone at St. John's who would be willing to check the admittance files for the last quarter of 2003.   If Syd Curtis had been brought in by Eric Templeton, he'd found his connection.

Travis glanced at the clock.   Seven-thirty.   Probably too late to follow up tonight; it would have to wait until morning.   In the mean time, he owed his client an update. He picked up his phone and dialed; he was sure Anne would be fascinated by the new revelations about the increasingly mysterious Syd Curtis.   Travis already had discovered enough to get Syd kicked off the police department – lying on your Academy application was cause for immediate dismissal.

But there seemed to be much more; Syd was a runaway, possibly a hooker and corpses littered her past.

Just the kind of dirt Anne was hoping for.

FORTY-ONE

Anne heard her phone vibrating in her purse but decided to ignore it. Ryan had just walked in and she didn't want to give him the impression that anyone or anything was more important than he was.

"Hey, Handsome," she said getting up and hugging him. She kept it businesslike, no genital grind, hopefully that would come later.

"Trader Vic's," Ryan said, sitting down. "I can't believe you picked Trader Vic's. I think I'm *still* hung over from that crazy night."

Trader Vic's was a Polynesian-themed waterhole and restaurant famous for lethal drinks and pupu platters. It was attached to the Beverly Hilton until a few years ago when the hotel relocated and downsized Trader Vic's to a poolside lounge. But the garish decoration remained, as did the delicious but deadly Tiki Bowl, Singapore Symphony and Rum Giggle.

Ten years ago Ryan and Anne came to Trader Vic's to celebrate their engagement. They ordered a Scorpion Bowl, a vicious concoction of rum, fruit juice and brandy, served in a bowl with a flower floating in the middle. The drink is so big it's served with four straws, so a party of four can share it. Ryan and Anne liked it so much they ordered another, and then a third.

By then they had invited everybody in the restaurant to their wedding, led a boisterous rendition of the Macarena, and to cap off the evening, made love in the middle stall of the men's bathroom. Anne's orgasm was so loud that Ryan and Anne got a standing ovation from the crowd as they walked back to their table.

"We had fun, didn't we?" she asked with a naughty

smile.

Actually, the next morning Ryan was completely embarrassed by their behavior. He thought they'd been silly and obnoxious. In fact, he was surprised the other patrons had put up with their nonsense. But over the years Ryan had seen other *we're-so-in-love-we can't-stand-it* couples make complete fools of themselves in restaurants and Ryan now understood what was going through the other patrons' minds: Look how crazy in love those two are, I remember feeling like that, God I *miss* feeling like that.

"We did have tons of fun," Ryan said, smiling warmly at the memory. "But if it's all the same to you, I think I'll stick to beer tonight."

Anne laughed. "Fear not, my Scorpion slurping days are behind me, too." And as if on cue, a waitress arrived with a vodka tonic for her and a Michelob draft for him.

"I hope you don't mind but I already ordered our drinks."

"Not at all, thank you," Ryan said.

"My pleasure." They toasted and drank. Anne was pleased; she'd chosen Trader Vic's not for the drinks but for the memories, and from the wistful look on Ryan's face, it worked.

It more than worked. In fact, Ryan had spent the drive over to the Beverly Hilton convincing himself that he was going to keep his relationship with Anne strictly business. He was in a relationship with Syd. Though he had feelings for Anne, she was the past. Syd was the future. But looking at Anne now, remembering those heady days, his resolve was melting. Could you be in love with two women at the same time, he wondered.

And then he found himself wondering what it would be like to kiss Anne again.

Stop it! You're here for business he scolded himself. "So," Ryan said. "I don't have a lot of time; anything I need to know before the big presentation tomorrow?"

Like a fly fisherman stalking a wily bass, Anne felt Ryan slip the hook. No matter, she knew time was on her side. "Okay, first things first; how much of the thirty-four million do you want to put in the foundation?"

"Funny you should mention that," Ryan said. "When I first agreed to take the money, I thought I'd put all the money in the foundation. But the more I think about it, the more I think I should keep some of it for myself."

"I agree completely," Anne said. We're going to need a few million to live on, she thought. But she said, "Once the money is in the foundation, you won't be able to use if for personal use. So if you put, say, half the money in the foundation to get it going – seventeen million dollars is an incredibly generous initial donation by the way – and kept seventeen million for yourself, that would enable you to take time to assess your personal needs, and if you decide you want to donate more to the foundation later, you can."

Seventeen million was a lot more than Ryan had considered keeping. But Anne was right; he could always donate more later. "Tell you what," Ryan said. "Let's start with a twenty-million-dollar donation; it just sounds better, you know, giving away more than half. That still leaves fourteen million for me, but I'm sure I'll donate most of it to the foundation later."

Not if I have anything to say about it, Anne thought. But she said, "Excellent idea. And the press will eat it up." She dropped her voice imitating a newscaster, "Cop donates tens of millions to charity."

"I'm really not comfortable with the media," Ryan said. "They're not exactly a detective's best friend."

"But they'll be the foundation's best friend. The more people who know about the foundation, the more people you'll be able to help."

Ryan was very uncomfortable with his face all over TV, magazines and newspapers. A natural modesty was one reason, but there was also a nagging concern about the tow truck driver. He could see Ryan on TV, remember him, remember losing his own Lotto ticket and realize the money is really his.

It's still not too late, Ryan thought. Once he took the money, he'd committed fraud. For the rest of his life he'd feel guilty about it. For the rest of his life he'd be worried about a phone call from the tow truck driver.

Anne saw the sudden concern wrinkle Ryan's forehead. She knew what that meant; he was worried about something, and for a righteous man like Ryan it could only be one thing. "Stop it," she said.

"Stop what?"

"Stop over-thinking it, Ryan. You're worried about the tow truck driver, aren't you?"

Ryan nodded.

"First of all, he probably doesn't even remember buying the damn ticket much less losing it. Second of all, even if he did, there is no way he would have remembered you. You were standing in line behind him. Third of all, even if he did remember you, he didn't see you pick up his ticket, because if he had, he would have asked you to give it back. And finally, there is no way he could know whether you bought your own Lotto ticket. He can't *prove* anything. He has absolutely no legal standing. Plus, remember, if you don't take the money, *nobody* gets it. You're going to do wonderful things with this money, Ryan. So, relax. Enjoy Fate's fickle finger."

Anne's words soothed Ryan. "I always knew you'd make a great lawyer."

Anne reached across the table taking Ryan's hand. "Reminds me of what you said the first time you kissed me? Remember?"

He smiled, remembering. "I do. I said, 'I always knew you'd be a great kisser.'"

Anne suddenly leaned across the table and kissed Ryan; a sweet, tender kiss, short but full of promise. "I've been wanting to do that since I saw you yesterday," she said, hovering, her lips inches from his, waiting for him to make the next move.

"That bitch!" Syd said. She was watching them through a pair of binoculars from one of the hotel's pool-facing rooms. She couldn't hear what they were saying, of course; there'd been no way for her to plant a bug with such short notice. But she didn't need sound to see what was going on. That bitch had kissed Ryan, whispered something to him and was now waiting for Ryan to kiss her back. "Don't do it, Ryan," she said to the empty room.

Syd had called her friend, Kevin Osaka, who was the Hilton's head of security. Syd had led an undercover sting at the Hilton when she worked vice. A string of hookers were using the Lobby Bar as a feeding pool and while the well-heeled male executives staying at the hotel appreciated the convenience of free cable, wireless internet and plentiful hookers, the many female executives staying in the hotel found the ladies of the night degrading. Or unfair competition. Either way the hotel management had to do something about it so the LAPD was happy to oblige. Kevin and Syd formed a friendship and when she called him a half hour ago asking for a room with a view of the Trader Vic's lounge, he hooked Syd up, no questions asked.

Syd wasn't surprised Anne was trying to seduce Ryan. It's what Liz predicted, and from Syd's limited exposure to Anne, what she expected.

This was the ultimate test, Syd realized. She'll finally find out if Ryan really loved her. She had her concerns. From the beginning of their relationship Syd had been the aggressor. She'd jumped him in the file room. She was the first one to say I love you. It took Ryan another two weeks before he said those magic three words, two weeks filled with Syd saying "I love you" followed by expectant gazes. In a way she felt she guilted him into it. A feeling reinforced when Liz told her that Ryan had trouble committing to relationships after Anne left him.

So, let's find out where we really stand, Syd thought. Okay, Ryan, your move.

Ryan's lips tingled. His heart raced, his dick was rock hard. Jesus God he wanted to kiss Anne. He wanted to ravage Anne. Her skin was so soft, her scent intoxicating. A montage of images from the hundreds of times they made love flooded his brain: fingers, feet, lips, the nape of her neck, the sweet taste of her clitoris, her deep-throated orgasms, the massage of a million small kisses, his explosive orgasms.

Ryan's eyes went from Anne's big brown eyes to her full, luscious lips. For years Ryan had wondered what he had done wrong. What had he done to lose Anne? He relived countless conversations looking for a clue. And he spent hours dreaming of a way he could win her back. He'd finally given up, feeling silly and juvenile.

But deep down he'd always hoped for a moment just like this, another chance to kiss her, another chance to make love to her, another chance to win her back.

And here it was.

And though a fleeting image of Syd seared his conscious, the biological beast that rules the subconscious blotted it out. After all, it's just one kiss. That can hardly be classified as a betrayal.

Just one kiss.

Ryan leaned forward, their lips met, and then their tongues. And she tasted just as good as he remembered.

"Oh, Ryan," Syd sighed. Syd lowered the binoculars, heartbroken. Syd knew that her world had just tilted; she didn't know what she was going to do about it.

Her cell phone rang. She answered. "Hello."

"Alex Cortez, here, Syd, how you doing?"

"Fine, Detective," Syd said, and her own problems vanished as she heard the excitement in his voice. "You're calling me with good news, aren't you?"

"Does the name, Alice Waterman, mean anything to you?"

Syd ran it through her mental database. "No."

"Jonathan Battle, one of the names you gave me, was very helpful. He remembered this incident in high school, pictures of one of their classmates emailed to hell and back. The girl was naked making love to a couple of guys. You could only see her face, the men's faces were never visible, but Battle had heard rumors, rumors that Colin Wood was one of the guys involved."

"And Adam Devlin? Were they both involved?"

"He couldn't remember. But he didn't think so."

"And Alice Waterman was the girl."

"Yep. Battle said she dropped out of school a few weeks after the incident, doesn't know what happened to her. I ran her name but she's not in our system. But I found out her parents still live in Santa Ana."

Syd had stuffed all her notes on the case into her backpack and brought it with her. She dug out the yearbook, found Alice Waterman's picture. "I'm looking at Alice Waterman's high school picture, Alex, and I've got to tell you, this girl looks nothing like the Lady in Red."

"People change," Alex said.

"Maybe," Syd said her excitement waning. But a lead was a lead, and Syd would run with it. "Good work, Alex. You got their address?"

"8276 Bella Vista. I can meet you if you like, but my little one's got her dance recital tonight and I promised I'd be there."

"No problem. My partner and I can handle it. I'll call you with a full report."

"Thanks, Syd. Good luck." Cortez hung up.

My partner, Syd said to herself. My backstabbing, bitch-kissing partner. She picked up the binoculars and looked, they weren't kissing anymore, they were talking again.

"Okay, that was a mistake," Ryan said. It's not what he felt, however; he felt like he wanted to kiss her again. Right here. Right now. But that would be wrong for so many reasons. "Look," he said. "I haven't been completely honest with you; I'm in a relationship."

"Really," Anne said, doing her best to seem genuinely surprised. "Who's the lucky girl?"

Ryan had never publically revealed their relationship to anyone, but since Anne was going to be around a lot now, he knew she'd figure it out sooner or later. "Syd," he said. "My partner."

"She's adorable," Anne said. "And a very lucky girl.

How serious are you? I mean, are you guys talking about getting married?"

"Way too early for that, I think, but I guess you could say we're pretty serious."

So am I, Anne thought, and your little redhead doesn't stand a chance. Time to wreak a little havoc. "That's wonderful, Ryan. I just hope your sudden wealth doesn't ruin the relationship."

"Why would the lottery affect the relationship?"

"Does she know about the tow truck driver?"

Ryan's expression went from confusion to understanding. "Yes. And frankly, she's not crazy about my taking the money."

"Wait a minute. She actually wants you to turn down the Lotto?"

He nodded. "She thinks it's dishonest to take the money."

"Even though you plan on giving most of it away?"

Ryan shrugged. "She's got high standards."

"So do I," Anne said. "And my standards demand we take that money and use it help scores of people in need."

"No need to get defensive, Anne. I agree with you. I'm taking the money."

"Sorry, I just have so little patience with… misplaced righteousness."

"She means well."

Time to sow a few seeds of doubt, Anne thought. "And she's not going to get angry every time you use some of the money for yourself? A new house? New car? A vacation for the two of you? She's not going to remind you the money you're spending isn't really yours?"

She may not say anything, Ryan thought. But there would certainly be that knowing look in her eye. "I don't know. I guess we'll have to wait and see."

"You know what, I'm sure it'll be fine," Anne said. "Syd seems like a lovely, reasonable girl." Okay, Anne thought. Time to move on the next part of her plan. She opened her briefcase. "You said you didn't have much time, so let's get down to business. I just have a couple of things for you to sign tonight." Her hands searched the inside of the briefcase and then she looked up, apologetic. "Shit, I must've left them in my room. You mind coming upstairs with me? It'll just take you a second to sign the papers and then you can be on your way."

Ryan looked at Anne with playful skepticism. "You just happened to leave them in your room? You sure this isn't a trick to get me in your room, ply me with alcohol and seduce me?"

You bet your ass it is, Anne thought. "No, not at all. Look, if you'd rather wait here, I'll bring them down." She quickly got to her feet. "I'll be right back."

"No, don't be silly," Ryan said. He got up, dropped twenty on the table for the drinks. "I'll come with you."

"Great. And no funny stuff, I promise."

"Deal."

So far so good, Anne thought as she slipped her purse over her shoulder. Now for the fun part. "The elevator's this way," she said and led Ryan out of the lounge.

Syd watched Ryan and Anne walk toward the bank of elevators. He's going up to her room, she realized. She'd lost him.

Syd considered calling Ryan, telling him about Alice Waterman. That would be one way to get him out of Anne's room. Ryan would certainly want to be in on the parents' interview.

But fuck him. He wants to sleep with his ex-wife, let him. Syd would handle it alone.

Syd collected her things, and with one last look through the binoculars at the man she loved, Syd left.

FORTY-TWO

Alice stared at the TV screen stunned. After all the years of wondering what exactly happened to her that night, now she knew. The blanks were filled in, and now that she'd witnessed the horror firsthand, it was so much worse than she'd ever imagined.

She'd been disgusted watching the three men rape her. But she expected that. What she hadn't expected was the fourth man, the man who appeared at the end of the video. And that changed everything. Because now one more man had to die.

But first she had to deal with Blake.

"So," Blake said. "Feel like talking about what you've just seen? Want to tell the world your side of the story?"

"Sure. But I'd like some water first."

Alice wasn't actually thirsty. But to get to the kitchen Blake had to pass in front of her. And maybe, just maybe...

"Water? Sure. Or maybe wine, it might help you relax. I've still got that bottle of Chardonnay."

"No thanks, lately I found white wine gives me a headache."

He looked at her, surprised at her wit. "You know, you're very hot when you're funny."

"Fuck you."

"That's more like it." Blake stepped out from behind his desk and headed for the kitchen. As he passed Alice, she kicked her feet into the back of his legs knocking his feet out from under him. He hit the ground with a thud. Alice rolled over, dragging her feet toward his face.

"Bitch," he mumbled and started to get up.

She kicked him in the face. His head bounced off her

feet and into the wall. WHAP!

"Cunt."

She kicked again and again and again. WHAP. WHAP. WHAP. His head bounced off the wall as blood erupted from his nose, his forehead and an eyebrow.

He was unconscious. Alice crawled over him and flipped onto her back. Since her hands were cuffed behind her back she had to fish blindly in his pockets for the handcuff keys. If he even had them in his pocket.

She came up empty in his front left pocket, but struck gold in his right front pocket. She twisted the fingers of her right hand trying to find the opening for the lock on her left handcuff. It was awkward, and painful, but finally the key slipped into the lock. She turned the key and the handcuff fell away.

Oh, thank God, she thought. She unlocked the right handcuff and tossed them across the room. Then she quickly untied her feet.

Blake was starting to stir. She thought about kicking him again, but the overwhelming desire to get her gun won out and she bolted into the living room to get her purse. She dug inside for the gun but couldn't find it. She yanked open the mouth of her purse, her hands and eyes desperately searching every nook and corner. It wasn't there.

Fuck! She had a terrible feeling about the missing gun but couldn't dwell on it now. She pulled out the only weapon she had left, the scalpel.

CLICK.

An unmistakable sound.

The sound of a gun being cocked.

Behind her.

She turned. Blake, blood pouring from the wounds on his face, stood in the kitchen, aiming the .25 at her.

She cocked her arm to throw the knife.

He fired.

FORTY-THREE

"I'm looking for Alice Waterman."

"Alice, why Alice is my daughter, but she doesn't live here," Betty Waterman said from her doorway.

The drive down to Santa Ana had been tough on Syd. She'd spent the hour and fifteen minutes obsessing on Ryan and Anne, trying to convince herself not to jump to conclusions. Anne had practically forced him to kiss her. And just because he left the lounge with her, didn't mean he was going to jump into bed with her.

Then Syd got pissed at herself for trying to excuse Ryan's behavior. He was just another asshole with a cock attached and she berated herself for thinking Ryan was somehow different.

Finally, she refocused on the case and the looming possibility that she was about to meet the Lady in Red's parents. And that thrilling prospect fueled the last, suddenly-hope-filled miles of her drive. So now, here goes...

"Alice lives in Hollywood," Betty said. "I'm sorry, I'm being rude. Come in, please."

Syd walked in and was hit by a wave of déjà vu. The layout of the house was almost identical to her Mom's house in Overland Park. Small living room with lace curtains draped across a narrow picture window, tiny dining room with red and orange paisley plastic tablecloth connected to the undersized kitchen by a swinging door.

"That hunk of blubber on the couch is my husband, Cliff. Cliff, this is a police Detective, Syd... what was your last name again?"

"Curtis. Syd Curtis." Syd stepped forward, shook Cliff's hand. He actually wasn't a hunk of blubber; he had a bit of a beer belly, but there was a lot of muscle on his body, and steel in his handshake. He had a friendly face, with rosy cheeks and a full head of gray hair.

Betty was thin with reading glasses perched on her slender nose, and shoulder length chestnut brown hair. "She wants to talk to us about Alice."

A frown creased Cliff's face as he indicated for Syd to sit in one of the chairs. Cliff and Betty sat across from her on the couch. "What'd she do now?"

"Well, to be honest I'm not sure she's done anything. I'd like to show you a picture." Syd had brought her backpack into the house; she fished out the surveillance picture of the Lady in Red. She handed it to Betty. "Do you recognize this woman?"

Betty and Cliff looked at the photo. "It's not a very good picture but that's her, all right," Cliff said, disapprovingly. "The new improved version, she calls it. Me, I think she looks like a slut."

"Cliff!" Betty said.

"You don't like it either, admit it."

"No, but I'm not going to call my daughter a slut."

Cliff looked like he was about to say something else, then his eyes cut to Syd, and he thought better of it and shut up.

"Have you seen the news today?" Syd asked.

"I never watch the news. It's all way too depressing for my taste. Cliff watches the news sometimes, though."

A light bulb seemed to go off in Cliff's head. He took the picture from his wife, looked at it. "Oh, no... Is this that surveillance photo from TV? The Lady in Red, that's what they called her, she's killing people, right?"

"That's right," Syd said

"Dear God," Betty said. "But I thought she was finally getting better. That the new therapy was working."

Hallelujah, thought Syd. Now for some answers. "I know something happened to Alice in high school, something involving Colin Wood and Adam Devlin, both killed by the Lady in Red. And I know there was some kind of financial settlement handled by Zachary Stone. He also killed by the Lady in Red. What I don't know is what happened. Could you tell me, please?"

Cliff's face hardened at the memory and he leaned back on the couch, his body language shutting down. Tears ran down Betty's face now and she turned away from Syd.

"I'm not here to judge," Syd said. "For Alice to act the way she has after so many years is a testament to the horrible things that must have been done to her. I'm just trying to understand why she is doing what she is doing."

Betty reached across her husband for the box of tissues. She wiped her eyes, blew her nose. Then her eyes met Syd's. "Do you have children, Detective?"

"No."

"There is no greater joy, or burden."

"We got little of the former and a more than our share of the latter," Cliff said.

Betty ignored her husband with practiced ease. "Alice was such a delightful child. We didn't have much money when she was growing up, but we spent a lot of family time together. Cliff always wanted a son so Alice was raised a tomboy; she loved sports and they would go hunting together every fall. And she was smart. She got into Camden Hall on a full scholarship. We'd talk about how one day she'd go to an Ivy League college and make a name for herself in corporate America. She promised us a ride on her first corporate jet.

"But things started to change when she turned fourteen. Boys suddenly became very important to her and Alice became very critical of her own looks. To be honest, Alice took a while to get pretty. She was a bit heavy, a little awkward and just didn't seem to fit in."

"This country's obsession with looks and sex is disgusting," Cliff said. "You want to blame someone for all this, blame Britney Spears, blame Paris Hilton, blame Lindsey Lohan. Blame all those bubble-headed, big-boobed, empty-headed teen queens on the cover of all the magazines and flaunting their skinny asses on TV. How's a normal girl supposed to compete with that?"

"Alice and I are about the same age," Syd said. "And I

know the feeling. I grew up in suburb of Kansas City but was nuked by the culture bomb, too."

"Alice used sex," Betty said. "That's how she competed. I didn't know at the time, but later she told me."

"Do we have to talk about this?" Cliff asked, clearly uncomfortable with the conversation.

"The more I know, the better chance I have of helping her," Syd said.

"You mean catching her, don't you," Cliff said. "You want to catch Alice and put her in jail."

"She's killed three men already; I'm trying to stop her before she kills anyone else."

"Even if they deserved to die?" Cliff asked.

I've been asking myself that same question, Syd thought. But gave the answer she was trained to give. "That's for a jury to decide. She's also in danger. She could be hurt or killed. The sooner I catch her, the safer she'll be."

Cliff didn't like it but he settled back in the couch, a scowl on his face.

Betty Waterman took that as permission to speak, and she did. "When Alice was fourteen, she discovered that giving boys sexual favors made her more popular. And if a boy paid attention to her, she flew to cloud nine, but the slightest inattention would send her spiraling down. In hindsight it was so clearly manic-depressive behavior, but kids act out, right? We now know she was sick, bi-polar the doctors say, but who imagines their little girl is mentally ill."

"I did," Cliff Waterman said. "I used to say there had to be something wrong with her, that she was just like your loony sister, but you wouldn't listen."

"Cliff, please." Betty Waterman turned back to Syd. "What Alice didn't realize, of course, was that her sexual behavior gave her a certain reputation and boys started taking advantage of her. They would be nice to her, she would reward them with sex, but once the boys got what they wanted, they'd dump her."

"And she'd go into a depression."

Betty nodded. "Then her senior year of high school she got this huge crush on a boy, Adam Devlin. They'd shared a bus ride on a school trip and he'd been very nice to her. He was very popular and she convinced herself that he'd ask her out and she'd suddenly become one of the popular kids. And then one day he asked her to a party. It was a dream come true for Alice. She went there with such high expectations, but there was no party. Just Adam and a couple of his friends playing pool and drinking."

"*She* was the party," Cliff said.

"That's right," Betty said. "They gave her a drink; it must've been spiked with something because Alice passed out. When she woke up hours later, she was on the pool table, naked. She had pain in her vagina and... well everywhere. And Alice realized they had drugged and had sex with her."

"They drugged and *raped* her," Syd said, anger burning inside her. "Make no mistake Mrs. Waterman, sex without consent is rape."

"But as bad as that was," Betty said, "for Alice, it wasn't the worse part. A couple of days later dirty pictures of Alice were emailed to all the kids at school. You couldn't see the boys' faces, but you could clearly see Alice, naked and having sex."

"And that's when the lawyer showed up," Cliff said. "They were suddenly worried Alice would go to the police and file charges so the lawyer basically threatened us. Take his money or he would ruin Alice's reputation. So we took the money."

"Our single biggest mistake."

"It was not a mistake," Cliff snapped and Syd realized she had stumbled into a well-worn argument. "If we hadn't taken the money, how would we have paid for all those doctors and that damned institute?"

"If we hadn't taken the money she may not have *needed* the doctors and institute." Betty turned back to Syd. "Three days after we agreed to the settlement Alice tried to kill herself."

"And you think humiliating herself in court, having the

world find out what a slut she was would have been better?"

"I didn't then, I do now." Betty's eyes found Syd. "Alice hates us; she thinks we sold her out." Betty turned back to Cliff and added pointedly, "And we did."

Cliff shook his head, defensive, angry and frustrated. "Well, we can't go back in time, so get used to it."

The friendly couple act was just a veneer, there was such obvious rancor between the two that Syd wondered how their marriage had survived. "Tell me about the suicide attempt. What did she do?"

"I had some sleeping pills, I'd have trouble sometimes, and she took them, all of them, a brand new prescription of twenty pills."

"If she hadn't knocked over a lamp when she passed out, we wouldn't have found her until morning," Cliff said. "But when I heard the crash I went upstairs to check on her."

"We put her into therapy immediately, that's when we found out she was bi-polar. They put her on drugs, lithium to stabilize her moods and an antipsychotic, but whenever she was feeling good, she'd stop taking her meds, then she'd get depressed and try to kill herself again. It was more than we could handle, frankly, so the doctors recommended putting her in a full-time facility. The Riverview Institute in Riverside. You know it?"

"No."

"A wonderful hospital."

"Wonderfully expensive," Cliff said. "And, if it was so wonderful, why'd they have to keep her for so many years?"

"She could get violent," Betty said to Syd. "When she got depressed she'd act out and sometimes attack the attendants or other patients. And every time she'd come home the old resentments about our taking the settlement would come up and well..." Betty trailed off, suddenly holding something back.

"Go ahead, tell her," Cliff said. "If Alice is killing people, a little arson won't matter."

"Three years ago she came home. Everything was fine at first, Cliff even got Alice a job at one of the Knott's Berry Farm gift shops."

"I maintain all the rides," Cliff said.

"I even began to daydream about Alice going back to school. She wasn't too old for college, so maybe some of those childhood dreams could still come true. Then Cliff did something really stupid."

"Damn it, Betty, don't say it like that. The car broke down, what was I supposed to do?"

"He bought a new car, a luxury car, a Lexus with all the trimmings."

"I was smart with that settlement money," Cliff said defensively. "I didn't blow it; I invested, carefully. Good thing, too, because Alice's medical expenses are ridiculously expensive. Anyway, my old Dodge was shot; I had hundreds of thousands of dollars in the bank, so why not buy a nice car?"

"Because it was rubbing Alice's face in your betrayal."

"She went with me to pick it out," he said practically throwing the words at Betty. Then, to Syd, "You have to understand that Alice's moods swing wildly. When we went to buy the car, she really enjoyed it. Hell, she even picked out the color, Amber Pearl."

"But at breakfast the next morning she had that look in her eyes – like someone else was inside her head – and she said we paid for the car with blood money."

"I'm sure she was off meds," Cliff said. "Though she swore she took them. She caused trouble at work too, yelling at customers and she got into an argument with her boss."

"She seemed calmer at dinner," Betty said. "But looking back I realized she was too calm. She had a plan."

"That night she doused the inside of the Lexus with lighter fluid and set it on fire," Cliff said. The car was a complete loss, we barely saved the garage and she almost burnt down the house."

"The police were going to prosecute her for arson," Betty said. "But when we explained she was bi-polar and promised to send Alice back to the Institute for treatment, they dropped the charges." Betty reached out and took her husband's hand. A gesture that shocked Syd considering the way these two sniped at each other. "When we brought Alice back to Riverview, she told us she never wanted to see us again. That we were dead to her."

"The doctors told us it might be a good idea for us to not see her for a while," Cliff said. "Being around us was a catalyst for her resentment and rage and we'd become a psychotic trigger."

"We've only seen her a of couple of times in the last three years." Betty said. "She'll call every so often and we get reports from the Institute. And the last report was very encouraging. Over the years they've tried a wide range of drugs and therapies, but just a few months ago they seem to finally find one that stabilized her."

"What was it?" Syd asked.

"The craziest idea I ever heard," Cliff said.

"It was an experiment. The doctors ran it by us first; I had my doubts, but they said it was very successful in a European trial, and we'd tried everything else so…"

"They lied to her," Cliff said. "Told her she had cancer and only a few months to live."

"The idea was to focus her," Betty said. "Give her a reason to apply herself. The risk, of course, was that she'd just give up, but Dr. Samuels 'sensed a stubborn spirit inside Alice,' his words; and felt that with a deadline on her life she might finally focus. If she did, they'd eventually tell her she beat the cancer, another *reinforcer* he called it, and she might finally be on her way to a productive life. And it seemed to be working. Dr. Samuels said it was almost like a light went off. She checked out of the Institute two months ago, she rented an apartment and got a job at the Best Buy in Hollywood. And she let us buy her a car so she could get around. She seemed to be doing so well the doctors said we could visit. So we drove up to Hollywood about a month ago and surprised her."

"Crappy apartment," Cliff said. "I wanted to get her something nicer but she said she was happy."

"The cancer-scare therapy seemed to really be working so we hoped that maybe this time..." Betty trailed off at the obvious reality of the situation. Alice's focus wasn't on getting a job and straightening out her life, it was on seeking revenge.

"What kind of car did you get her?"

"A white Prius," Betty said. "She really cares about the environment."

The irony of someone who cuts off men's cocks caring about global warming wasn't lost on Syd. "You know the license number?"

"Sorry, no."

"Do you know Alice's address and phone number?"

Betty frowned. "I don't remember her apartment address, do you, honey?"

He thought about it. "No, I think I threw it away when we got home. It was near a famous corner, though. Just a couple blocks south of Hollywood and Vine. It was on Vine, though, I remember that."

"How about a phone number?"

Betty looked embarrassed. "She wouldn't give it to us. She said she would call us if she wanted to talk to us."

Syd knew they could canvas the buildings south of Hollywood Boulevard but that would take time. Syd's best bet would be to figure out who Alice's next victim might be and get to him as soon as possible.

Syd asked, "How many boys raped Alice that night?"

"Three," Betty said. "Adam, of course. Colin Wood, it was his father who offered the settlement and the third boy was..." Betty shook her head, unable to remember. "Cliff, do you remember?"

He thought about it and then shook his head. "No, sorry, I don't."

Syd reached inside her backpack and pulled out the list of names she'd culled from Wood and Devlin's phone books. She handed it to Betty. "Do any of these names seem familiar?"

Betty went over the list. "A number of them, but I don't know which of them might have been the third boy."

She passed the list to Cliff who glanced at it, then shook his head. "Sorry." He started to hand it back to Syd then stopped. "Wait a minute," he pulled the list back. "This name here, Blake Hunter, I remember the name Blake. I had an Uncle Blake, and I remember thinking about that when we heard the name eleven years ago."

"So, Blake Hunter was the third boy," Syd asked, excited. "You're sure?"

"No. I'm not sure. I remember the name Blake is all. If there was more than one Blake, I'd have no idea which one it was."

Syd took the list, double-checked. Just one Blake, Blake Hunter, and he lived in Malibu. Syd stuffed the list back in her backpack, stood up. "Mr. and Mrs. Waterman, thank you very much."

"Detective," Betty said, "Do you think Alice is right? Do you think we sold her out?"

"Don't ask her that," Cliff said. "She won't give us an honest answer. I mean, you can't really, can you?" Cliff asked Syd. "You're just going to say what we want to hear."

"And what is it you want to hear?" Syd asked.

"Betty wants to hear that we did the right thing," Cliff said. "Which we did."

"Let me ask you this," Syd said. "When the lawyer offered the cash settlement, did you ask Alice which she would prefer, the money or a trial?"

"Of course not, she was just a kid, besides she was in no state of mind to decide."

Syd nodded. She knew what she should say, and Syd also knew the truth. She chose. "You did do the right thing, for you. You spared yourself the embarrassment of everyone learning in open court that your daughter was promiscuous. But you did a terrible disservice to your daughter. You prevented her from fighting back against the men who raped her, from punishing the men who raped her. The men she is punishing now. So not only did you betray Alice, you are responsible for turning your daughter from rape victim into a murderer."

235

Cliff stared at Syd, stunned by her honesty. Betty was shocked too. But it didn't stop her from turning to her husband with an, *I told you so* glare on her face.

"Is that what you wanted to hear, Mr. Waterman?" Syd left without waiting for an answer.

Syd drove quickly. With luck she was just over an hour from Malibu. Of course, she could call dispatch and have the place surrounded in a matter of minutes, and she almost made that call. But Syd wanted to catch the Lady in Red herself. Not for the glory of the capture, but so she could have a chance to talk to her.

And now Syd had an answer for the question, why now? Why had Alice Waterman waited eleven years to get revenge for the rapes? Because she was given a death sentence by one of her shrinks. And since she thought she was going to die, she had nothing to lose by killing the men who attacked her. She wouldn't be risking jail or the needle for her murders because she was doomed already.

Except the diagnosis was a lie.

A trick to help poor Alice straighten out her life.

Syd felt a growing affinity with Alice Waterman. And seeing the house she grew up in tonight, the weak mother, bullying father, hearing about how she was betrayed by her parents and abused by men only made Syd want to meet her more.

She'd still have to arrest her, of course. She had no illusions about somehow helping the Lady in Red get away with murder. But she felt a bond with Alice, a bond she wanted, needed to share.

Now the only question was, what to do about Ryan? She wanted to share these feelings with him. Wanted to tell him about who she really was, why she understood the Lady in Red.

Could they actually be a couple if he didn't know all of her secrets?

More importantly, were they even a couple now? What was he doing, right now, with that bitch, Anne?

One way to find out, Syd decided. Call him.

She picked up her cell phone and hit the one on her speed dial.

FORTY-FOUR

The trouble started on the elevator. Ryan and Anne were alone and Anne shot Ryan a mischievous look. "Should I hit the Stop button?"

Ryan laughed, the memories flooding back.

When they were married, Ryan and Anne loved to make love in public. Trader Vic's was the first time, but so exhilarating they found themselves daring each other to have sex almost anywhere. Anne climbed into Ryan's lap when they were stuck in a traffic jam on the 405 and, to the delight of Fed Ex driver stuck next to them, she pulled out his cock, pulled down her panties and mounted him. The *Anne-on-Ryan's-lap* became a favorite position. They used it in movie theatres, Starbucks' bathrooms, during the half-time show at a Rose Bowl game, and in the back row of a lecture hall during one of Professor Moylan's interminable Psych classes.

They also used a variety of other positions depending on where they were; standing when Ryan pinned Anne to the wall in the Travel section of Barnes and Noble, missionary when Ryan took Anne golfing and she couldn't find her ball in the woods, doggy style in the back of L.A. County Natural History Museum's dinosaur display, and reverse cowgirl when Anne dragged Ryan into the empty break room of a Ralph's grocery store.

But their favorite spots were elevators. In high rises they used to wait until they could get a car by themselves, press the button for the top floor and see if they could finish before the car stopped. In smaller buildings they'd press the Stop button, the alarm would always sound but it actually served to drown out Anne's orgasms.

Good times, he thought. He was a different guy then, he suddenly realized. Less serious, certainly less structured, much more spontaneous. He'd closed down after Anne left him. He became much more conservative, cautious, not nearly as much fun, he realized.

Or was it just that he was a different person with Anne? And if they got back together, would he revert back to a more carefree persona? He glanced at her and she was smiling.

Standing so close to Anne, feeling her body heat, her scent, Ryan's hand dangling just inches from hers, was such a turn on. And Syd be damned, there was something unfinished here. What if, okay, he knew it sounded stupid, but what if they were meant to be together? What if his getting the lottery ticket was all part of some huge master plan to get them back together? And as insane as he knew that kind of thinking was, Ryan was having a visceral reaction to Anne that he never felt with any other woman.

Anne felt it, too. She had to admit she missed those crazy days herself. Anne and Ryan's love affair was filled with wild abandon. Sure they were kids, but during those first couple of years she felt electrified. A feeling she hasn't had since. Not with Rick, never with any of her lovers. And she suddenly wondered if she was a different person with Ryan? If, no, *when* they got back together, would they be able recapture that exultation? And suddenly, more than ever, she wanted to find out.

DING. The elevator arriving interrupted both of their reveries. But as they stepped out of the elevator and walked down the thick carpet, something palpable had changed. They walked closer together, Ryan's hand brushed Anne's hand with every step until he finally wrapped his fingers around hers.

They faced each other as they reached the door to her suite. Anne slid the keycard into the door but her eyes never left Ryan's face. Ryan pushed open the door; they were still holding hands as Anne led him inside. The door swung closed behind them. Without a word, Ryan pulled her close and kissed her.

It ignited a wildfire. Hands started flying, jackets hit the floor, he pulled out her blouse, she ripped open his shirt, undid his belt, he pulled up her skirt and pulled down her panties, she pulled down his pants and slipped his penis out of his boxers. Then, in a move they practiced while still UCLA undergrads, she leapt up throwing her legs around his waist as he caught her under the arms, then lowered her onto his cock.

They both gasped as he entered her.

And they stood there, staring into each other's eyes, neither moving, both just enjoying the feeling of being a part of the other; a completeness neither had felt for so long.

"You feel so good," he whispered.

"No," she replied. "*We* feel this good." As she began to gently rock her hips, he responded and seconds later the passion that had been building between both for the last two days exploded in simultaneous orgasms.

They lay in each other's arms an hour later. Naked now, sated after another less frantic lovemaking session, Anne cuddled contentedly. She was surprised by the passion of their lovemaking. And she knew that something monumental had happened. She'd had a life changing epiphany. She loved Ryan.

Ryan.

Not his lottery money. Not the chance at a job running his foundation. But the flesh, blood, synapses and dimples of Ryan Magee.

She felt safe in his arms. Protected in his arms. At home in his arms.

This man, she realized, was her soul mate. She'd been a fool to leave him. The humiliating poverty of her childhood had skewed her priorities, and seven years ago, when she bolted from that cramped studio apartment, she made the biggest mistake of her life.

But now, somehow, she'd been given a second chance and she wasn't going to blow it. She knew Ryan still loved her. She saw it in his eyes, the way he touched her, the way he made love to her. Now she needed him to realize what she now knew to be a cold hard fact; they belonged together.

Ryan propped himself up on an elbow, looked at Anne. "You lied to me," Ryan said.

Fear rattled Anne. "I did?"

"You promised no funny business."

Relief flooded Anne. "If I'm not mistaken, you kissed me. So, from a strictly legal point of view, you were the funny business instigator and I, the helpless victim."

"There's nothing helpless about you, baby," he said kissing her.

Okay, Anne thought. Let's see how he feels. "Regrets?" Anne asked.

No, more like a revelation Ryan thought. *Wanting* to be in love with Syd was different than actually being in love. Ryan cared deeply about Syd, knew how much she loved him and wanted to love her back because well, it would make Syd happy.

But the depth of his affection for Syd didn't compare to the feelings suddenly unleashed in Ryan for Anne. A giddy, intoxicating, euphoria he forgot existed.

"No regrets." Ryan said.

Okay, then here goes, thought Anne. "Leaving you was the stupidest thing I've ever done. I love you, Ryan. I've always loved and I'll always love you. If this was a revenge fuck, fine, I deserve it. But if it was more, if you feel the way I do, then please, take me back."

There they were, the words Ryan wanted so desperately to hear in those misery soaked months after Anne left him. He'd fantasized about a midnight phone call, a frantic knock on his door, an apology-filled email. He checked his cell phone obsessively hoping for *the* call.

Then, slowly, his heart healed. Albeit a cell at a time, the way the body heals itself, and it took a long time.

But deep down, Ryan realized, he never stopped hoping that one day he'd get that call, hear that knock, read that email. And now, finally, here it was.

Please, take me back.

He stared into Anne's beautiful brown eyes, smiled "Welcome home."

Anne squealed with delight, threw her arms around his neck and kissed him. "Thank you, thank you, thank you," she said, punctuating each *thank you* with another kiss. Then her fingers slid down his chest to his understandably exhausted penis. "Got anything left down there, big boy?"

Ryan laughed. "Yeah, a full bladder." He slipped off the king size bed. "Be right back." He walked naked into the bathroom, closed the door.

Anne fell back on the pillow nearly dizzy with joy. Somehow she'd turned Rick's financial disaster and her own career debacle into a gold-plated life with the only man she'd ever loved. Life, go figure.

She heard the muffled sound of a cell phone vibrating. She scrambled across the bed to her purse, but her cell phone was silent.

She heard another vibration from Ryan's clothes piled on the floor. She climbed off the bed, dug through the clothes and found the phone in Ryan's jacket pocket. She looked at the Caller ID, Syd.

Shit. Anne did not want Ryan talking to her now.

The phone vibrated again.

Anne turned the cell phone off, dropped it back into Ryan's jacket then leapt back into the bed.

Uh oh, Syd thought as she picked her way through traffic on the northbound 405. Ryan *always* picks up his phone. Possible exceptions: One, he's already on the phone, and even though his phone would beep and tell him he had an incoming call and identify it as Syd, he's so engrossed in the conversation he can't possible pick up; two, he's fucking the shit out of that bitch; three, he's dead.

Well, Syd thought. If it's not one, and it is two, he's going to wish it was three.

His message came on, "Hi, this is Ryan Magee, sorry I missed your call. Please leave a message."

Syd thought about just hanging up, but there actually could be an innocent reason for the call not going through, so she said, "Hey Ryan, it's me. Three boys raped Alice that night: Colin, Adam and a guy named Blake Hunter. He lives in Malibu, 22756 Pacific Coast Highway. It's nine forty-five now, I should be there in less than an hour. Call me."

She disconnected then refocused on her top priority. The Lady in Red.

FORTY-FIVE

The Vest Pocket Colt .25, with its miniscule two and a quarter inch barrel was designed to shoot at targets five to eight feet away. After that, luck has as much to do with hitting a target as skill.

This was only the second time Blake had ever fired a weapon; the first was high school when they took Adam's father's .44 Magnum to the city dump and shot at rats, so his skill level was low. But Blake's luck was good and he hit his target.

Alice screamed as the bullet ripped into her shoulder, blood spurted as the slug shredded her deltoid muscle, just missed the cephatic vein before nicking her clavicle bone, tumbling through the trapezius muscle and bursting out of her shoulder before finally plowing into the living room wall.

The force of the bullet hitting Alice spun her around, and her brain was already calculating how she was going to survive a battle with a man with a gun when she's just got a small scalpel.

So she instinctively let the spin knock her off her feet and she tumbled to the ground. There was no way for Blake to know exactly where he hit her, Syd realized, so she shuddered once and then went still.

Dead still.

Blake stared at the lifeless body. God damn her, he thought. He was counting on a lengthy interview to stitch together his documentary. And her murder trial would have been the icing on the cake. Fiery statements from the D.A. intercut with righteous indignation from the defense. Mix in a few shots of the beautiful defendant and you've got real drama. But now, all he'd have was a funeral.

Of course, a funeral makes for a much more definitive

ending, and his own role in the story had been enhanced. Enhanced big time, he suddenly realized; he's become the fucking star. After capturing the Lady in Red, he had to fight it out with the desperate serial murderer, finally killing her with her own weapon.

And then it hit him, documentary, hell! This should be a feature fucking film. Someone sexy but deadly would play the Lady in Red: Angelina Jolie, Scarlett Johansson, or maybe Keira Knightley. And an A-lister like Brad Pitt or Matt Damon would play Blake.

He'd write and direct, the first time ever a victim/hero told his own story on screen. What a publicity dream.

He looked at Alice's body.

Did she just breathe?

He thought he saw some movement. He aimed the gun at her. He should put a couple of more shots into her to make sure, he decided. He centered the muzzle at the back of her head, tightened his finger on the trigger and squeezed.

Then stopped.

The cops would be able to figure out the trajectory of the bullets, determine that he was standing and she was on the ground. Realized he'd shot a defenseless victim.

Not very heroic.

How would an audience feel watching Brad Pitt shoot the inert body of Scarlett Johansson just to make sure she was dead?

They'd hate it. It seemed so cowardly.

But what if she was still alive? He was sure he saw her move.

Keeping the gun aimed at her, Blake slowly stepped toward the body. When he reached her he saw a pool of blood gathering beneath her.

That's good, he thought. But blood alone wasn't enough to prove she was dead. He nudged her stomach with his foot.

Alice's right hand shot out, the scalpel slashing Blake's ankle, severing his Achilles tendon.

Blake's leg collapsed. Furious he pulled the trigger,

but too late, his aim ruined by the fall. Three shots went harmlessly into the ceiling.

His back hit the ground first, followed by his head and gun hand. The force of the impact popped the gun out of his grip and sent the Colt skittering across the floor.

Alice pounced on him. She straddled his chest and began slashing his face with the scalpel. Blood spurted as the tempered steel of the #10 blade sliced down his left cheek, up his right cheek, across his chin.

Blake screeched in pain. He looked into Alice's maniacal face; she was pure animal now desperately fighting for her survival.

In his periphery vision Blake could see the gun on the floor, eight or nine feet away. He had to get her off him and reach the gun.

She slashed again, this time the knife sliced across his forehead, opening a flap of skin and sending a river of blood into Blake's eyes.

He let out a roar, placed his hand on her chest and shoved as hard as he could. Alice fell back, tumbling off him. He was free.

Blake clambered toward the gun. His right leg was useless, so he pulled himself across the floor with his hands as his blood drenched the floor.

He could hear Alice scrambling to her feet behind him. He reached out, his fingertips touching the gun. Got you, he thought.

But as he tightened his grip on the Colt, Alice drove the scalpel through the back of his hand pinning it to the floor.

He screamed in agony.

Alice plucked the gun off the floor, turned it on Blake. Blood poured from the gashes in his face. He looked at her, terrified. "Don't shoot."

Hate simmered off Alice. The rape was Blake's idea. She'd watched him *direct* her degradation. He was actually going to try and use her rape to re-launch his movie career. And now he was begging for mercy.

"I know people," Blake pleaded. "I can help you get

away, out of the country with a new identity and plenty of money. Just please, don't shoot."

Alice thought about it then slowly lowered the gun.

Unexpected hope filled Blake's eyes.

And that's when she shot him – right between those hope-filled eyes.

Alice dug through the medicine cabinet in Blake's bathroom. It was a veritable drug store. Her bloodstained hands shuffled through bottles of Xanax, Ativan and Valium. Depressed much, Blake, she thought.

There were also bottles of Viagra and Cialis, for fun she assumed. There were bottles of Vicodin and Percocet, no doubt for pain. She wasn't looking for pain pills, but she knew the dull pain in her shoulder would detonate later into agony so she pocketed the Vicodin. There were bottles of Ambien and Lunesta for sleep. There was also a bottle of Valtrex which she knew treated herpes. No surprise there.

She pawed through a variety of drugs she never heard and didn't care about. What she wanted was an antiseptic, something to disinfect her shoulder wound. And a couple of thick bandages.

Nothing more in the cabinet so she looked under the sink.

Bingo.

She pulled out a bottle of Betadine and a first aid kit with a variety of bandages. She poured the Betadine onto a washcloth then applied it to the entrance wound. She gasped and nearly collapsed as pain engulfed her.

She sat on the toilet, poured more Betadine onto the washcloth and using the mirror to guide her, pressed the washcloth onto the exit wound. This time a soft moan escaped from her lips as the pain crested quickly, then slowly receded.

She ripped open one of the large bandages. She dribbled a little Betadine onto the gauze then placed it over the entrance wound and pressed hard attaching it. It stung like crazy but she was getting used to it. Then she ripped open a second bandage, added a little antiseptic and, using the mirror as a guide again, stuck it on. Okay, she thought. That should stem the bleeding and take care of any infection.

She looked at herself in the mirror. Her white tube top was drenched in blood. Some of it his, most of it hers. And blood was splattered on her face and skin.

In fact, her blood was everywhere. In the living room, dripped on the floor all the way into the bathroom and now all over the sink, floor, and soaked into the washcloth.

There would be no way to clean up this crime scene. The cops were sure to get her DNA this time. But hell, they've got her picture, and once they connect Blake, Colin, Adam and Zachary Stone, they'll know who she is. And until an hour ago she wouldn't have cared. She wanted to kill four men and she'd done it. The police can pick her up, big deal. Thanks to the Big C she wouldn't live long enough to stand trial.

But now everything had changed. One more man had to die.

She peeled off the tube top, dropped it to the floor. She grabbed a fresh washcloth, ran it under warm water and started cleaning herself up.

She'd had weeks to prepare for her attack on Blake, Colin, Adam and Stone. She'd researched each one, knew where they lived, worked, ate, drank. She planned their executions down to the tiniest detail.

She wouldn't have that luxury with her next victim. The cops would be on her tail. The one advantage she had is they would have no idea who she was after.

Alice grabbed a shirt out of Blake's closet, a tan Tommy Bahama luau shirt that was too big for her, but the shirt tails covered her bloodstained skirt.

Time was the issue now. She had very little of it. Once the cops talked to her parents, they'd find out about her car and apartment and it wouldn't take too much digging to find out where she lives. So Alice had to move. Fast.

And she'd need more money, enough for a cheap hotel

and food for a week or two. She had about twenty two hundred, which would be cutting things close. She needed more.

She searched Blake's bureau looking for cash or his wallet. Found nothing. It must be on him. So she went back into the living room. She had a horror movie fantasy for an instant that she'd walk into the living room and he'd be gone, and then suddenly appear behind her.

But he lay dead on the floor.

Alice knelt down, patted his pants pockets, felt the wallet in back and fished it out.

Nine hundred and twenty-three dollars. Not bad. She took the money, dropped the wallet onto his chest.

Next she went back into the office. She wanted the video of her rape.

At some point she'd make sure the cops got a copy. She wanted the world to know exactly what happened to her. She wanted the world to know that those scumbags got just what was coming to them.

But not yet. If the cops saw the tape, they'd see the fourth man and figure out what she was up to. But once he was dead, she'd make sure Blake's masterpiece got a worldwide release.

While Alice watched the video, Blake controlled it with a remote so she didn't know where the tape itself was. She searched the bookcases found a stack of components: receiver, DVD player, cable box. No VHS player. The recording was made on a video camera so there should have been a tape – unless he burned it to a DVD. She hit open on the DVD player and a disk slid out. It had a white paper label with the title **High School Pool Party** scrawled on it.

Alice grabbed it, found an empty plastic DVD case and stuck it inside. Then she noticed the video camera in the corner of the room. The one Blake used to record her reactions as she watched the rape.

The red light was still on. It was still recording.

She walked to the camera, looked at the small LCD monitor on the back. The camera was aimed at the middle of the room where the Lady in Red had been sitting, but it also saw through the door into the living room and Blake's dead body was on the right hand side of the frame.

The camera had recorded their fight, her attacking him in the office, his shooting her in the living room and their final battle.

Alice laughed. It would have been incredible footage for his documentary. Not the ending Blake had in mind, though. Thank God.

She hit the button to stop recording. Found the button to open the camera and reached for the tape – then hesitated.

The tape showed her bound hand and foot, held captive by Blake Hunter. It showed her fighting to free herself, getting shot by Blake before finally overpowering him.

She was clearly the victim here simply defending herself. The police should see that. Realize she wasn't just a cold-blooded killer. She cued it to the beginning of her tripping Blake in the office and struggling to get out of the handcuffs.

Then she remembered it also showed her shooting Blake in the face after he'd begged for mercy. Maybe she better take it after all. Alice grabbed the tape.

She was moving quickly now. She grabbed her purse and dropped in the DVD and tape. She did a final look around the room to see if she'd forgotten anything. Her eyes alighted on Blake's still camera.

He'd taken those shots of her in the sunset.

She considered taking the camera then decided the cops already had those crappy surveillance photos of her; might as well let them have a couple of glamour shots.

She stepped over Blake's body and then stopped. If there was going to be a fifth victim, she needed to finish this crime scene. After all, she had her legacy to think about.

Let's see, he was victim number four, so… Alice spotted a deck of cards on the kitchen pass through. She picked them up, fished out the four of hearts and dropped it on Blake's chest.

She definitely wasn't looking forward to the next part. The thought of touching Blake again repulsed her. Alice crouched down next to Blake, unzipped his fly. He wore boxers. She reached in and pulled out his flaccid penis.

Not much now, are you, hot shot?

She grabbed the tip and pulled, stretching it out so she could lop off as much as she could – because as every woman knows, size does matter.

Slash, slice, cut, cut. And that was that. Then she opened Blake's mouth, and jammed in the penis.

One final detail left; Alice picked up Blake's wallet, checked inside and yes, there it was, a Platinum American Express. She took it and dropped the wallet.

Okay, time to go. Alice crossed the room, threw open the front door and let out a startled scream.

Syd stood in the doorway, her Glock pointed at the Lady in Red's heart. "Hello, Alice," Syd said. "I've been looking for you."

FORTY-SIX

Syd's going to totally freak out.

That's what Ryan was thinking as he showered in Anne's hotel room. Syd had been worried about Ryan spending so much time with his ex-wife and Ryan had assured Syd and re-assured her she had nothing to worry about.

Yeah, right.

Ryan knew firsthand the emotional devastation of being dumped and wanted to find a way to spare Syd. He cared deeply about her, loved her even, he did. But not in the same way as he loved Anne. Would she understand that if he tried to explain it?

No, of course not. How could she?

And Syd was a fabulous partner. Would there be any way she would want to remain his partner?

No, of course not. How could she?

The big question then became when and how to tell Syd about Anne? Ryan thought of something his father told him. When Joseph Magee got tired of one of his wives, he'd start doing things he knew she hated. He'd drive her crazy so that she'd be the one who wanted to end the relationship. Now that took a lot of time and patience. And it certainly wasn't a very honest way to solve a problem. But it did put the women in the control position, saved them the humiliation of being dumped and the subsequent heartache. Ryan's dad was also convinced it saved him a little alimony since the women filed first and felt guilty about it.

Syd certainly deserved better than that. And they were in the middle of a crucial murder case and he didn't want personal business to jeopardize the Lady in Red investigation.

In Cold Blonde

So it would be prudent to wait. At least a few days.

Ryan dried himself off and stepped into the bedroom. Anne had put on a black nightgown. She'd also retouched her make-up. Ryan's heart did a little flip when he saw her. She just looked so... beautiful.

"I better go," he said slipping into his boxer shorts. "I need to touch base with Syd before the presentation tomorrow."

"Speaking of Syd," Anne said. "What're you going to tell her?"

Ryan stepped into his pants. "That I care deeply about her, but I've realized I'm still in love with you and that you and I have reconciled."

"Reconciled," she said, pronouncing the word slowly as if tasting it. "Not a very pretty word for such a wonderful thing. It sounds so legal."

"I thought you loved legalese."

She got up, moved to him. "I speak legalese, I love you." She put her arms around him and gave him a quick kiss. "Stay with me tonight. I want you to be the first thing I see when I wake up tomorrow."

Ryan was tempted, but shook his head. "I just can't, I'm sorry." He picked up his shirt, put it on.

Anne reached out, started buttoning his buttons. "Are you going to tell Syd about tonight?"

"No, I thought I'd wait a few days, at least until we've wrapped up the Lady in Red investigation."

"A couple of days? What're we supposed to do until then, pretend there's nothing going on between us?"

She'd finished with the buttons. Ryan tucked in his shirt. "If you don't mind. I've got a feeling it's going to be pretty ugly and I don't want anything jeopardizing the case right now." He picked up his jacket. The cell phone tumbled out and hit the floor.

Anne's eyes locked on it. Would he notice she turned it off?

Ryan picked up the phone and stuck it in his pocket without even looking at it. "Syd's a good kid and this is going to kill her. I just want to make sure I handle it the best way possible."

"You're sweet. Have I told you that?"

"Not in seven years."

"You're my sweet boy." She kissed him again, deeper this time.

"You taste so good," Ryan said. "I love you, Beautiful."

"Me too, you, Handsome."

Ryan crossed to the door, opened it.

"You know, it's kind of funny," Anne said. "You've now got two women in your life you have to pretend with. You're hiding your relationship with Syd from the police department and you're hiding your relationship with me from Syd."

"Soon everyone will know about us. I promise." He blew her a kiss and closed the door.

Ryan walked down the hall as happy as he could remember. There was a bounce to his step and he felt absolutely wonderful.

He pressed the button for the elevator thinking about tomorrow. So much was happening tomorrow; the lottery presentation and the Lady in Red investigation on the brink of an arrest. He was filled with confidence about both. About everything.

Ain't love grand?

The elevator arrived and Ryan got in, pressed the button for the Lobby. It suddenly occurred to him that Syd hadn't called. The last time he talked to her she was knee-deep collating Colin Wood and Adam Devlin's phone books and she should have checked in by now. He reached into his pocket for his cell phone and flipped it open checking for messages.

The phone was off. Ryan never turned his cell phone off. He even kept it on as he recharged it. What's with that? Must be a technical thing, he decided. He pressed the button turning it on.

The phone beeped as it started up. His screen lit up – just the shrink-wrap Verizon logo – Ryan never downloaded a personal picture. Didn't know how and didn't care.

DING. The elevator door opened as he reached the lobby. He stepped out of the elevator. Sure enough, there was a missed call from Syd. And she had left a voicemail. Ryan was about to play the voicemail when he was interrupted. "Detective Magee?"

Ryan looked up to find a handsome blond man in a Brooks Brother's suit. "Yes?"

"Could I have a minute of your time?"

There was something about the man that was vaguely familiar. And he was intense, a man on a mission.

"Sure." Ryan put his phone in his pocket.

The man stuck out his hand. "I'm Rick Rogers, Anne's husband. Or should I say soon to be *ex*-husband."

Ryan shook the man's hand warily. Every cop knows jilted husbands can do crazy things. "I don't want any trouble," Ryan said.

"Don't worry," Rick said. "You carry a gun, I carry a Blackberry. But there are some things about Anne I think you ought to know." He indicated a couple of chairs in the lobby. "Shall we?"

Ryan wasn't comfortable having any conversation with the man who stole Anne from him seven years ago, but he was curious about what Rick Rogers would have to say. They sat down.

"You were in Anne's room a long time," Rick said with a knowing look.

"Are you following her?"

"Let's just call it idle curiosity."

"I think the legal term is stalking."

Rick sat back in his chair, smiled. "She's good, I'll give her that."

"What're you talking about?"

"Did Anne tell you she was leaving the firm?"

"Yes. She said she was sick of the rat race and she's decided it's time for her to give something back. She's going to run my charitable foundation."

"Did she mention that she was given an ultimatum by my father, resign or go to jail?"

"What?"

"Look, Ryan, I feel bad about what happened to you
seven years ago. I'd never met you so there was nothing
personal. But now that I'm the one who's been dumped
and I've got a taste of what you must have gone through.
And it sucks, big time."

Rogers was rambling a bit and Ryan began to think
he'd been drinking. "What does this have to do with your
father's ultimatum?"

"It's the reason I'm telling you all this in the first
place. To warn you. About Anne."

Ryan had heard enough. "Thanks, consider me
warned. Nice to meet you." Ryan got up, started to walk
away.

"Doesn't it strike you as a little coincidental that Anne
suddenly appears back in your life the day after you hit the
Lotto?"

That stopped Ryan.

"Did she tell you we were broke? That we're filing for
bankruptcy?"

That turned Ryan around.

"Did she tell you that we forged my father's signature
to get a loan?"

That got Ryan back into the chair.

"Our marriage was shit, I'll be the first to admit it,"
Rick said. "But as long as Annie lived in a great house,
drove a German car, wore French designer clothes and had
a black AMEX card, she didn't seem to care. But the
minute we lost all our money, she started looking around."

"Tell me about the forgery."

"I bet wrong on the market. I lost all our money and
our beach house. I went to my father on bended knee and
he bought us a condo. Suddenly we were living on a
budget and Anne hated it. Then I got a tip from a friend
that a new stock was going to double. It was supposed to
be a sure thing. A chance to get back on our feet. So Anne
and I forged dad's signature and took out a million dollar
loan on the condo. The plan was to get in and out quickly,
pay off the loan, and have a nice little profit left over. But

the stock went down instead of up and we lost everything."

"And your father found out?"

Rick nodded. "We couldn't pay the mortgage and the bank called him. Now he's threatened to go the police and the California Bar Association unless we resign from the firm immediately." Rick waited a moment to let his words soak in. Then he continued, "So, let's be very clear, Anne wants to run your foundation because she doesn't have a job. And Anne wants you back in her life because she doesn't have any money. That's all Anne cares about, it's all she's ever cared about, money."

Ryan didn't want to believe it. He'd held Anne in his arms, looked into her eyes. He saw love there, the same adoration he remembered from college, he was sure of it.

Rick saw the denial in Ryan's face. "Let me ask you a question," Rick said. "How did Anne first reconnect with you?"

Great question, Ryan thought. And the answer should convince Rick that Anne's motives aren't as diabolical as the lawyer imagines. "At my office, at the Hollywood Station. She was there on business for another client and dropped by to say hello."

Rick shook his head with an expression that said you dumb son of a bitch. "Anne is a corporate litigator, Ryan. She does her business in boardrooms and courtrooms. She has *never* represented a criminal case. I doubt she'd ever been in a police station until she *accidently* bumped into you. *Accidently* bumped into you the same day as the lead story on every newscast is about lucky cop, Ryan Magee, winning forty-seven million dollars."

"Thirty-four after taxes," Ryan mumbled, shell-shocked.

"Look, I'm sorry to be telling you all this. I could have kept my mouth shut, I know. But she played you for a sucker once, played us both for suckers. Just don't let her do it again." Rick Rogers stood up, and started to walk away.

"Wait," Ryan said, still desperately trying to hold onto Anne's version of the truth. "I met Anne for drinks last night and she told me your law firm has represented a number of Lotto winners. Is that true?"

Rick looked sympathetically at Ryan. "Sorry, Detective. Rogers, Middleton and Roberts has never represented a Lotto winner." And with that, Rick left.

Ryan sat there, the implications of Anne's manipulations and lies flooding his brain. She'd pursued him, no doubt about it. From her appearance in the bullpen to her phone call later that day suggesting drinks at Musso and Frank. And tonight, picking Trader Vic's instead of any of the hotel's other restaurants or bars. Trader Vic's where they had their alcohol-fueled love fest. Then she discovered she *accidently* left the papers in her room.

Premeditated. All of it.

And Ryan fell for it

A roar filled Ryan's ears. Ryan was embarrassed, humiliated. He suddenly stood up, walked toward the elevators. He was going to go back up to the room and confront her. He wanted to say something to her, to hurt her as much as her betrayal had hurt him. He pressed the Up button and the elevator door opened.

But instead of walking in, Ryan just stood there, imagining himself standing in her open doorway, saying what exactly? *You lying bitch? You hurt my feelings? Fuck the foundation and fuck you?*

Just what the hell was he supposed to say at a time like this?

And didn't he risk making a bigger fool of himself than he had already?

The elevator door closed.

Ryan knew that sometimes the best thing to do was nothing, and this was clearly one of those times. Let it go, for now. Go home and think about it.

Ryan turned around and headed for the parking lot.

Meanwhile, happy as she ever remembered being, Anne ran a bath. The suite had a Jacuzzi tub and Anne loved luxuriating as jets of hot water pummeled her body. The hotel provided a bathing salt, which she liberally sprinkled into foaming water. And then Anne remembered the phone call she'd ignored when Ryan first arrived at Trader Vic's.

The tub had a little more time to fill up so she pulled out her cell phone and checked her messages. She had one from Travis Taylor. His message asked her to call him. She did. He answered on the first ring. "Travis Taylor."

"It's Anne Rogers, Travis, I hope it's not too late."

"Sleep is for sissies."

Anne laughed. "You've got some news on Syd Curtis?"

"I do. Syd Curtis is quite a remarkable young woman. She's from Kansas City, not Riverside. She ran away from home when she was seventeen, came straight to Hollywood. She's been connected to a pimp named Ernesto Sian so I suspect she was a hooker at one time. But here's where it gets interesting, I tracked down Syd's mother and spoke to her. I pretended to be one of Syd's classmates and wondered whatever happened it her. Get this, her mother hasn't heard from Syd since the day she left almost ten years ago."

"She doesn't know she's a cop?"

"She doesn't even know if Syd's alive or dead."

The more Anne heard, the happier she got. Anne wondered if Ryan knew all this? Somehow she doubted it. "Did you tell the mother Syd was alive?"

"No. Not sure there's an angle in it yet. I've got some more work to do, but here's the bottom line. We can prove she lied on her LAPD application so we've already got enough evidence to get her fired. And I've got a feeling I'm going to find another surprise or two. I'll call you tomorrow with another update."

"Great work, Travis, thank you." Anne hung up. She was hoping Travis would get enough dirt to drive a wedge between Ryan and Syd. Well, he'd found a whole lot more. She was a teenage runaway and a hooker? Fabulous. And lying on her LAPD application was the icing on the cake. All Anne would have to do is leak Travis' report to the press and Syd would be kicked off the force and out of their lives forever.

But then another thought struck Anne. A much better one. She'd confront Syd with Travis's report and make her an offer she couldn't refuse. Ask for a transfer out of Homicide and out of the Hollywood division. Something in the Valley maybe, or South Central. Something far away from Ryan. Ask for a transfer or Anne would leak the report to the press. And if Syd told Ryan about Anne's blackmail, Anne would leak it to the press. Syd would have no choice.

Now the only question became when to spring the surprise on Syd.

Anne stepped into the tub and settled beneath the churning water. She sighed happily as the hot water swallowed her. And then the answer came – she'd talk to Syd tomorrow, at the lottery presentation. Syd was sure to be there, and what better way was there for Anne to cap off what was certain to be one of the best days of her life than by checkmating that perky redhead.

FORTY-SEVEN

It was only forty degrees outside but Ryan had the top down. The heater was on and kept his feet warm, but the crisp air whisked the heat away from Ryan's upper body and face, so he was cold. Freezing actually, but that was fine. He wanted to be uncomfortable. He wanted to suffer.

A familiar ache filled his heart. The perfect world Anne had helped construct in Ryan's imagination – living happily ever after with the girl of his dreams, millions of dollars in the bank and running a foundation for the needy – was suddenly gone. What was he supposed to do now about the lottery money, about the foundation, about Syd?

Syd.

Jesus, before Ryan was waylaid by Rick Rogers he was checking his Voicemail. Ryan took out his cell phone, brought up Syd's message.

"Hey Ryan, it's me," Syd's recorded voice said. "Three boys raped Alice that night: Colin, Adam and a guy named Blake Hunter. He lives in Malibu, 22756 Pacific Coast Highway. It's nine forty-five now, I should be there in less than an hour. Call me."

Nine forty-five, Ryan thought. Ryan remembered glancing at the clock as he was going to the bathroom. It read nine forty-five. So when his cell phone rang, Anne must have heard it; she checked to see who the caller was, saw Syd's name and turned off the phone.

That bitch.

Okay, this was good, he thought. I'm starting to get mad. Fuck Anne. Fuck that manipulative, lying bitch. I let her ruin my life seven years ago but I'm not going to let her ruin my life again. I was a happy, satisfied man before she popped into the bullpen, so just forget about the last forty-eight hours, man up, act like they never happened and focus on something constructive, like catching the Lady in Red.

Ryan aimed the Mustang toward Malibu and hit the speed dial for Syd.

Syd's cell phone rang. She took it out of her purse and stared at it. It rang again. Syd saw the Caller ID, Ryan. She just stared at it. It rang again.

"You going to get that?" the Lady in Red asked.

"No," she said. "He can leave a message." Syd turned off her phone.

A lot had happened since Syd met the Lady in Red at the door with a gun in her hand...

When Syd pulled up to Blake's Malibu home, she saw a white Prius parked in the driveway. Alice's parents bought her a used white Prius so Syd knew she'd found her. She pulled her automatic as she approached the door. She was about to try the doorknob when the door swung open and she was face to face with the Lady in Red.

"Hello, Alice," Syd said. "I've been looking for you."

Oh, shit, Alice thought. Not now, not yet. I have one more man to kill.

"Get down on your knees and put your hands behind your head or I will shoot you."

Alice looked at the redheaded cop. She looked young, but there was steel in her tone and a *don't fuck with me* glint in her green eyes.

Alice wondered if all handcuff keys were the same. She'd pocketed the keys to Blake's handcuffs after she'd freed herself. Here's hoping, she thought as she dropped to her knees.

With practiced precision Syd cuffed Alice. "Where's your gun?" Syd asked as she slipped on a pair of surgical gloves.

Alice's eyes dropped to her purse. Syd opened it, saw the Colt and scalpel. She took them out of the purse, slipped them into her jacket pocket. Then, just to be sure, she searched Alice. And found just one thing, a handcuff key.

What the hell, thought Syd.

Shit, thought Alice.

Syd was about to ask about the handcuff key when she noticed a crimson stain soaking through the shoulder of the Lady in Red's shirt. "You're bleeding."

"You should see the other guy," Alice said.

My thoughts exactly, thought Syd. Where the hell was Blake Hunter? She grabbed Alice by the handcuffs and pulled her to her feet. "Let's go," she said.

It was only a few feet from the entry hall to the living room and Blake's bloody corpse. Syd clocked the cock sticking out of his mouth. There was blood everywhere, his face a bloody pulp. "Jesus Christ," Syd muttered. "Not up to your usual surgical standards."

"Yeah, well, shit happens."

Syd checked the body for a pulse, found none. She noticed the playing card on Blake's chest, four of hearts. Then her eyes took in the rest of the crime scene. There was a trail of blood from the body to the middle of the room, where a small pool of blood stained the wood floor. Then she noticed something shining in the doorway to another room – a pair of handcuffs. That explains the key, Syd thought. Syd bent down picked them up. They were fur-lined. "Curiouser and curiouser," Syd said.

She needed to search the rest of the house, make sure they were alone. "Don't move," she said to Alice and then quickly made her way down the bloodstained hall to the guest room and master bedroom, both clear. Then she stepped into the master bath. "Holy shit," she muttered as she saw the bloodstained sink and towels.

She hurried back to the living room; Alice was where she left her. "You want to tell me what happened here?"

Alice stared at Syd in stony silence.

"Look, Alice," Syd said. "I know what Adam, Colin and Blake did to you. I just came from your parents. I know what *they* did to you. I understand what you've been through. Why you've done what you've done. And I'd like to help you. But I can't help you unless you help me help you. So please, tell me what happened tonight."

Alice could hear the honesty in Syd's words. She sensed she could trust her. "I could tell you, or you could watch it yourself."

"What're you talking about?"

"Blake Hunter wanted to make a documentary. He knocked me out, handcuffed me and was videotaping me when I tried to escape. It's all on a tape, in my purse."

Syd grabbed Alice's purse, pulled out the tape. Then her eyes settled on the DVD case. She took it out, turned it over and saw the handwritten title, **High School Pool Party.** "Is this what I think it is?"

Alice nodded.

"He was videotaping you watching yourself get raped?" Syd ask, astounded.

"That's right."

"Motherfucker."

"You should watch the rape, too. But start with the other one."

Alice showed Syd where the camera was in the office. Syd loaded the digital tape.

"You'll have to watch it on the camera's monitor," Alice said.

Syd flipped open the monitor, it was a small screen, maybe six inches wide, certainly big enough to watch the video.

"It's cued up," Alice said. "Just hit Play."

Syd did.

The angle is over Blake's shoulder to a handcuffed and bound Alice. She says, "Fuck you."

"That's more like it," Blake says then walks towards her on his way to the door. Alice suddenly kicks Blake in the back of the knee, he falls down.

"Bitch," he says as he tries to get to his feet. But the Lady in Red has dragged her feet toward his head and she kicks him in the head. His head hits the wall with a crack.

"Cunt," he says as she kicks him again and again. Finally his body has gone limp and she stops kicking.

The Lady in Red crawls over him, flips onto her back

and fishes the handcuff keys out of his pocket. She unlocks the handcuffs and tosses them away, then quickly unties her feet and hustles out of the room.

"I ran into the living room to get my gun out of my purse."

Blake stirs, leaps up and dashes into the kitchen.

"But Blake had obviously found it earlier and hid it so I took the only weapon I had, the scalpel."

The kitchen is visible through the office doorway. Blake re-enters frame, pulls open a drawer, takes out a gun, aims and fires.

"He hit me in the shoulder, but I went down like he'd killed me and played dead," Alice said.

Blake stands there a moment, trying to decide what to do. He aims off screen, seems about to pull the trigger then reconsiders and walks out of frame.

"Fuck," Alice said. "He was about to shoot me from the kitchen."

"Thank God he changed his mind," Syd said, completely wrapped up in the video.

Syd's sympathy caught Alice by surprise. Just who the hell was this cop?

There's a scream from off camera and three quick shots, a loud THUD and the gun slid into the right side of the frame.

"When he got close to me, I slashed his ankle with my scalpel. I cut him and he went down. I jumped on him slashing his face, but he shoved me off."

A bloody Blake pulls himself into frame and reaches

for the gun. Alice suddenly appears and jabs the scalpel through the back of Blake's hand. He screams in agony as she picks up the gun.

He looked at her, terrified. "Don't shoot. I know people. I can help you get away, out of the country with a new identity and plenty of money. Just please, don't shoot."

Alice slowly lowers the gun, Blake looks surprised, pleased; then she quickly raises the gun and fires.

Blake Hunter's head jerks once then drops to the floor.

Syd hit the stop button, looked at Alice. "You're lucky to be alive."

"I'd be luckier if you weren't here."

Syd turned off the video camera. Her eyes fell on the DVD. She picked it up. "You sure you don't mind if I watch this?"

Alice was surprised by the compassion in Syd's voice. She really didn't want to see it herself again, but she wanted this cop, this woman, to understand exactly what happened to her. "I don't mind," she said. "In fact, you need to see it."

Alice pointed out the DVD player, Syd loaded the disk.

"You know," Alice said. "Every time I watch this DVD I'm in handcuffs. Kind of ironic, don't you think?"

Syd smiled cheerlessly. "Yeah." Syd picked up the remote control and hit Play.

A hand held camera sweeps across Colin Wood's game room and comes to rest on an unconscious Alice Waterman. Adam and Colin kneel next to her. "Fuck, that shit works fast," Colin says. "Help me get her on the pool table, Adam."

They pick her off the floor and lay her on the pool table. Colin holds her neck but he lets go too soon and her head thuds on the table.

"Careful," Adam says, looking very uncomfortable. He looks directly into the lens. "You sure taping this is a good idea, Blake?"

"It's a brilliant idea, bro. When we're old and gray and snorting Viagra, we're going to cherish the chance to relive our glory days."

And that's when Syd's phone rang. She hit Pause.

"You going to get that?" Alice asked.

"No," Syd said after fishing out her cell phone and checking the Caller ID. "He can leave a message." Syd turned off her phone and looked back at the screen. She hit Play.

"Get her clothes off," Blake says from behind the camera. Colin pulls off her sandals as Adam peels off her tank top.

"How convenient," Blake says, zooming into a close up of Alice's bra. "It unhooks from the front. She was making things easy for you, Adam. She wanted you to suck her titties."

Blake zooms out as Adam says, "Shut up." He unhooks the bra then lifts her back up a bit and slips it off.

"Nice," Colin says cradling her breasts in his hands. He sucks on her left nipple. "Hey, she put some perfume on her tits." Colin looks at Adam. "She went all porn star for you, buddy."

Adam leans down, sniffs her right breast. "Wow," he says surprised. Then he looks at her face. Blake follows his look with the camera and zooms in on Alice's face. Her eyes are at half-mast and her mouth gaps open. She looks drunk.

"She looks bad, man," Blake says. "Maybe we should stick her head in a bag," Blake says. He zooms out, pans to Adam.

"You are such an asshole," Adam says, but he's smiling as he says it.

"Bet she doused her pussy, too," Blake says. "Colin, get her panties off."

Blake pans to Colin as he unzips her jeans and pulls them off revealing black boyshort panties. Blake zooms in, black curly pubic hairs stick out from the sides of the panties. Colin peels off the panties revealing a thick black patch of hair trimmed into a triangle. Colin leans down and smells it. "Yep, perfumed for your dining pleasure." He takes another sniff. "I think its ode de lick-my-clit."

"Dive in," Blake says.

Colin spreads her legs and nestles his face between Alice's legs. His hands massage her breasts as he gives her head.

Alice stirs beneath him. Moans. Blake zooms in on her face as she mutters, "Oh, Adam..."

"She's got it bad for you, Adam," Blake says. "Least you could you do is kiss her."

Blake pans to Adam who was staring into the lens. He looks unhappy. "Fuck you, Blake," Adam says.

Blake says, "You're no fun." He pans the camera back to Colin who stands up wiping his mouth with the back of his hands. "She tastes good, man. You should try it."

"Okay." The picture whips wildly as Blake hands the camera to Colin. A close-up of Blake now fills the frame. "I'm going in." Colin pans Blake to Alice's breasts as Blake gently kneads them and then settles in to suck the right breast. "She does smell good," he says with a mouthful of nipple. Then he bites down, hard.

Alice yelps.

"You don't have to hurt her," Adam says from off camera.

"Ignore him," Blake says. "He's in love." Blake now settles in between Alice's thighs. He pulls back skin exposing her clitoris. "Colin, zoom in on her pussy." The camera zooms in on the exposed pink flesh. "Sweet," Blake says, then his tongue enters frame. Colin widens a bit as Blake gives her head.

"Excellent technique," Colin says. "Hey this could be an invaluable instructional video." He pans to Adam. "What do you think, professor? Any tips for our audience?"

"No," Adam says sourly and walks to the bar. He pours himself a stiff shot of Jack Daniels and tosses it

down.

"Hey are we here to fuck or drink?" Blake says from off camera. Colin pans the camera back to Blake. He pulls off his shorts and underwear together. He's got an erection. "Lets see if she's able to give head." Blake slides Alice's head around so it's now on the rail, near the edge of the pool table. He gently opens her mouth and slips his penis inside. He begins to gently move it in and out. "Come on, baby," he whispers. "We've heard you give great blow jobs."

Alice moans again, looks at Blake, seeing but not seeing; and her lips wrap around Blake's penis. Her head begins to move and, before long, she's doing all the work.

"Amazing," Colin says from behind camera.

"You sure she's not going to remember any of this," Adam asks from off camera.

"Guaran-fucking-teed," Blake says, leering at the camera. "Hey, Colin, zoom in tight so you just see her sucking my cock." The camera zooms in. "Oh, yeah, Alice, suck it baby..."

"Don't come in her mouth, Blake," Colin says. "My dad would kill me if she dribbled your jizz all over the felt and ruined the table."

"Don't worry," Blake says, I'm not going to waste my first shot in her mouth." He pulls out. "Hand me the camera; your turn." The picture swishes violently as Colin hands the camera to Blake. "Drop trou, dude. The water's fine."

Blake focuses the camera on Colin's midsection as Colin unbuckles his belt and pulls down his jeans revealing a pair of pale blue boxer shorts, tented by Colin's erect penis. Colin strips the boxers away and then proudly displays his cock for the camera.

"He came to play ladies and gentlemen," Blake says. Colin steers his manhood toward Alice's mouth then hesitated. "Go ahead, bro, stick it in her mouth." He does and, after a few moments, Alice's lips wrap around him and she goes to work.

"Yeah, suck it baby," Colin says as Blake zooms in

tight, so only the penis and her face are on screen.

"I recognize that angle," Alice said to Syd. "You know about the pictures of me that Blake emailed to everyone at school?"

"Yes."

"This was one of them. Me sucking a cock. Sent to *everybody.*"

Syd could imagine the mortification. She was terrified in high school that one day the kids there would find out what her stepfather was doing to her. She couldn't even imagine how she might have felt if people actually saw pictures of it.

"I always wondered whose cock it was," Alice said. "Now I know. Colin fucking Wood. And as humiliating as it is to watch them strip, maul and mouth fuck me, I'm absolutely mortified when I remember all the time and energy I put into deciding what I was going to wear that night."

"Your mother mentioned you had a crush on Adam."

"I was head over heels in love. And when he invited me to this party, I was so excited. I thought my life was going to change forever that night. Boy was I right."

Colin pulled his penis out of her mouth. "Okay, Adam, your turn."

The camera swings across the room to Adam, still standing at the bar, another drink in his hand. "Nah, you guys go ahead, I'm good here."

"Don't go getting all limp dick on us, man," Blake says. "We had a deal, all for one and one for all. Now give her a taste of your tumescent tonsil tickler."

"Mrs. Reynolds would love your use of alliteration," Colin says from off screen.

Blake laughs from behind the camera but the lens never leaves Adam's face. "What's the problem, bro? We've got a naked girl on the pool table willing to do whatever we want."

"We've got an unconscious girl on the table, Blake."

"Hey, inviting Alice was your idea. You're the one who told us she was practically stalking you. You're the one who said she'd be an easy mark. Now come on, Adam, give her what she really wants. You."

Adam didn't look happy, but he put his drink down and walked over to the pool table. He reached down, stroked Alice's breasts, and then cupped a hand over her vagina. Blake zoomed in as Adam slipped a finger inside. "She's dry as a bone," Adam said.

"That's why God invented K-Y," Blake said. Blake swung the camera to Colin. "There's a tube on the bar, dude, and a stack of condoms. Why don't you fix our boy up?"

Colin finds the lubricant and condoms. He tosses the tube first, and then detaches one of the condoms and, as he throws it, the camera pans back to Adam. "Showtime, bro," Blake says.

But Adam just stands there, the K-Y and Trojan in his hand, staring at Alice.

"What's a matter, Adam," Colin says from off camera. "Can't get it up?"

"Fuck you," Adam mutters. "And fuck this." He sets the K-Y and Trojan on the edge of the pool table and starts for the door.

Oh, my God, thought Syd. Adam didn't rape her. She killed him for nothing.

"Faggot," Blake calls stopping Adam at the door.

"I don't think he can get it up," Colin says. "From now on we'll have to call him limp dick Devlin."

"Or LDD for short," Blake says. "And when everyone asks why we call you LDD, we'll tell them it's because you can't get it up."

Adam turns, embarrassment burning his cheeks. "You want to see me fuck her? Fine," he says strutting back to the pool table. He pulls down his cargo shorts and underpants revealing a fully erect penis. "That hard enough for you," he sneers.

Then Adam rips open the condom package and slips it on.

"Ribbed for her enjoyment," Colin jokes from off camera.

Adam grabs Alice by the thighs and pulls her hips to the edge of the table. He steps between her legs.

"Don't forget the K-Y," Blake says.

"Fuck the K-Y," Adam says and thrusts.

Okay, Syd thought. He deserved that bullet to the face.

Then Syd watched as first Adam, then Colin and finally Blake raped Alice. Colin actually shoved his cock in Alice's mouth as Blake raped her. The boys hooted and howled having a great time with their comatose victim.

Those hoots and howls, grunts and groans triggered a flood of horrific memories. During her drug-addicted hooker years Syd had been the *girl-on-the-pool-table* many times. There was a frat house at USC, five or six rowdy bachelor parties, a drunken fiftieth birthday party, five Merrill Lynch brokers celebrating an IPO, a limo full of rappers celebrating a gold record. All those men, their hands, tongues, cocks inside her. Taking turns poking and prodding, sucking and fucking, reducing her to nothing more than a hunk of meat, a human receptacle.

Of all Syd's drug-drenched memories, the gangbangs were the worst, the most demeaning, the most repugnant. And now watching Alice's gang rape first hand, not reading about it in a police report, not hearing it from shell-shocked victim, but seeing it with her own eyes touched a chord in Syd that both broke her heart and enraged her.

Syd's eyes drifted to Alice; she was watching her own molestation with a forlorn expression on her beautiful face. She looked so desolate, so… disillusioned, yes that was the word disillusioned. Because on that night, on that pool table, all Alice's childhood hopes and dreams were stolen from her.

Syd looked back to the screen.

Blake pulls up his pants. "Jenna Jameson she's not,

but hey, I've had worse."

"Now what?" Colin asks from behind the camera.

"Now we have a little more fun," Blake says. He picks up a pool cue. "I saw this in a porno, always wanted to try it."

He takes the cue and slowly slides it into Alice's vagina. He sticks it in deeper, deeper until he finally stops. "I've hit bottom, boys."

"Wow," Colin says, "She took like fifteen inches of that thing."

Blake slowly pulls the cue stick out of Alice as an idea lights up his face. "Hey," he says. "Who's up for a trip down the Hersey highway?"

"Count me in, bro," Colin says.

Blake rolls Alice over and slaps her on the butt. "Her face may not be much to look at, but she's sure got a fine ass."

"Think she's ever had anal sex?" Colin asks.

"Don't know," Blake says. "Hey Adam, you ever hear if she takes it up the butt?"

Colin pans the camera to Adam at the bar. "No. Tim Schroeder just mentioned a blow job and a three way with Davey Winder."

"Actually, I don't think it matters," Blake says as Colin pans the camera back to him. "It's not like we need her permission."

Colin laughs. "You are bad, D-man."

Blake picks up the tube of K-Y, squeezes a dollop into his palm, and then applies it to the shaft of the pool cue. "Time for a little recon," Blake says. He inserts the end of the pool cue into her anus and gently pushes. The shaft disappears into her butt, an inch at a time.

"Next time you invite me over to play pool," Adam says. "I'm bringing my own cue."

Then a new voice is heard: "What the fuck are you doing?"

The camera swings to the door where a man is standing. He's got a long face, bushy eyebrows and a full head of salt and pepper hair.

"Oh, Jesus," Colin says. "Dad. I --"

"Get that thing out of her," Nick Wood says as the camera pans him to the pool table. Blake removes the pool cue, drops it to the floor and backs toward the bar. But the camera stays on Nick Wood as he stares at Alice.

"What's wrong with her?" He slurs his words a bit, like he's been drinking.

"Nothing, Dad. She's the school slut. She came over to party with us and got drunk." Nick Wood's eyes go to the floor; the camera follows his gaze to the pile of used condoms, then whips back to Nick Wood's face.

"You all fucked her?"

"Yeah, but it was her idea. She's like this crazy nympho chick. She wants to be a porn star and begged us to film her."

"She beg you to stick a pool cue up her ass, too?" he snaps as he rolls Alice over puts a finger to her carotid to check her pulse. As he does, his eyes drift down to her breasts.

"I thought you were going to be in Cabo until Sunday, Dad."

"I decided to come back early. Next time I'll be sure to warn you." He takes his finger from neck. "Her pulse is strong."

"I told you she just had too much to drink."

Nick Wood looks directly into the lens. "Get that camera out of my face. Turn it off, Colin. Now."

The picture swings wildly as Colin carries the camera to the bar and sets it down. The picture is suddenly rock steady. In the right foreground of the frame is the bottle of Jack Daniels, in middle of the frame are Colin, Blake, Adam. Nick Wood stands in front of the pool table. Alice is visible on the left side of the frame.

"Well, boys, the party's over. Everyone out!" The boys hurry for the door. "And Colin," Nick Wood says. "You are so grounded."

The boys exit the room.

"Thank God Nick Wood showed up," Syd said. "No

telling what they would have done to you next." Syd reached for the Stop button on the remote control.

"Wait," Alice said. "It's not over."

Syd was confused. "But they all just left the room."

"True. But I'm still not alone."

Shock filled Syd's face as the implication registered. No. Fucking. Way.

She turned back to the screen.

The angle hasn't changed. The camera is on the bar pointed toward the pool table. Nick Wood closes the game room door, stands there thinking for a moment, then locks it. He walks back to the pool table, looks at Alice.

"So young," he says.

He walks toward camera, picks up the bottle of Jack Daniels, pours himself a drink. Only half of his face is visible on the right side of frame. "So damn young," he repeats.

He sips his drink and his eyes spot something behind the camera. His hand reaches past the camera, and then comes back into frame holding a condom. He stares at it for a long time, thinking, and then a mischievous smile tugs his lips.

He turns back to Alice. He takes a long pull on his drink as he slowly makes his way back to the pool table. He weaves a bit as he walks.

"Hello," he says. "Can you hear me?"

No response.

"Hello," he says, gently shaking her naked shoulder. Nothing.

His hand is still on her shoulder. He slowly lowers it until his hand covers her breast. He begins stroking the breast, watching her face for any reaction.

He puts down his glass and now both hands are on her breasts.

He bends down and kisses the breasts. One of his hands drifts past her stomach and buries itself in her pubic hair.

He suddenly stands, shakes his head. "This is crazy,"

he mumbles. He veers toward the door, looks like he's going to leave, but no, he just double checks to make sure it's locked. He turns back to Alice.

"What the fuck," he says and pulls down his pants. He rips open the condom, slips it on and inserts himself into the naked, unconscious girl.

The sight of a fifty-year-old man raping an unconscious seventeen-year-old girl horrified Syd. She remembered meeting Nick Wood in the morgue. And then pieces of the puzzle started to fall into place.

Zachary Stone was Nick Wood's lawyer. Nick Wood must've heard Stone had been killed on Saturday night. And when his son Colin was murdered by a woman on Monday night, Nick Wood realized who the killer was. But instead of telling us he hid out. Why? Because he was afraid he might be on her hit list.

Nick Wood grunts as he comes, pulls out of Alice, rips off the used condom and tosses it into the trash.

"Thank you for a lovely evening," he says, and laughs. Then he pulls up his pants, grabs the bottle of Jack Daniels and leaves the room.

"Unbelievable," Syd said.

"Mr. Wood had no idea his son had left the camera on. Blake told me he didn't realize either until the next day when he was fast-forwarding through the tape looking for some frames to email. Then when the shit hit the fan at school and he got worried about me going to the cops, he called Mr. Wood and told him he knew what he did to me."

"And that's why Nick Wood was willing to pay so much," Syd said. "He couldn't risk this tape going public, so he was willing to pay anything to stop your parents from going to the cops."

"My father sold me out for a million dollars."

The amount shocked Syd. She'd known there'd been a settlement, but not how much. A million dollars, wow. And that got her thinking... If Nick Wood hadn't been recorded raping Alice, if he wasn't personally in danger of going to jail, would he have coughed up a million dollars? Not likely.

So if Nick Wood hadn't raped Alice, there would have been no payoff so Alice would have gone to the police with her parents and gotten her day in court. She might never have tried to kill herself. She might never have gone to the Institute. She might have had all her childhood dreams come true.

The real bad guy here, the ultimate bad guy, was Nick Wood.

"So now you've got a problem," Syd said. "You have another man to kill."

Alice looked at her, surprised. "That's right. My plan was to just kill the four of them, Blake, Adam, Colin and that lawyer. After that, it didn't matter. I actually wanted to get caught by the police so I could tell my story." Alice laughed. "I had this crazy thought my story might inspire other women to fight back, stand up for themselves the way I didn't. Men take advantage of women every day and we just let them! Well, I was sending a message with every bullet, with every amputated prick. And if other women started fighting back, started to make men pay for their cruelty, maybe, just maybe, scumbags like Colin, Adam and Blake would think twice before they rape somebody."

Okay, thought Syd. That's a little nuts, but hey, she's spent the last eleven years in a psychiatric hospital, what do you expect.

And Syd thought she knew the answer to the next question but she asked it anyway. "Why now, Alice? Why wait eleven years?"

"I've got cancer. The doctors just gave me a few months to live. They told me to use the time as productively as I could. I don't think they had my becoming a serial killer in mind, but hey, it seemed like a good idea at the time."

So she was living a lie, Syd thought. A psychiatric trick gone horribly awry. The question was, should Syd tell her that?

"I am a little ashamed that it took a death sentence for me to take my revenge," Alice said. "But I was never willing to throw my life away to get back at them. You know, go to jail or get killed trying to get even. As crappy as my life was, at least it was my life. That's what keeps most victims down isn't it, the law's crazy insistence on even punishing the innocent if they want a little payback?"

Syd was about to give her the standard answer about civilization being built on laws and blah blah blah, instead she blurted out, "It didn't hold me back. I killed my stepfather."

Alice's eyes went wide. "You what?"

"He'd been sexually abusing me for years and one night I just... killed him. I never told anyone that before. Never even said it out loud."

"Why'd you tell me?"

"I don't know. Because I wanted you to know I understand how you feel, I guess. And my road from there to here hasn't been easy. I barely made it. Yet, even knowing that, if I had it to do over again, kill him I mean, I would do it in a second."

"Justice."

Syd nodded. "Justice."

Then they sat for a moment, both lost in their own thoughts, the only sound the crashing of waves on the beach.

Then Syd made a decision. She stood up, pulled a key out of her pocket, leaned down and unlocked Alice's handcuffs. "Nick Wood is in hiding. I'm not sure where he is, but a good place to start may be his house."

Syd helped Alice to her feet. "You're letting me go?"

Syd shrugged. "By the time I got here you were gone." Syd reached into her jacket pocket, handed Alice her scalpel and gun. "I don't know how much time I can buy you, so act fast."

"Thank you..." Alice laughed. "I don't even know your name."

"Syd. My name is Syd."

"Thank you, Syd."

And now it was time to tell her the truth about the cancer, Syd thought. "There's something you should know Alice..." Syd trailed off as she saw Ryan step into the living room. Alice saw Syd's reaction and turned to see who was there.

And that's what Ryan saw, the Lady in Red turning toward him, a gun in her right hand. Years of training kicked in and purely on instinct, Ryan raised his Glock and fired twice even as Syd called, "Ryan, no!"

Both shots hit Alice in the chest. She staggered back and then crumpled to the floor. Syd dropped next to her. Blood pumped from the two chest wounds. "Alice," Syd cried as she tried to stem the bleeding. But it was too late. Alice placed her hands over Syd's, looked her new friend in the eye, managed a feeble smile, and died.

FORTY-EIGHT

Ryan rushed to Syd, knelt down. "Are you all right?"

Syd stared at Ryan, a bit dazed, trying to make sense out of what just happened. "I'm fine. What're you doing here?"

Ryan looked at her, confused. "You called me, left a message. I called back but you didn't answer. You sure you're okay."

No, thought Syd. But she said, "I'm sure, yeah, I'm fine."

The sound of distant sirens cut through the night. Syd reacted, surprised. "You called for backup?"

"When I pulled up, I saw your car. You didn't answer your phone, so yeah. I called Hanrahan, told him to send the cavalry." His eyes slid off her to the Lady in Red. "Want to tell me what happened before I got here?"

Syd had a decision to make. Trust Ryan or lie. Finally telling someone about her stepfather had felt good. Syd would love to tell Ryan about her stepfather; what he did to her, why she'd felt a bond to the Lady in Red, how she was about to let the Lady in Red go. She wanted to trust Ryan with everything. Tell him about those first terrible years in Hollywood, about Ernesto, the EMT, Eric Templeton, his sister, Andrea. To trust him with everything. Yesterday it would have been a no-brainer, yesterday she trusted him with her life.

But tonight, after seeing him in Anne's arms, she wasn't so sure.

Syd said, "I only got here a few minutes ago, saw the body on the living room floor and started searching for the Lady in Red. But I fucked up, Ryan. When I was looking here in the office, she got the drop on me."

Syd could see doubt in Ryan's eyes, but she plowed

ahead before he could poke at her story. "I was actually talking to her when you showed up, trying to get her to turn herself in. She came here to kill Blake Hunter, but he got the gun away from her, shot her in the shoulder; she fought back with the scalpel, got the gun back and killed him."

Ryan glanced at the Lady in Red, saw the bloodstain on her shoulder.

"Take a look at what she did to Blake Hunter, Ryan. He's a mess."

Ryan hesitated, he knew Syd well enough to know he wasn't getting the whole story, but he figured no need to rush it, especially since he had a bagful of his own deceit to deal with.

So he stood up, stepped carefully around the bloodstains to examine Blake Hunter. "Jesus fucking Christ," Ryan muttered. "She filleted him."

"They must've had one hell of a fight," Syd said. "Check out the master bathroom, there's blood everywhere."

Ryan was happy to look at anything but Blake's butchered face.

"Down the hall to the left," Syd said, pointing. As soon as Ryan disappeared down the hall, Syd hustled to the DVD player and hit the eject button. The **High School Pool Party** disc slid out. She stuck it in her jacket pocket. Next she grabbed the digital tape out of the video camera and tucked it safely away.

In the bathroom Ryan stared at the bloodstained towels, discarded bandage packaging, open medicine cabinets. Something on one of the bottles caught his attention; he put on his surgical gloves, carefully picked up the bottle. A bloody fingerprint was on the label. Then he noticed the same fingerprints on other bottles. The Lady in Red had gone through Blake's drugs. Looking for what? Then he saw the open bottle of Betadine; she was looking for antiseptic he realized. She wanted to disinfect the gunshot wound.

He looked back at the fingerprint on the label again, the fragment of an idea stirring in the back of his head.

Syd stepped into the bathroom. "She left plenty of DNA this time," Syd said.

"And fingerprints," Ryan said. "Either you interrupted her before she could clean up or she didn't care anymore."

"I don't think she cared anymore. She'd finished what she started."

"What do you mean?"

"She'd killed the men who raped her. I talked to her parents, Ryan, found out what happened. Eleven years ago, when Alice was a high school senior, she was invited to a party by a boy she had a crush on, Adam Devlin. Only there was no party, just three horny high school boys, Adam, Colin Wood and Blake Hunter. They drugged her then gang raped her. Blake videotaped the whole thing. The next day he emailed nude pictures of Alice having sex to all his friends. She wanted to go to the police but a lawyer representing the three boys showed up and paid Alice's family a million dollars to walk away."

"And let me guess, the lawyer's name was Zachary Stone."

"Give the smart detective a cigar."

Ryan digested the story; the refocused picture of the Lady in Red didn't sit well. She'd just been transformed from serial murderer to victim. And he'd killed her. He sagged a bit as the implications pierced his soul.

Syd saw remorse flood his face. "You had no choice, Ryan. You saw a suspect holding a weapon turning toward you. You had to shoot." Syd meant every word. If anything, she knew it was her fault Alice was dead. If Syd hadn't been pissed at Ryan and just answered his phone call, he wouldn't have charged into the house with his gun drawn.

The sirens had been steadily getting louder. Now they reached a crescendo and suddenly stopped.

"We've got company," Syd said.

Chaos. That was the best way to describe the crime scene an hour later. Since Malibu falls under the L.A. County Sheriff's jurisdiction, when Lieutenant Hanrahan got the call from Ryan, Hanrahan phoned the Sheriff's Department and they scrambled two patrol cars to secure the scene.

Officially, the murder of Blake Hunter would be a L.A. County Sheriff's investigation, but since LAPD had processed the scenes of the Lady in Red's last two murders, and since an LAPD officer was involved in a shooting, it became a dual investigation. So detectives and crime scene technicians from both departments soon swarmed Blake Hunter's beach house.

That kind of manpower can confuse any crime scene but it was nothing compared to the gathering media circus.

The press monitors LAPD and Sheriff's Department frequencies so it wasn't long before word of a murder in Malibu spread throughout the city. And if that wasn't newsworthy enough, minutes later it was confirmed that it was a Lady in Red story. She had murdered another victim and then she had been killed in a shootout with an LAPD detective. But not just any detective, it was Detective Ryan Magee, the lottery-winning cop who was about to get a check for tens of millions of dollars.

And though it was midnight, cell phones rang, engines started, helicopter blades whirled; every resource was scrambled to cover the story. Soon the Pacific Coast Highway was clogged with satellite trucks, the sky was filled with news choppers and the shoreline outside Blake Hunter's beach house was choked with camera-toting boats.

Sheriff's deputies and police barricades kept the Press at bay, but the reporters, photographers and cameramen knew that Ryan Magee would have to come out at some point and they wanted to be there when he did.

Inside the house, Tony Ramirez and his SID team, aided by the Sherriff's Department forensic experts, scoured the house. Liz finished her examination of Blake Hunter's body and crossed to the Lady in Red's corpse.

Off to the side and safely out of the way, Ryan and Syd stood with Hanrahan. Hanrahan sucked on a cherry Tootsie Roll Pop. Ryan and Syd had declined Hanrahan's offer.

After Syd summarized Alice's high school rape and Syd's abridged version of the Blake/Lady in Red battle, Hanrahan said, "Wait, you're saying the rape was videotaped."

Syd nodded. "Blake Hunter taped the whole thing and then he used frames from the tape to send out those disgusting emails."

"Where's the tape now?" Hanrahan asked.

Syd planned to *discover* the DVD in a day or so. She wanted the world to see what happened to Alice Waterman. To understand what drove the Lady in Red to kill those men. And maybe help realize Alice's hope that her rape and ultimate revenge would inspire and empower other rape victims. But she couldn't turn the tape over. Not yet.

"I don't know," Syd said.

"Blake Hunter's office is full of tapes and DVDs," Ryan said. "And he's got stacks of hard drives. It could be here, but it'll take us a while to go through them all."

Tony Ramirez joined them. "Well, unlike all the other crime scenes, this one is teeming with evidence. Some familiar, like the Lady in Red numbering her victims; she used the four of hearts this time. And the severed penis, I get it already, she hated these guys. And he's got a missing American Express card, which I found in her wallet. But we've got a lot of new stuff; I found five .25mm shell casings, one in the kitchen floor and four in the living room. In the past the Lady in Red always picked up her brass. We've got blood in the living room, on the floor leading into the master bath and all over the master bath. Bloody fingerprints galore in the master bath; I did a quick check with the Lady in Red's fingers, they match. There also signs of a struggle in the office; there are fresh bloodstains and tissue fragments on that wall," he said pointing.

"That would be Blake Hunter's blood and skin," Liz said joining them. "Besides the scalpel lacerations and that bullet hole between his eyes, he shows signs of blunt force trauma to his face and forehead, and his Achilles' tendon has been severed."

"And let's not forget his cock," Hanrahan said.

"I've seen bigger." Liz said.

Hanrahan grunted.

Liz went on. "The Lady in Red has the three gunshot wounds as well as a huge contusion on the top of her skull and abrasions on both wrists."

"Probably from these," Ramirez said holding up an evidence bag containing Blake's fur-lined handcuffs. "I found them on the floor of the office."

"Yep," Liz said. "Those would do it."

"And this is interesting," Tony Ramirez said, holding up Blake's camera. He turned it on and showed them the digital screen in back. A stunning picture of the Lady in Red backlit by the sunset appeared. Tony hit a button and scanned through three more poses.

"Wow, classy shots," Liz said.

"Wait, he was taking pictures of her, too?" Hanrahan said. "So let me get this straight, he takes her picture, knocks her out, handcuffs and shoots her. She bangs his head into the wall, cuts his ankle, slashes his face and shoots him in the head."

"I've had worse dates," Liz said.

"God, I'd love to know exactly what happened here." Hanrahan said.

"I don't think we'll ever really know for sure," Ryan said.

Oh yes you will, Syd thought. She intended to *find* the videotape of Alice and Blake's fight to the death when she *discovered* the rape tape. The image of Alice, bound and handcuffed, being forced to watch her own rape was too heartbreaking not to release. And Alice's brave fight to save herself was downright inspirational.

But once again, not yet.

"You guys finished?" Hanrahan asked Liz and Tony. They both nodded. "All right, good work."

Liz turned to her two assistants. "Let's bag them up." They dropped the first body bag next to Blake and unrolled it.

Tony Ramirez headed into the kitchen where he left his

crime scene kit. He started boxing the evidence. "Excuse me a minute," Ryan said to the others and went to join Tony.

"So," Hanrahan said, turning to Syd. "Looks like you and Ryan have still got the only perfect record in Homicide. You're my Dream Team."

Some dream team, Syd thought. A bitch-fucking, backstabbing, lottery stealing Ryan and a lying, evidence stealing, murdering Syd. "We make a great team, all right," Syd said.

And, Syd thought, there was a very good chance their partnership wouldn't last past tomorrow. If, as she feared, Ryan and Anne hooked up, she'd be asking Hanrahan for a transfer.

Hanrahan drifted off leaving Syd alone. She glanced into the kitchen. Ryan was huddled with Tony Ramirez, Tony was shaking his head and laughing. What the hell were they talking about, Syd wondered.

A body bag was unrolled next to the Lady in Red. Syd watched as the coroner assistants picked Alice up, slipped her into the bag and zipped her up. Was there anything more dehumanizing than being zipped into a black plastic bag?

"There's a lot of sympathy in those green eyes," Liz said joining Syd.

"I feel sorry for her, Liz. She was a good kid just trying to get by before those boys raped her. And I can't help but wonder what her life would have been like if she didn't go to that party."

"I call it the Domino Theory," Liz said. "The innocent single event leads to an inevitably tragic conclusion. This morning I had a six-year-old boy on my table, shot once through the head. Last night he found his dad's handgun in a bedside drawer and started playing with it. He dropped it, it went off and killed him. So when did the first domino fall? When the kid found the gun, when his dad put the gun in the drawer instead of the top shelf of the closet, when his dad bought the gun, when his dad read the newspaper article about a home invasion in their neighborhood that sent him to the gun store in the first place? Sometimes it gets a bit murky, but it's always there, the first domino. And if you could just stand it up again, stop the chain reaction, then so much needless tragedy could be undone."

Was tonight's domino the bus ride eleven years ago when Alice fell in love with Adam, Syd wondered. Or her saying yes when he asked her to the party, or Adam not walking out the door of the game room that night, or Nick Wood raping Alice, or Alice's father selling her out, or the doctor's lying to her about the cancer or Syd not answering Ryan's phone call?

Liz asked, "And what was the first domino in your relationship with Ryan? The day you first met him... or the day he first met Anne?"

Syd recalled her binocular-enhanced view of Ryan kissing Anne. A melancholy smile touched Syd's lips. "I'm afraid it was the day he met Anne."

Liz touched Syd's arm. "I'm sorry, sweetie."

"Well, it's not over until the greedy bitch sings."

Liz laughed.

From the kitchen Ryan watched Syd and Liz. What was Liz laughing about, he wondered. But Syd didn't look amused, if anything, she looked downright miserable.

Ryan knew Syd lied to him. She'd said she'd just arrived at the house a few minutes earlier, but when Ryan arrived, he put his hand on the hood of Syd's car. It was cool, so she'd been there at least a half an hour. Plus, she told him to check out the mess in the master bathroom, but if the Lady in Red had gotten the drop on Syd in the office, how would she have known what was in the master bath?

He wanted to know why she lied. He wanted to know what really happened inside 22756 Pacific Coast Highway.

And then there was the bigger question. What was to become of them? Looking at Syd he knew he still loved her. But after the way Anne so easily seduced Ryan, he had to wonder if he loved Syd enough. And what does he tell Syd about what happened at the hotel? If he tells her the truth, could she ever forgive him? Should he lie to protect her feelings?

Syd's attention returned to Ryan. He was tense, tenser than she'd ever seen him. And ever since he first walked into Blake Hunter's house, there had been a reticence to Ryan, like he was holding something back. Anne? She wanted to ask him what happened at the hotel, but she was terrified he'd lie to her and she could never forgive him if he lied.

And so there they stood; two people looking across the crowded room at each other, with so much to say to one another, and no idea how to say it.

The sky outside the picture windows lightened as sunrise approached. "Okay, people, time to feed the sharks," Hanrahan said. "Ryan, you're the reason every reporter in Southern California is camped outside this house. You want to make a statement?"

Ryan felt bad about killing the Lady in Red and worse about the lottery. The last thing he wanted to do is face a barrage of questions. "It's been a long night, Lieutenant; if it's all right with you, I'd just like to get home and grab a little sleep before tomorrow's lottery presentation."

"No problem. Syd, this is your chance to get famous; want to go out there and tell everyone how you broke the case?"

My chance to get famous, Syd thought. For years that drive to get famous had fueled her career in the LAPD. But now, somehow, it didn't seem as important as it did a few days ago. "I'm kind of beat, too, Chief. I'll pass if you don't mind."

Hanrahan reacted, surprised. "No problem," he said. "I can handle it. You and Ryan head home and we'll run interference."

"Sounds good," Syd said.

"Thanks, Lieutenant," Ryan said, and then something occurred to him. "Wait, we still need to go through all of Blake Hunter video material, see if we can find the high school tape."

Syd panicked for a moment but was saved by Hanrahan. "It's late, you've been up all night. We'll seal the house, come back tomorrow after the Lotto presentation."

"Great," Ryan said stifling a yawn.

Ryan and Syd weaved their separate ways through the crowded room and met at the door. "Are you coming to the presentation?" Ryan asked.

"Do you want me there?"

"Of course I do. You're the one who got me into this mess. You're the one who found the ticket."

Oh, shit, Syd thought. Maybe that was the domino in her relationship with Ryan, finding that stinking ticket.

"I'll be there, Ryan, but I need to go home and grab some sleep."

Ryan got her meaning. She wanted to go to her apartment, alone. And honestly, so did he. Ryan needed time to figure out what the hell to say. "Yeah, me, too," he said.

As they stepped outside, the army of reporters, cameramen and photographers burst to life. Strobes flashed, camera shutters clicked, video cameras zoomed in, the helicopters swooped low and questions were hurled at them over the police barricades.

Syd stared at the frantic faces of the massed media; part of her still yearned to step up to the gathered microphones and bask in the limelight and part of her was revolted by their scavenger-like behavior.

"Detective Magee, is it true you shot the Lady in Red?"

"Do you know why she went on a killing spree?"

"Can you confirm reports that she killed a man in Newport Beach last week?"

They ignored the questions as Sherriff's Deputies cleared a path so Ryan and Syd could back out of the driveway. Ryan opened Syd's door. Syd got in, and was about to ask Ryan about his meeting with Anne. But she was afraid of the answer; afraid he'd lie, so she hesitated.

"I'll see you later, sweetie," Ryan said and closed the door. He headed for his car.

Oh, fuck it, Syd thought. She hit the button to roll down her window. "Hey, Ryan."

He stopped and turned.

"I almost forgot to ask, how'd your meeting with Anne go tonight?"

Ryan paused, measuring his words. "Let's just say, it was full of surprises."

Shit, Syd thought. A non-answer! But, hey, at least he didn't lie. Yet.

"I'll give you the details later," Ryan said, waved and got in his car. As Ryan backed up, he'd wished he put his top up because the reporters were literally shoving their microphones into his face shouting questions:

"Who was the Lady in Red?"

"What was the final body count?"

"Did she know all her victims?"

Finally, his old friend, Patricia, from KNBC stuck her beauty pageant winning smile in front of him and said, "Solving the biggest serial killer case this town has seen in decades and winning the lottery – this must be a great day to be Ryan Magee."

A great day to be Ryan Magee, Ryan thought. Yeah, right.

He put the Mustang in gear and pulled away, leaving the unhappy media in his wake.

FORTY-NINE

Anne couldn't believe it. As she drank her room service coffee, she flicked between the morning news shows. They were all covering the same story: The Lady in Red.

Why hadn't Ryan called her to tell her the good news? He'd not only solved the case but also killed a notorious serial murderer.

This was huge.

Getting publicity for someone winning the Lotto was one thing, getting publicity for someone winning the Lotto who is also a genuine American hero was a whole different ball of wax.

This was great for the foundation. Additional money should come pouring in. But new avenues for revenue had suddenly opened up. Books, movie offers, personal appearances. Ryan Magee was about to become an industry.

And he was all hers.

Which made her wonder again why he hadn't called? Probably didn't want to wake me, she decided and reached for her phone. She called him but it went straight to voicemail. Anne said, "Hi, honey, it's me. I'm watching TV and I see you've had a busy night. Congratulations, this is wonderful news. Call me as soon as you get up. I want to hear all the details. I love you."

Anne hung up, excitement rippling through her. Today was going to be a wonderful, unforgettable day.

Syd never got to bed. When she left Blake Hunter's house, she took the Pacific Coast Highway to the Interstate 10. She drove east to the 405, but instead of taking it north to head toward her apartment, she suddenly took the ramp leading south to Orange County.

It was just a little after dawn so traffic was light and before she knew it, she was knocking on the front door.

Betty Waterman answered the door and was surprised to see Syd. What was the detective doing back here?

She obviously hasn't seen the news, Syd realized. And no one had called the Waterman's because the Lady in Red's identity hadn't been released yet.

Then Betty read the expression on Syd's tired face and put two and two together. "Oh, no," she whispered.

"I'm so sorry," Syd said, and the next thing Syd knew she was holding Betty and they were both crying.

Cliff Waterman greeted Syd brusquely and took the news stoically, as if he always knew his daughter's life would end like this. And Syd sensed something else, too. Relief. He was scared of Alice, she realized. Well, she had tried to burn down the house. And now she was killing people, so he was probably afraid he was on her hit list, too.

What do you say to the parents of a slain serial murderer? How do you console them? Syd couldn't tell them about the DVD or video yet. They had to remain secret for the time being. So she said, "In a few days everyone will know exactly what happened to Alice. In a few days everyone will know that Alice was the real victim." Then Syd told them who to call to claim Alice's body, and left.

Syd got in her car and shut the door. Now what? Instinct had brought her to Orange County to tell the Watermans their daughter was dead. Or, was it something else?

Someone else lives in Orange Country. In nearby Newport Beach not eight miles from here. Nick Wood.

Syd hadn't actually thought it through when she took the DVD and video from Blake's beach house. But she took them for a very specific reason. She took them because she didn't want anyone else to see them until she'd finished what Alice had started.

Until she killed Nick Wood.

And now here Syd sat just a few miles from his house. Of course, he might not be home. He'd been in hiding since his son's murder.

But if he'd seen the news, if he'd heard the Lady in Red was dead, then it would be safe for him to reappear, wouldn't it?

Syd pulled out her cell phone, looked up Nick Wood's number from her notes and dialed. It rang once.

Pick up, you sleazy bastard, Syd thought.

It rang again. Alice is dead, you coward, pick up.

Another ring. Shit, answer, God damn it.

Then, a click and "Hello?"

"Mr. Wood, hi, this is Detective Curtis from the LAPD. We've been trying to get a hold of you."

"Yes, I'm sorry, I got the messages, but I've been so upset by Colin's death I haven't wanted to talk to anyone."

Horseshit, Syd thought. You just watched the morning news, saw the Lady in Red is dead and have crawled out from under your rock. "Well," Syd said. "Good news, the Lady in Red won't be hurting anyone else."

"I know, I just saw the news. Great work, Detective."

I knew it, thought Syd. "Thank you. Mr. Wood, there are a few personal items of your son I'd like to return to you. I've just come from a meeting in Newport Beach and could be at your home in ten minutes or so; would it be all right if I dropped by?"

There was a longer-than-there-should-have-been pause; obviously Nick Wood was trying to figure the angles, trying to guess how much Syd knew and didn't know. But he must've realized that refusing to see her would have seemed suspicious so he said, "Sure, I'm at 1412 King's Road." He gave Syd quick directions and hung up.

The house was a beautiful Mediterranean-style home sitting on an acre of land with an ocean view. Syd imagined an excited seventeen year-old Alice walking up the stone steps to the front door eleven years ago, fantasizing about her upcoming evening with her crush, Adam Devlin.

Oh, Alice…

Syd rang the doorbell. A few moments later Nick Wood opened the door. Though it was only seven-thirty in the morning, he was dressed; Bali loafers, khaki's and another Polo shirt, light green this time. But Nick Wood looked a bit tired, a bit stressed.

"Come in, come in," Nick said. Syd stepped into the entryway. The house was spectacular with hardwood floors, a thirty-foot spiral staircase, artwork draped walls and the soft tic/tock/tic/tock from an unseen Grandfather clock.

"You have a beautiful home," Syd said.

"Thank you," Nick said leading her down the hall and into the living room. It was surprisingly feminine, with a thick white carpet, giant tan couch that could seat twenty of your favorite people, two loveseats, a coffee table and vases of fresh cut flowers. Everything faced the picture window, of course, and the to-die-for view of the ocean.

Syd needed to know if they were alone, so asked, "It must take a lot of help to keep a house this big."

"Not really," Nick said. "It's just me now. So I only have a housekeeper stop by three days a week."

Monday, Wednesday and Friday, Syd assumed. Today was Thursday, excellent.

"Can I get you some coffee, Detective? Or a latte? I've got my own machine in the kitchen."

A latte would take him longer to make. "A latte would be wonderful, thank you."

"Be right back." Nick Wood left.

Syd wanted to look around. She drifted out of the living room, down the paneled hallway to another open doorway.

The game room.

It all looked so familiar; the pool table sat in the middle of the room, the bar at the far end. There was a flat screen TV hanging on the wall that wasn't there eleven years ago, otherwise, it looked the same. Syd walked in.

She wasn't exactly sure what she was going to do. Unlike Alice, Syd had a lot to lose if she murdered Wood.

It would be difficult to put a bullet in his brain, walk out the front door and escape prosecution.

A simple investigation would reveal she was in Orange County at the time of the murder, and there was a phone call on her cell phone to the victim only minutes before he was killed. So she had opportunity.

She was a cop with a gun. Means.

Ryan knew Syd felt sympathy for Alice. Motive.

Was Alice's revenge really worth Syd's own life?

"Oh, there you are," Nick Wood said. He handed Syd her latte, then asked, annoyed, "What are you doing in here?"

"I wanted to see where it happened," Syd said, watching his face for the reaction.

There was the slightest twitch from one of those bushy eyebrows. "Where what happened?"

"The gang rape of Alice Waterman."

Nick Wood studied Syd. He's wondering how much I know, thought Syd. The police killed Alice in Blake Hunter's home, so Wood knows we've figured out the connection between Adam, Colin and Blake. What he doesn't know is if we've seen the video, if we know about his involvement.

"That's why we were calling you, by the way. We figured out something happened when your son was in high school; we heard you'd made a payoff to one of Colin's classmates. But we didn't know who was involved or what happened. If you'd returned our calls, you could have told us Blake Hunter was the third boy. We would have warned Mr. Hunter, sent officers to his house and he'd still be alive today."

"I'm sorry, but I told you. I was so upset I didn't talk to anyone the last couple of days. To tell you the truth, my doctor prescribed me some heavy-duty tranquilizers and I've basically been in bed. I haven't called my office or checked my messages."

"And what about when we first met you in the morgue? I'm sure you suspected Alice Waterman then. If you had been honest with us and told us about the high school rape, we could have saved Adam Devlin's life, too."

"I didn't suspect Alice, then. I mean, it happened eleven years ago, why would I suspect her for killing Colin now?"

"Do you own a gun, Mr. Wood?"

The sudden change of direction threw Nick. "What's that got to do with anything?"

"I'm guessing you do. And I'm guessing you've been holed up here, with that gun close by, waiting to see if the Lady in Red showed up to kill you."

"Why would she have wanted to kill me?" he asked, but with failing conviction. He obviously knew where this conversation was going.

"I've seen the video, Mr. Wood. I assume you demanded the video from Blake Hunter eleven years ago when you agreed to buy Alice Waterman out. And Blake gave it to you. But deep down you were always afraid he kept a copy, weren't you?"

Nick Wood played his last desperate card. "A video of what?"

"You raping an unconscious Alice Waterman right here on this pool table."

The air seemed to come out of Nick Wood. He sagged against the bar. "Who else has seen the video?"

"Now that you mention it, only me." Hope flickered in his eyes. "But, sorry, no, it's not for sale."

"So you're here to arrest me?"

"I wish I could. But the statue of limitations on rape is ten years, even for a disgusting animal like you."

Now Nick Wood looked confused. "If you don't want money and you're not here to arrest me, what are you here for?"

"To kill you."

Wood jumped like an electric current hit him. He stared at Syd, waiting for her to pull her weapon, but she just stood there.

"But I've decided to just destroy you instead."

"I don't understand."

"I'm going to send a copy of that tape to a friend of

mine. Before you can say YouTube, your flabby ass is going to be seen on every computer screen in America. Then I'll send copies to all the television networks. How will your friends and neighbors feel about you raping a defenseless teenage girl? How many of your clients will want to work with a sexual predator?"

"But that was years ago! I was drunk. I told you before, I'm sorry for the way I used to behave. And now I'm impotent, doesn't that... I mean..." he tailed off as he realized how empty, how meaningless his excuses sounded.

"I want the world to see what you and those boys did to her. I want the world to understand that Colin, Adam and Blake *deserved* everything that happened to them. Alice killed them as an object lesson for women everywhere. As a call to fight back. And she did something else you'll read about in tomorrow's paper. She cut off the cocks of her attackers so that men everywhere would know there is a price to pay for rape. And just so you know, she was on her way over here to kill you, to slice off your useless cock when she was killed by my partner. I was upset at first; I wanted Alice to finish her revenge. But now that I think about it, I've decided your punishment may actually be worse. You're going to become the most hated man in America. Every woman will know your name. Every woman will know what you've done. Wherever you go, whatever you do, you'll be the scummy bastard who raped that poor high school kid. The press will haunt your every step. Paparazzi will be camped on your front lawn. And once the initial outrage is over, and the media moves on to its next victim, maybe, just maybe, some woman out there will finish what Alice started. I want you to think about that, every day; the next woman you meet, the next corner you turn, the next doorway you walk through may be your last. And I hope that whatever woman finally kills you, cuts your cock off first."

Syd turned and headed out the door, but then she turned back to a devastated Nick Wood. "Or, you could do us all a favor and take that gun of yours, stick it in your mouth and pull the trigger."

Syd watched Nick Wood's reaction to see if her words landed. Nick Wood lifted his head, mulling a seemingly once unthinkable option.

Without another word, Syd left.

FIFTY

Ryan desperately wanted to get a few hours sleep so he took the unusual step of turning his phone off. When his alarm woke him at nine-thirty, he opened his eyes and stared at the ceiling.

Decision day.

Ryan stood at a crossroad, his life would change forever today and he, and he alone, controlled the outcome.

Heady stuff.

Ryan had made a lot of decisions on the ride home last night and he knew what he wanted to do, but he was going to need some help to pull it off. He grabbed his cell phone off the night table, turned it on and checked his messages. There were four.

Anne's message was first. She sounded so fucking happy, he thought. Hard to believe it was all an act. Ryan had no intention of calling Anne back. He'd scc her soon enough.

Hanrahan called reminding Ryan to schedule his interview with the Force Investigation Division. Whenever an LAPD officer uses deadly force, they are required to get cleared by the FID. Ryan would call them as he drove to the California Lottery office.

Ryan's stepbrother, Johnny, called suggesting they meet at Santa Anita racetrack next week so Ryan could look at a promising two-year-old filly. Ryan decided he'd call Johnny back, never.

The last call was Newport Police Detective Alex Cortez, offering his congratulations and wanting to schedule a meeting, hopefully at a bar serving cold draft beer, so he could hear the blow by blow. Ryan liked Cortez and would call him as he drove to the lottery, too.

But that was it, just four messages. Not the one he was

hoping for. Not the one he was counting on.

Ryan showered and dressed quickly. He put on his blue suit instead of his usual sport coat and slacks. He knew he'd finally have to face all those microphones today and he wanted to look his best.

He thought about his father's last appearance in front of the press. He stood atop the steps of the Criminal Courts Building declaring his innocence and predicting a jury of his peers would find him not guilty of tax fraud.

It was a marvelous performance that convinced everyone but the jury.

Years later, when his father was dying, Ryan went to visit him in prison.

"Any regrets?" Ryan asked.

"Yes," his father said recalling that fateful day in court. "I should have worn my blue suit."

But that was Ryan's father. Live life and never apologize. "Life is not a dress rehearsal," he'd tell the young Ryan as one wife would leave and another would move in. "There are no second chances, no do-overs. Savor every day."

And his father did. Even his time in jail. He never looked back, never second-guessed. He'd come to his crossroad, made a decision and walked proudly to the end of the road.

But Ryan's father never considered other's feelings in his calculations. As far as Joseph Magee was concerned, the world revolved around him; he was the star of the show and everyone else was an extra.

It must have been nice to be that emotionally isolated, Ryan thought. It may have been wrong by a lot of people's standards, but it gave his father comfort every day. Right or wrong, his father knew who he was.

And up until this moment, Ryan thought he had a pretty good idea who Ryan Magee was. He tried to be fair, honest, hard working, not too judgmental (tough when you're a cop) and a fair arbiter of right and wrong.

But Ryan suddenly realized that a man can't really define himself until every tenet he thought he believed in is pushed to the limit. Ryan never thought of himself as greedy, but he suddenly understood the value of committing fraud to collect thirty-four million dollars. The hopes and dreams of so many people depended on him taking that Lotto money, and as Anne said, if you don't take it, *no one* gets it.

Ryan never thought of himself as naïve, but Anne had manipulated him with ease.

Ryan cherished his integrity, yet he'd slept with Anne, betraying Syd.

Ryan's carefully constructed self-image had disintegrated under pressure, and he had to accept the fact that life is not black or white. We're often forced to live in the gray area and our ability to navigate those waters is what really defines you. And so far, he wasn't doing too well.

Ryan looked in the mirror and straightened his tie. But all that was prologue, Ryan decided. All that mattered now was what he did today.

But he still needed a little help from his friends.

FIFTY-ONE

Lucinda McCarthy, vice-president of the California Lottery, was thrilled. "Just look at all the media," she said to Anne. "I haven't seen this much excitement since Raul Hernandez won fifty-four million dollars in 1985." They were standing in the middle of the Studio City Holiday Inn ballroom as news crews from CBS, NBC, ABC, FOX, Channel 5, Channel 9, CNN and even Univision set up around them. There were also a growing number of well-wishers; uniformed cops, detectives, friends Ryan had made over the years. "Of course, that was only the Lotto's second year," Lucinda went on. "And it was our biggest jackpot to date so simply everybody was clamoring for an interview. These days we have to give away handfuls of Scratchers just to get the local channels to show up."

"Yeah, well, Detective Magee has become quite the celebrity."

Lucinda's eyes searched the room. "Is he here yet, I'm dying to meet him."

Anne scanned the room, too. "No, not yet." And he hasn't called me, Anne thought. I hope nothing's wrong. Then Anne spotted someone she wanted to talk to almost as much as Ryan. Syd. Okay, Anne thought. This should be fun. "Excuse me, Lucinda, there's someone I need to see."

"Of course, I'll see you in a bit and, oh, before I forget," Lucinda handed Anne a manila envelope. "Here's what I call my Survival Guide for Lotto Winners. A list of names and numbers of some wonderful professionals who can help Ryan access the full potential of good fortune."

And all related to you, no doubt Anne thought. "Thank you, I'll make sure Ryan gets this." Anne tucked the envelope under her arm, weaved her way through the camera and cables to the other side of the room where Syd was pouring herself a cup of coffee from a refreshment table.

Syd saw Anne coming. And Anne's body language and attitude sent alarm bells ringing in Syd's brain. Anne projected a sense of smug superiority and worse, ownership; ownership of the thing Syd held most dear. Ryan.

"Detective Curtis," Anne said, extending her hand. "Anne Rogers, we met in the bullpen."

"I remember," Syd said with a smile, but she ignored Anne's outstretched hand, leaving it hanging awkwardly between them.

"So it's going to be like that," Anne said. "And I was hoping we could be friends."

"No you weren't," Syd said.

"You're right," Anne said, lowering her hand. "I wasn't." Anne decided to play a bit with her prey before she finished her off. "Actually, I'm surprised you're here."

"Really, and why's that?"

"Well, after what happened between Ryan and me last night, I thought..." Anne trailed off correctly reading the desperate curiosity in Syd's face. "Ryan is such a wonderful lover," Anne said, knowing each syllable pierced Syd's heart. "I was a fool to ever leave him, a mistake, by the way, I won't make again."

So there it was, Syd thought. Ryan did sleep with her. The final, delicate strands of hope elevating Syd's spirit snapped.

"Did he happen to mention our *reunion* last night?" Anne asked.

It took a real effort for Syd not to slap the smugness off Anne's face. But, not willing to give this bitch an inch, Syd said, "No, we were a little preoccupied."

"Ah, yes, the Lady in Red, of course. Congrats." Something caught Anne's eye, Ryan was walking into the ballroom, and as much as Anne was looking forward to delivering the coup de grace on Syd, she wanted to talk to Ryan more than anything. "Let's talk later," Anne said and stepped past Syd, crossing the ballroom toward the door.

Syd turned to see what had distracted Anne, and as she'd expected, it was Ryan. Well, Syd thought, he can have his greedy bitch and he can have his stolen Lotto money. I'm out of here. Syd stepped back out of sight, and as reporters and friends called out to Ryan, Syd slipped out the ballroom door.

Anne noticed Syd's exit and smiled victoriously.

Meanwhile, Ryan's eyes were riveted on his cell phone. He just received a text message and as he read it, he smiled. He snapped his phone closed as Anne reached him.

"Darling," she said opening her arms and stepping towards him.

He put his hands out, catching her at the waist and keeping her at arm's length. "Morning," he said stiffly, his eyes searching the room.

Whoa, thought Anne. Something's up. What the hell's happened?

"Have you seen Syd?" Ryan asked.

"No," Anne said innocently, making a show of looking for her.

"She told me she'd be here," Ryan said, frustrated.

"Is everything all right, Ryan?" Anne asked. "I've called you a couple of times this morning and -- "

"Everything is great," Ryan interrupted. "But I've changed my mind about a couple of things."

"What things?"

"You're about to find out. Wait here." Ryan took a step toward the stage, then stopped and turned back to Anne. "Oh, by the way, Rick says hello."

Anne's face fell as Ryan walked away. Rick? Oh, no, what did Rick tell Ryan? The worst thing possible, Anne realized. The one thing she couldn't afford for Ryan to know.

The truth.

Anne rushed forward, grabbed Ryan by the arm spinning him around, then pulled him close and said in a desperate whisper. "You can't believe anything Rick says, he's a pathological liar."

"He told me Rogers, Middleton and Roberts has never

represented a lottery winner. You told me you had. So, simple question, have you ever represented a lottery winner?"

Anne stared at Ryan, her mind racing, trying to figure out what to say, how to parse the awful truth. Finally, shaken, her voice barely above a whisper, Anne said, "No."

"Rick told me you and he forged some mortgage papers. Did you?"

"Yes," Anne said and then regrouped. "Okay, I might have had an agenda when I first went to see you in the bullpen, I admit it, but all that changed last night. I love you, Ryan. I don't care about the money. I don't care about the foundation. All I care about is you, I swear it."

Ryan could hear the sincerity in her plea, and felt a twinge of sympathy. But his mind was made up. "Sorry, Beautiful, we're done."

Crushed, Anne watched Ryan step on stage.

Lucinda was standing with a couple of Lotto officials and a heavy-set man in a suit he must've bought about twenty pounds ago. Behind them on a display stand was a six-foot check made out to Ryan Magee for thirty-four million dollars.

"Detective Ryan," Lucinda said shaking his hand. "I'm Lucinda McCarthy with the California Lottery, congratulations."

"Thank you," Ryan said.

"And this," Lucinda said, indicating the heavy-set man, "is Farid Nouri, he owns the store where you bought your ticket."

Ryan shook his hand. "And how much did you win?"

"Twenty-three thousand, five hundred dollars," Farid said.

"The store gets .5% of the winning jackpot," Lucinda said.

"Does he get a giant check, too?" Ryan joked.

"No," Lucinda said, laughing. "Just the Lotto winner. So, would you like to get started?"

"Just another minute or two," Ryan said, eyeing the crowd. The now familiar faces of the press looked up at him expectantly, as well as friends and colleagues from the LAPD including Hanrahan, Chen, Katz, his former mother-in-law, Liz, and a distressed looking Anne. But no Syd.

Syd was hurrying across the crowded lobby toward the front door when she noticed Tony Ramirez running toward the ballroom with a man in tow. The man was big, with an unremarkable face but a very distinctive wardrobe – greasy coveralls. They rushed past Syd and Syd's jaw dropped when she saw the logo on the back of the coveralls, **Valley Tow and Salvage**.

Tony reached the ballroom door, whispered something to the tow truck driver, then Tony stepped inside while the tow truck driver remained in the hall.

Fascinated, Syd started back toward the ballroom.

On stage, Ryan saw Tony walk in. Tony gave Ryan a thumb up. Ryan turned to Lucinda. "Okay, let's get started, but first I need to tell you something." Ryan pulled Lucinda to the side of the stage and whispered furiously in her ear.

As Ryan huddled with Lucinda, Syd walked back into the ballroom and up to Ramirez.

"Hey, Tony," Syd said.

"Hey, Syd," he said, but his eyes never left Ryan.

"Want to tell me what's going on?"

Now his eyes met hers. "You mean, you don't know?"

"No."

Tony barked out a laugh. "You've got one crazy partner, I'll tell you that."

On stage, Ryan turned to Tony and spotted Syd. A smile exploded on Ryan's face. Then he turned back to Tony and nodded.

"Excuse me a second," Tony said to Syd and then stuck his head outside the ballroom door. "Okay, buddy, you can go on up."

The slightly baffled, though clearly excited man walked through the door and headed for the stage.

"Is that who I think it is?" Syd asked.

"The tow truck driver," Tony said. "Ryan told me the whole story."

"But, how did Ryan find him?"

"He got an idea at the crime scene last night when he saw the Lady in Red's bloody fingerprints on the medicine bottles. It occurred to him that if the tow truck driver had any grease on his hands, there was a very good chance he left a print on the Lotto ticket."

"That's what you guys were talking about in the kitchen."

Ramirez nodded. "He gave me the Lotto ticket and when I got to the office, I was able to bring up a print. Ran it through the computer, got a hit, Alan Moll. He had a commercial class C California driver's license, which you need to operate a tow truck. I emailed his driver's license picture to Ryan and he recognized him. So forty-five minutes ago I walked into Valley Tow and Salvage and changed Alan's life forever."

"So he did the right thing," Syd said, surprised. "He gave up all that money..." And then Syd thought about Anne, did she know about this? Syd searched the crowd then found a surprised, stricken-looking Anne staring at the stage. She looked absolutely miserable. So she didn't know; interesting, Syd thought. Very interesting.

On stage, there was a flurry of activity. Ryan shook Alan's hand and introduced him to Lucinda, Farid and the others. Lucinda was on her cell phone in the middle of an agitated conversation with someone.

"Let me get this straight," Alan said to Ryan. "You could have kept all this money and no one would have thought twice about it. But instead you decided to track me down? We're talking millions, man!"

"I know," Ryan said. "And it was tempting. But, ultimately, Alan, they weren't my millions."

"Okay," Lucinda said, hanging up. "I've just talked to our legal department. Mr. Magee, if you are willing to sign an affidavit that you saw Mr. Moll drop the lottery ticket and that you have just now been able to track him down, then the jackpot will be awarded to him."

"Great," Ryan and Alan said together.

"But you better get back on that cell phone," Alan said.

"Because I want to give a finder's fee to Detective Magee." Alan turned to Ryan. "How'd ten percent sound?"

"That's four point seven million dollars," a surprised Lucinda said.

"Three point four after taxes," Ryan said. "But Alan, there's no need. What's yours is yours."

"Then let me do what I want with it. Take the money, please."

Ryan looked into the grateful tow truck driver's face and smiled. "Thank you, Alan."

"No, you crazy fool. Thank you!" Alan said, and then he threw his arm around Ryan and hugged him.

The press had no idea what was happening yet, but the frenzied conversations on stage had certainly piqued everyone's interest so all the cameras were rolling when Alan locked Ryan in a bear hug. Clips of that embrace would lead every news story that night and grace the front page of tomorrow's *L.A. Times* with the headline: **Honest Cop Stuns Crowd.**

FIFTY-TWO

"We have to talk."

After a raucous forty-five minutes of answering questions about finding the lottery ticket and the Lady in Red investigation, Ryan climbed off the stage and made a beeline for Syd. As the reporters now lobbed their questions at the dazed tow truck driver, Ryan grabbed Syd by the arm and steered her to a quiet corner of the hotel lobby.

"About last night," Ryan said.

"You fucked that greedy bitch."

Syd said it matter of fact. No accusation in her tone, no indignation, no anger even. That surprised Ryan, he'd expected a scene of some sort. But, of course, Syd knew him better than he knew himself. She probably figured it out last night. Probably the instant she saw him.

"Yes, I fucked that greedy bitch. We can talk later about why. I'm not sure what it says about me, or about us, but I want you to know that it's over, finally, completely, irrevocably."

"I fucked over seven hundred men."

"What?"

"And I killed two of them."

Syd had decided if Ryan was going to level, so would she. In fact, she decided she'd never lie to Ryan again. "My stepfather abused me from the time I was fourteen years old. When I was seventeen, I killed him. I ran away from home and came to Hollywood, fell in love with a pimp who got me hooked on heroin and put me out on the street. Two years later I overdosed, was saved by a paramedic named Eric who helped me kick and get off the street. Eric was killed by my pimp, and I killed the pimp in self defense. Eric's sister took me under her wing, helped

309

me get through school and into the police academy. But when I was a hooker, I kept count for a while, how many men I'd slept with; I gave up at six hundred and seventy-one but didn't get off the street until four months later. So seven hundred, give or take. And you fucked that greedy bitch, so the way I figure it, we're even."

Ryan laughed. "I always sensed there was more to Syd Curtis, but I had no idea..." Then he took Syd in his arms and hugged her.

Anne watched them from the ballroom doorway. The freckled face redhead looked ecstatic. Well, at least Anne knew she could destroy Syd's career whenever she wanted.

Then Anne realized Syd wasn't her enemy. Syd had done nothing wrong. Syd hadn't stolen Ryan; Anne had lost him by lying. Anne knew that if she'd been honest with Ryan from the beginning, things might well have turned out differently. If she'd been honest with Ryan, it could very well be her in Ryan's arms now.

So, Syd Curtis, Anne decided, you are getting a pass, for now.

"Excuse me," Lieutenant Hanrahan said, brushing past Anne as he charged into the hallway. He spotted Ryan and Syd as they broke their embrace. "Cut that shit out," he said joining them. "Or I'll have to break up my best team."

"You mean, you know?" Ryan asked.

"Please. *Everyone* knows. The way you two look at each other is downright combustible. So, play it cool in public and the LAPD's most famous homicide detectives can remain partners.

"Now, I just got a call from our pal, Alex Cortez, in Newport Beach. Nick Wood is dead. He put a bullet through his brain."

Ryan was shocked. "Grief?" wondered Ryan.

Hanrahan shrugged. "I don't know."

I do, thought Syd. And soon so would the whole world.

Not grief but justice.

Nick Wood was dead. Rest in peace, Alice. Rest in peace.

EPILOGUE

Alice Waterman's funeral was a media free-for-all. Video crews from around the world descended on Good Shepherd Cemetery in Huntington Beach. In a show of respect to the deceased, the FAA banned all air traffic over the cemetery to prevent the inevitable onslaught of helicopters from disrupting the ceremony.

The funeral was held a week after Alice's death; but more importantly, just one day later, the LAPD released two videos: Alice's gang rape and Alice's courageous escape from Blake's handcuffs, their ensuing battle and Alice eventually killing him. But it was a third video that got the most attention, the Lady in Red's manifesto.

Syd found the cell phone video Friday morning when they finished cataloging the crime scene evidence and Syd thought to check Alice's cell phone files. Syd was worried the D.A. would try to suppress the video so she sent it to a friend and it debuted on YouTube that night.

In a slightly distorted close-up the Lady in Red looks directly into the lens.

"My name is Alice Waterman. I was a rape victim. If I had been smarter, it never would have happened. If I had been braver I would have gone to the police. But I was weak and did nothing. The men who attacked me flourished while I suffered every day for years.

"Well, I got smart, got brave and did something. I killed the men who raped me and mutilated their precious cocks.

"Men everywhere are going to hear what I've done.

"Men everywhere will know it can happen to them.

"If I could do it, you can do it.

"Be brave, be smart, fight back."

311

Simply put, those three videos transformed the Lady in Red from serial killer to folk hero. While the talking heads on FOX News, CNN and MSNBC debated Alice's cold-blooded vengeance, every woman who watched Alice shoot Blake between the eyes was filled with grim satisfaction. Alice's wish for inspiration and empowerment was realized.

And the lives of many people on the case were changed forever. The Watermans were deluged with offers for books and movies but were proceeding cautiously; they were determined to honor Alice's memory.

Liz was interviewed by Bill O'Reilly and her blunt, irreverent personality made her an instant hit. She became a sought after TV commentator whenever a new murder case captured the nation's imagination.

Lieutenant Hanrahan was bumped to Captain and offered a desk downtown. But Hanrahan liked Hollywood Homicide so he said thanks, but no thanks. However, his dental checkup was a disaster. The sugar from sucking so many Tootsie Roll Pops had ravaged his teeth. He had to have six cavities filled, gave up the candy and went back to sucking Marlboros.

Tony Ramirez was working harder than ever. Besides his job at SID, he spent every evening working on the launch of the first Mirabelle's Meatballs restaurant – because the first thing Ryan did when he got his three point four million dollars from the California Lottery was to write Tony a check for two hundred thousand dollars to get his franchise dream started.

Ryan and Syd refused all requests for interviews. Ryan didn't want to discuss having to kill the now beloved Lady in Red. And Syd's quest for fame now seemed childish. A homicide cop's business is other people's tragedies, and to seek celebrity at their expense was just plain sleazy. Besides, with fame comes examination and Syd wasn't particularly interested in people digging into her past. Some things are best left secret.

Thousands of people filled the cemetery as Father

O'Malley read his eulogy over Alice's open grave. Syd stood off to the side with Ryan. Her eyes traversed the faces; the friends, the family and the strangers who were so touched by Alice's story they felt they had to be there to pay their respects. Syd finally settled on Betty Waterman. The woman whose heart ached the most.

Tears ran down Betty's face. The depth of Betty's grief touched Syd. And Syd couldn't help compare Betty to her own mom. Did she cry when she realized Syd had run away? Did she ever cry now? Was she even alive?

Suddenly Syd felt an overpowering desire to know.

As Alice's body was lowered into the earth, Syd whispered to Ryan that she'd be right back and she walked to a private spot on a tree-lined hill facing the Pacific.

Syd took out her cell phone, closed her eyes trying to remember her old phone number and dialed.

It rang.

Eleven years is a long time; odds were if her mother was still alive, she'd probably have moved.

It rang again.

And what would she say to her? Hi, mom, it's me. How you doing?

It rang again.

And if she gets a machine, should she leave a message or call back?

It rang again.

Okay, Syd thought. Nobody's home and no machine. Sorry, Mom, you missed your chance. She reached to hit End when the phone was answered.

"Hello."

Her mother's voice; even after all these years Syd recognized it instantly.

"Hello?" Amanda Stevens repeated.

Her mother's voice triggered a fearful little girl inside Syd, ashamed and terrified.

"Hello? Is anyone there?"

Syd's heart pounded, tears flowed. But somehow she fought back the temptation to hang up. "Mom," she said finally. "It's me. Syd."

There was stunned silence then, "Oh, my God, Syd. Where are you, baby? How are you?"

And Syd told her.

THE END

BUT WAIT!

Before you go, we've included an excerpt from another novel by James L. Conway – a wild and wicked thriller full of humor, unforgettable characters and nonstop action – *Sexy Babe*…

ONE

The worst day of my life began with an orgasm.

His, not mine. So what else is new?

His name was Jason Settles, an actor who had that bad-boy thing going on. Jason had long sun-bleached hair, brown bedroom eyes, a perpetual three-day beard and these incredibly perfect white teeth, well, caps really, but this was Hollywood and everyone had caps, or wanted them.

Jason was usually typecast as Sexy and Dangerous, and his girlfriend, Grace Taylor, that's me, was usually cast as the cute, perky, blonde, blue-eyed Girl Next Door. Which, I guess I looked but rarely felt like.

Jason lived on Wonderland Drive just off Laurel Canyon in this little blue bungalow with a hot tub in back. It seemed like every house in Laurel Canyon had a hot tub, some kind of weird remnant of the 70s, I think. It was in that hot tub that Jason and I had first made love. And the answer is no, I didn't get off that night either. To be perfectly frank, I generally need a little mechanical help, if you know what I mean. It kind of freaks guys out, though, when you ask them to use a vibrator on you. Makes them feel inadequate or something. So I usually just fake it and take care of myself later.

Okay, that's probably too much information. Anyway, after Jason's wham bam thank you Grace, he climbed out of bed and went into the bathroom. "You want the shower first?" he asked.

"No," I said. "I need to get home and change. I've got an audition at ten." Then I bolted up in bed. Shit! My agent was supposed to fax the scene to me here at Jason's house. I leapt out of bed and raced to Jason's fax machine. Thank God, the scene was there.

It was three pages. Not bad, I thought, walking back to the bathroom. Usually, the more pages the better the scene. Then I read the character name: Sexy Babe.

"Oh, no," I muttered as I joined Jason.

"What is it?" he asked through a mouthful of toothpaste.

"My character. It's Sexy Babe."

"The role's not even big enough for a character name?"

I scanned the material, just two lines in a three-page scene. This was bad. I was supposed to be reading for guest star roles, leads in pilots, break-out parts in edgy independent movies, not two lines as a nameless bimbo on *NCIS*. "I may not have worked in a while," I said, insecurity filling every pore of my being. "But I'm not doing another bit part."

"Hey," Jason said, "look at the bright side; at least it's not Sexy Babe #2."

The bright side, of course. I'm good at looking at the bright side. In fact, I've got a deep well of eternal optimism. I just have to remind myself to tap it.

"No, Jason," I said. "The bright side is realizing that this must be some kind of mistake. Someone must've sent me the wrong sides. I'll just call Lucas when the agency opens and straighten it all out."

I stepped on Jason's medical scale, reached to adjust the weights, and then stopped. "Who weighs 94 pounds?"

"Who, what?"

"Weighs 94 pounds. The scale is set at 94 pounds, it's usually set at either 185ish, your weight, or 105ish, my weight. Hey, I know," I said, trying to be funny. "You're probably banging the model next door. She looks like she weighs 94 pounds."

"Really," Jason said, as he stepped back into the bedroom and started getting dressed. "I hadn't noticed."

Okay, about a hundred things wrong with that answer. First, no man could *not* notice how skinny Melody was. She was five-foot-ten, all legs, tits and ass. Second, she traipsed around the backyard in a band-aid sized bikini doing weird Tai Chi exercises every morning. Third, Jason may be gorgeous, but he's not a very good actor, so he could've definitely used a take two on the "Really, I hadn't noticed," delivery. And now that I thought about it, he looked guilty as hell.

Then it hit me. "You're sleeping with her, aren't you?"

"Don't be ridiculous."

Whoa, that reading was even worse than "Really, I hadn't noticed." Now I was sure. "Jason, stop lying to me. Why don't you just man up and admit you're sleeping with her."

This was where he was supposed to sweep me up in his arms, tell me how stupid I was being, how much he loved me, and then shut me up with a passionate kiss. Instead, he looked at me and said, "All right, I'm sleeping with Melody."

His words seemed to hang in the air in front of me. I'd asked for the admission, hoping he wasn't sleeping with her. But actually hearing him say the words hurt more than I could have imagined. I didn't know what to say, what to do next.

"In fact," Jason said, filling the awkward silence. "I think I may be in love with her."

Any confusion I felt was suddenly washed away. "Wait," I said. "You think you're in love with another woman yet you screwed me ten minutes ago?"

"I was trying to find the right time to tell you."

"Yeah, tough decision. Do I dump Grace before I fuck her or wait until I'm done."

"See, I knew you would turn this around on me."

"What?"

"That you'd find a way to blame me."

"I do blame you. Hello! You're fucking another woman!"

"Because..." He trailed off like the rest of his sentence was obvious.

I tried to think of what would come next and drew a blank. "Because, what?"

"Think about it," he said, staring hard at me. "It's all your fault."

"My fault?"

"I'm not the one with intimacy issues."

"So you're saying that if I didn't have intimacy issues, you wouldn't have cheated on me?"

"There you've said it. And I forgive you."

"You forgive *me*?"

"What we had was great, Grace. Awesome, even. But it's time we moved on." He grabbed his keys off the counter. "I'm going to the gym. It might be best for everyone if you were gone when I get back." He walked out the door.

Okay, Jason was a jerk. I knew that. But for the last six months he was *my* gorgeous jerk.

And I always knew Jason was just an in-between guy – the guy after my last less-than-perfect boyfriend and before the long-dreamed-about Mr. Right. But still... Ouch.

Oh, and the worst thing – I weighed 109.

I burst out Jason's front door fifteen minutes later. My arms were filled with the detritus of our six months together. A box filled with make-up, tampons, toothbrush – you know, that stuff. I balanced a pile of clothes on top of the box and tried to talk into the cell phone wedged into my shoulder. "Sexy Babe? Come on Lucas, it's got to be some kind of mistake."

Lucas Abrams was my agent. We hooked up when I first got to town — yes we slept together and no, I didn't. Actually it was more a fling than a thing; he came to a showcase where I performed a scene from *Carnal Knowledge*. He'd just been promoted to an agent at Pinnacle Artists after making the "mail room to assistant" odyssey. He liked my work, and signed me. We went out that night to celebrate, had too many Cosmos, and ended up back at his place. We both admitted it was a mistake in the morning, agreed our working together was more important than our sleeping together, and we've been platonic ever since.

"Actually," he said. "The fax was a mistake."

"I knew it." I reached my seven-year old red Miata convertible, dumped my crap in the back seat, and took proper hold of the phone. "I mean, you promised me no more bit parts. So when I saw --"

"Not that kind of mistake," Lucas interrupted. "More like the 'you're not a client anymore so we're not sending you out on auditions' kind of mistake."

"What?"

"Times are tough, Grace. Too many actresses, too few parts. So the partners have decided to trim the client list."

"If this is a joke, it is so not funny."

"No joke. Look, I fought for you, I did. But the partners just looked at the bottom line. Each year you've booked less and less work."

"But we've been so close! I almost landed that Cameron Crowe comedy six months ago. And you said I was the second choice for the CBS pilot."

"I was being nice, Grace. You were a bust in both auditions."

"What?"

"You've got tons of talent, don't get me wrong. But you're just not the same actress I met five years ago. It's like the passion's been sucked out of you."

"Do you have any idea how hard it is to learn two or three parts a day, drive all over town auditioning -- seeing the same actresses trying out for the same roles -- and almost never getting hired?"

"I do. But you used to be excited to have all those auditions. Now you dread them. Does that tell you anything?"

"It's hard not to get discouraged, Lucas. But I'll do better, I promise. Give me another chance; I'll be the new improved Grace Taylor, you'll see."

"I'm sorry, it's out of my hands. Stop by anytime to pick up your head-shots and demo reel."

"Lucas, no, please..."

"Prove us wrong, kiddo. Go out there and become a star." He hung up.

I promised myself I wouldn't cry on the drive home. I made it twenty feet. Tears of anger, frustration and humiliation poured down my face. I was crying so hard traffic was a blur so I turned on the windshield wipers. They scraped uselessly against the bone-dry glass and when I realized how stupid I was, I started laughing.

Then my old optimism came roaring back. Hey, it'll all work out, I told myself. I had tons of actress friends who would be happy to introduce me to their agent. And guys hit on me all the time. So fuck Jason Settles. Grace Taylor was available again and Hollywood was full of hot guys.

It was about a fifteen-minute drive from Jason's house to my apartment in Westwood. Or should I say, apartment about to go condo.

Would you pay $560,000 for a 400 square-foot, one bedroom apartment in a thirty-year-old building? Me neither. Never mind the fact I had no money and lousy credit. The apartment was shabby, the walls were paper-thin, the refrigerator rattled, the toilet ran, and the shower stall smelled like rotten cheese.

My lease was up and, since I wouldn't buy the shithole, they were kicking me out. I had twelve days to vacate the premises. To be honest, I hadn't even started looking. I was kind of hoping Jason would ask me to move in with him.

Idiot!!

I heard the phone ring inside the apartment. I was holding the box in one arm and the armload of clothes in the other, but I managed to dig my keys out of my purse and let myself in. I dumped my stuff on the chair and dove for the phone like a lifeline. "Be someone I know and love."

"Will I do?" I recognized the voice instantly. Madison Stone, one of my best friends. We met at an audition for the TV show, *House*, both reading for a newlywed who's got a brain tumor and only Dr. House's quirky brilliance can save her. If I was the Girl Next Door, Madison was usually cast as the Drop Dead Gorgeous. Madison had incredible red hair, a killer body and this oozing kind of sexuality that usually left guys tripping all over themselves. And, if she'd been a better actress, she could have been a star. But to be honest, and she was the first to admit it, Madison was a little stiff. She always seemed to be "acting," was never able to disappear into the role. But she worked it. She was in two different acting classes, and a cold reading workshop. Madison did book a lot of print work and enough commercials to keep her in a nice apartment, let her shop at Barney's, and treat us to hundred-dollar lunches at the Ivy.

"Oh, thank God, Madison. You won't believe the day I'm having. Jason dumped me and my agent fired me."

"Oh, sweetie, I'm so sorry. I never liked Jason, though. None of us did. But your agent is a different..." Madison tailed off. A beat later her voice was louder, angry. "What the hell are you doing here?" She was talking to someone else in her apartment.

"Madison, who's there? Are you all right?"

"Get away from me." She sounded scared now. Near panic.

"Madison!"

She screamed. Then I heard what sounded like a punch, followed by another scream, shattering glass, the thud of the phone hitting the floor, and then the line went dead.

Oh shit. I quickly called her back, but it just rang. And rang. Not good.

Madison only lived a couple of blocks away, so I thought about running over there and rescuing her, then got real. I'm an actress, not the Bionic Woman. I called 911. It was busy. Ten-fifteen on a Thursday morning and 911 is busy! I called again. Busy. Goddamn L.A. I grabbed my purse and bolted out the door.

I started running. If I cut through the alley and caught the light on Santa Monica Boulevard, I could be at Madison's in a couple of minutes. And while I may not have been the Bionic Woman, Madison and I did take a self-defense class from Charlie Wang's Women Empowerment Academy.

I reviewed Charlie's Five and Five. The five target areas: Eyes, Nose, Throat, Jaw and Groin. The five attacks: Palm Strike, Throat Strike, Head Butt, Elbow Blow, Knee Kick. Charlie was also a huge proponent of mace. We drilled using it when attacked from the front and attacked from the rear. On graduation day, we each got a diploma and a four-ounce can of mace. I'd never fired it in anger, so to speak, but it was in my purse and ready to go.

I looked for help as I bolted out of the alley and raced down Kelton Avenue. No cops, anywhere. No hunky guys standing around who might want to help a lady in distress, either. The light blinked from yellow to red as I got to the intersection. Screw it, I thought, and I darted into the street. Screeching brakes and blaring horns greeted me, but I made it across Santa Monica unscathed and stopped in front of Madison's building. There was an exterior staircase leading to the second floor landing and Madison's apartment.

I pulled out my cell phone, tried 911 one final time and couldn't get a signal. I had a copy of Madison's key, part of Charlie Wang's Buddy System. I grabbed it and started up the stairs. When I reached the apartment, I put my ear to the door, heard nothing. Tried to look in the window, but the drapes were drawn.

I thought about knocking. But if some evildoer was inside, I was afraid they would just shoot me through the door. So I unlocked the door, traded the key for my can of mace and slowly stepped inside.

The living room was empty, but a complete mess. Stuff was tossed everywhere. I inched forward, peeked into the kitchen. Madison was sprawled on the floor. I rushed to her, blood dripped from a gash on her forehead. She was either dead or unconscious.

"Madison!" I whispered urgently. I put two fingers to her carotid artery — I played a nurse on an episode of *The Mentalist* and the technical advisor had taught me how to do it. The pulse was strong, thank God. "Madison," I whispered again. I looked for something to staunch the bleeding. There was a dishtowel on the counter. I grabbed it, but when I pulled it, I realized it was sitting under a nest of copper measuring cups. They went flying; with a loud clang, they hit the floor.

There was a thud from somewhere in the apartment, then the sound of running footsteps. Crap!

I whirled toward the kitchen door, the mace aimed in front of me. A man burst into the kitchen. Big, mean and ugly. Not him, the gun in his hand. He was short, but all muscle, with a pockmarked face and maniacal eyes.

As he raised the gun, I sprayed him full in the face. He screamed and dropped to his knees, his hands clawing at his eyes. I bent over Madison, tried to get her to her feet, but she was still out and dead weight. No way I could pick her up.

Then the thug, still frantically rubbing his eyes, got to his feet. He was recovering fast. I reached out to spray him again, but he knocked the can out of my hand.

Shit!

He dove at me but I darted to my left and he missed. Then I made a beeline for the door.

I half ran, half fell down the stairs. As I hit the ground, I looked back to see the thug flying out Madison's apartment after me. I hurtled myself into the middle of Santa Monica Boulevard waving my arms, screaming, "Help! Somebody help me!"

WE HOPE YOU'VE ENJOYED THIS EXCERPT FROM *SEXY BABE.*

IT'S AVAILABLE NOW AT AMAZON.COM

And, thanks to Camel Press, we've included an excerpt from another novel by James L. Conway – a Hollywood thriller full of mystery, murder, mayhem, and humor – *Dead and Not So Buried*

Prologue

Lightning ripped the sky like a knife through flesh.

Okay, that's a little much. Fact is, there was no lightning. Hell, there wasn't a cloud in the sky. But kidnapping is a heinous crime, heinous enough for a little atmosphere. So even if there was no lightning, there should have been.

The Kidnapper broke in through the rear gate. A crowbar snapped the rusted chain. His size eleven boots left a clear path across the dew-sodden grass, past the flowers, through the statues, to her chamber.

Having long since vacated her body, she couldn't hear the scratching and scraping as he broke into her sanctuary. Couldn't see him as he entered her cold, white room. Never felt him sweep her into his arms.

The Kidnapper shuddered. She looked terrible, much worse than expected. Her white gown was streaked with dirt and mildew. That shock of blond hair was reduced to just a few sparse, wispy patches. And her face was a mess. At least she didn't smell.

She fit easily inside the oversized burlap bag. He pulled the cord. Outside once more, he scanned the grounds with his sharp green eyes. Nothing. He cocked an ear. Just a solitary siren destroying someone's peace a few miles away.

He placed the ransom note in the doorway then tossed the bag over his shoulder and retraced his steps toward the rear gate. Except for stealing Marvel comic books from Harmon's Drug Store when he was a kid and doing a little coke when he first got to Hollywood, this was the first time he'd ever broken the law. He'd expected the anxiety buzz, but the hard-on was a complete surprise.

His car was parked a block away. The top was down on his black SL 550. He placed her carefully on the back seat. He didn't bother buckling her in, though; after all, his victim had been dead for almost forty years.

He slipped behind the wheel of the convertible. Once he got the ransom he'd pay off the leasing company. He was getting sick of their repo threats. Everybody's repo threats.

The car purred to life. The kidnapper smiled as he put the car into gear and drove away from the cemetery. Unbelievable. He'd actually pulled it off. He'd kidnapped one of Hollywood's greatest icons.

And now everyone would have to pay.

The Beginning

I was in my office when the call came. Sitting at my desk admiring the front cover of a paperback novel. My paperback novel. *Rear Entry*, by Gideon Kincaid. That's me. Ex L.A. cop turned private detective turned novelist. The Joe Wambaugh of the PI set.

I should be so lucky. The book had only been out for two weeks. Too soon to tell if anyone would buy it. Dreams of fancy cars and private planes were on hold as I continued to earn a living poking through other peoples' lives.

Hillary came in from the outer office. "I'm sorry, Gideon," she said, her features twisted in compassion.

My own features were twisted in confusion. "Sorry about what?"

"I understand if you don't want to talk about it."

Hillary's my secretary, a smart twenty-five-year-old with all the good stuff—blond hair, blue eyes, great body. But there's a sweetness to Hillary, an endearing naivety that makes me look upon her as a little sister. All my thoughts about Hillary are pure. Well, almost all of them.

"I'll be happy to talk about it," I said. "If I had any idea what we were talking about."

"Death."

"If you're asking me to take a stand, I'm definitely against it."

I've known Hillary since she was ten years old. Her father, Jerry, was my partner for a couple of years when I was driving a black and white out of the West Valley Division. A couple of years ago she showed up looking for a job. I'd just lost my secretary, and Hillary needed the job, so I said sure. She didn't just want to be a secretary, she told me, she wanted to be a PI like me. I told her I'd show her the ropes but never really got around to it. Truth is, she's so good in the office I'd hate to lose her.

"Okay," she said. "I didn't think you'd want to talk about it. But it won't do you any good to, like, keep all that grief inside. It'll fester and feed on itself. Eat away at your insides until your soul dies and you become one of the walking dead. A spiritless zombie going through life like a blind man in a garden." She did that from time to time—rattled on in New Age nonsense. Something to do with her being a native Californian. "Anyway," she said. "Alex Snyder's on line two."

"Alex Snyder?"

"From the mortuary ..." She said it like only an idiot wouldn't know what she was talking about.

"Of course, the mortuary ..." I said, as if I knew what the hell she was talking about. It's never a good idea to let your secretary think you're an idiot. I picked up the phone. "Gideon Kincaid."

"This is Alex Snyder, from Westside Cemetery. I wonder if we could meet."

"Look, if this is some kind of sales call, I—"

"No, Mr. Kincaid. This is business. Important business. Please, I need to see you right away."

Somebody must've stolen a headstone, I thought. Or maybe his teenage daughter had run away. It didn't really matter. He needed help, and that's what I did for a living. "All right, Mr. Snyder. I'm on my way."

My office is in Sherman Oaks, in a strip mall on Ventura Boulevard. Above a pet store called The Bunny Hop. My romantic soul felt I should have an office in one of the funky old buildings on Hollywood Boulevard—much more Chandleresque. But I get the creeps in Hollywood. Frankly it scares the shit out of me. Not the weirdos, the gangs, or the homeless. But the decay. If society can let the Boulevard of Dreams turn into an urban nightmare, what chance does the rest of the city have?

Westside Cemetery is in Brentwood, about twenty minutes from Sherman Oaks, so I used the time in my car to catch up on my literary career.

"Bad news."

"Sales are slow?"

"Slow would be good. They're nonexistent. The publisher's decided the title's the problem. *Rear Entry* sounds like a sex manual for gay men."

I was talking to my agent, Elliot. He's got a boutique agency for writers on their way up. Or down. I wasn't sure which category I belonged in. "Elliot, the title was their idea."

"Everybody makes mistakes."

"Let them make mistakes with Grisham's next book."

"Almost nobody writes a bestseller their first time up. Not even Grisham."

"It took me three years to write *Rear Entry,* and now you're saying I have to write another book?"

"You told me you wrote for the pure joy of it."

"I was lying."

"I warned you writing was a tough way to get rich."

"I thought *you* were lying."

"Never fear, Bubele. It's not over until the buyer for Barnes and Noble sings. If they give us a doorway display, hell, who knows ..."

"Anything I can do to help? Interviews? Book signings?"

"Reality check, Gidman. You're nobody. James Patterson does interviews because he's famous. People will watch a show to see him. Ratings go up, he sells more books. It's a help you/help me kind of simpatico. Stephen King does a book signing because he's famous. People come to a bookstore just to see him. More people in the store mean sales go up. We've got that help you/help me thing going again."

"But they got famous writing books."

"Correctamundo, but they wrote bestsellers. Writing bestsellers made them famous. And fame is the ultimate passkey. Before you can hit the interview/book signing trail, *Rear Entry* needs to become a bestseller."

"But how will it become a bestseller if I can't do any interviews or book signings?"

"Welcome to Catch 22 Land—chicken and the egg and all that."

"So that's it? There's nothing I can do?"

"You could get famous first. Break a big murder case. Solve a million dollar diamond heist. Marry Lindsey Lohan. You need something to single you out, something to make people sit up and take notice."

Yeah, right, I thought. *Who's going to notice a two bit PI?* "All right, Elliot," I said. "Thanks for the advice."

"Wait, I've got one more piece of bread to throw upon the waters."

"What?"

"Don't give up your day job."

Dead and Not So Buried

There's something very soothing about cemeteries—all that grass, the flowers, the fountains, the birds. It's a shame they're wasted on the dead.

The Westside Cemetery is in the heart of Brentwood. It's small—only about two acres—but some of Hollywood's biggest stars are buried there.

I was shown into Alex Snyder's office by his secretary—a middle-aged woman who oozed warmth and compassion. Alex Snyder also oozed warmth and compassion. He was the kindly grandfather type—late sixties, thick gray hair, natty moustache, reassuringly plump. He smiled as I entered, shook my hand. "Mr. Kincaid, a pleasure to meet you."

"Please, call me Gideon."

"Gideon," he said, smiling.

"Will there be anything else?" the secretary asked.

"No, Bernice, thank you."

She closed the door. Snyder pulled a .45 Smith and Wesson out of his desk and shoved it in my face. "Where is she?"

"Get that gun out of my face before I make you eat it," I said. It's tough to talk tough with a gun an inch from your nose, but I didn't think he'd really pull the trigger.

He pulled the trigger. The bullet blew a hole in the wall a micro millimeter from my left ear.

There was a scream from outside the door then a fearful Bernice asked, "Alex, are you okay?"

"Just dandy, Bernice," he said, his eyes never leaving mine. To me he said, "The next one is between your eyes. Now, where is she?!"

"Who?"

"Christine."

"Christine who?"

His eyes nearly bored holes in mine before he said, "You don't know, do you?"

"No."

A little more cornea drilling, then: "I believe you." He lowered the gun, backed away and sagged into his desk chair. "I'm sorry, Mr. Kincaid. I hate violence, but this kidnapping's got me a little crazy."

"Maybe you should start at the beginning."

"I got a call this morning at five-fifteen. One of the gardeners found Christine Cole's crypt open and her body missing."

Holy shit. "Christine Cole?"

Christine Cole was one of the biggest movie stars of the sixties. A model turned actress, she vaulted to fame the year after Marilyn Monroe died and took her place as Hollywood's "it" girl. A sultry blonde with a killer body, Christine oozed sex. And she used it. To the gossip columnists' delight, Christine unabashedly slept her way through the rich and famous. And she battled some personal demons with drugs and alcohol. But Christine also had talent, and she made a string of hit movies. Four, to be exact, and only four. Because, on a foggy April morning, a drunk Christine lost control of her silver Jaguar XKE on the Pacific Coast Highway and plunged to her death. She was thirty-three years old.

Her death had shocked the world. And, like that of Bogart and Monroe, Christine's fame had only increased since her passing. Her image was on everything from tee shirts and coffee mugs to perfume and push-up bras. A true Hollywood icon.

Someone had robbed her grave. Stolen her corpse.

Who steals a corpse?

I said, "There can't be much of her left after forty years. Just bones, right?"

"Bones. The gown she was buried in. And some jewelry. She was buried wearing a bracelet, necklace and diamond ring."

"Valuable?"

"On another body, no. But these were on Christine Cole."

"How much is the kidnapper asking?"

"Two million dollars."

It suddenly hit me. "Wait a minute … why'd you think I knew where the body was?"

"Your business card was attached to the ransom note."

"What?"

"The kidnapper says you have to deliver the money." He handed me the note. The words looked like they were cut out of a variety of magazine articles.

> IF YOU WANT TO SEE CHRISTINE AGAIN, HAVE GIDEON BRING $2,000,000 IN USED $100 BILLS TO THE NORTHWEST CORNER OF HOLLYWOOD AND VINE AT 3 P.M. TODAY, OR I'LL SELL THE BODY, BONE BY BONE.

My business card was paper-clipped to the top of the page. In the six years I'd been a PI, I must've given out hundreds of business cards. Was this guy an ex-client? Someone I'd interviewed? Someone who'd picked up my card from a desk? No way of knowing. "I'll be happy to deliver this ransom free of charge." I wanted to find out who this son of a bitch was.

"I appreciate that, but I'll pay for your time—as long as you promise me you won't do anything to jeopardize the safe return of Ms. Cole's remains."

In other words, don't let it get too personal. "I won't." Something was nagging at the back of my brain. There was a familiar aspect about all this, but I couldn't get it to bubble to the surface. "I'd like to see her crypt."

"The funeral itself was small, only thirty-five guests. But outside the gates stood hundreds of reporters, photographers, police officers and fans."

We were standing in front of the open crypt. The marble facing had been pried off, the bronze casket slid open. The only thing inside was the dried remains of a few roses.

"I played the organ," Alex Snyder said. "You know what they requested? 'Yesterday.' Christine loved the Beatles."

A set of footprints in the still-wet grass led to a rear gate. The chain had been broken, snapped by a crowbar, from the looks of it. Probably used the same crowbar on the crypt. "I could talk to a few neighbors," I said. "See if anyone saw anything last night."

"Absolutely not! Don't talk to the neighbors. Or the police. Anyone. We'll be ruined if the tabloids find out we lost Christine Cole's body. I just want to pay the money and get her back."

"You realize the kidnapper might take the money and not return the body."

"I'll take that chance. Will you help me?"

I fingered the ransom note and my business card. "I don't think I have a choice."

WE HOPE YOU'VE ENJOYED THIS EXCERPT FROM *DEAD AND NOT SO BURIED.* IT'S AVAILABLE NOW AT AMAZON.COM

www.ingramcontent.com/pod-product-compliance
Lightning Source LLC
Chambersburg PA
CBHW062021170626
46813CB00001B/246

9 780988 549920